Family Games

Family Games

Jean Stubbs

St. Martin's Press
New York

Library of Congress Cataloging-in-Publication Data

Stubbs, Jean.
    Family games / Jean Stubbs.
       p.   cm.
    ISBN 0-312-10437-5
    1. Family reunions—England—Cornwall (County)—Fiction.
2. Christmas—England—Cornwall (County)—Fiction.   3. Cornwall
(England : County)—Fiction.   I. Title.
PR6069.T78F36   1994
823'.914—dc20
                                                            93-44054
                                                            CIP

First published in Great Britain by Macmillan London Limited.

First U.S. Edition: May 1994
10 9 8 7 6 5 4 3 2 1

To Gretel and Robin and The Great Years

ACKNOWLEDGEMENTS

I should like to thank Jennifer Kavanagh, Tom and Sandra McCormack, and Jane Wood for their enthusiasm, encouragement, patience and perspicacity – and my husband for listening to each book.

CONTENTS

'Families are dangerous places.'
Gretel McEwen
Speech and Language Therapist/Counsellor

Invitation

October 1989

There could not have been two more different women than Sybil and Blanche Malpas, mother and daughter: the one rooted in tradition and faintly bewildered by progress; the other in the vanguard of the modern age. And yet their telephone conversation, moving from one voice to the other, a Wimbledon of opposites, was tender to both sides, because they had built their relationship over thirty-five years and they loved each other.

'Blanche? Darling, it's me. Mummy.' She recollected that her daughter preferred names to titles. 'Sybil,' she said in amendment.

Her daughter's voice was deep, dark and pleasing.

'Sybil. Where are you?'

'Back in Clifton. We arrived home last night.'

'I was going to ring both places this evening to ask how the funeral went.'

'Very well, but very wet.'

Blanche sat in the ground-floor flat of a Clapham house and thought of Cornwall in the rain. Dripping black umbrellas, subdued West Country voices, the villagers out in full strength. Outside, London drizzled darkly. Inside, the room radiated light and warmth, was rich in creative clutter. A makeshift table, which ran the length of three tall sash windows, was heaped with fabrics. The dress-maker's dummy wore a multi-coloured tabard that harked back to medieval times, but when teamed with a pair of tights would become up-to-date. Pictures on the walls were a mixture of photographs, prints and original fashion sketches. Books on the shelves in both alcoves represented a lifetime of reading, from Beatrix Potter and nature books, through a catholic taste in novels and a left-wing glance at politics, to art, costume, textiles, design and designers. A sofa and two easy chairs sat

3

round the fireplace, and the coffee-table between them was covered with fashion magazines. Blanche called this room 'the shop', though its function was a mixture of living and working, and she sat in its centre, wearing a loose-fitting gown that could be made glamorous but at present was simply comfortable and elegant.

Sybil was still talking.

'Darling, I thought you always worked at home on Tuesdays. I've tried to ring you several times today and only got the answerphone.'

That sat on a desk near the long windows: a silent secretary.

Blanche said, 'I've been out all day working with a new music group. No, you've never heard of them and you probably wouldn't like them. I'm designing clothes for their first tour. I took my sketches over, and we spent ages discussing them. You should have left a message. I would have rung you as soon as I got back.'

'I hate machines, and what I wanted to say was personal.'

Blanche smiled, lifted her eyebrows, made an affectionate grimace.

'Darling, have you a few minutes to spare?' Sybil's tone changed to teasing intimacy. 'Are you sitting comfortably?'

Mentally, Blanche became four years old again, sitting in a miniature chair that had belonged to her mother as a child, listening to the radio. Afterwards they would go for a walk in the park, pushing Edward, the new baby, in a coach-built pram. She smiled again, stuffed a cushion behind her head, relaxed against it.

'Yes, Sybil. I'm sitting comfortably, wearing what the Victorians would have called a *peignoir*, drinking a gin and tonic, and Aaron's fast asleep.'

One chubby arm outflung, dreaming the immeasurable, unfathomable dreams of childhood.

'Dear little fellow!' said Sybil tenderly. 'Such a good baby.'

There were a few moments' silence. Blanche could picture her mother in the hall of the family house at Clifton: doodling on the telephone pad, ash-grey head bent in contemplation of Aaron.

'Darling,' Sybil said, 'what I really wanted to talk about was Christmas. And Uncle Jack.' She dealt with the second subject first, faintly reproachful. 'I was sorry that you felt you couldn't come down to Cornwall for the funeral.'

4

Blanche answered drily, 'Since my father isn't on speaking terms with me, and won't acknowledge Aaron, I thought it best to keep out of the way. And,' anticipating the next gentle hint, 'as I detest wreaths I sent a cheque to Helston Cottage Hospital instead.'

Sybil said quickly, 'Oh, Jack would have approved of that idea. Anyway, there were so many flowers that they needed an extra car to carry them. And the whole village turned out.' But that had not been enough. 'Still, it was sad that none of you three children came. Uncle Jack was so good to you all, and I know you loved him too . . .'

Blanche's mouth tightened. She frowned into her glass.

'. . . but of course it's difficult for Edward, living up in Yorkshire, and Lydia can never organize herself. Have you heard from her lately?'

Defensive, annoyed, Blanche said, 'No. Our paths never seem to cross.'

'I can't understand that, since you both live in London.'

Crisply, 'London is a big place. I don't even know most of my neighbours.'

'I shouldn't like that,' Sybil said decidedly, and there was another short silence. 'Anyway, she's having man-trouble again. That dreadful Philip person actually turned her out. I hadn't heard from her for over a month, and when I rang up – not realizing what had happened – he told me she was looking after an antique shop for a friend. What on earth does Lydia know about antiques?'

Diverted, Blanche asked, 'Who's Philip? The last man I met was called Billy.'

Sybil swept this question aside. 'Well, it doesn't matter now, darling, because it's all over. Philip gave me the number and I rang her. No apologies or explanations, of course. She sounded very bright as usual, and said she was busy and couldn't talk for long – have you ever known Lydia to be busy? – and she's staying with this friend who owns the antique shop while she looks round for somewhere to live. I hinted that perhaps it was too early to be involved with another man, but apparently this friend is a woman. So that makes a change.'

Blanche smiled to herself, saying, 'It's extraordinary how Lydia always finds someone to look after her. I haven't seen or heard from her – or Edward – for months.'

5

Sybil's voice strengthened. It had come upon home ground, upon a fixed principle.

'So I gather. And that's one of my reasons for ringing you. We are all drifting further and further apart, and that seems wrong. When you were children all three generations knew each other. We used to be a proper family.'

But this was an Edwardian dream from some mythical family album. A sepia vision from the past, covering heaven knew what awful truths. And Blanche gave an impatient sigh, remembering that Sybil's parents were old and hardly ever saw them; that the occasional state visit was depressing; and that they had died within a year of each other before she was twelve. On the paternal side, meetings had been just as infrequent and even more of an ordeal. And the only contact with her father's sister was the rare letter to him and sporadic presents to Blanche, since that constantly travelling lady seemed not to realize that Edward and Lydia existed.

The ensuing silence suggested that Sybil was also travelling, but in some region of the mind. Blanche returned to the point. 'We were never a proper family.'

Sybil defended her principle vigorously. 'We always spent Christmas with one or the other set of grandparents, and when Grandpa Outram died Grandma made her home with us for the last year of her life . . .'

In mourning of every sort, which did not diminish.

'Yes, I remember that. It was hell.'

'Oh, Blanche, my dear girl. I'm sure you're not a cynic, but you do sound like one.'

'I'm not a cynic. I'm a realist. Individuals and friends are all right, but the family is a diabolical institution. Anyway,' as her mother seemed about to protest further, 'tell me about Uncle Jack's funeral.'

Sybil paused to reconsider the event. 'Very sad and beautiful,' she said at last. 'Daddy and I drove down from Clifton on Thursday and came home yesterday, having gleaned the news and heard the rumours.' Here she hesitated, as if uncertain what news and rumours to impart.

'Are we going to lose Minions?' Blanche asked.

'Well, nothing is actually settled because Jack's private papers are in rather a muddle, so we only know the obvious bequests. The colonial nephew, Ralph, will inherit the estate. He couldn't be present at the funeral but he sent a splendid wreath.' And as her daughter did not answer, 'Darling, are you there?'

'Yes. Yes, I'm here. I was just drinking steadily,' said Blanche, who had been stricken motionless, glass in hand. 'Was Minions not mentioned at all?'

'I had a word with Jack's solicitor, and he advised me to wait until the nephew arrives, some time at the end of this year, to see how he feels about the tenancy.'

'This nephew – won't he continue renting it to you?'

'He could, but I should imagine he'd charge a price we couldn't possibly afford. People are paying nearly two hundred pounds a week for a holiday chalet these days. What do you suppose a seventeenth-century farmhouse would be worth? And the death duties will be heavy ...' Her voice trailed off, as if unwilling to speculate further.

Blanche's silence had underlined a concern that she now expressed forcibly. 'I should hate us to lose Minions. It was wonderful to bring Aaron down there this summer, and to find you and the house waiting for us at the end of the journey.' She could not resist adding waspishly, 'And my father absent, busy with his own concerns. Just like being back in my childhood – the good part, that is.'

Sybil began vigorously, 'Now don't play the White Queen, crying before you're hurt!' And then veered away in delight, 'Oh, Blanche, the Virginia creeper has turned the most astonishing shade of crimson.'

But her daughter was not to be distracted by chiding or beauty. 'I don't see why we should lose it, anyway. Surely you and Tony don't want to rattle round in that great house at Clifton once he retires next summer? All those high ceilings and flights of stairs. Why don't you sell it and make an offer for Minions?'

'I did test the waters to find out how Daddy felt about the idea, but he wasn't very forthcoming.'

Blanche answered with some asperity. 'Why not? I thought he'd been waiting all his life to write the ultimate book on anthropology. Minions would be an ideal place for him to work, and a more convenient size for you to run.'

'He says it would be a mistake to withdraw to Cornwall completely, and lose touch with our friends and connections here. I think the truth of the matter is that he still plans to keep a finger in the university pie.'

'May God help his successor!'

Sybil decided not to continue this discussion. 'Anyway, darling, I really rang to talk about Christmas. And I've discussed this matter with Daddy, so it isn't just hope and fancy.'

Blanche reached for the bottle of gin, and compressed her lips, knowing what was to come. She gave the impression of being remote, controlled, sophisticated. But the hand on the bottle trembled slightly, and inwardly she quaked.

'Darling, I know that you and he have had your difficulties in the past, and the row over Aaron crowned everything, but I do think it's time you both made an effort. It was a shock when you decided to be a single parent and bring up the baby by yourself. Tony would have understood a mistake, or a man letting you down, but a deliberate choice on your part was beyond his comprehension. And I'm bound to say,' with a tinge of humour, 'that it was beyond mine, too. But you were my daughter, so though I couldn't understand or approve of your decision I accepted it.'

Blanche said ironically, 'Sybil, you're like the lady who stands in the dock and says of the serial murderer, "But he was always a loving husband, Your Honour!"'

Her mother did not intend to encourage frivolity.

'Now you're teasing me, and I'm serious. Blanche, I want to see our family gather together for Christmas at Minions.'

As if she were the mother and Sybil the daughter, Blanche replied, 'Why *do* you keep on trying? Why not accept the fact that as a family we don't work? Some of us like some others but no one, apart from you, likes everybody.'

Sybil rode over this remark, saying, 'I've rung Edward, and he's prepared to drive down with Henny and Ben. And Lydia said yes, but could she invite Freddie, whoever he may be . . .'

'Oh dear!'

'Yes, that *will* be a trial. They're always such ghastly men. But I did mention it to Daddy and he says he'll put up with it for my sake.' Sybil braced herself. 'Anyway, it's important that Aaron should meet us all and that everyone should meet him. I realize that you must have some good reason to exclude his father, but a child needs the balance of both sexes. If not a father, then a grandfather, an uncle, a cousin. Children need the family as much as the family needs them.'

Blanche translated sarcastically. 'You want me to turn up with my illegitimate child under one arm and a celebratory bottle of bubbly under the other?'

Sybil fired a broadside. 'I want you to come home for Christmas and bring our grandson with you. It's high time that Tony acknowledged Aaron, and that you and he tried to understand each other instead of playing the irresistible force and the immovable object.'

Blanche was silent.

Sybil pleaded, 'I'll see that Tony comes half-way, if you will. It's such a hurtful situation. Ignoring birthdays. Not speaking. Not writing. Do try, Blanche, my dear. And if you could bring him some personal gift, however small, which shows thought and care, he would be so delighted. He always gave you such wonderful presents. Marvellously clever presents. He always knew how best to please you.'

'And how best to hurt me.' Sombrely.

Sybil became conciliatory, thinking perhaps she had said too much. She ended the conversation swiftly, lightly. 'Well, well, we'll say no more about it. Let me know when you make up your mind, and whatever you decide is right by me. Take care of yourself – and give Aaron a special hug and a kiss from his gran.'

Guests

CHAPTER ONE

Saturday, 23 December

'The first to come and the last to leave,' said Anthony Malpas, putting on his spectacles and studying the bill. 'What better compliment can we pay you?'

'Always a pleasure to see you, sir,' said the restaurateur.

Anthony drew out his wallet and selected a credit card. 'Our thanks to you for making this such a memorable evening. And, as always, our compliments to the chef.' He added a tip, exactly judged.

'Oh, thank you, sir!' And as the rest of the party began to collect their outdoor clothes, 'Allow me, madam . . .'

But Anthony was there before him, to settle his wife's old blue velvet cloak carefully upon her shoulders, for Sybil expected such small personal attentions, and he remained punctilious in paying them. In their sixties, they were a handsome couple still. Sybil had the air of a woman who had been much admired. The rings on her fingers bore witness to an engagement and four decades of marriage. The garnets in her ears and on her neck had been a wedding present from her father to her mother. All paid tribute to a beauty that had not so much vanished as been transformed and rendered harmless by age. She had kept her figure and her erect carriage. Almost as tall as her husband she accepted his homage with grace, but also as her due, and smiled upon the proprietor. 'So kind of you to fit us in at such short notice, Mr Tregembo,' she said, having expected nothing less.

'And so many of us,' said Anthony, waving a lordly hand, exacting his tribute as patriarch of a large and handsome tribe.

The six adults and two children had occupied three tables made into one in the centre of the converted barn. They had been aware of dominating the bistro with conversation and laughter, with both personal and seasonal festivity. In the depths of

Cornwall, and in mid-winter, they must have been a welcome influx. The other few diners had either enjoyed or ignored them: three elderly people, glad of diversion; a middle-aged man and woman who no longer had anything to say to each other; a young couple totally absorbed by love. What an example the Malpases had seemed, especially at that time of the year and in this unbelieving age, of the happy and united family.

Sybil took the proprietor into her confidence. 'Nowadays, we tend to stay in Clifton for Christmas, because it's easier for everyone to meet there. But this year, with the future so uncertain, we thought we'd come to Cornwall instead.'

This implied that the family always celebrated Christmas together, which was not true.

'Ah, yes, of course,' said Richard Tregembo, adopting a reverential tone. 'There'll be many changes, I'm afraid, now that Mr Maddern is dead.'

Anthony cleared his throat, and said, 'We were all at university together, Jack Maddern and my wife and myself. Known him for most of our lives. We shall miss him frightfully. His death is a great loss to the village, too.'

'Is it true', asked the proprietor, curious, 'that some cottage rents are as low as a pound a week?'

Anthony's colour rose a little higher because the rent for Minions had also been ridiculously low, originally tailored to fit the income of an academic man. Still, he answered loud and clear. 'Oh, absolutely. Peppercorn rents in return for service. You might describe it as a feudal system. But it worked. Undoubtedly. Oh, yes, it worked.'

'And we look on Minions as our second home,' Sybil murmured. 'Holidays, half-terms, weekends. We've been coming here for nearly forty years.'

'Forty years!' This was echoed deferentially.

'I shall be retiring next summer,' Anthony announced.

He did not believe that statement, did not expect it to be believed, but Richard Tregembo missed his cue.

'Had you not thought of buying the farmhouse and retiring down here, sir?'

'Oh, that's out of the question!' Anthony said vehemently, also giving the wrong answer, for the proprietor was Cornish and regarded retirement in Cornwall as a precursor to Paradise.

Sybil amended both their statements. 'We couldn't afford the price they are likely to put upon Minions,' she explained, 'unless we sold our own house. That would be a big step to take and will need a great deal of thought. But anyway, with Mr Maddern's affairs unsettled no one can make any definite decisions.'

Reproach underlined her diplomacy, and Anthony added in a lower, propitiatory tone, 'No, no. Can't make definite decisions yet.'

Richard Tregembo saw that he had blundered into some personal controversy and hurried out of it.

'Naturally. Of course not.'

Now that they were all warmly wrapped and ready for the journey home, final words, final thanks and final smiles were in order.

Sybil held out a gloved hand, saying, 'Let us hope that this won't be our last visit as a family group.'

It was a poignant moment, ruined by her nine-year-old grandson, Benjamin.

'But *why* don't you sell the house in Clifton and buy Minions instead, Grandpa? You'd make a fab profit! It must be worth two hundred thousand at least.'

Sybil laughed and pulled him to her, saying, 'Ben! It's high time you were in bed.'

Even with his cheek pressed against the faded folds of her cloak his voice still clamoured. 'Dad reckons that Minions is worth about a hundred and seventy-five thousand . . .'

His father, embarrassed, passed one hand over his smooth light-brown hair and glanced uneasily at his parents.

'Ben, darling!' Sybil warned.

For Anthony's nostrils were twitching, and he was beginning to frown.

'. . . so you'd be twenty-five thousand pounds to the good. Think of that! Twenty-five thousand—'

'Can't anyone silence that young chatterbox?' Anthony demanded, trying to sound as if he did not mind.

Mr Tregembo was smiling with professional indulgence. 'Children are welcome,' the smile said.

'Ben!' said his father, sharply for him.

'Ben!' said his sister Henrietta laconically. '*Do* shut up!'

He reddened, and stared at them indignantly. 'Oh, *you*!' he muttered, and was silent.

Everybody laughed then, and trooped out to a cold night and a sky full of stars.

Anthony was organizing his flock. With his flowing wings of grey hair, his imperious black eyes, expansive gestures and resonant voice, he was a prophet come to judgement. 'Edward, you take Blanche and the two children this time, and we'll have Lydia and her friend Betty.'

'Freddie, Daddy. Her name's Freddie,' said his younger daughter persuasively.

'Freddie. Of course. Edward, *I'll* lead the way.'

'So long as he doesn't take that short cut again,' Ben said audibly, and was shushed.

'Sybil! Sybil!' the leader commanded.

She had wandered away, and was standing by a ghostly group of cast-iron garden furniture. Bereft of customers and cream teas, they were awaiting no one. Yet chill white chairs tipped up against chill white tables as if the seats were being held for absent persons. A good witch, very tall and still in her damson blue cloak embroidered with tarnished silver thread, Sybil seemed about to rouse them from enchantment and restore their summer afternoons.

Cries of 'Sybil! Mummy! Gran'ma!' failed to animate her.

Blanche walked rapidly back and touched her shoulder. 'Tony's huffing and puffing, darling.'

She was far away, one hand tracing the curlicues of painted iron. But she turned at the sound of her daughter's voice, saying plaintively, 'It's so pathetic to see their little legs sticking up in the air.'

Blanche's tone was amused but kindly. 'They'll be back on their little legs again at Easter. The season's over.'

'So are many things that Easter won't resurrect,' Sybil replied sadly, thinking of Jack Maddern and the years of friendship. 'Blanche, I was wondering whether we should hold open house on Christmas Eve, as Jack did at Predanick Wartha. Not on his scale, of course, just inviting the villagers we know best. But I don't want people to think that we're trying to take Jack's place — that we're being presumptuous.'

'I'm sure they won't,' said Blanche, 'but why not consult Mrs Laity when we get back, and invite them through her? She's the village mouthpiece. What she says goes.'

'How clever of you, darling.' Momentarily relieved. 'Yes, I could do that.'

The patriarch was stamping his feet and slapping his arms, giving a tremendous performance of a man being cold. 'Oh, do come on, Sybil. You can talk to Blanche any time, for God's sake. Here, Lydia. Fetch them back!'

Unmindful of her husband's impatience, Sybil was busy catering. 'But how many will there be? Twenty or thirty or more? That means an extra shopping expedition tomorrow, and borrowing plates and glasses, and baking dozens of mince pies, and possibly a few other things such as sausage rolls, and perhaps cutting sandwiches. And then there are the drinks to consider — both soft and alcoholic — and whether we should serve coffee afterwards . . .'

Now Lydia scurried up, saying, 'Daddy's about to explode! What's the problem?'

She had inherited her mother's light, quick voice but not her earnestness. Indeed, she found it difficult to take anything seriously at the moment, for the family had accepted her friend and she was happy.

'Sybil is thinking we should hold open house on Christmas Eve,' Blanche explained to her sister, 'but she's fussed about feeding the multitude.'

'What a splendid idea!' said Lydia, who never fussed about anything. 'We'll help. I can concoct an eye-crossing wassail bowl, and Freddie's a first-class cook, and the children will adore being scullions. Problem solved.'

'Sy-bil!' Exasperated.

His wife returned to the moment, lifted her head, brightened her tone, and called, 'Coming, darling!'

She even smiled for him, though at that distance and in the semi-dark he could not have seen it; but perhaps the smile was implicit in her voice for he stopped slapping and stamping, and opened the car door and held it out for her in readiness.

She was sombre again, accepting the proffered arms of Blanche and Lydia, as she began to negotiate the cobbled yard. 'So long as Jack and Minions were here,' she said, 'and all of you came to Cornwall for holidays now and again, family life didn't seem to be over.'

Lydia and Blanche raised their eyebrows at each other. Time lay ahead of them like a long white winding road full of adventure. Their mother, it seemed, had come upon a cul-de-sac.

'Now, suddenly, I feel that everything is over,' said Sybil. And left the chairs and tables to their winter vigil.

CHAPTER TWO

Anthony took Sybil's arm possessively, as if her daughters had been guilty of attempted abduction, and settled her in the ramshackle old Vauxhall he should have traded in years ago.

Blanche chided him lightly, coolly, but in an undertone, 'There's no need to play the ringmaster. We were only organizing Christmas to create the least possible disturbance to yourself.'

Lydia raised her eyebrows and whispered to Freddie. Demurely they took their seats in the back of the car, while Anthony swung round on his elder daughter as if she had stabbed him. She waited, chin up, hands thrust deeply in the pockets of her scarlet greatcoat. The stand-up collar and quilted front, the ballooning sleeves, the aureole of frizzed black hair and pale oval face gave her a medieval look. Different ages suit different women. Her late thirties suited Blanche. She wore them like a crown.

Anthony replied coldly, deliberately, 'Indeed? You always gave me the impression that you liked disturbance.'

Sybil said in a pleading tone, 'Oh, please don't start quarrelling. You haven't seen each other for nearly two years, and we've had such a lovely evening.'

They checked themselves, exchanged deep looks: the looks of Sumo wrestlers judging whether to engage. The moment was over. The contest not yet ready to begin. Anthony moved heavily into the driver's seat. Blanche turned on her heel and walked to her brother's car.

Edward had a new white Mazda. Was it bought, or borrowed for the occasion to make an impression? Blanche made a mental note to ask the children. Henrietta always knew the whys and wherefores, and Ben would have found out how much it cost.

In this age of separated and divorced parents, Blanche reflected, children had to become street-wise to survive. Her son Aaron, though facing a different problem, would be spared that trauma at least. She had chosen his father, but chosen not to marry. She preferred to be a single parent. It cut out the costly middle-man of marriage.

Edward, having overheard their exchange of words, said hopefully, nervously, 'Everything all right, Blanche?'

Tall and slim, ruled by a sensitive disposition, he had inherited his mother's pleasing nature and failed to live up to his father's expectations. The state of Anthony's temper and Sybil's happiness worried him, who desired peace at almost any price. At this precise moment he wanted Blanche to tell him that everything was fine, but she would not.

'No, it's all wrong. I don't understand why Sybil keeps trying to patch up a set of family relationships that should have been ditched years ago.'

'Strong words!' Edward said, and laughed, and patted her knee affectionately, and changed the climate of the conversation. 'Wonderful to see you, anyway, and you're looking amazingly well. Postcards and phone calls excepted, we haven't been in touch for ages. How long has it been?'

'Two years ago exactly. A disastrous family Christmas that Sybil arranged at Clifton.'

He swerved away from this reminder. 'I don't know why you and Lydia and I all wait for Mama to gather us together,' he went on, in his light pleasant voice. 'We should meet as individuals. I know we live a fair way from one another but it's only a matter of making the effort. I meant to visit you in the hospital when Aaron was born, but somehow it didn't happen.'

She smiled in recollection, knowing good intentions to be his weakness. 'I forgive you, because you sent those amazing dark red roses instead.'

'Did Lydia visit you?'

'No. She sent a bottle of champagne – and I forgave her, too!'

'But you weren't entirely alone? Mama came, didn't she?'

'Oh yes. Yes, of course she did,' said Blanche. 'She came from Clifton the moment I telephoned to say I was in labour, and sat in the hospital all day and night while I wrestled Aaron into the world. Then came up again to stay with me for the first week I was home.'

She was silent for a few moments, unsmiling, remembering. Without Sybil that would have been a cruel beginning.

She returned to the present, and asked, 'How are things with you, Teddy?'

For he was also a single parent, but by default. That marriage, between an amiable unambitious husband and a competent worldly wife, had teetered from crisis to crisis for twelve years, with Sybil acting as peacemaker and occasional child-minder. Then six months ago Katrina, who had met another man, abruptly and unexpectedly left home. She also left a note, saying she needed time to be apart, time to find herself.

He shrugged, and said in an undertone, 'We're managing. The trouble is that Kat always organized the domestic side so I'm a bit new to it all. We still have her cleaning lady, who comes in three times a week and does washing and ironing. I'm not home until five o'clock, and I usually have books to mark, so we live on fry-ups and take-aways. I try to make a game of it all. The kids have been marvellous. If they're not staying the weekend with Kat, the three of us spend Saturday morning shopping in a supermarket and have a milk-shake to celebrate afterwards. Then I take them to the cinema, or hire a video for the evening. I spend Sundays on them. I've been teaching Ben cricket, and Henny's learning how to cook, and teaching me. Neighbours and friends help. But how long that will last I don't know. You can't be everyone's good cause for ever. Mama's been a life-saver. She took the kids down to Minions for a month in August while I earned some extra money.'

'I know. Aaron and I joined them for a fortnight of that time.'

He jerked his head towards the back of the car and added, 'But as little pitchers have big ears, we'll talk later.'

For Ben was moving forward, resting his arms on the back of the driving seat, speaking confidentially into his father's ear. 'Dad, why did Grandpa get shirty when I said he should buy Minions? Gran'ma would rather live here than in Clifton and it'd be cheaper.'

'Oh, I don't know,' Edward replied evasively. 'It was late in the evening, and he'd had a long day. I expect he was feeling tired.'

But Blanche believed that when a child asks for information it should be given, thoroughly and truthfully. 'Grandpa got shirty because he and Gran'ma are having a private battle about Minions. As long as the rent remained at twopence a week—'

'Twopence a week?' cried Ben, eyebrows peaked. 'Is that all it cost?'

'No, no. I mean that it was terribly cheap and they could afford to run both houses. But now Uncle Jack's dead, and Grandpa's retiring, they must choose one or the other, and they can't agree to which.'

Anthony's old Vauxhall roared into life and careered off down the narrow lane, just missing a white gate-post.

Ben said sincerely, 'I'm glad I'm not in *his* car.'

'So's he,' said Henrietta tersely, having the last word.

'Pass the caramels, Hen!' said Edward, restoring order with indulgence.

'Has Grandpa always driven that badly?' Ben asked.

And was answered with a laugh, and a twin chorus of 'Yes!'

The Mazda's headlights picked out an avenue of windblown trees, the golden glance of a passing fox, chilled hedgerows, dark ditches.

'Remember how we used to drive down to Cornwall late at night, at the beginning of the holidays?' Edward asked his sister.

'Three of us half-asleep in our pyjamas, with the current Labrador in the back, luggage in the boot and on the rack, and a potty under the driving seat,' Blanche answered.

'And Minions waiting for us at two o'clock in the morning, with all the lamps and fires lit, and a cold supper on the table.'

'Halcyon days, Teddy.'

They were reliving a Cornish idyll which his two children were about to lose.

'Daddy?'

'Yes, Hen?'

'How long have Gran'ma and Grandpa had Minions?'

'Oh, since they were married. Back in the nineteen fifties. It was part of Uncle Jack's estate and he let it to them for a song.'

'How old is Minions, Dad?' Ben asked, chewing a caramel.

'How old would you say, Blanche?'

'The original part of the house goes back to the reign of King Charles the Second. Three hundred and twenty years? One of Uncle Jack's Royalist ancestors built it, and the Madderns used to live there.'

21

'Used to live in Minions?' Henrietta cried on a high note of disbelief.

'Yes, until the nineteenth century. Then they wanted something larger and grander, so they built Predanick Wartha on a hillside half a mile away.'

'I like Predanick Wartha,' Henrietta said. 'There are lots of places to play hide and seek. But I love Minions best. Minions is large and grand enough for me.'

'Minions is older than Predanick Wartha,' said Ben, determined to outdo his sister.

'It was fairly primitive when we first had it,' said Edward.

'No running water, electricity or sanitation,' Blanche chimed in. 'Chemical closets and oil lamps. And much smaller than it is now.'

'Do you remember the year Uncle Jack gave us a pony for Christmas, and we learned to ride it in the paddock? He did a lot for us, one way or another.'

'He was in love with *her*, of course,' said Blanche cryptically. 'But Superman got there first — otherwise you and I would not be having this conversation.'

'Who was? Who did? What conversation?' From the back of the car.

Blanche and Edward laughed.

'It was an old love story that happened long, long ago,' said Blanche flippantly. 'In the days when a gentleman could offer his heart and hand to a lady in exchange for a lifetime's devotion.'

'Yuk!' said Ben.

'Good bargains men got in those days,' Edward remarked.

'What bargains?' Ben asked, alerted. 'Where, Dad?'

'I was joking.'

'Some joke! Can I have another caramel?'

22

CHAPTER THREE

The family was welcomed in the hall by Sybil's dog, Gracie, latest of a line of yellow Labradors. Elderly, sedate, languidly waving her tail, she led them into the warmth of the living room where she sank down again in front of the fire, duty done. Alone and aloof on top of the television set, perched Blanche's Siamese cat, eyes flashing crimson as they caught the light. Patch, the black and white resident tomcat who kept Minions free of rats and mice, stayed at a respectful distance from both. And in the midst of this private zoo sat Demelza Laity, who had spent the evening either reading *Woman's Weekly* or knitting one of its patterns.

Mrs Laity had fulfilled most village roles in her long lifetime: wife and mother, amateur midwife and layer-out of corpses, friend, neighbour, adviser and repository of secrets. And for the Malpases, caretaker, house-cleaner and babysitter. In her old age she was a short, vigorous, sturdy woman with white curly hair, freshly cut and permed for Christmas, and a pair of keen dark eyes. Now she rose stiffly from her armchair to greet them, and answered Blanche's question before she could frame it. 'Your Airing's been as good as gold, Blanche. Only woke up once, and I give him that fruit juice you left. Shouldn't wonder if he isn't cutting a back tooth. I rubbed his gum with a drop of brandy from the kitchen cupboard. He went off comfortable after that.'

'Airing was pissed,' Ben whispered to Henrietta, and sniggered.

Mrs Laity folded her hands across her stomach and gave him a look, the meaning of which could not be mistaken.

'It's long past your bedtime, Ben,' Sybil reminded him gently.

He allowed her to kiss him, waved casually to the others to ward them off, and said, 'G'night, everybody!'

Henrietta, officiating for her mother, said, 'Ben, what do you say to Grandpa?'

'What? Oh, yes. Thanks for the dinner, Grandpa. It was great.' Then he changed tactics, pointing accusingly at his sister and saying, 'It's past *your* bedtime, too.'

'I'm *going*,' said Henrietta indignantly, 'as soon as you've stopped littering the place up.' And she tossed a haughty head, drew her long brown hair over one shoulder and began to plait it.

Ben stuck out his tongue at her, put it in again quickly as he saw Anthony glaring at him, and stumped up the stairs, one by slow and heavy one.

Sybil stepped quickly into the breach. 'Tea or a nightcap, anyone? Mrs Laity? A cup of tea?'

'Not for me, Mrs Malpas, thank you. I'll be off home now.'

Blanche followed her into the hall, opening her handbag, saying, 'Mrs Laity, let me pay you.'

'Oh, no hurry about tha-at.' Politely.

Sybil was behind them. 'Mrs Laity, may I have a word with you before you go?'

Anthony, back to the fire, warming himself, called after them accusingly, 'I thought you said something about tea?'

'We're going to make it in a minute, darling!' Sybil called back.

Her mind was elsewhere, but the instant response, the sweetness in her tone, were automatic.

She was saying confidentially, 'Mrs Laity, I wondered if you'd like to drop in for a mince pie and a glass of punch on Christmas Eve?'

Henrietta came running out, singing, 'Polly, put the kettle on . . .' closely followed by Lydia and Freddie, chorusing, '. . . we'll all have tea!'

Sybil concentrated again on Mrs Laity. 'And perhaps you'd like to bring your sister – so helpful always at the post office – and her husband. Oh, and Matthew Kellow – so useful in the garden. And I was wondering . . .'

As Mrs Laity buttoned a bottle-green coat over her stomach purposefully, and said, 'That'd be handsome.'

'You see, Blanche and I were remembering all the lovely Christmas Eves we spent up at the Hall, and this will be the first year that Mr Jack hasn't . . . and we wondered if anyone else in the village would like to drop in . . . those who feel they know us

well enough . . . of course, it's short notice and nothing special
. . . just seasonal goodwill . . .'

Mrs Laity pulled a mouse-coloured felt hat down on her head
and closed the conversation. 'You'd like me to ask around the
village, Mrs Malpas? Not everybody. Just they that knows you. A
mince pie and a glass of punch. Well, I'll do that for you. But
you'll need to put some time limit on it or you'll have that Mat
Kellow with his feet in the hearth at midnight – and his head too,
if he keep on drinking!'

'Then shall we say between eight and ten? They can come and
go as it suits them. Will that be all right?'

'Good as gold. Don't you think no more about it, my dear.'

A freckled face and two gleaming eyes appeared between the
landing banisters. A husky wheedling whisper addressed Sybil.
'Gran'ma, can I have some cornflakes for Clementine? She's
woken me up, running round in her wheel.' His hamster was the
present love of Ben's life.

'Darling, you've only just gone to bed. I'm sure you woke *her*
up, not the other way round. I'll see what I can do.'

Blanche said, 'I'm going up to see Aaron. I'll take some
cornflakes.'

'Darling, that *would* be kind.'

Mrs Laity swathed herself in a coral wool scarf and picked up
her patchwork leather holdall. 'I'll be off then, Mrs Malpas.'

She stumped forward to put her head round the living-room
door and say, 'And goodnight to *you*, sir!'

'Goodnight, goodnight!' cried Anthony cordially, rocking on
his heels, lord of the hearth and master of the house. 'God bless
you, Mrs Laity. Has no one come to fetch you? Have you a torch?
Can I not drive you home?'

'No, no, sir. I haven't far to go, and once I'm down the lane
there's a street-lamp on the corner,' said Mrs Laity, understanding
that his invitation was not meant to be accepted, but appreciating
the attention all the same.

'Good, good, good.' He reached his pipe from the mantelshelf
and began to fill it. Mrs Laity completed her farewells.

'Goodnight then, Edward.'

His tone was airy, his answer frivolous but hinting at cultural
depths, to conceal the lack of ease he always felt in his father's
presence. 'Goodnight, Mrs Laity! May flights of angels sing thee
to thy rest!'

'Very kind, I'm sure,' said Mrs Laity unmoved, having known him all his ineffectual days. 'See you tomorrow evening, then, Mrs Malpas, Blanche.'

Sybil closed the front door, and leaned against it for a moment as if she were unexpectedly tired.

From the kitchen they could hear Lydia's and Freddie's gusts of laughter and Henrietta's high, light giggle.

'Aren't those happy sounds?' said Sybil, nodding towards them, brightening, looking younger. 'Do you know, when Lydia asked if she could bring her friend Freddie I thought, naturally enough, that it was one of her awful men. Blanche, my stomach actually *clenched* at the thought of coping with him and Daddy throughout the holiday. Tony still hasn't forgotten that Christmas at Clifton two years ago when she brought Billy Derwent. I *almost* asked her not to come. But now I'm glad I did, because it was such a lovely surprise when Freddie turned out to be Frederica! I like her very much. And Daddy likes her. Do you like her?'

'Yes, I do. She makes a refreshing change. Lydia's friends are usually male, moneyed and moronic.'

'And they have an unfortunate way of bringing out the worst in her — she's so easily influenced. But Freddie seems to be having a beneficial effect. I was wondering if . . .'

Sybil was edging her way into an earnest conversation, but Blanche did not intend to be drawn further.

'We must all wear buttons saying *I Like Freddie*!' she replied lightly, and went to find the cornflakes.

They were laughing so much that they failed to see the kettle boiling. Blanche rescued it from the Aga and made two pots of tea: one Indian, one China. The kitchen was large and square, dominated by a pine dresser that held a history of the Malpas family in the remnants of old tea and dinner services and children's ware. Henrietta had found her personal mug and was mixing cocoa.

'This child,' said Lydia to Blanche, 'is killingly funny. She's been telling us about the journey down from Yorkshire. Mimicking everyone. She's exactly like Teddy at the same age. Do you remember how Teddy used to make us laugh when we were children?'

Henrietta was smiling round, touchingly pleased with this reception.

'She's a Rock of Gibraltar, too,' Blanche said fondly. For her niece had always been a favourite. 'She keeps those two men of hers in order.'

'I wish to God I could!' said Henrietta devoutly.

She was such a quaint eleven-year-old that they all laughed, but the little girl dropped her spoon and burst into tears. Then they saw that she had been serious, and was finding life difficult.

'Touched on a nerve, eh?' said Freddie kindly.

Lydia mouthed across to her sister, 'Missing her mother?'

'Just a bit tired. Very sorry,' Henrietta sobbed.

Blanche placed one arm round her thin shoulders and hugged her. 'I'll bet you've been up since the crack of dawn, packing for everyone.'

Henrietta found a handkerchief tucked under her jersey sleeve, wiped her eyes in a businesslike way and visibly pulled herself together. The three women were amused and sorry, careful not to smile.

'Here, Henny, let me mix your cocoa for you,' said Freddie kindly.

'And have a couple of chocolate biscuits with it,' said Lydia in sympathy.

'Can't eat – too much – chocolate,' Henrietta sniffled. 'It – makes me – spotty.'

She hiccuped, blew her nose, looked round at them and managed a giggle.

'How about a couple of shortbread fingers instead?' Lydia asked.

'Nothing, thank you. I was extremely piggy at the restaurant this evening.'

Blanche said, 'You've had a long hard day, Hen. Come to bed and bring your cocoa with you. You can put the bedside lamp on and read if you like. Aaron won't mind. I'm bringing him up to be adaptable.'

Her son was wide awake, standing up in his cot in the crimson gloom of a nursery light, staring round his new world with the air of a Magellan. He was one of life's explorers and discoverers,

27

finding strange people and places fascinating rather than frightening. But at fifteen months old, after a long day's travel and an evening with an unknown babysitter, even the most intrepid hero is glad to see his mother. He gave a long low crow of excitement and pleasure and jiggled the side of his cot. Blanche lifted him up, kissed him passionately, and inspected his condition. 'Lord above, he's a lake! Hen, would you be a love and pass me that packet of disposables?'

Aaron tried to twist over, pointing through the bars, saying, 'Ba! There!'

'Ba's on the floor,' said Blanche. 'Who threw poor old Ba out of the cot?'

Aaron lay on his back and kicked in glorious abandonment, chanting, 'Ba. Ba. Ba.'

'That's an extremely peculiar creature,' said Henrietta, of the long limp dirty-white wool toy. 'What is it supposed to be?'

'It's meant to be a lamb. That's why we called it Ba. Mrs Patel knitted it for his birthday and he loves it.'

'Who's Mrs Patel?'

'She's the lady who looks after Aaron during the day while I'm working.'

'H'm. Daddy's been reading us stories of ancient Greece and Rome,' said Henrietta, quite recovered, 'and Aaron does remind me of the infant Hercules. I'll bet if you brought a couple of serpents in he'd strangle them with his bare hands. Oh, by the way, don't suggest that to Ben. He's likely to find two grass snakes and try it out.'

She switched topics without pausing. 'It's a tight squeeze in here for the three of us, isn't it? Still, we've got a bigger bedroom than anyone except Gran'ma and Grandpa. And I like this room. Was it always yours?'

She was still enough of a child to be unselfconscious about her body, and began to undress, folding her clothes and hanging them neatly on the back of a chair as her mother and grandmother had taught her. Her shoulder-blades were budding wings.

'Yes, but I shared it with Lydia until the extension was built. Then she was given Edward's room next to this one, and your father moved into the new bedroom next to Gran'ma and Grandpa – where he and Ben are now.'

Henrietta pulled a nightgown over her head, saying, 'He and Ben and Clementine, you mean. I'll bet she rolls round in her wheel all night and keeps them both awake! Should I take those cornflakes to her?'

'Oh, yes, please. And tell Ben I'm coming in to put the light out.'

Blanche made a dry and tidy parcel of her son and tucked him back in his cot. She heard Henrietta giving her brother a sarcastic run-down of his behaviour throughout the day, ending with, 'And for God's sake go to sleep!'

Ben held his ground sturdily. 'You go to sleep, too,' he answered. 'Bossy-boots!'

She bounced back, saying, 'That boy is impossible!'

'He's a boy,' Blanche replied peaceably. 'He's supposed to be impossible.'

Slithering through the open door on paws of silk came the Siamese, and immediately Henrietta scooped her up, crooning, 'My darling Salome, come to bed with me!'

'No, Hen. I must take her out, otherwise she'll jump into Aaron's cot.'

'Oh, please, please. I won't let her. Oh, please. Oh – all right,' forlornly, handing over the cat.

'You can read until I come to bed,' Blanche reminded her. 'Have you brought a book with you, or do you want one from downstairs?'

'Oh no. I've brought one,' importantly, taking a paperback from her travelling case, and making a great play of hiding the title.

'What is it?'

'It's a secret,' said Henrietta, dying to tell. 'Promise you won't be shocked?'

'I'm not very shockable.'

'*Lolita.*'

No point in asking if her father had allowed this extraordinary choice. His attitude towards his children was one of easygoing disregard.

'Dear God. At eleven years old. What do you make of it?'

'I don't know,' she replied honestly. 'I think it's a bit yukky myself, but I must read it because Sally Fosdike did and it's all about a nymphet. Blanche,' hopping to the next question, 'do very young girls like having sex with grown-up men?'

'Not if they're sensible.'

'I shan't,' said Henrietta positively, 'but then I shan't have sex, anyway. Sally Fosdike told me what people do and I think it's very rude. I'll bet Ben will. It would be just his sort of thing.'

'Goodnight, Hen,' Blanche said, and could not help shaking with laughter as she hugged her.

Henrietta kissed Blanche's cheek and Salome's head. 'I don't know why people think I'm so funny,' she said pensively. 'Actually, I'm dead serious.'

The intrusive and indomitable male world was threatening to disturb her peace once more. Blanche's son had pulled himself up again, standing this time at the end of the cot where he could contemplate his cousin at close range. Henrietta's tone changed to one of command.

'Aaron Malpas! Lie down immediately!'

His face assumed a truculent aspect. He sought among the rare specimens of his vocabulary.

'No,' said Aaron.

Blanche closed the door and left them to it.

In Ben's room a sturdy striped figure was sitting cross-legged by the hamster's cage, and a voice that could have breathed o'er Eden was saying, 'One cornflake for you, Clemmie. And one for me.'

Salome yowled and Ben jerked round, saying urgently, 'Don't let her in!'

'I won't. I'll put your light out later. Goodnight, Ben.'

'Night, Blanche,' briskly, then again with zephyr-like softness, 'and another one for you Clemmie, and another for me . . .'

The hamster sat up with the cornflake in its paws, nibbling fast and daintily while Ben watched her with the absorption of love.

CHAPTER FOUR

Christmas Eve

Each member of the family had been allotted a task for the evening. Anthony and Sybil were to play host and hostess; Blanche to act as general manager; Edward to be the barman, with Lydia and Freddie as waitresses; Henrietta and Ben would answer the doorbell; and Aaron would go to bed.

Minions had been made ready for the occasion. The dividing doors between living room and playroom were folded back to form a spacious reception area. In the room across the hall both leaves had been let into the dining table, and chairs sat round the walls as if waiting for a dance. Mounds of warm mince pies, powdered with icing-sugar, stood by piles of folded green paper napkins and red paper plates. An assortment of glasses, on loan from the Cornish Arms, surrounded a steaming bowl of Christmas punch. Lydia had made the punch in her image: slapdash, inspirational and generous. It was eye-watering. Henrietta and Ben tried a surreptitious sip or two and, in a mood of seasonal goodwill, stuck out their tongues, crossed their eyes, and staggered about, arm in arm.

Anthony was completely at ease. With the air of conferring a favour on the assembly, he took up his favourite position in front of the living room fireplace, smiling genially.

'Darling, you look incredibly handsome,' said Sybil, straightening his white bow tie, 'but are you sure it's the right thing to wear formal dress? It might seem—'

'Nonsense. Jack and I always wore our penguins for this occasion.'

'Yes, I know. But that was at Predanick Wartha, and Jack was local gentry.'

'And this is Minions and I'm the host,' said Anthony positively. 'Besides, I like people to dress up for an occasion.'

'Quite right,' said Blanche, on her father's side for once. 'If people didn't dress up I'd be out of business.'

He addressed his complaint to her. 'In my youth the girls made an effort to look pretty, and the men to be clean and smart. But youngsters never do, these days. I see my students turn up for a university dance – and God knows from their appearance whether they're male or female! – with unwashed hair, scruffy jeans and a T-shirt bearing some such slogan as *Kiss Me Kate!* printed across the front.'

'More like *Do You?*,' Ben said under his breath, and was shushed by his sister.

Nevertheless, when she had ceased to be officially scandalized, they put their heads together and giggled.

'Students haven't money to spend on clothes,' Sybil reminded them.

'It isn't money,' said Blanche flatly, as positive as her father. 'It's a question of style and flair. At art college, in the dress design department, we could run up something gorgeous that cost practically nothing.'

'You looked outlandish most of the time,' said Anthony mildly, gratified to find her concurring with him.

'But not unwashed or shabby, and certainly individual, wouldn't you agree?'

'I'll grant that.'

Reassured, Sybil slipped her arm through his and surveyed the family. 'I think we're all very elegant!' she remarked.

'I wanted to stay as I was,' muttered Ben, suffering from a shirt and tie.

Anthony looked at Sybil approvingly. She had developed a personal style over the years: a flowing line, soft materials, subdued colours. Privately, Blanche dubbed it 'White Witch' and had created this silvery-blue gown for her.

Anthony lifted his wife's hand and kissed it in homage. 'There's no one here to match you!' he said, with conviction.

They smiled at each other. And as always Sybil, wanting others to share his praise, singled out her new guest. 'Don't you think Freddie looks chic?'

'I was about to say so,' said Anthony courteously, inclining his head towards her.

A stocky woman in her early forties, Freddie held herself well and made herself handsome. Her greying fox's brush of hair was beautifully cut. She wore the minimum of make-up and, like Sybil, had developed her own style. This evening she wore a severely tailored black suit and a frivolous white silk shirt that evidently caught Henrietta's fancy.

'You look like a highwayman,' said Henrietta enviously, 'with the ruffles peeping under your cuffs and all down your chest. I wish *I* looked like a highwayman.'

She was disconsolate in last year's finery, now a fraction too tight and too short.

'And *I* wish,' said Freddie, kindly and perhaps truthfully, 'that I was a slim young willow wand, with long brown hair and all my life before me!'

'Thank you.' Unconsoled. 'Lydia looks lovely, too.'

Now the girl was desiring a woman's body, which could be draped cunningly, seductively, in plum-blue jersey wool.

'Can that be a Bruce Oldfield?' Blanche asked, only half believing.

Lydia must be in funds.

'Yes. It's an early Christmas present from Freddie, actually,' said her sister.

'Lucky you! Do you mind if I stare at it intently?'

'Stare away. I'll hand it over when I've taken it off tonight, and then you can give it a professional inspection.'

Anthony cleared his throat, preparatory to making a statement.

'You may think us old-fashioned and sentimental, Betty,' he remarked pleasantly, putting Lydia's rich friend in her place, 'but in our family we feel that Christmas presents should not be exchanged before Christmas Day.'

'That one was a pre-Christmas gift,' Freddie answered him, equally pleasantly. 'I have another for the day.' She paused fractionally before putting him in his place. 'Alan.'

She was so composed, and her tone so good-natured, that the challenge took a few seconds to register. Blanche bit her bottom lip, and her eyes gleamed. She winked at Lydia, prepared to join the fray.

Then her father laughed and said, 'Sorry, Freddie. Never could remember names!'

The moment passed.

'Let's have a glass of that punch while we're waiting,' Edward cried, relieved.

Ten minutes to eight.

Freddie, moving over to Blanche, drink in hand, said, 'Lydia tells me you're a dress designer.'

'Yes. But not on the Bruce Oldfield level.'

'Is that one of yours?' Indicating her glittering evening jacket.

'Yes. Quite an ancient effort. It was the first thing I made when I left college, so you can guess how old it is. I spent hours and hours, mesmerized, sewing on the beads.'

'I like it. A touch of the Byzantine. And a classic shape that doesn't date.'

'It does wear well,' said Blanche off-handedly, but she was deeply pleased.

'You look a touch Byzantine yourself,' said Freddie, sizing her up. 'Tall, too. You're fortunate to be such a good advertisement for your own clothes. Do you work with or for someone, or by yourself?'

'Dress design is a sideline, for the moment. It's a perilous profession at the best of times, which these are not, and I have a son to bring up now. I teach three days a week at an art college. The rest of the time I do private commissions. My latest job is dressing a new pop group for a tour. It's amusing and original, and they pay well.'

'What else have you done?'

'Weddings for the newly rich. They aren't yet confident enough to walk into the big salons, so I'm easier to approach, and cheaper. Sometimes I dress the female sides of both families. And they recommend me to their friends. It's shrewd of you to spot the Byzantine influence. I love heavy brocades, rich colours, jewels and embroidery. I made a glorious dress for one bride, with floating panels . . .'

The doorbell rang, and the children sprang forth.

Sybil's fears had been ill-founded, her antennae too sensitive. The villagers accepted the invitation at face value: a chance to see inside Minions and to enjoy themselves. They arrived more or less together, and showed no signs of departing earlier than was

34

necessary. In a sense they took over the occasion, and the Malpases had only to follow. By nine o'clock the punch bowl was emptied, the mince pies decimated, and the house filled with the joyful noise of a party in full swing.

Anthony and Edward were being affable with their guests and each other.

Henrietta, to the accompaniment of sonorous voices, was earnestly playing 'God Rest Ye Merry, Gentlemen' on the play-room piano.

In another corner of the room, surrounded by an admiring audience, Ben was showing off Clementine, who rolled hither and thither inside a transparent plastic ball. 'And I've got a stick insect,' he was saying, 'in my bedroom.'

Sensibly, the other animals had retreated and were sitting upstairs, shedding hairs on the visitors' coats.

In the kitchen the Malpas women met: entertained, elated.

Brewing more punch, warming more pies, Lydia and Freddie sang, 'Oh, they won't go home 'til the mor-ning. They won't go home 'til the mor-ning!'

Sybil said, 'They'll certainly be here until midnight at this rate!'

Blanche, coming in for a dustpan and brush, added, 'Well, they'll have to carry Mat Kellow when they do go! He's been drinking since he arrived, and he's already tripped up and smashed a wine-glass.'

Round the door came the face of Demelza Laity, unused to being idle while others worked.

'No, no,' they chorused, waving their arms at her. 'You're not allowed to help tonight, Mrs Laity. Go back to the party.'

But she wanted to sweep up the broken wine-glass. 'It's that Mat Kellow,' she said. 'I did say.'

They protested. She insisted. The doorbell rang and silenced them all.

'I thought everyone was here. Who's the latecomer?' Blanche asked.

'I don't know nobody else,' said Mrs Laity. 'I'd best see, hadn't I?'

The four women waited and watched, interested, as she plodded down the passage. No one was ushered in from the cold. Some conversation or explanation seemed to be in progress. Then Mrs Laity partly closed the door and plodded back to report.

35

'It's three folk as we don't know, Mrs Malpas. A tall elderly lady as did the talking, and a small lady standing behind her, holding a bundle, with a scarf to her mouth. And a man lurking by the 'edge holding some great box. They stood well back, and it was dark and I couldn't see them proper. And the lady she say she want to speak to you. But I didn't like to let none o' them in so I ask her to wait.'

Her disquiet was transmitted to them.

'How very odd,' said Sybil, frowning.

'Perhaps it's D. H. Lawrence's three strange angels,' said Blanche lightly.

'In which case,' said Freddie, picking up the quotation, ' "admit them, admit them" !'

Yet no one made an offer to move.

Mrs Laity's imagination ventured further forth. 'Might be some o' they hit and run folk.'

Blanche laughed and relaxed. 'There are too many of us to hit,' she remarked.

'And we can hardly leave them standing outside,' said Sybil.

'I'll go, if you like,' Freddie offered, seeing that they still hesitated.

'Nonsense!' Sybil said. 'Why should you?'

'I'll go, for heaven's sake,' said Blanche, and she walked rapidly down the hall, and opened the door, crying, 'Awfully sorry to keep you waiting.'

The three figures did look ominous. They hung back, just as Mrs Laity had described them, and she could not see their faces. For a moment they were all silent. The atmosphere was tense, fragile, apprehensive. The air was cold. Their breath steamed. Then the spokeswoman came forward into the porchlight, smiling but not at ease.

She was much the same age as Blanche's parents, and seemed faintly familiar. It was a harsh, handsome, hawk-like face, and the voice matched it. She was wearing a black cape lined with fur, which had once been very beautiful and very expensive. She had pulled her fur hat well down over rebellious white hair. This, and the high leather boots, gave her a Russian appearance.

She said, almost brusquely, 'I asked for Sybil so that I might introduce myself by degrees. It's many years since we last met and none of you children would know me. My name is Natalie Malpas.'

She had been a family legend: a photographer by profession, a wanderer by nature, someone who sent extravagant presents when they were least expected, whose rare letters were a sheet of paper wrapped round a bundle of pictures, on which she had scrawled 'love from Tasha'.

Some family bond reasserted itself between them.

Blanche cried in joyful disbelief, 'Aunt Tasha? I'm Blanche.'

The woman smiled spontaneously then, and said, 'So I thought.' And more quietly, 'Yes, I would have known that.'

Still she stood back, uncertain. Surely this was the moment for words of delight and surprise, hugs and kisses? At least, that was how Blanche felt. But Natalie apparently wished to dispense with outward shows of affection. Introductions over, she waved an imperious hand in the direction of her companions. 'The three of us arrived early this evening at the Cornish Arms, and had a meal together. We're staying there. They told us you were giving a party tonight. So we came bearing gifts, hoping to be invited.'

Blanche was saying, 'Oh, Aunt Tasha! I can't believe it's you.' Then recollecting the hospitality of the house. 'Come in, come in – and do bring your friends with you.'

Still the other two hung back.

Natalie said, 'They aren't friends exactly. None of us has met before now. But as we were staying in the same place, and had the same destination in mind, we came together.' Then she cried mockingly, jokingly, 'Advance and reveal yourselves!' And to Blanche, 'They seem shy – and from what they've told me, they might well be.'

Anthony, coming splendidly into the hall, cried, 'Who the devil is it? Bring them in, for God's sake, and shut that door before we all freeze to death!'

'He doesn't change!' said Natalie, and walked past Blanche, saying in her harsh contralto voice, 'How are you, you old bastard?'

He answered under his breath, as if he were informing himself, 'Tasha?'

Sybil came to his side, one hand lifted to her mouth. Natalie paused, temporarily losing her air of command. Then she strode forward, looking more Russian than ever, and held out her arms to them both.

Sybil embraced her sister-in-law more in astonishment than pleasure. Then they stepped back and stared at each other, smiling self-consciously, remarking that neither of them had changed a bit. Well, perhaps a little bit, but not much. They would have known each other anywhere.

Anthony cried heartily, 'Well, well, well! Tasha, of all people!' and placed a benevolent arm round her shoulders.

But Blanche had registered the first expression on her parents' faces, and guessed that this visitor was not welcome to either of them, though both were making a public show of reunion.

'You needn't worry,' Natalie was saying loudly, hoarsely, 'I haven't come to land on you. I've booked a room at the Cornish Arms for a few days. And if you can't bear me I can always disappear.'

Sybil had taken charge of the situation and was issuing different orders. 'You'll do no such thing! Disappear indeed! What nonsense — after all this time! Tony, darling, will you get Tasha a drink? We have punch and wine, or something stronger if you prefer that. Whisky? Darling, a large whisky for Tasha, please. This is a long lost sister, everyone. Isn't that wonderful, at Christmas time?' Remembering the other latecomers, 'Blanche, will you take care of our other guests while I . . . ?'

The small woman with the bundle clutched to her chest was moving into the lighted porch. For a moment Blanche did not recognize her. But Henrietta and Ben, sidling into the hall, anxious to miss nothing, immediately scurried past Blanche crying, 'It's Mummy! Mummy! Mummy!'

'Of course,' Blanche said to herself. 'Katrina!' And to her sister-in-law, 'Kat, you idiot! What are you playing at? Hiding away! Come in, come in!' And to herself, 'You don't recognize the person you least expect!'

Katrina and her children were laughing and crying and clinging, while between them a small animal stuck its head from the top of the bundle, and strove for freedom and recognition.

'This is my Christmas present to you, Henny,' said Katrina, extricating the puppy and presenting it. 'It's a King Charles spaniel.' And she stood the little creature, whimpering with terror, on the floor.

The other animals, drawn by instinct to the very place they were not wanted, had descended the stairs. Salome leaped on top of the hall table and let out a chilling howl of non-welcome.

Gracie padded forward growling softly, to smell and inspect this new visitor. Patch arched his back and spat. And into the throng rolled Clementine, roving distractedly in her transparent bubble. The puppy wet itself immediately.

Henrietta cried, 'Oh, my darling! It wasn't your fault. Hen will mop it up!'

She took the newcomer into her thin young arms, and pressed it lovingly to her flat young chest. The puppy licked her lavishly.

'What on earth's going on here?' cried Edward, coming out of the dining-room. And stopped short, and turned so pale that the freckles stood out on his face like a rash. He passed a hand over his hair, saying distractedly, 'Good God. It's Kat!' He started towards her, unsure of his welcome, but hopeful.

'Hello, Teddy,' said Katrina pleasantly, but her eyes kept him at a distance. She turned to her mother-in-law. 'Sybil, I do apologize for crashing in like this, but it was truly important.'

In the background Lydia held Natalie's fur-lined cape and explained the intricacies of the situation to Freddie, who was saying, 'Je-sus H. Christ!'

Although the hosts were now totally distracted, the party went on around them all as if it had never been interrupted. Aware of the third stranger, Blanche turned to the figure lurking by the hedge. 'Come in, come in, whoever you are!' she called gaily.

To be transfixed.

A large untidy man with a mop of rust-red curly hair moved forward into the light, abashed. He was carrying a box full of Christmas parcels. He was comfortable in his old brown car coat, but beneath this a navy-blue chalk-striped suit sat oddly on him, as if his body was used to wearing more casual clothes. He set down the box, held out his hand, unsure whether it would be taken or bitten, and spoke in a tone half-mocking, half-beseeching, whose caressing lilt came of Irish ancestry.

'Hello there, Blanche. I happened to be passing the door, and thought I'd drop in to wish you a Merry Christmas!'

Blanche neither moved nor spoke, but by this time Sybil had pulled herself together, and amazingly well considering the circumstances. She came forward, with her hospitality smile pinned well on, saying, 'And this gentleman is . . . ?'

'Aaron's father,' Blanche replied bluntly. 'I don't believe you've ever met. His name is Daniel Kidd.'

CHAPTER FIVE

Blanche had never admired her mother more. Daniel, uninvited and previously unknown, was someone outside Sybil's experience in every way. His relationship to Blanche and the child would be seen as irresponsible, heartless, contrary to all Sybil's beliefs in marriage and parenthood. Yet she welcomed him in, and introduced him to the company with aplomb.

'Everybody! This is *not* Father Christmas – though you might think so from that enormous box of Christmas presents – but Blanche's friend Daniel Kidd. Put the box over here, Mr Kidd. Yes, in that corner by the tree will do nicely.' Then to her elder daughter, 'I expect, Blanche, that Mr Kidd would like a word with you in private before he joins the rest of us.'

Her brow furrowed slightly as she considered the problem of privacy. Minions was jammed from end to side. Enlightened, she cried, 'Tony's study! You can take him upstairs to your father's study, Blanche. Now, what would you like to drink, Mr Kidd? We have rather a good punch—'

Here Natalie broke in with, 'He doesn't like punch any more than I do. He's a whisky man. Irish if you've got it and Scotch if you haven't. I should know. We've all been drinking and talking together since seven o'clock!'

Daniel bowed his unruly head, picked up Sybil's hand, kissed it, and said in a voice of velvet, 'Gracious lady, I would sooner go thirsty than inconvenience you further!'

Sybil's smile came and went impishly. She appreciated the charm, but would not yield to it without good reason. 'That's very sweet of you, but I don't think we need demand a sacrifice of that magnitude.'

She guessed that he had already been drinking to nerve himself for the encounter.

'Blanche, take our bottle of whisky upstairs with you. I don't know whether it's Irish or not. We shall be serving coffee later. Mr Kidd?' He straightened up and looked at her earnestly with deep blue reverent eyes. 'Would you like anything to eat?'

'I thank you, but I have already eaten.'

'Would you like something more?' She could not help adding, 'Perhaps a home-made mince pie?'

He judged his hostess shrewdly. 'A home-made mince pie I could not resist,' said Daniel.

'Very well. Blanche, take a plate of mince pies with you.'

Blanche said to her mother, *sotto voce*, 'I didn't invite him and I don't want to have anything to do with him.'

'Nevertheless,' Sybil answered, softly but adamantly, 'he is Aaron's father, and presumably must have meant something to you once, and he is your guest, and you must deal with him! Now please take him away while we cope with the others.'

'This is one of mine,' said Daniel, fishing out a bulky badly wrapped package, and tucking it under his arm.

Watched by every member of her family, Blanche preceded him haughtily up the staircase. Humble but determined, he followed her.

They entered the sacred study together, and he placed the parcel on Anthony's desk. She motioned him to sit, and stood as far away from him as the little room would allow.

There was a brief silence, then Daniel said reproachfully, 'You never let me know when he was born.'

'You didn't ask me to let you know. In fact, you said that the pregnancy was my idea and you wanted nothing more to do with it.'

He bowed his head at the reprimand, but began again. 'I bought *The Times*, the *Telegraph*, the *Independent*, and the *Guardian* for weeks, and looked in the birth columns, trying to find out when he was born.'

Blanche asked, not looking at him, 'How did you know I'd put it in the paper anyway? It isn't the sort of thing I usually do.'

'I thought you'd be flying the flag,' he said. 'You were always a great one for flying the flag. It'd be your way of saying you didn't care what people thought, and that you'd done what you felt was right.'

She inclined her head, acknowledging that he understood her.

Although they were apart, the current on which they had first been borne away together was beginning to flow again. She was aware of him staring at her and her flesh prickled. She sensed anxiety in the way his big hands smoothed his knees. She guessed that he had dressed up to meet her family, and that his jacket and tie restricted him. And his voice both pleased and troubled her.

'I found it in all four of them,' Daniel continued. 'You made sure nobody missed it. "To Blanche Malpas, a son. Aaron."'

Blanche took her bottom lip between her teeth and bit it reflectively.

'It's a grand name,' said Daniel, 'and I like it. But why Aaron?'

Then her tongue was loosened. For the experience had been costly, and she still remembered the loneliness of labour, the tearful exhilaration of birth, the vulnerability of this new human being, the shock of being totally responsible for him, the terror of loving him enough to die for him if need be. The Malpas virago, her father had once named her. She reared up now, facing Daniel Kidd, blazing away at him: a Byzantine figure in her stiff beaded jacket and heavy gold earrings, with her narrow black eyes and her frizzed black bob and a brave red lipstick on her mouth. 'I called him Aaron because I loved the name, and there was no one in my family – or yours, as far as I was aware – called Aaron. I wanted him to begin life unencumbered. No uncle, cousin, father, grandfather to be placated. No ready-made model for him to waste emotional energy in copying or rejecting. *His* name. *His* life. That's why.'

'You were always eloquent,' said Daniel, who had not ceased to regard her, 'and beautiful and vital, and utterly and cruelly desirable. Mother of God, Blanche, how did we come to lose each other?'

She did not answer him, did not know what to say, and was afraid to begin saying anything lest she said too much and could not stop. She was shattered in every way by his presence, possessed by anger and fear and apprehension.

'And I've never even set eyes on the boy. Could I not have a glimpse of him?' Daniel asked, very low. 'Just a glimpse. I won't wake him up. He doesn't have to see me. I've brought him a Christmas present,' gesturing towards the parcel, 'but I'll take it and go away again if you want that.'

Blanche reflected that she should not have to feel so vulnerable. The Daniel she left was a man who set his freedom above all else, as she did; a man who shunned permanent bonds and social ties; a man who avoided the daily round and the common task. The joy of the coming child had softened a separation she would otherwise have found unbearable. The demands of Aaron had diminished the claims of Daniel. She had believed herself to be free of the man and was not now so sure.

'What do you mean by coming out of the blue like this?' she demanded. 'What can you want of me or my son?'

'It's not exactly out of the blue,' said Daniel, very low. 'I did write to you, but the letter was returned, marked address unknown.'

'I moved just before Aaron was born.'

'I sent it off again, care of the art college.'

'I returned it unread.'

'I found your Clifton address and sent another letter, care of there.'

'I returned that one unopened.'

He spread his hands to indicate that he was, and had been, at a loss.

'So finally,' he said, 'I decided to call on you both.'

She cast up her eyes and spoke to whatever mocking god was presiding over this rendezvous. 'He *calls* on us. At a private family occasion, on Christmas Eve, in the depths of Cornwall. My God! Now I've heard everything.' She addressed him fiercely, 'Did it not occur to you that you might be pushing your luck?'

He smiled sheepishly at his hands.

'Listen to me!' cried Blanche, forcefully. 'Two years ago . . .'

'A year and nine months,' he dared to say.

'. . . we agreed to go our separate ways, if you remember. I can quote you chapter and verse if you like.'

He shook his head, motioned this offer away. 'I'm not after proving a point,' he said pacifically. 'I remember what happened. We'd been wrangling about nothing at all—'

'It may have been nothing at all to you, but to me it was a great deal. You benefited by our living together. I did not. You worked, slept and ate when you felt like it, and if the flat was a mess you didn't notice. I'm organized and tidy by nature, so my work was being disrupted, and too much of my time was spent in keeping the place decent and looking after both of us.'

'But', he said, hoping for justice, 'that was just me being what

43

I am, and you being what you are.' As she showed no signs of relenting, he added, 'And then you flummoxed me entirely by telling me you were pregnant, and intended to keep the baby.'

In a fury, she said, 'You told me I was welcome to make a fool of myself, if I wanted to, but not to make a fool of you.'

'Well, I couldn't make head or tail of what you were driving at,' said Daniel, with some reason. 'A baby is more trouble than I could ever be, and takes up more time than any man on earth. I ask you now, as I've asked myself a thousand times, where was the logic in your argument?'

She dismissed logic with a wave of the hand, crying, 'Then you insulted me, by hinting that I'd got pregnant on purpose so that you'd marry me!'

He surveyed her sorrowfully. 'I couldn't help feeling that it was no accident,' he suggested.

'Of course it wasn't an accident, but I didn't have marriage in mind. If I found it hell to live with you, why should I marry you, for God's sake? I was in my middle thirties and I wanted a child while there was still time. It wasn't simply a want either. It was a need. I was hungry for a child, aching for one.'

He said cautiously, 'I accept that now, but you didn't explain it to me at the time—'

'Explain? Who was explaining? We were at the point of throwing things! I told you I was pregnant and you could go to hell if you didn't like the idea.'

Some of the rage and bewilderment he had suffered, then and afterwards, reddened his face and roughened his tone. 'And I felt I'd been used without being asked, and I was damned if I'd play Joseph to your Mary! Did it not matter to you that I was the boy's father?'

She stood up, turned her back on him, folded her arms. This was going to be even more painful than she had supposed. She said with difficulty, 'Certainly it mattered. Just as you had mattered. Yes, to be fair, I wanted *your* child.' Then she found the answer. 'But I didn't want *you!*'

His eyes glinted for a moment, as if he too had found an answer. His anger cooled. 'Well, I couldn't make head or tail of the situation by that time,' he said reasonably. 'What should I have done? What did you want me to do?'

She flung up her arms in despair, and even in despair the gesture was graceful. She faced him now, answered him passion-

44

ately. 'Oh, God knows! Certainly not to be shallow and cynical. I suppose I hoped you might respond to me truthfully and closely, in some way. To ask me why. To look at our life together as I had, and wonder what it amounted to. It wasn't very much, was it? Living from day to day, with no particular purpose, apart from our work.'

He ventured to defend their past. 'It was magic in the beginning. You have to admit that, Blanche.'

She leaned against the wall, folded her arms, and addressed him directly. 'You and I had no future, Dan. Our relationship was either fun or nothing.'

'I deny that!' he cried. 'We were more than that. Why would I be roaming the country on Christmas Eve if we were no more than that?'

Blanche said emphatically, 'We were hollow people. And I *felt* hollow. Aaron made me whole, and I intend to stay whole. So don't waste either your charm or your lust on me because they won't work!'

He was silent then, staring at his clasped hands, struggling with himself. Then he said, 'I'm hollow without you, Blanche. And I had to lose you before I knew that.' He pleaded with her for recognition. 'The old rogue's died in me, Blanche. I've grown up, if you like. I've changed. I see things in a different light.'

Blanche clenched one fist and struck her breastbone for emphasis. 'But – I – haven't!' she cried. 'I feel now as I felt then. I don't want to live with you or any other man ever again. I don't want to know anyone else that well.' She paused, and added, 'I'm not talking about lovers. I don't mind a lover. In fact,' defiantly, 'I've been thinking about someone.' That was the truth, but thinking was as far as it had gone.

'I'm not asking you to take me over,' he said. 'I don't mean that I'm tired of living in a muddle, and I'd like a woman to sort it out. I mean that I want to learn to know you all over again. I want to love you properly this time, to love you as you deserve, if you'll give me the chance.'

Her indrawn breath was a captured sob. She did not answer, could not answer.

He looked at her for a long while in silence, ran one hand through the wilderness of his hair, sat forward, elbow on knee, and thought. And she looked sad, looked away, plucked at a loose bead in her jacket, would have liked to cry wildly and hit him

45

again and again, because he had walked into her life and disrupted it.

He stood up slowly, and reached for the package. 'I'll be on my way, then,' he said, 'and I won't trouble you further. But if you need me for anything at all, any time at all, this is where you'll find me.' And he laid a business card on the desk.

Blanche said rapidly, harshly, 'You can see him before you go. No, don't thank me. Don't say *anything*. I'm not up to talking. He's in the room at the end of the corridor, on the right. It's this way.'

Aaron was awake at the prow of his cot, negotiating the boisterous seas of a Minion's party. His tight-curled halo of red hair glowed in the semi-light. He straddled the bedclothes with confidence, gripped his craft firmly, hailed the approaching vessels amiably. 'Ma-ma-ma-mah!'

Blanche picked him up, heart pounding, and nuzzled his face. She knew that he would be staring at the stranger, fearless, curious. And Daniel would be staring back, in such a whirlpool of emotions as she could well imagine.

Daniel said submissively, 'I wouldn't want to frighten him, but could I hold him for a minute?'

Cutlasses flashed and clashed in her heart. Yet the man had a claim, of sorts.

She said curtly, 'He doesn't like being handed about. He'll come to you if he chooses.'

And she set the boy down on the floor. 'You'd better give that present to me for the moment,' she said.

Obediently, he handed it over, saying, 'It's an Indian outfit.'

An Indian outfit! She could have laughed, screamed, struck him with the parcel, and gone mad.

Father and son took the measure of each other in silence.

Walking was a relatively new experience for Aaron, who clung to his mother's skirt while he balanced himself and thought out the opening move. His gaze travelled from the decorum of Daniel's polished shoes to the blue appeal of his eyes.

Blanche waited to see what would happen next.

Suddenly her son loosed his hold, took four lurching purposeful steps forward, clutched the legs of Daniel's one and only suit, and commanded, 'Up!'

46

'He wants you to pick him up,' Blanche said, dry-mouthed.

Daniel hoisted him reverently aloft. She watched him caress Aaron's red curls that were his, and look into the glinting black eyes that were hers.

'Strange,' Daniel marvelled aloud. 'Most wondrous strange.' His voice was full of tears, but then he had never been ashamed to show his emotions.

Held to the breast of this man, Aaron was also staring his fill. He loved Blanche more than anyone else in the world, but she could not fulfil all his needs. Already he was intrigued by the manners and appearance of his own sex. He watched and mimicked them, as if to teach himself what he must be one day. He would admire the strength and power of Daniel, she knew. Perhaps he would dream about him later, twitching his fingers and eyelids, making little restless movements of remembrance.

Daniel was having a very quiet and intimate conversation with his son. 'I'm sorry I haven't met you before,' he was saying. 'It wasn't that I didn't care about you. I just didn't know what to do for the best. And then, again, you wouldn't have had much time for me before now. The first year belongs to the mother, and last Christmas you were no more than a tadpole. But I couldn't let this year pass me by entirely. I've had to play the detective to find out where you and your mother were, and then to come a long way on a train. But I'm glad I've seen you. You're a fine big fellow. And a handsome fellow. And a credit to the pair of us.'

Blanche, head bent, felt that she should not be hearing this confession, but Daniel was not self-conscious.

He turned to her and said hopefully, 'Could I give him my present?'

She nodded curtly, and replied, 'If you sit him on the carpet and take off the string he'll open it himself. He'll like that.'

Daniel reverted to his intimate tone. 'There then, my bold boy. Down you go, and see what your dad's chosen.'

Aaron plundered the brown paper excitedly, throwing laps of it aside in his haste to find the treasure. When he came to the gift itself he drew a deep breath, gave a deep 'Oh!' of delight, and looked up at them both to make sure that they were appreciating the glory with him.

Involuntarily they knelt beside him, smiling.

He held up the head-dress and enquired on a long curving note, 'Bi-i-ird?'

'It's a head-dress, Aaron.'

'You put it on your head, Aaron.'

Their hands and voices came together, to show him how it was worn. Then Daniel held him up to the mirror so that he could see how fine he was.

'Oh!' said Aaron. Then, 'Down!'

Blanche helped him into the fringed suit, and Daniel put the miniature tomahawk into his clutching fingers.

'I don't think that the tomahawk is a good idea!' she remarked, but not censoriously.

'He can't hurt anyone with it. It's made of rubber. I did ask.' He was anxious to show her that he had thought out the implications, that he understood his responsibilities.

'You'd be surprised what Aaron can do when he's on the warpath!' she replied, amused but unimpressed. 'I'll bet he blips quite a few people with that!'

Aaron commanded, 'See!'

'He wants you to hold him up to the mirror again, so he can see himself.'

'Then up you go, my boy! Ah, will you look at that for a fine figure of an Indian warrior? What shall we call you? Big Chief Aaron.'

'He can't be a big chief right away,' Blanche chided. 'He's an Indian brave.' She came over, arms folded, smiling on them both. 'You're a brave, Aaron. Say – brave.'

He frowned with concentration and mimicked her. 'Bave.'

'Now isn't he quick on the uptake?' said Daniel, uncritical, admiring.

But Blanche was intent on correct pronunciation. 'Br-r-r-rave, Aaron. Br-r-r-rave. Br-r-r.'

He concentrated. 'Br-r-r . . .' The sound appealed to him. He flipped Daniel on the head with his tomahawk saying, 'Br-r-r . . . Br-r-r!'

Sybil, coming in, found them all laughing together, and her small frown of anxiety vanished.

She said, 'I thought you might be here. Blanche dear, a word with you. People are making going home noises. Would you like to help us speed the parting guests? I don't mean you, of course, Mr Kidd . . .'

She paused fractionally to allow him to take his cue, which he did with alacrity.

48

'Now could you not find it in your heart to call me Daniel?'

'Daniel, then. And you must call me Sybil.'

With exasperation Blanche noticed that, though he had still to prove himself worthy, her mother's smile was ready to include him as a possible member of the family.

'As I was saying, we don't expect *you* to go, Daniel,' said Sybil, smiling. 'In fact we're planning to send the children to bed and have coffee and sandwiches. So if you could follow me down, Blanche, when you've settled Aaron.'

She paused on the threshold to muster enthusiasm. 'What a marvellous surprise! Three reunions to celebrate.'

And none of them bringing great joy, Blanche felt, and all to be regarded as highly suspect.

CHAPTER SIX

On her way downstairs Sybil reflected that Blanche had always been a difficult and divisive child, though she was closer to her in many ways than to Edward or Lydia. Or was it that she had always needed to give more time and thought to Blanche, who from an early age had taken up arms against a cruel world? She had never known anyone love or hate quite so passionately as Blanche, and she was headstrong still.

'Tony,' Sybil had often said to her husband, 'if you forbid her something outright, or insist that she do something else, she feels bound to take the opposite stance.'

'You spoil her,' he had replied. 'What she needs is a firm hand. Discipline.'

Renowned for his excellence with students, he was never good with small children. He lacked understanding and patience, and expected far too much of them. And he had a way of giving orders that made them either silently mutinous, like Edward and Lydia, or openly mutinous, like Blanche, who made them suffer her childhood tantrums, her adolescent disputes and her adult rages.

'She should have been called Mary, Mary, Quite Contrary!' Anthony said once, when his elder daughter had particularly infuriated him. 'I have never known such an arrogant argumentative nature.'

Although he had.

And then her insistent honesty almost made a vice out of virtue. What demon possessed her to blurt out, in front of everyone, 'This is Aaron's father, Daniel Kidd!'

So explicit. So unwise. Why toss that particularly fat bit of gossip into their midst, on top of the shock created by Natalie's entrance, and the rifts known and perceived between Edward and Katrina? Tomorrow the news would be all over the village. Not

50

that scandal mattered any more. This evening might well be the Malpases' swan song, after all. A double wake, as it were, combining a final family gathering at Minions with a lingering goodbye to Jack. 'Oh, my dear Jack!' Sybil said to herself, momentarily stilled by the realization that he no longer existed.

But her daughter's peccadillos continued to preoccupy her, and she continued her descent and her inner dialogue. Imagine saying, 'This is Aaron's father!' Like a challenge. Well, Blanche had always challenged the conventions, and provided the village with most of the Malpas gossip, but this was open provocation to her father, and just as things were going well between them.

By great good luck, owing to Edward having to come all the way down from Yorkshire, and Lydia and Freddie starting out late, Blanche and her boy were the first to arrive. So there was plenty of time to become . . . what? Reacquainted was possibly the word. Both of them had tried, though conversation was stilted.

'You're looking well, Blanche,' Tony had said. And then with an effort, 'So this is Aaron, is it? He seems a healthy specimen.'

Blanche had concentrated on university news, and certainly showed great tact about his approaching retirement, neither ignoring the fact nor asking awkward questions. Then they all had afternoon tea together, and he cut a little square of his sponge cake for Aaron, which was rather nice. Yes, it had gone pretty well, apart from Blanche stirring him up about the Christmas arrangements yesterday evening. And today they had been careful not to cross swords.

So wouldn't you think that Blanche would have more sense than to say, 'This is Aaron's father!'

Yet her elder daughter was such a lovely vital person, and so clever with her designing and dress-making. She had created this house-gown, like something a film star might wear, with the back panel cut long so that it trailed slightly behind her, and the material so soft that it fell and flowed and floated with a life of its own: all exquisitely stitched by hand. Such a talented woman and, contrary to all the prophecies, an excellent mother: loving and practical, treating her child with firmness yet with respect, and spending every hour she could with him, playing, teaching him words. Sybil called it good mothering, but nowadays they had a name for it. They called it 'quality time'.

Lydia, on the other hand, couldn't sew, cook, look after herself or anyone else, or do anything much apart from being pretty and lively, and finding some appalling man to keep her. A party-time girl. Had they spoiled her, perhaps, the baby of the family, who had arrived when there was more time and money to spend on her? Or had that disastrous early marriage wounded her more deeply than they thought, rendering her null and void to other relationships? Stupid, really, to allow her to wed at eighteen, though Colin was older and more mature and seemed right for her, and they were so much in love. But it had all gone wrong, and Lydia never seemed to learn from her mistakes.

'Out of the frying-pan! Into the fire!' Tony said, whenever she turned up with a new man.

The problem was that youth and beauty didn't last for ever. Someday there would be no one to pick up the pieces, or the bills. If only Lydia had a career like Blanche. If only she could be persuaded to train for something. If only she were not so extravagant.

And talking of extravagance, how on earth had Edward afforded that Mazda? He suffered from a contradictory nature: he believed in plain living and high thinking, and yet liked to cut a dash now and again. For months he would jog along, uncomplaining, and then suddenly kick over the traces. He had probably been saving up to replace his old record-player, and used the money as a deposit on the Mazda instead. Heaven knows how he managed his finances now Katrina had gone. Tony once said in a bitter moment, 'There is nothing wrong with Edward that a large private income wouldn't cure!' And though he was a kind and loving person, with a delightful sense of fun, he was not made of the stuff that produced great men. Tony had said years ago, 'The boy is bright enough, but he lacks the essential ingredients for success – drive, stamina, and an overwhelming desire to win!'

He had married far too young, and neither he nor Katrina understood each other's needs. She wanted to be somebody in the eyes of the world, to live in a residential suburb, to have her children privately educated. But, even had he wanted the same things, he could never have afforded her life-style on his income as a comprehensive-school teacher. Katrina had accepted this in the early years, making the most of a modest household, looking after Edward and the children beautifully, while attempting to prod him forward but without success. When the children began school she went back to work to provide a few of the luxuries she thought essential, and probably she worked too hard – perhaps pushed herself to breaking point before she walked out on them all.

She had written a long letter to Sybil soon afterwards, trying to explain why she had left home. Sybil appreciated the thought, but it did not help the situation, and it was fairly obvious that the main inducement was this other man. No use giving abstract reasons.

Incompatibility. Who was compatible, after all? The family doctor had once said to Sybil, during a very stressful time in her own marriage, 'None of us is naturally compatible. We all have to work at it!'

The needs of the individual. Surely those needs must be relegated to second place, until the children grew up?

Loss of personal identity. Well, that was true during the early years of mothering, but childhood lasted such a little while, and then they were gone.

Self-fulfilment. Yet at whose expense?

And Edward was no better, saying he didn't know what had gone wrong, he always let Kat have her own way and do what she liked. Which meant, in truth, that he left the domestic worries and responsibilities to her, and brought home the occasional bunch of flowers to show he loved her. Most men did that. Most women had made the best of it, until the women's liberation movement became vociferous. It must have been under their influence that Katrina had written that defiant postscript to her letter, 'I have rights as well. So let Teddy try coping for a change!' Certainly, Edward had done his best and he loved Henny and Ben, but he was not a practical person, and a father is not a mother.

So, in consequence, while Katrina looked for a compatible partner, thought only of her individual needs, regained her personal identity, and attained fulfilment, her children were trying to bring themselves up. Henrietta was much too thin and excitable. Ben needed his hair trimming and his neck scrubbing. And both of them squabbled and looked neglected, and were growing out of their shoes and clothes, while their father spent his savings on a new car and their mother bought her way into their affections with a pedigree puppy.

Sybil took each stair slowly for her body felt heavy, her feet hurt in their high-heeled shoes, and her ankles were beginning to swell after the evening's effort.

Anthony was waiting for her, hovering at the foot of the stairs. The arrival of their uninvited guests had troubled him, as it troubled her. There was something uncanny about three people, unknown to each other and for unknown reasons, deciding to come to this remote end of the country on Christmas Eve and take their chance on being welcomed in.

Anthony spoke her name, almost in entreaty. 'Sybil?'

Whenever he was worried he turned to her for reassurance, but how could she restore his confidence in the situation when she herself had none? The thought of grappling with the difficulties and desires of their estranged visitors, as well as the usual traumas of a Malpas family gathering, appalled her. What she needed now was a husband who would support her, not lean on her. Sometimes, when he demanded too much, she did wonder whether she should have married Jack Maddern instead and lived at Predanick Wartha. What a long, tranquil, charmed backwater of a life that would have been.

Still the entreaty. 'Sybil, my dear?'

She had met Jack at university when he was a light-hearted, fresh-complexioned young man with a boyish brown lock of hair forever falling over his forehead. He had gained weight as he grew older, lost his hair, taken to laughing in what she sometimes thought was a stagey fashion, though people liked it. But his nature remained as sweet as a nut. He had such an expansive manner, such a constant desire to give of himself and his possessions. Good-humoured, good-tempered, easy-going: all the qualities that her husband lacked.

Anthony was looking up at her, seeking refuge, covering the real tremor with news of a surface ripple.

'Sybil? I believe our guests are thinking of leaving.'

This understatement made her smile to herself, for the villagers were milling round Mrs Laity *en masse*, demanding their outdoor clothes.

She took the last step gingerly because of her swollen ankles, and slipped her arm through his, saying, 'Yes, my dear, I know,' and took charge of them all.

'Mrs Laity, would you show the ladies up to our room? Teddy and Ben, could you bring down the gentlemen's coats?'

What were the rest of the family doing? Ah, yes, Henny was collecting glasses and plates, and Freddie and Lydia were ferrying trays into the kitchen. Those three had been marvellous this evening. And the two family visitors? Conversation had evidently guttered out between them. Long-legged Natalie lay back in Tony's easy chair, boots crossed, whisky glass in hand, eyes half closed. Stylish little Katrina perched on an ottoman by the fire, and cuddled the puppy, who stared out from the fortress of her arms with round dark glistening eyes.

'Isn't he a darling?' Henrietta cried, her voice high-pitched with excitement. 'I'm going to call him Mr Silk.'

It would not be easy to keep the puppy happy and reconcile the other animals to its presence. Katrina had not thought of that, nor of the poor little creature's lack of house-training. Katrina had thought only of herself as a bountiful giver, and the effect the puppy would have on her daughter.

And here was Blanche at last, coming down the stairs as if nothing had happened: beautifully bizarre, with her head held high, and an expression that forbade anyone to ask what she was thinking or how she was feeling.

Blanche, Edward, Lydia.

The Russians had a proverb. Many children, many sorrows.

'I want six or seven children!' Sybil had cried in the height and might and ignorance of her youth.

Three had been enough to fill her life from end to end and side to side, and she never had a quiet heart about any of them. Was there something she had not learned? Something she should, or should not, have done?

CHAPTER SEVEN

Blanche paused for a word with Mrs Laity, nodded and smiled at others, and joined her parents. 'They all seem to have enjoyed themselves,' she said.

'Where's that fellow of yours?' Anthony growled.

'Staying with Aaron. He thought he'd only be in the way here.'

'H'm. What does *he* do for a living?'

'He's an artist, an illustrator. Quite well known, well established.'

'Good God.'

People were filing sedately up the stairs in their party best; squeezing themselves down again, bulky in their outdoor clothes; threading their way in and out of the throng. At the front door Sybil and Anthony stood shoulder to shoulder, smiling, shaking hands, thanking each person separately for coming, to be thanked most heartily in their turn, and wished a Merry Christmas. At length the last reveller disappeared into the night, the mist thickened, and peace descended on the house.

Sybil squeezed her husband's arm. 'I would call that a highly successful occasion.'

'It's gone well so far,' he answered drily, 'but it's not over yet.'

And he nodded towards Natalie and Katrina, and jerked his head in the direction of the staircase.

'I'll make coffee,' she answered, skimming over the suggestion that there were further obstacles ahead.

'Oh no, you won't,' said Blanche, putting an arm about her shoulders. 'You'll sit and take off your shoes and relax for once.'

'Yes, yes, come and sit down,' said Anthony protectively,

tenderly. 'You do too much, work too hard. Let these youngsters take care of you for a change.'

Yet, despite their entreaties, she could not let go the household reins at that minute, but must shoo the children off to bed – since neither of their parents made a move – suggest how the puppy be settled down for the night in the playroom, worry about a makeshift dog basket and litter tray, send a message to Daniel to join them all, and finally summon up the last of her energy to make conversation with her sister-in-law and daughter-in-law. But no sooner had she sunk gratefully into an armchair, sighing a little to herself, than Gracie padded forward and slithered luxuriously down at her feet, and Patch jumped onto her lap and purred.

'You haven't changed,' said Natalie with caustic humour. 'Children and animals could always take advantage of you.'

'I know I'm a fool,' Sybil answered wryly. 'I used to spring the mouse-traps that Tony set, and let them eat the cheese.'

She looked away from her sister-in-law at the richly glowing flames, and was immediately reminded of another task. She summoned her husband. 'Tony, we must bring in more logs tonight and make up the fire. The children will be down early to open their presents – oh, heavens, we haven't set out the presents or done the stockings yet – and they'll probably forget to put on their dressing gowns and slippers. We must keep the room warm for them . . .'

And Henrietta's dressing gown was half-way up her legs, and the armholes were tight, and Ben's slippers were fit for nothing but the dustbin. She must look round the January sales . . .

This sorry reverie was broken by the sight of Lydia and Freddie wheeling in a rattling trolley, and now the laws of hospitality knifed her conscience. 'Oh, really, this is too bad of us. Freddie is our guest, and she's cooked mince pies all day and waited on everybody all evening.'

'Perhaps she's hoping to be regarded as a member of the family,' said Freddie.

'Mummy, do stop worrying,' said Lydia. 'We can sort out the presents when you've gone to bed.'

'Aunt Tasha, would you like a cup of coffee?' Blanche asked, presiding over the trolley.

'I'd rather not. It keeps me awake. I'll stay with this,' holding up her glass.

'Let me know when it's empty. Here's your cup, Sybil. Do sit back and drink it, and forget Christmas preparations for half an hour.'

'She needs a small glass of cognac to pick her up,' said Anthony, exploring the sideboard cupboard. He liked to care for her in little easy ways, and liked to be seen caring for her.

Blanche was saying, 'Coffee for you, Kat? Daddy, are you having coffee or do you want something stronger?'

'I'm having whisky when that fellow brings my bottle back!'

In answer, Blanche said over her shoulder, 'Teddy, would you mind hurrying Dan up? And ask him to bring the bottle with him – if there's any left, that is!'

'Why do you say that? Is the man a heavy drinker?' Anthony asked, disquieted.

'Only at parties – and he could hardly mistake a coven of Malpases for a party,' Blanche replied flippantly. And as he continued to look annoyed and perplexed she said, 'Daddy, that *was* a joke!'

Daniel reappeared self-consciously, grinning with nervous goodwill. He had found the bathroom, washed his face, even combed his hair, to appear fresh and presentable. He handed over the whisky, whose level had not descended perceptibly, to which he added another larger and more expensive bottle, and then held out a broad frank hand. 'For you, sir. In thanks for your kind hospitality.'

So what could Anthony do but shake the outstretched hand, welcome him to the gathering, and offer him another glass?

'Come and sit by me, Daniel,' said Sybil, as Blanche kept her back to him, made no comment, and gave him neither instruction nor encouragement.

She was summing him up as Blanche's possible husband and Aaron's father. He was eccentric, she could see that, but then she had a weakness for outsiders, so much more interesting. And he needed someone to look after him, which made her like him all the more. He had loosened his tie, revealing that his maroon shirt lacked a button. His suit was fairly presentable but crumpled, and should have been cleaned. She guessed from the way he wriggled his feet inside his shoes that he usually wore sneakers. She could picture him in daily life: a man who lived on a diet of pub meals and fry-ups, ate when he was hungry, slept when he was tired, and had little idea of time. Occasionally he would surface for

58

sociable or business reasons: hilarious among friends, and tending to drink slightly too much whatever the occasion.

She wanted him to be happy, to expand, to confide, to engage her on his side against Blanche, who was being unresponsive. She smiled upon him. 'If you're too warm in this room – we tend to coddle ourselves in the winter, I'm afraid! – do take off your jacket, Daniel,' she said.

Outside her magic circle, Anthony roamed round, glancing from time to time at his easy chair where Natalie reclined: boots crossed, glass refilled.

'Here, Daddy. Come and talk to Fred and me,' said Lydia, patting the sofa in friendly invitation.

He sat despondently between them, and sighed.

Daniel removed his jacket and fixed his hostess with a reverent blue gaze. His voice was honey and black velvet.

'Sybil, forgive me for trespassing on your hospitality, and at this time of the year, but I had to see the pair of them. And Aaron's a fine boy, isn't he now? And I want to make things right with Blanche, but I'm getting nowhere at all, and to tell you the truth she frightens the life out of me.'

Sybil threw back her head and laughed aloud, and her husband turned to look at her enquiringly.

'Nothing. It's nothing!' she said to him, still laughing. And to Daniel, 'People do tend to be frightened of Blanche. I think it's her defence. I shouldn't take any notice, if I were you. Just act as you think best.'

'God bless you, I'll do that!' he said, encouraged.

Sufficiently restored to take a grip on events, Sybil addressed her three visitors at large. 'So you're all staying at the Cornish Arms? Has Mary Sampson made you comfortable?'

She was genuinely concerned, and they were quick to reassure her that the Cornish Arms was a cross between home and the Savoy.

'We would, naturally, put you up here if it were possible,' said Sybil, 'but as you can see . . .'

Oh, they did see. She must not trouble herself in the slightest.

'And Mrs Sampson is doing Christmas lunch tomorrow, and I'm sure they can rustle up a slice of turkey for us,' said Natalie, still acting as spokeswoman for the uninvited guests, 'so we haven't come a-begging.'

This statement hung on the air, hoping for a different response.

'What nonsense!' Sybil cried automatically. 'I won't hear of it. We expect you to share our Christmas dinner.' Though it would be a squeeze, and all the shops were shut and wouldn't be open for days, and Daniel looked as though he ate a lot, given the opportunity.

'Besides,' said Blanche, from the outskirts of the conversation, 'I think you'll find that Mrs Sampson's full up on Christmas Day.'

'That's true,' said Sybil. 'And all the restaurants round here are booked up for Christmas dinners by the middle of November. So you have no choice!' she cried vivaciously, though her heart failed her a little. 'You'll have to take pot luck with us.'

'I don't suppose any of your meals could be called pot luck,' said Natalie drily. 'You were always an accomplished home-bird.'

Katrina, who was not fond of cooking, though competent, said, 'Sybil's Christmas dinners are out of this world.'

From the sofa, Anthony spoke proudly. 'We hardly had room in the car for the two of us. Sybil brought everything down with her. Luggage. Presents. Two puddings. A cake. Candied fruits. Home-made mincemeat. A box of ornaments. A blasted Christmas tree sticking out at either end of the roof rack. I was afraid the police would stop us for dangerous driving! *And* we collected a damned great turkey that she'd ordered from the farmer at Baripper.'

'I told Freddie,' said Lydia, 'that your Christmases were legendary.'

Hearing of these fabled feasts, Daniel smiled at Sybil, and sat like an overgrown child at her side, trusting her to feed him. She saw the look he gave Blanche, saw Blanche ignore him, and was sorry. She patted his hand. 'I shall expect you to do justice to my cooking, Daniel,' she said kindly, wishing she had ordered a larger bird.

The clock chimed eleven. Anthony stood up, gave a little cough to attract their attention, and consulted his father's fob-watch to check its accuracy. This piece of theatre brought even Natalie slowly to her feet.

'Well, time to be going – or we shall be locked out,' she said.

'And then there'll be no room at the inn!' cried Daniel, gaining sufficient courage to make a joke.

'Oh, well, if you really must,' said Sybil, relieved.

60

Still her conscience prodded her to say more, to show them that they need not go at once, though this was what she wanted.

'Amazing, actually, that you found room in the village at all. And you haven't told us how you discovered that we were here. That must have required some detective work!'

So the three of them again sat and compared notes, which were very similar.

The spirit of Christmas must have entered them, they said airily, laughing at the idea and at themselves.

But Christmas, Sybil could not help thinking, was the loneliest festival in the year for a single person to endure.

Anyway, the desire to be with their family had cut across all other considerations, for which they apologized yet again to their hosts. Daniel's purpose in coming was simple and self-evident, but Natalie and Katrina hinted that the full intent of their visit had yet to be revealed.

'Another day, perhaps?' Sybil suggested tiredly.

Oh yes, certainly. Yes, later, when the festivities were over, and they were given time and space. But to continue.

There had been the last-minute decision to contact the Malpas family. Telephone calls to the house in Clifton, where Sybil had left two married students in tenancy, who gave full information. The realization that they must provide their lodging. Looking up the village of Minions in an RAC/AA guide, and finding that the Cornish Arms did bed, breakfast, and dinner by arrangement, and still had three rooms available. The miracles performed to book train tickets. The journey. The arrival. The coincidence of meeting. The tripartite discussion. And subsequent revelations.

Sometimes they spoke together, sometimes one took up a thread of the story while the others listened. Occasionally they contradicted or expanded or corrected a statement. They tried to cover the enormity of gate-crashing a family Christmas by magnifying their efforts. To be safely here, to be accepted and even welcomed, made them garrulous with relief.

'Oh, God!' Anthony muttered to himself. 'Will they never be gone?'

Lydia and Freddie chuckled.

The clock chimed twelve.

'It's Christmas Day!' cried Lydia, like a delighted child. 'Merry Christmas, everyone!'

The answering chorus was a little ragged. Everyone had called on their inmost resources. Only Natalie, rounding up her troops, still sounded forceful. 'Pumpkin time, everyone! Now, when do you want us tomorrow, Sybil?'

'After breakfast, perhaps?' Sybil proposed.

Katrina said, awkwardly for her who was so self-possessed, 'I know I've given Henny her present already, but oh, I *should* like to see the children opening their presents.'

'Which will be about five o'clock in the morning,' said Sybil, resigned. 'Do you want to come as early as that?'

Katrina hesitated. 'I think it might be difficult leaving the pub at that hour. I don't want to put Mrs Sampson out. She's stretched several points for us already.'

Sybil summoned herself up for a final effort. 'Then suppose we ask the children to wait for their big presents until you've arrived? They can have their stockings as soon as they wake up. But come as soon as you can. A child's idea of time is different from our own.'

Katrina's face struggled. Last year the children had been her undisputed province. Finally she said, 'Yes. Thank you. I'll do that,' and handed the puppy over to Sybil.

'I shouldn't think there's the same urgency for you two,' Sybil said hopefully to Natalie and Daniel, as Mr Silk licked her fingers. 'So come round at your leisure and we'll be waiting for you with coffee or sherry. I'm afraid,' she added, with genuine regret, 'that we have no presents to give you . . .'

No, that didn't matter in the least, they reassured her. Not in the least.

'Well, then . . .' said Sybil, all duties done at last.

Edward helped Katrina into her smart dark overcoat. They had kept apart from one another, had not exchanged more than those initial words all evening. 'See you tomorrow, then?' he said, trying to sound at ease.

'Yes. Tomorrow,' she answered pleasantly.

Anthony held out Natalie's fur-lined cloak. 'Takes courage to flaunt this sort of thing these days,' he said, attempting to chide her while paying a compliment. 'People have been known to shout insults at women in fur coats, even to throw paint. Sybil's old musquash has been hanging at the back of the wardrobe for some years now. She says she feels she can't wear it.'

'I was born in the roaring twenties, and I bought this cape in Austria in the sexy sixties,' Natalie replied indifferently. 'So it doesn't matter a toss to me what other people think. And if anybody throws paint at me I'll crown them with the can!'

Edward helped Daniel into his old brown car coat, and announced over his shoulder, 'I'm going to run you all round to the pub.'

Cries of, 'No need. It isn't more than half a mile . . .'

Anthony said gratefully, 'My dear boy, I was about to offer . . .'

'That's all right, Dad. Ladies and gentleman, your chauffeur and limousine await!' Edward cried, and smiled most charmingly, and saluted and clicked his heels.

Daniel. 'Ah now, we don't deserve this kindness . . .'

Katrina. 'But it's much appreciated, Teddy . . .'

Natalie. 'And it's a bloody *long* half mile. Let's face it . . .'

Blanche folded her arms and glowered as Daniel approached, so he turned away, but gave a little bow of thanks to Sybil, and kissed her hand.

'Good night, everyone!' cried the householders, relieved at last.

'Goodnight. Goodnight. Goodnight.'

Closing the front door behind them, Anthony said, 'Thank God for that. I thought they'd never go. Sybil, why in the name of everything that's sacred . . . ?'

She did not answer him, repeating a Christmas litany under her breath. 'The presents. The logs. The little dog – Mr Silk.'

'Mummy,' said Blanche, taking over, 'do go to bed. Daddy, make her go to bed.'

'Yes, yes, yes. Quite right. Those people have tired her out. Come along, my love.'

Yet on her way upstairs, from the possessive harbour of her husband's arm, Sybil had to pause for a special word with the one remaining visitor. 'Freddie, I do apologize for these shortcomings. You must be thinking that Lydia's brought you to a madhouse. What a tempestuous first visit you've had so far! We'll make it up to you tomorrow. We aren't usually as fraught as this.'

But from the living-room doorway Blanche replied soberly, 'Oh, yes, we are, Freddie. Every bit as fraught. And every time.'

CHAPTER EIGHT

Christmas Day

Blanche heard Henrietta trying not to disturb her while disembowelling a Christmas stocking, and tactfully, gratefully, did not allow herself to be disturbed. But Aaron crawled to the end of his cot, intrigued, pulled himself up, threw his knitted friend to the floor, and gave a shout to encourage the dawning day.

'I'll get him. I'll get him!' cried Henrietta, as Blanche sat up.

'No, sweetie. He's too heavy.'

'I can manage. I'm very strong. Oops-a-daisy,' slightly breathless as she lifted him. 'Come to Hen.'

'He'll be wet,' said Blanche, and swung her legs out of bed. 'What time is it?'

'Only ten to six, I'm afraid.'

'You've done well to last that long. We once woke up at three. *Not* a popular hour.'

'Blanche, I forgot. Merry Christmas!'

'Merry Christmas, Hen! You carry on with your stocking while I change Aaron.'

'And Blanche, Blanche. Guess what I thought when I woke up. I thought – Mummy's come back, and I've got a puppy!' She dropped the stocking. 'Oh, Mr Silk. I must see how he is!'

Her thin face was pink with elation. Her tone slightly shrill.

Blanche said calmly, to steady her, 'One thing at a time, Hen. It's rather early to be dashing downstairs. The puppy will wait another few minutes. If I can leave Aaron with you I'll look after Mr Silk, and bring up a tray of tea and biscuits.'

'And Mr Silk, too. Bring Mr Silk.'

'That really wouldn't be a very good idea. Even Gran'ma would mind if he made messes in the bedroom and chewed the sheets.'

Henrietta opened her mouth to protest, and then screwed it tight shut as they heard a subdued but persistent knocking. 'Guess who this is?' she said, resigned.

The door was opened very quietly and left ajar for a moment, then into the room rolled Clementine, pedalling furiously in her bubble. She was followed by a creeping figure in shrunken pyjamas, a freckled face split by a seasonal grin, and a husky congenial whisper of 'Merry Christmas, everybody!'

'Merry Christmas, Ben. Do stop tiptoeing round and sounding like a ghost with a sore throat,' said his sister briskly. But the spirit of the day entered her, transforming her from a childish shrew to a child. 'Ben, Mummy's come back!'

'I know, I know. I thought that first when I woke up. Even before thinking it was Christmas Day.'

'So did I. I thought about Mummy, and then my puppy – I wonder what Mummy's got for *you*? – and then about Christmas Day. Have you brought your stocking with you? You can come into my bed if you like and bring Clementine. Ben, I've got a chocolate assortment in my stocking. Would you like some? Shall we give Clemmie a bit?' Momentarily distracted. 'Oh, Blanche, what a gorgeous kimono with a gold tree climbing up the back! Did you make it or buy it?'

Blanche was wrestling her son into his first nappy of the day.

'It was one of the costumes for a light opera that didn't happen. I sold the other costumes, but kept this because I liked it so much.' In a mock-stern voice, 'And what about Gran'ma's rule? *No chocolate until after breakfast.*' Then, 'Oh, my God!'

Her capable hands were stilled as she thought of Daniel, sleeping not more than half a mile away, and due to arrive soon after breakfast. But I will not be cajoled, she thought. Her mouth was mutinous.

In that brief space of time Aaron struggled free, rolled over, pointed imperiously towards the children, and said, 'There!' To indicate where he wanted to be.

Blanche returned to everyday life and rolled him onto his back. 'In a minute, you impatient toad!'

Henrietta was saying, 'Ben, I think it would be a good idea if you put Clemmie back in her cage. We can't look after her *and* Aaron.'

'I should take her back to your bedroom and let her travel

round,' said Blanche. 'Why should your father sleep in peace while others toil?'

Edward, appearing at the doorway, said, 'And a Merry Christmas to you, too, you heartless vixen!'

He was tying the cord of his dressing gown, eyes half closed, yawning and smiling amiably. He gave the impression of being young and boyish, but Blanche noticed that his hair was thinner, the lines on his face more deeply etched, his scholarly stoop more pronounced. He winked at his children. 'Merry Christmas, kids!'

'Merry Christmas, Daddy!' In joyful chorus, as they scrambled off the bed to embrace him.

'Teddy,' said Blanche, in her most winning voice, 'are you feeling charitable?'

'Meaning a mug of tea? You don't deserve it! But I always was a good-natured beast. Do you kids need feeding and watering?'

Cries of, 'Yes, please, Daddy. Ribena. Orange squash. Biscuits.'

'And rose hip syrup in warm water for Aaron, please. God bless you, Teddy!'

Outside on the landing Lydia's light, bright laugh encompassed him. 'You'll never remember all those orders,' she cried, teasing.

'Ssh!' he whispered, putting one finger to his lips and nodding towards their parents' room. 'Let's go down and have a private natter before all the Malpases are let loose on one another.' Then he kissed her cheek and said, 'Merry Christmas, Sis.'

She looked fresh and astonishingly pretty in her quilted cotton housecoat, hair brushed back into two pale-gold wings. Face, figure, voice, gestures: everything about Lydia was attractive, and she spoke in a pretty, inconsequential fashion to match them. 'Merry Christmas, darling. Wasn't it amazing when Blanche's man and Aunt Tasha and Kat showed up last night? I'm making coffee for Freddie and me. How long are you staying, Teddy?'

His own smile vanished at the mention of his wife's name. He looked anxious. 'Not sure. I shall keep my eye on the family barometer, and scoot when it swings to stormy. What about you?'

She shrugged and smiled, slipping one arm in his, descending the stairs. 'Just as long as Daddy's nice to Freddie and me.'

The kitchen was clean and peaceful, waiting for the day to begin. It was a room that had been made larger and lighter by knocking down a partition and whitening the ceiling joists and the rough-cast walls. Physical warmth radiated from a scarlet Aga, sitting snugly in its granite alcove. The floor was quarry-tiled in rust-red. A pale-green painted dresser, on whose doors Blanche had stencilled bronze leaves and flowers, held an assortment of cottage china. An old-fashioned clothes-rack hung from the ceiling. Shopping lists, children's drawings, and favourite post-cards were pinned on a large cork board. And in the middle of the kitchen, surrounded by stick-back chairs, stood a nineteenth-century farmhouse table, bought many years ago at a local auction, and vast enough to seat ten people comfortably and twelve at a squeeze.

Gracie rose from her basket and padded across the tiles to greet them, and Lydia opened the door to let her out. Salome sat up at the side of the Aga and yawned, wide and pink and insolent. Patch sneaked off through the cat flap, leaving a mouse in front of the kitchen sink which had been tormented to death. Edward picked it up with the tongs and dropped it in the pedal-bin.

'Horrid puss-cats!' Lydia said, searching the dresser shelves for their personal pottery.

Their three mugs, roomy, sturdy and pot-bellied, had been made a generation ago by a craftsman at a Cornish fair. *Blanche* in white on billiard-table green, with tall blue irises growing from base to lip; *Edward* in scarlet on a creamy ground, flanked by black and scarlet soldiers; *Lydia* in yellow on royal blue, decorated with blobby primroses.

'The old man may be retiring next summer, but he's still got plenty of fire in his belly,' said Edward, filling the kettle, 'and despite Mama urging us to love one another I can't even relax in his company. Childhood minus our father would have been perfect. I used to love those holidays when we came down early, or stayed here without him.'

'I'm sure Mummy did, too, though she always said dutifully at regular intervals, "Wouldn't it be lovely if Daddy were here?"'

'But it never was and we knew it, because he always hogged her attention and we had to keep out of his way – unless he took us for an educational botany walk, which was worse.'

'All those dreadful Latin names. And I got blisters on my heels.'

'And though Uncle Jack did the grand old pals act with Daddy, I got the impression that he preferred having us by ourselves, too.'

Lydia paused, coffee pot in hand. 'Teddy, didn't you feel strange yesterday evening, going through the Christmas Eve routine without Uncle Jack presiding, gin and tonic in hand, and that great laugh bellowing out? He was the only person I ever knew who actually went *Ha! Ha! Ha!*'

'He laughed a lot. I don't know whether that meant he was happier than other people.'

'He liked *us* to be happy,' said Lydia, who had been a favourite with him. 'He could even coax Blanche out of a bad mood. Teddy, hasn't Blanche mellowed? I used to be frightened of her when I was little.'

'You and me, both!' Edward said devoutly. 'She was possessive about Mama, too.'

'*And* about her toys. I cuddled her teddy bear once and she went berserk.'

'When she was on the rampage you and I hid in the cupboard and held hands!'

They both laughed.

'Still, she was always ready to tackle Daddy on our behalf,' said Edward. 'She liked being the leader and protector.'

'And she's so sweet with Aaron. And isn't he a dear little boy?'

'Rouses your maternal feelings, does he?' Edward asked, mocking, curious.

But Lydia laughed and pushed back a lock of hair, saying, 'I'm such a child myself that I couldn't possibly want one! Freddie calls him Blanche's Little Buster! Isn't that perfect?'

Edward was assembling his orders on a flowery National Trust tray.

'Has Kat come to kiss and make up?' Lydia asked suddenly, curious in her turn.

Edward looked suddenly bereft. 'I hope so,' he said, so sorrowfully that his sister was relieved to hear footsteps in the passage, and to change the subject playfully, 'I'll bet this is Mummy, coming to scold us!'

But it was Blanche, saying, 'The kids are champing at the bit, and Henny's fretting for that wretched puppy.'

'Everything under control,' Edward assured her.

Lydia was warming herself at the Aga and watching the coffee percolate. She said, 'Blanche, how long is everyone staying?'

'I think Sybil would like the immediate family to see the New Year in together, but I don't hold out much hope of that.'

'Christ Almighty! We shan't last that long,' said Edward. 'Dad's already lowering his antlers. By the way, I like your bloke, Blanche. A bit of a wild card, but you never had much time for the ordinary sort of guy. How long had he been around?'

'We lived together for two years,' said Blanche with some difficulty, aware that they were watching, listening, assessing. 'We even shared a flat, which was a great mistake, because I'm a loner and I like my privacy and he's gregarious and loves company.'

'You never brought him home,' Lydia observed, arranging four biscuits on a plate.

'I never brought *anyone* home who mattered.'

'Whereabouts does Aaron come into this?' Edward asked.

'Oh, Dan and I were getting on each other's nerves. And I wanted a baby before I grew too old, so I allowed myself to get pregnant. We had a final flaming row, rather like a public firework display, and he roared out and I threw a table-lamp after him.'

Lydia giggled, crying, 'Temper, temper — as Mummy used to say!'

In a lower tone, Blanche remarked, 'We'd both rather loved that lamp. I was sorry about it afterwards.'

'I can imagine,' said Edward. He did not have to imagine. He and Katrina had indulged in equally destructive rows, and he was silent, pondering his own predicament. The atmosphere became sombre.

'Bye-bye, you lovely people!' Lydia cried, lifting her tray and departing in relief.

Blanche and Edward were silent for a few moments after she had gone, and then he said, 'What do you think of Lydia's new friend?'

'She's riding the family waves and troughs extraordinarily well, so far.'

'It's an odd sort of friendship. Lydia never had much to do with women before, and this one seems to have taken her over.'

'Yes, but you know Lyd. She never thinks through any relationship. She's probably making use of Freddie, unconsciously, until the next rich man turns up.'

They were both silent.

Then Edward said awkwardly, head bent, 'I need a private natter, Blanche . . .'

She sighed, and said, 'I'll be glad to lend an ear and a shoulder when I can, Teddy, but right now I must get back to the children or they'll set fire to themselves and stick beans up their noses. Oh, Lord, and I must see what's happened to the pup.'

He attempted a jaunty stance and tone.

'No matter. Here's your tray. Ah! And here's our mama, with *stuff-the-turkey* etched into her forehead!' Kissing Sybil's cheek. 'How are you, lovely lady? Did you sleep well?'

He had adopted the role of favourite son, and she patted his cheek indulgently. 'Pretty well, thank you. Weren't the children good to sleep so long? Is that Gracie scratching at the door? Gracie – da-arling! Yes, darling, and I'm pleased to see you, too. Oh, dear, licked before breakfast . . .'

Edward said, 'I'll look after the puppy, Blanche. You pop off to the kids. And you, my dear Mama, will sit and drink my tea. I'll be back in five minutes and make some more.'

Blanche mouthed at her, 'Teddy needs a sympathetic ear!'

Sybil raised her eyebrows and nodded.

'I'm glad,' said Blanche impishly, 'that you're still wearing that very respectable Granny-type wool dressing gown.'

'Why?' Sybil asked, laughing. 'Nostalgic memories?'

'No. It's far too dull for you. I have plans to replace it with something more glamorous.'

'It's not worn out yet,' Sybil protested, pleased.

'It wouldn't even make decent dusters.'

Edward returned with Mr Silk in his arms, all rolling eyes and drooping ears, uncertain of his fate.

'He's peed everywhere *except* the litter tray, and he's chewed hell out of that blanket you put in his basket.'

'Poor little creature,' said Sybil, holding out her arms. 'He doesn't know what's happening to him. We must make him some bread and milk.' She was diverted by another consideration. 'Oh dear, I haven't made the forcemeat yet, and it's seven o'clock. The turkey weighs eighteen pounds, at fifteen minutes a pound – I need Ben here to do the arithmetic for me – Blanche, would you pass me that notepad, please?'

Edward exchanged meaningful looks with his sister.

'Another Christmas Day dawns in the life of Mother!' he said.

Blanche stood immobilized, at the foot of the stairs.

Heading the procession of children came Ben, carrying all

three stockings, awkwardly crammed with goodies. Behind him followed Henrietta, holding Aaron's left hand. His right hand grasped each banister rail as he took the downward slope one perilous step at a time, and she was finding his progress distressingly slow.

'Let Hen carry you!' she pleaded.

'No!' Aaron said, and continued to plod resolutely down.

Blanche laid the tray on the hall table and came half-way up to meet them. Henrietta's eyes shone with tears. 'I did take good care of Aaron but he kept asking for you, and I had to see Mr Silk. He won't know where he is or what's happening.'

'Gran'ma's giving him bread and milk in the kitchen. Off you go, Hen. I'll take over. Come on, obstinate! Leg it!'

Aaron turned a blissful smile on her, took another step into space, mouth pursed, and landed safely.

'Legit!' he said, savouring the word. 'Legit!' he cried, triumphant.

Oh, God! Blanche thought, Dan will adore him. I'll never be able to keep him away.

Ben spoke confidentially, fingers plucking her sleeve, 'Blanche, do you think Mummy's come back to us for good?' He was looking to her for a miraculous answer, but there was none.

'I don't know, Ben. Let's enjoy Christmas and see what happens, shall we? Would you like to take that tray into the living room? Walk slowly and hold it carefully. Well done.'

Henrietta was scampering back, clutching a bemused and slobbering puppy. Sybil's voice floated after her through the open kitchen door.

'Be careful not to joggle him about, Henny. He's full of bread and milk. And don't go in the playroom until we've cleaned it up. And . . .'

Ignoring her, the children sat in front of the Christmas tree gloating over the glories to come, drinking their fruit juice, feeding biscuits to Mr Silk, talking in high excited voices.

Aaron stood still, clutching Blanche's hand, watching them.

'There!' he commanded, forefinger outstretched to the glittering tree.

'No, you're coming with me to have something to eat. Eat. Yum, yum.'

His black eyes gazed imperiously into hers. Weak with love, she nuzzled his neck and snorted like a pig. He pushed her head away, laughing. They went down the hall together, wrapped in their own world.

'. . . and you had no idea that Kat was coming?' Sybil was saying, bemused.

Edward reached for the sugar basin, embarrassed. 'Not an inkling. She has the kids for the weekend twice a month by arrangement. I don't see her. Haven't seen her since she left. Don't even know where she lives.'

'But surely you have her address and telephone number for emergencies?'

He mumbled, 'Oh, Henny knows where to get hold of her,' and as Sybil set down her mug and stared in disbelief, he added nervously, 'That's how Kat wants it, and I respect her desire for privacy.'

'Well, I do not. The fact that she is leading a secret life, and connives with your children to keep it secret, is downright disgraceful.'

'That's putting it rather forcefully.'

'Not forcefully enough!' said Sybil. 'You shouldn't put up with it.'

He helped himself to too much sugar and stirred it round and round, disconcerted.

Blanche strapped Aaron into his high chair, gave him his feeding cup, sipped her tea and listened. Sybil was in full flight, and her daughter-in-law's name was given its full and bitter length.

'And apparently Katrina is not the only one to have secrets. She expected you to be in Clifton for Christmas.'

Edward said uneasily, 'I think the kids assumed that. I may not have made it clear to them. Anyway, Henny said that Kat would be away for a few days over Christmas, skiing in Scotland. So why should it matter where we were?' He added, 'Henny and Ben are supposed to be spending the New Year with her.'

'Supposed? Has *that* arrangement not been made clear?'

He huddled further back in his chair as if to evade her questions. 'I don't know what's happened. I don't know why she's here, yet.'

'And if the children are to spend New Year with her, which is the first I've heard about it, when do you plan to take them home?'

'I hadn't thought that far ahead.'

Sybil made a sound of exasperation, something between a *tut* and a *tcha*, and Edward roused himself to find a more acceptable answer. He said haltingly, 'Henny said that they were to spend Christmas with me, and Kat was having them for New Year. That's all I know.'

Sybil lifted her eyebrows at Blanche, and returned to the inquisition. 'Are you telling me that there is no communication between the two of you?'

He shook his head.

'Then you must both talk things out while she's here,' Sybil said roundly. 'You can't leave the situation hanging in the air.'

His face was as pale as it had been when his wife appeared the previous evening, and his freckles stood out like a rash. When he spoke he sounded as though the words were being pumped out of him. 'How can I talk to her? You know Kat. If she makes up her mind . . . she will have her own way. There's this man . . . whoever he is . . . he's been in the background . . . for ages. I thought if I let her have her head . . . if I sat tight . . . she'd get over it. Come back to us.' Momentarily illuminated, he said, 'She might have come back!'

'But what I don't understand,' Sybil cried, incensed, 'is why you don't *ask*! Why are you content to know nothing about this man, or where he lives, or she lives? Why have you not insisted on talking this out?'

He put his head in his hands then, and sobbed once, and said, 'I can't bear it. I don't want to hear about it. Don't want to think about it. Can't manage without Kat.'

Sybil exchanged a long, sad, speaking look with Blanche. Her face softened. She put one hand on his shoulder and patted it. 'Oh, my dear boy,' she said, 'when will you learn that we must fight to live, fight for what we want and what we think is right? Well, well. Never mind, for the moment. We'll see what can be done. As you say, she might have decided to come back to you all.' And then in a different tone, 'Who's that coming down the hall?'

Freddie, clad in black silk pyjamas and a fine wool dressing gown, opened the door and peeped round it, smiling the guarded smile of one who is not quite sure of a welcome.

73

'Sorry to bother you,' she said, 'Lydia forgot the demerara sugar.'

Edward lifted his head, wiped his sleeve across his eyes, and became another person. 'Where's that waiter?' he cried, rapping the table. 'Waiter! Waiter! I'll fire the fellow.' He jumped up, pulled a lock of hair over his forehead, hung a gingham napkin over one arm, and replied obsequiously, 'Coming, sir. Here, sir. What can I do for you, sir?'

'Demerara sugar for the ladies – and be quick about it!'

'At once, sir. If not sooner, sir.'

Aaron laughed aloud and banged his feeding cup on the tray of the high chair, crying, 'Sir! Sir! Sir!'

'I'll come to you in a moment, sir!' Edward said, swinging round to bow to him. 'May I recommend the Aga porridge, sir? With cream and brown sugar, sir?'

'Sir! Sir!' Aaron shouted with delight, and threw his plastic cup on to the floor.

But as Edward scurried about, keeping up a running commentary between waiter and customer while he brewed coffee and served porridge, Sybil rose from the table and made a brief excuse. 'I must see what those children are doing.'

She departed in dignity and chagrin, and Freddie looked after her, uncertain whether she had inadvertently offended her.

'Nothing to do with you, Freddie. Simply a touch of Malpasia,' said Blanche.

'I've had a slight disagreement with Mama about my domestic arrangements, Freddie,' said Edward cheerfully. 'It's all over now.'

'Don't you believe it,' said Blanche. 'That was just a short and nasty dress rehearsal for the long and important scenes ahead. I know my family.'

The back door opened, and disclosed two of the three strange angels, hesitating on the threshold, unsure of their reception, crying, 'Merry Christmas, everyone!'

'We couldn't wait a minute longer,' said Katrina.

Daniel's eyes were alight for Blanche in her shimmering Chinese kimono, for his son spattering porridge over the high chair.

'We crept out without so much as a bite of breakfast,' he said.

'But Natalie's still in bed, and I think she'll be quite a while before she surfaces,' said Katrina, in propitiation. 'She took a couple of sleeping pills last night.'

She was smiling round nervously, including her husband in her remarks without addressing him personally. Now Edward kept them on this footing by flourishing his gingham napkin and bowing low. 'Welcome, sir and madam, to the Malpas Hotel. Nothing regarded as too much trouble. Toast and tea shall be yours in abundance, and porridge was made in the Aga overnight. As you can see, we already have one satisfied customer who can recommend it heartily. Umbrellas will be provided while he eats.'

Daniel laughed out of sheer enjoyment, and walked towards his family, hands outstretched. But Blanche plucked Aaron from his high chair and held him to her, despite the porridge, so that Daniel stopped in his tracks.

'Where are the children?' Katrina asked, looking round.

She was soon to be answered.

Sybil appeared on the threshold, saying distractedly, 'Why will no one listen to me? I did warn them. Oh, hello, Katrina and Daniel! Do please excuse me, but we have a domestic crisis. No! Not now, Gracie, go away! Teddy! Teddy! Stop playing the fool – as if you hadn't been fool enough already! – and find me a floor-cloth and a bucket of water.'

Close on Sybil's heels came Henrietta full of apologies, and Ben vociferous with explanations, followed by a woebegone puppy. But at the sight of Katrina all was forgotten.

'Mummy! Mummy! Mummy!'

'Oh, my darlings!' said Katrina, laughing and holding out her arms.

Instantly restored, Mr Silk jumped up and round them, yapping animatedly.

'What's the matter, Sybil?' Blanche asked wryly, over Aaron's tight red curls.

Her mother's answer was terse. 'The puppy has been sick on three Christmas presents.'

CHAPTER NINE

The turkey was hissing placidly to itself in the Aga. Fires had been lit, rooms dusted, vegetables prepared, children persuaded to wash and dress, breakfast accomplished in relays, and everyone brought to the requisite pitch of seasonal exhilaration. In one corner of the living room the Christmas tree was reflected in the mirror over the swagged mantelshelf. Brought from Clifton, strapped to the roof of the car, it was over six feet tall, and though daylight robbed its electric candles of drama they still shone beautifully on an array of ornaments, some of which went back to the younger Malpases' childhood. And beneath its lowest boughs, already being explored by slinking cats and sniffing dogs, were nine piles of presents: imposingly wrapped, enticingly ribboned, seductively carded and bowed.

Blanche walked over to the tree, marvelling, and said, 'So you still have the peacock? I remember him when we were young!' And gently stroked his iridescent spray of feathers.

Now Anthony entered, hospitable and immaculate, carrying a tray of sherry, which was offered – in the whispered opinion of Henrietta and Ben, far too slowly – to the adults. When everyone was served he gave his two impatient grandchildren a long look, and raised his glass as if to toast them.

' "I see you stand like greyhounds in the slips, straining upon the start!" ' he quoted, chuckling a little at his wit. 'And all parents are present. So – let the celebrations begin!'

Henrietta and Ben leaped to the heaps they had marked as their own and plunged their arms deep into the shimmering mass.

Blanche sat with Aaron by his small treasure trove, handed him a parcel and watched his face intently. She did not see the interchange of nods and winks between Edward and her parents, nor notice that her brother had left the room, until he wheeled a vermilion-red pedal-car forward saying, 'This is with love from Grandpa and Gran'ma!'

Both mother and son gave a long-drawn, 'O-o-o-h!' of wonder and delight, and Blanche jumped up to hug and kiss Sybil and Anthony, crying, 'How brilliant of you to think of it, and how generous. Oh, thank you a thousand times!'

Their action and her response brought them close that moment.

'We wanted it to be a surprise,' said Anthony, pleased with himself, 'so Mat Kellow hauled it up to the attic for us, and Edward very kindly brought it down just now.'

'I award these grandparents first prize and four gold stars for their choice,' said Blanche very brightly, feeling close to tears. 'The only problem being that Aaron will drive round recklessly all day, bashing our legs.'

The three lingered for another moment in a glow of harmony, gave each other a final hug and moved apart.

Aaron, enraptured, had been helped into his vehicle by Daniel and was attempting to scoot right into the Christmas tree. Briskly Henrietta diverted him, while Lydia and Freddie nudged each other in the ribs and exploded with laughter.

When they could speak, Freddie said, 'He reminds me of Ben's hamster, aiming madly at all the wrong places!'

Henrietta, opening a long box, suddenly shrieked like a train whistle, scrambled up, threw her arms round Blanche's neck and kissed her passionately on both cheeks.

'It's too beautiful for words!' she cried. 'I'm going upstairs this minute to put it on! Daddy! Mummy! Look at the dress Blanche has made for me. Madly fashionable. Dark-green plaid with a wide sailor collar. And her very own label in it. Just when I hadn't a rag to wear!'

'Blanche! Blanche!' Ben clamoured. 'Thanks a million for my camera. Stand still. I'm going to take the very first photograph, and I want it to be of you and Aaron – oh, and Daniel too, if he likes,' he added politely. 'Can you come closer together?' As Blanche drew back. 'And will you pull Aaron's pedal-car forward so that he's in front of the picture?' They complied: Daniel smiling, Blanche secretly fuming. 'That looks brill! Say *sex*!' And, glancing at his grandfather, changed this to, 'Say *cheese*! Smile, please!'

While Henrietta and Ben had been exploring and exclaiming

with ecstasy, Sybil was saying to herself in quiet despair, 'I suppose it's useless to expect Teddy to take note of the presents the children have opened, and Kat isn't doing so, and now the labels are mixed up. Should I try to sort it out? No! Enough is enough. For all I know, it's out of fashion for youngsters to write their thank-you letters on Boxing Day. Good manners seem to have flown out of the window . . .'

The first excitement was over, and her family was demanding that she begin.

'Yes, yes. You start off the grown-ups, my love,' said Anthony, adding, 'and open my present last!' Desiring the greatest and final accolade.

Sybil looked round to see who most needed her attention. Henrietta and Ben had disappeared. Lydia and Freddie were playing with the puppy. Daniel and Blanche were teaching Aaron how to steer, Edward was pouring himself a large whisky surreptitiously, and Katrina was looking isolated.

With unerring instinct, Sybil drew a silver-clad gift towards her, feeling its shape, judging its weight. She could guess what it was. Marrons glacés. An extravagance from someone who wished to propitiate her.

'My dear Kat!' Sybil cried. 'How delightfully wicked of you! You know what a weakness I have for marrons glacés!'

Ah, poor thing! she thought, as Katrina's smile registered joyous relief. And went over and kissed her, to show that though she could not comprehend a mother leaving her children she would not be the first to cast a stone.

'Sybil,' Katrina whispered, as lips met cheek, 'I really must have a private talk with you.'

'Later!' Sybil promised, smiling, but her spirits sank a little, and then lifted again as she drew out Blanche's padded cotton morning gown, resplendent with cabbage-roses. 'Oh, my darling girl! Oh, but it's much too beautiful to use now, with the Christmas cooking! Oh, but I must try it on! And tomorrow I'll wear it to Boxing Day brunch!'

Then she praised each of her other gifts, to the complete satisfaction of their givers, ending with a special kiss for her husband, who had bought her a Victorian velvet choker embroidered with seed pearls. 'You always know what I like, Tony,' she said, and drumming up an audience for him, 'Such perfect taste, don't you think?'

'Perfect taste! And absolutely *you*!' they all agreed.

In softer mood, Blanche examined the choker carefully, and pronounced it exquisite.

Anthony refilled their glasses. 'Who's next?' he asked, replete.

Blanche insisted on waiting until the last. To give was even more delectable than to receive. From the moment Sybil suggested that they spend Christmas together, she had invested all her spare hours and income, her imagination and ingenuity, in finding and making gifts for each member of the family, to mark the occasion. They sat invitingly in their black and gold striped packages, waiting to ravish their recipients. Aaron's alphabet building blocks and Ben's first camera had been obvious choices. But Henny's dress, Lydia's nightdress, Edward's hand-blocked cravat, Sybil's new housecoat and the smoking jacket and cap for her father had been created with anxious care. They meant to say, 'I am giving you part of myself. Wear me, and remember that.'

She savoured their faces, their remarks, the utterly satisfactory gloat of success.

'So this is how you see me?' Anthony growled engagingly. 'The Victorian patriarch in the bosom of his family!'

This was another rare moment of truce. Blanche lifted her face, smiling, and he kissed her cheek in courteous homage. 'You are an exceptionally accomplished woman,' he said.

From a man who valued achievement above all else it was the ultimate compliment.

'Your turn now,' said Sybil to her elder daughter.

The family's gifts to Blanche had been chosen mostly after careful consultation with Sybil, to fulfil a need or please the eye, and to keep up the standard she set herself. A fine new folding work-table from Anthony to replace the old one, two needlework cushions worked by hand from Sybil, a nineteenth-century fashion-plate print from Edward, a beribboned and satin-clad wardrobe pomander from Henny and Ben, and a zany multi-coloured linen basket from Lydia and Freddie. Even the untutored guests had made wise choices: a German fashion doll from Natalie, Samsara perfume from Katrina.

Finally, bowing before her, came Daniel with a box that had evidently been professionally gift-wrapped. Her heart began to beat rapidly, with fear, with pleasure. She gave him a quick upward look, a smile that was almost an apology. Delicately feeling its shape, unfolding the layers of tissue paper, breathing

79

more quickly, she brought forth a silver mask on a stick, and gave an involuntary cry of awe, of delight, of disbelief.

'Oh, *Dan*!' And then, knowing she had betrayed too much feeling, she repeated ruefully, 'Oh, Dan!'

'I saw it in a shop called Masks for Dreams,' he said quietly, knowing he had enchanted her. 'And it said Blanche to me.'

They crowded round her to view this princely presentation. She held it up, smiling very wide to prevent her mouth from quivering. Then, as they voiced their admiration, she placed the silver mask over her face and hid behind it gratefully until Sybil said she wanted a closer look.

There was no gift for Daniel, of course. 'I'm afraid I have nothing for you,' she said to him, holding out her hands in mute apology, palms upwards.

'I need nothing,' he replied, 'more than this.'

And he touched first her hand, and then Aaron's head.

Which is too much, Blanche thought, watching father and son together. Far too much.

She saw Sybil smile to herself, and guessed that she had decided they were on the right track, and could now lavish her maternal attentions on Edward and Katrina. Blanche wondered whether, in years to come, she would become so involved in Aaron's marital problems. But when she imagined him in his young manhood, bruised, rejected, barred from Eden, she was riven, and understood. But my mother's involvement is threefold, Blanche thought, looking at her brother and sister, and, if we are to be honest, none of us is very satisfactory or has become what perhaps she wished we would be. Does she question sometimes whether we were worth her life?

The ceremony of opening presents was over. Sybil and Anthony disappeared. Blanche and Daniel sat in silence, leaving their son to learn to pedal. Katrina was lavishing attention on her children to the exclusion of Edward, who hovered about them uncertainly. Freddie began to pick up discarded papers and ribbons, and Lydia to smooth and fold them, while Mr Silk, pine needles sticking to his fur, pounced joyfully on each retrieval.

Natalie arrived at mid-day, just as Sybil was checking the state of the giblet stock, and Anthony was opening three bottles of Nuits St George and grumbling about the company's drinking habits.

80

'We must have soaked up the best part of a bottle of whisky last night. If that fellow of Blanche's hadn't brought a bottle we'd be right out by now . . .'

'Oh, good!' Natalie said cordially, producing another two. 'I did choose the right offering after all. Merry Christmas to both of you. I think it's Bell's. Is that all right? I bullied them out of Mr Sampson at the pub.' And she put an arm round each of their shoulders, and kissed their cheeks.

'Dear Tasha!' they cried in obedient unison.

'Can I do anything?' she offered, out of social habit rather than intention for she was useless domestically and both knew it.

'No, thank you,' said Sybil firmly. 'I like the kitchen to myself until we're dishing up. Everyone else is in the living room. So do go in. We've opened our presents, by the way. We thought you wouldn't mind.'

'No, you're right. I don't give a damn about all that nonsense. How are the kiddiewinks and animals behaving?'

'As well as can be expected,' said Sybil absent-mindedly, basting the turkey. 'Tony, do take Tasha into the living room with you and give her a glass of whatever she wants to drink. And will you ask Freddie and Lydia to come and buttle for me? They can carry things.' She added to herself rather than to them, 'Freddie really is so helpful and thoughtful, such a good influence.'

Natalie was diverted. She made no effort to move.

'That's an odd alliance. How long have they known each other?'

'Not long. A few months, perhaps. Lydia's wretched man was being difficult about money, and Freddie gave her a job in one of her antique shops. Then this same man actually turned her out into the street, and Freddie offered to put her up.'

'And how much do you know about the helpful and thoughtful Freddie?'

'Very little,' Sybil replied. As she registered the mockery in Natalie's voice a small frown gathered between her brows, and she made her voice ring with confidence and cheer. 'But we like her very much. Don't we, Tony?'

'Yes, yes. Just about the only decent person Lydia's ever brought home.'

'She's a self-made woman,' Sybil continued, 'and Lydia tells us that she's almost too generous. People tend to take advantage of her. She was married once, but it didn't work out. And there were no children. Oh, damn!' As the fat splashed up.

She needed to be left alone to concentrate on the cooking. It was typical of Natalie not to understand, and to ignore all hints.

Sybil said to her husband in despair, 'Tony, could you possibly . . .'

He came to her rescue at once. 'Tasha, my dear, let's leave the chef to it, shall we?'

'And, Tony, will you ask Blanche if she can put the finishing touches to the table? She does that sort of thing so beautifully – oh! and she was delighted with your doll, Tasha. How clever of you!'

'So Lydia has shacked up with Freddie now?' Natalie asked blandly, not moving.

Anthony answered her while Sybil persuaded the turkey back into the oven. 'A temporary arrangement until she finds somewhere else.'

'So it's been man-trouble with Lydia so far?' Natalie continued, with an ironical smile, as if she were about to shock innocent children.

'I'm afraid her taste in men is quite damnable,' Anthony replied coldly, frowning.

'Let's say she's been *unlucky* with men,' said Sybil loyally, topping up the simmering pudding pan. 'She tends to accept them at face value.'

'Then perhaps she'll have better luck with women,' said Natalie smoothly. 'I'll lay a pound to a penny – or whatever currency you bet with these days – that the delightful Freddie is a member of the sisterhood.'

Their faces closed against her. Their alliance became impregnable.

'Darling?' Sybil said to her husband, eyebrows arched.

'Yes, of course. You want us to disappear, and to send in Lydia, Freddie and Blanche. Allow me to take your cape, Natalie.'

But Natalie shrugged off the snub with the cape. Her smile remained ironical. She said, 'I never know whether to despise or admire you two for your ability to disguise the truth.'

They laughed together, and cried, 'Oh, Tasha!' As though she spoke in jest.

Anthony escorted her out.

✻

By three o'clock they were all swooning with food and drink, and the disenchantment that always follows any great event was already threatening to set in. Unless they were diverted, Sybil reckoned, the party would topple over into indigestion and bad temper, and that spelled danger all the way round. 'Constitutional, everyone?' she suggested. 'The children should have some fresh air and exercise after all these indulgences, and we can walk the dogs. Besides, Natalie and Daniel have seen nothing of our Cornish countryside. It isn't at its best, of course, in mid-winter, but the coast has a rugged beauty all the year round.'

'We shan't manage a coastal walk at this time of day,' said Anthony, not helping her. 'Too far to go on foot, and too complicated to go by car. Besides, it will be dark soon.'

'I should have thought . . .' Sybil began, but seeing how deeply he had sunk into his chair made contingency plans. 'Oh, well, we can do that another day. What about a local walk to Mrs Wish's farm and back? It won't take more than half an hour or so.'

Reluctantly, each in their different way, the members of the family party prepared for healthful exercise.

'Never did think much of English countryside,' Natalie grumbled, to anyone who might listen. 'When you've seen one green and pleasant field you've seen them all.'

'You can stay behind if you want to rest, Tasha,' said Sybil crisply.

'No, no. I'll drag my overfed carcase along with you. Don't want to be anti-social. Let's see this glorious countryside of yours.'

'It isn't pretty, of course,' said Sybil defensively.

'I never cared for prettiness. Always preferred character.'

'This has plenty of character. Hasn't it, Blanche?'

She appealed to her elder daughter, who replied agreeably, 'I should have said it was eminently photographic, Aunt Tasha. I presume you've brought your camera with you?'

'Have you brought your needlework with you?' Natalie asked abruptly.

Surprised that she should have taken offence, Blanche answered lightly, 'I do know what you mean. A busman's holiday is no holiday.'

Hastily, Natalie rephrased her remark. 'Usually I feel naked without a camera, but I'm taking a break from it for a while.'

Blanche discerned an asperity, a readiness to take up arms,

which had been hers before Aaron was born. That advent had wrought many changes. Nowadays only her father could rouse the virago in her. So she answered in comradely fashion. 'Actually, I always do bring sewing with me, in case I find myself sitting down in the evening with my hands unoccupied. It's a reflex action. I like to sew and listen, or sew and talk.'

Natalie's face cleared. She had been understood and accepted. 'Would you walk with me?' she asked.

'I'd love to. But do you mind walking at snail's pace with a rumbustious child and a knitted animal in a push-chair?'

'I'll carry Aaron on my shoulders, if you like,' said Daniel, hovering, 'and then you and Natalie can walk and talk in peace.'

Blanche protested, as nicely as she could, 'But he's used to a push-chair.'

Aaron had a finer grasp of meaning than of words. He struggled in his mother's arms, and pointed a magisterial fore-finger at Daniel, crying, 'Up!'

'Darling, you'll be much more comfortable in the push-chair.'

Aaron made himself unmanageable. He stiffened his arms and legs and body, and turned a dark malignant red. He yelled, 'Up! Up!' fighting for liberty.

'I should let him go if I were you,' said Natalie, amused by his determination.

'Here he is then!' Blanche said to Daniel, defeated.

'I'll take good care of him,' he promised, exultant.

With a whoop and a lift, father and son were united.

Aaron patted Daniel's head and cried peremptorily, 'Go!'

From his father's shoulders he stared out regally upon a wider world.

'It's a curious thing about Christmas Day,' said Sybil, as they set off at a lethargic pace. 'I wake up earlier, but my schedule always runs late, and everything takes longer to do.'

There was no answer to this. The party sauntered on in small divisions. Freddie and Lydia, though friendly to all, were happiest by themselves. Ben clung to Katrina's hand. Henrietta, though encumbered by Mr Silk and his lead, tugged Edward towards them, making a semblance of a family group. Sybil and Anthony had elected to walk one on either side of Blanche and Natalie, with Gracie padding behind them.

'And what do you think of our wild retreat, Tasha?' Anthony asked.

Resentment coloured her reply and struck them to the heart. 'Fine to look at, fun for a weekend, but utter boredom to live in. You're surely not going to retire here, are you, Tony? It might suit Sybil but you'd be dead in six months.'

A curious expression crossed his face, as if he were wondering how to phrase his agreement. Before he could answer, Sybil spoke with unexpected force. 'It's a common fallacy that people need the city for stimulation. I've always found that I could be more relaxed and creative without constant distractions.'

'Perhaps some of us don't want to be relaxed and creative,' said Natalie, enjoying this reaction. 'Perhaps some of us want *all* the orange: juice, pith and zest. I think I can safely say that my only fear in life is of missing something.'

Again Anthony seemed about to speak, and again his wife answered before he could. 'If you've treated life like a fairground, and spent all your time in the sideshows, then you've missed the essential meaning.'

'Assuming there is a meaning,' Natalie replied coolly, 'which I doubt.'

This time Anthony managed to make his opinion known. 'I must admit that I, too, have doubts. Personally, I would call myself a good old-fashioned Victorian agnostic, which means,' laughing, so that they would know he could see a joke against himself, 'I keep my options open.'

'I've no time for sitting on a fence,' said Natalie scornfully.

'That', said Sybil swiftly, 'is because you know nothing about balance.'

It was rare for her to thrust and parry. Natalie was amused, Anthony uneasy. Blanche listened and watched, waiting for the next move. Something between the three elders was being raised again, some old Lazarus of a grievance brought back to life.

Yet instead of pursuing the subject Sybil smiled, turned round, held out her hands to Henrietta and Ben, and said, 'Leave your mummy and daddy to talk, and let's go on ahead to see Mrs Wish at the farm, shall we? She might have some eggs to spare, and then you can collect them from the hens.'

She called up Gracie, quickened her pace and walked ahead of the family group, head held high, a flush on her cheekbones.

Blanche would have expected Anthony, who relished any argument, to continue the conversation with Natalie. Instead, he dropped back and joined Lydia and Freddie, appointing himself as teacher-companion. Although he lacked feeling for natural beauty he was widely read in the study of nature. As he expounded on winter bird life Freddie listened with interest but Lydia yawned and yawned.

Left unwillingly alone, Edward and Katrina were silent for a minute or two. He was seeking for a conciliatory opening. She was brooding over some imagined injury.

She said, 'I had hoped to speak to Sybil. I made a point of asking her, but she seems to be avoiding me.'

Irritated, he replied, 'Why should you think that?'

Katrina replied directly. 'Perhaps she doesn't want to hear what I have to say. Perhaps she's made up her mind how I should behave and is giving me every opportunity to conform.'

'Rubbish!' he cried, so forcefully that Lydia turned round. 'You always think my family is criticizing you.'

She did not answer. Her face closed up: a door slammed shut against him. They were silent, trudging on together, heads bent.

He began again, seeking for an acceptable opening. 'You're looking very smart.'

'I've got a well-paid job,' she replied unforgivingly. 'I have to look smart.'

'A well-paid job?' he answered, retaliating. 'I thought you'd found a well-paid man.'

'I've done both.'

'Oh, lucky, lucky you. What happened to the skiing holiday?'

'We've postponed it. I have something important to discuss with you. I didn't choose to come down from Yorkshire simply to fight my way through another lousy Malpas Christmas.'

His face lost what colour it had. Sensing trouble, his instinct was to avoid it. 'Who would?' he replied. 'Excuse me a moment, there's something I must ask Lydia.'

He joined the educational group, playing the ignoramus so that his father could enjoy correcting him.

Alone, Katrina dug her hands into the pockets of her overcoat, and walked on, head held high.

Blanche and Natalie strode side by side: two tall, long-legged women, kicking the dark wet leaves of autumn aside with their leather boots.

'I'm surprised', said Blanche, to break the silence, 'that Sybil hasn't said, "*Leaf-mould!*" and dashed back to the house for a bag to collect it.'

Natalie's expression conveyed no interest in this statement. Seemingly at random she asked, 'Are *you* a keen gardener?'

'No. I used to play gardener's boy to Sybil, at Clifton and here, and I quite enjoyed it, but city window-boxes are more my style.'

'Cities, travel, night-life, the passing show, being in touch with events, meeting crazy people, having lovers, living high on transient moments, creating your own life and your own private world?'

'You put it very well,' said Blanche, glancing at her, surprised.

'I've lived that way all my life.'

They strode on, thinking.

Then Natalie said, as if she were trying to form a picture of Blanche, 'And yet you're a devoted mother, which doesn't quite fit in with the rest.'

This had also puzzled Blanche and she did not know the answer. 'I adore Aaron, and he's changed me a great deal, but I was a very late recruit to motherhood, and I certainly wouldn't describe myself as the maternal type.'

'Will you have more children?'

'I shouldn't think so. He takes up all the time I can give him, and I want to do other things as well. I doubt if I have the energy or the hours to manage more than one child, though Sybil would say that was selfish.'

'Sybil doesn't want to do the other things we mentioned. Tell me . . .' Natalie began.

As if she had been alerted that their conversation was becoming too intimate, Sybil turned round, and called to her daughter. 'Blanche, do bring Aaron and Daniel along to see the hens!'

Daylight had waned when Sybil wheeled in a late-afternoon tea, saying, 'Indian or China, with milk or lemon? Scones, clotted cream and bramble jelly? Christmas cake?'

'It looks utterly delicious but I couldn't manage a morsel,' Freddie said, putting up one small capable hand. 'Lydia boasted about the quality of the Malpas cuisine, but never thought to warn me about the quantity! China tea and lemon for me, please.'

The other women agreed, but the men prepared to do justice to the spread.

'I'd be sick if I ate anything,' said Ben ominously, shaking his head.

'And he means it,' Henrietta warned. 'So don't make him!'

Games

CHAPTER TEN

Eight o'clock. The hill of dirty dishes had at last been washed up and put away, the children sent unprotesting to bed, small talk exchanged, and yesterday's papers read from cover to cover. The evening stretched before them, empty of entertainment, and the party spirit was slumping again. Natalie's mouth had settled into a disagreeable line that signalled trouble. Katrina, who had been avoiding Edward and seeking refuge in her children's company, was looking at him speculatively. Something about her expression, nervous yet exhilarated, warned Sybil to prevent them from talking. And Daniel, who had been understanding and patient so far, was now openly courting Blanche and making her tense and irritable.

Sybil did not intend playing referee to three simultaneous fights. There must be a major diversion. 'I know what we'll do!' she cried triumphantly, and clapped her hands together before her face, as if applauding herself. 'We'll play charades.'

And stopped all the protagonists in their tracks.

'Oh, Christ,' said Edward under his breath.

'We haven't played charades for years,' she said, delighted. 'I can't think why, because everyone was so good at it.'

'My dear Mama,' said Edward, speaking as to a child who needed instruction, 'the reason we haven't played charades for years is because the game always ended in a flaming row.'

'No, it didn't, darling. We used to play it with lots of people besides ourselves – Daddy's students, and Uncle Jack's friends, and your school friends – and they all loved it. I remember charades as being great fun.'

Blanche was leaning back against the piano, arms folded, one foot crossed in front of the other. Now she looked straight at her mother and spoke frankly. 'I think you should know,

Sybil, that charades may have been fun for you but it was hell for us!'

She addressed their visitors as if they sat in judgement upon the Malpases. 'We played in teams, and it was highly competitive, with a sliding scale of praise and blame. And there were some very nasty undercurrents which brought out the worst in everyone. Sybil ran one team, trying to improve our morals, and Daddy ran the other, trying to improve our intellects. The feelings of outsiders, such as students, Uncle Jack's friends, and school mates, were spared out of courtesy. They hadn't a clue what was going on, but we three children were in the front line, being rectified or educated.'

'Do I hear the rattle of childhood skeletons?' Freddie enquired, trying to lighten the tone.

Natalie had been listening intently. 'Serious-minded parents can be a great drawback,' she observed. 'My mother and father were fanatical for our success. Tony did brilliantly, of course, but I struggled to impress them for years. Then I thought, what the hell, and gave up.'

'There is nothing wrong with being serious-minded,' said Sybil firmly. 'My parents set a good example and expected us to do well, but they never pressured us. We worked hard because we wanted to please them. My two brothers were showing great promise at college, but they both died in the second world war. And I was considered very bright, but I got married – so naturally . . .'

Her sentence, like her early promise, was cut short. She resumed her defence of the game. 'I remember lovely times when we spent Christmas down here and played charades at Predanick Wartha, and you all enjoyed yourselves thoroughly. You can't deny that!'

'It was entirely different when we were down here,' Lydia protested, 'because Uncle Jack organized the games, and he just wanted everyone to have fun.'

Daniel was sketching, seeming not to listen. Katrina knotted her hands in her lap and stared down at them. Sybil gave a despairing shrug and lift of the eyebrows. Natalie took out a silver case, fitted a cigarette into an ivory holder, lit it, and blew smoke-rings at the beams in the ceiling. But Anthony was incensed, and made his views known.

'Damned nonsense!' he exploded. 'I always had the best interests of you three children at heart. This is *you*, Blanche, making trouble again, twisting the truth and encouraging the others to follow your lead. If you'd paid attention to me you'd have had a university degree and a sensible life-style by now, instead of being a one-woman sweatshop. Good God,' he cried, looking more like a prophet than ever, as he gestured towards his offspring, 'what has any of you ever done that was worthwhile, either personally or professionally? You can't even summon up a decent marriage between the three of you—'

'Tony!' Sybil warned him, low-voiced but firm.

He came to a blustering halt, muttering to himself, 'Oh, no. It's easier to blame me and stew in your ignorance!'

No one answered him or looked at anyone else.

Into the silence, Freddie said, 'Can't we play charades without having teams? Just act a word each and let everyone guess what it is.'

'And without Daddy giving marks for performances,' Blanche said, refusing to forgive him for past or present.

'Oh, did you have marks?' Freddie asked, startled.

'Personal marks and team marks, and a short summary of each person's proficiency. Like an end-of-term report.'

'Holy shit!' Natalie said to her cigarette.

'You have to give marks if you're going to award prizes!' Anthony roared. He appealed to his guests for fair play. 'She hasn't mentioned the prizes, of course. Oh, no! We gave prizes for the most unusual word and the best interpretation. Prizes!'

'A Mars bar apiece for beating your brains out,' Edward said sourly.

'You also gave booby prizes for the easiest word and the worst performance,' Lydia said, stung by recollection. 'Jelly babies, to illustrate our mental capacity. I've loathed the things ever since, so much so that I'd never give any child jelly babies!'

Her brother and sister agreed.

He turned on them, shouting, 'That was intended as a joke, and everyone apart from you three blasted kids thought it was jolly good fun.'

For the first time Katrina entered the conversation. She spoke in a detached tone, looking back at a situation that had caused her rage and anguish, and was still evidently capable of wounding her. 'But I remember this, too, and I wasn't a child. We played charades when Sybil first invited me to Clifton. The weekend Edward and I became engaged.'

She addressed Natalie and Daniel, not seeking sympathy so much as stating her case. 'Edward and I met at a comprehensive school in the Midlands, where he was a junior English teacher and I was a junior secretary. I'm not an intellectual person and my family weren't academic like the Malpases, but I was a bright, competent girl, and people generally liked me. Yet as soon as Tony and Sybil realized that I wasn't one of their sort they had no more time for me.'

'That's not so, Katrina. I made every effort to welcome you,' Sybil cried, her sense of hospitality outraged. 'I asked Teddy beforehand what you liked to eat, and gave you the best guest room.'

'You did everything beautifully and were very kind,' Katrina agreed, and then spoiled the effect by adding, 'but then you always are with everybody.'

Anthony, whose choler was rising again, said accusingly, 'And we threw a special party for you, and Sybil went to a dickens of an amount of trouble over it!'

'Yes, you gave a very elegant wine and cheese party,' Katrina agreed, 'and invited a bunch of favourite students and close colleagues round to meet me. I made the same sort of impression on them as I had done on you. They thought I was a pretty girl who didn't count, and saw that you agreed with them, and treated me accordingly — with the utmost condescension. And when the conversation naturally began to flag Tony had a wonderful idea. "Let's play charades!" he said. The students were all vying for his attention, and bent on being absolutely brilliant. By that time I was completely demoralized, and Teddy was no help either. He never would stand up for either of us. And I'd only played charades for fun, like Uncle Jack, so we didn't shine.'

She had never come to terms with that humiliation, never forgiven them, and now relived it in the telling.

She said tightly, 'We were awarded the booby prizes. Two jelly babies. One black. One red. I felt as if I'd been smacked and sent into a corner.'

'Accompanied by jocular remarks and patronizing laughter,' Edward added, with considerable rancour. 'It was a bloody

94

nightmare. Kat wanted to break off the engagement. It took me the rest of the weekend to persuade her not to chuck the ring at me and walk out.'

With one accord the company glanced at the fourth finger of Katrina's left hand. It was ringless, and they were silenced by the thought that she had, as it were, come full circle.

'Do you see what I mean, Freddie?' Blanche cried, swinging round, hands on hips. 'Charades are the Malpas equivalent of Christians versus lions in a Roman circus.'

Daniel chuckled, and shook his wild and curly head, but whether in mild disagreement or in appreciation of Blanche's fighting spirit was not certain.

Sybil spoke up now, with great dignity. 'Well, I had no idea that all of you took this so personally, but you have entirely misinterpreted our motives. I think that Kat has a special case. She was young and sensitive, and perhaps we were less perceptive than we should have been. But neither of us ever intended to make anyone feel miserable and inadequate, and we should be very sorry to think we did.'

'I'm not sorry,' said Anthony peremptorily, 'I'm fed up with the damned lot of them. The only thing I'm sorry about is that you ever persuaded me to ask them all here for Christmas.' He added hastily, sincerely, 'That doesn't include you, Freddie!'

A smile lit her eyes and departed.

He said politely, but without enthusiasm, 'Or our other guests, of course.'

Natalie inclined her head. Katrina tightened her lips.

'I'll say this for Daniel,' said Anthony, softening towards one of his unexpected visitors. 'He's got a sense of proportion and a sense of humour, which is more than Blanche has or ever did have, and I—'

'I think I've had enough, Tony,' said Sybil quietly, sternly.

They stared at her in astonishment.

In the hush that ensued, Sybil said wearily, 'For some reason the members of this family seem bent on raking up past grievances instead of enjoying each other's company. So I suggest we give up the idea of doing something together, and amuse ourselves as we please. That way everyone will be satisfied.'

Anthony came over and put his arm round her shoulders. 'Now, now, now,' he said, repentant. 'You mustn't take it to heart. I won't have them upsetting you.' Adopting the role of cheer-leader, he exhorted the company, 'We all want to play charades, don't we?'

An uncertain murmur from the guests. Silence from the family.

'And we'll open a couple of bottles of wine to start us off on the right foot!' Anthony continued, becoming expansive. He embraced his wife tenderly, 'Are you happy about that, Syb?' he asked.

'If everyone else is,' she replied, unconvinced.

'Well, I think it's a jolly good idea of yours!' he said heartily. 'Here we all are. The entire clan gathered at Christmas time. Why can't we join in a good old-fashioned game of charades?'

His eyes, his voice, accused them. Freddie, Daniel and Natalie agreed warily, intrigued. The other four were grudging but resigned.

Recovering a little, Sybil asked, 'Then who wants to dress up?'

This sparked off a reaction. They all wanted to dress up, and now entered the spirit of the occasion.

'Where's the dressing-up box?'

'In the attic. We'll need a ladder.'

'Oh, it'll be such fun seeing what's in the box!' Lydia cried. 'Come on, Freddie, let's help to carry it downstairs!'

'Blanche, as a professional *couturière*, should be in charge of the wardrobe,' said Sybil, mindful that her husband had insulted his daughter's profession.

Appreciating this sidelong reproach, Anthony became more cordial. He could not bring himself to apologize, nor to address Blanche directly, but he did his best at second-hand.

'Don't make too much noise,' he advised the box-collectors, 'or you'll wake up young Aaron,' and added, for good measure, 'Daniel, could you give me a hand with the wine?'

To be answered cordially, 'With all the pleasure in life, sir!'

'Good God,' Edward said *sotto voce* to his siblings, 'the old man's positively quivering at the idea of playing charades again. It's a power game, you know. It always was.'

Katrina said resentfully, 'Whatever it was, you and I lost it.'

'But of course we lost it,' said Edward, speaking to her naturally for once. 'I'd left home, taken a job that he didn't think was up to scratch, and become engaged to someone he didn't know and wouldn't have chosen for me. Worst of all, we were obviously happy. He had to cut us down to size.'

Blanche said, 'And now you know the reason why I never brought Dan home.'

Natalie, sitting near them, interposed. 'Then you were mistaken,' she said. 'You could have done, because Dan has no pretensions. Tony can't hurt him, and he respects that.'

Thin-skinned Katrina said, 'Are you suggesting that I *had* pretensions and he didn't respect *me?*'

Natalie was impatient with her. 'I mean that he's a bully, and if he can safely kick someone he will. You and Edward probably invited the jackboot – if you don't mind my saying so.'

Katrina fired up. 'Well, I do mind, as it happens.'

They confronted each other: the one quivering with injured pride; the other cool, sarcastic, amused. Sybil, registering a commotion in their corner, began to make her way towards them.

Blanche said crisply, 'I should save your ammunition if I were you, comrades. You have no idea of the number of troubles that can fly out of our dressing-up box when the lid is opened, nor how many old grievances are preparing to be rebirthed. In my judgement, you'll need every bullet you've got to fight this battle – and I would advise you to keep the last ones for yourselves!'

While the box full of clothes was being angled, bumped and coaxed down the narrow staircase, Anthony sat in the dining room at the head of his table. He was in his element. He had changed into the ruby velvet jacket Blanche had made for him, and wore the smoking cap at a rakish angle. He had brought down a writing pad from his study, and was busy unscrewing the top of an elegant fountain-pen.

'Never could stand those modern biros and felt tipped articles,' he remarked, to whoever cared to listen.

Then he became the ringmaster. 'Sybil! Would you be kind enough to call everyone together for a preliminary conference?'

The late revelations had had a salutary effect on him. His children had thrown mud pies at the image of brilliant academician and benevolent father, and stuck up a tyrant in its place. He did not accept that what they had said was true, but he acknowledged some misunderstanding on both sides. This, in the first place, he set down to Sybil spoiling them, with the inevitable result of making them vain and touchy. In the second place, he admitted a personal error: that of believing them to be as intelligent and gifted as himself. He supposed that natural fondness had misled him. He had thought them all swans who insisted on behaving like geese. Now he knew they were simply geese. So he could forget his ambitions for them. He wished he had known this years ago. It would have saved many trials and tribulations, particularly with Blanche.

He reflected on her, as she sat opposite him, hands clasped, eyes cast down, and in spite of his displeasure he thought her beautiful: that wonderful unmanageable hair with a life of its own; her strength and slimness; the way she wore all her vivid clothes like distinctive skins; the keenness of intelligence, the quickness of retort, the driving force. No, he had not been wrong about this daughter's potential. She could have gone far in his world, if she had been so minded. Instead of that she was wasting her brains on dressmaking.

Their eyes met. A chary glance on both their parts.

So she and the others had thought him overbearing, even deliberately unkind, had they? Blast them. Well, he would show them that he could take criticism, however unjust, and be as liberal as the next idiot.

He said, truthfully as it happened, 'This smoking jacket is surprisingly comfortable, Blanche. Did you get my measurements from Sybil?'

'Of course.'

'H'mph.' But as perfection did not exist he must add, 'The cap feels odd.'

'That's because you should wear it further forward, and straight on.'

He gave it an impatient tug and push.

'Let me,' said Blanche, and came round to him and adjusted the cap.

Her scent was provocative, spicy and delicious. He was reminded of something Natalie used to wear — what was it? — L'Heure Bleue?

'Is that perfume L'Heure Bleue?' he asked, momentarily melted.

'No. Ma Griffe.'

Her tone was crisp and he could not resist saying, 'Your claw? How appropriate!'

Nor did she prevent herself from replying, 'You should know!'

She returned to her seat and did not look at him again. Yet, for a moment, they had been together in a good place.

Anthony observed the others filing in. He thought them a motley crew, and no one up to standard except for Sybil. But, then, Sybil was part of him. He had always thought that fairy-tale of Adam and Eve a charming one. There was something appealing about woman being created from man's rib. It did not make women more comprehensible, but at least the origin had been sound.

Electing himself as chairman of the meeting he stood up, eyes alight, bearing majestic, and considered his notes.

'Just a couple of points!' he assured them genially. 'First, I agree that the game should be pure entertainment. Secondly, I have a proposal to make, which I shall put to open vote.'

Here he paused and looked round impressively to make sure he had their attention.

'Although I'm sure we all feel obliged to Freddie for her recommendations, I still think we should have teams, otherwise the game will lack focus. But there will be no prizes or personal comments of any kind, only team marks, and in view of recent criticisms I think that Sybil and I should not lead either group. Indeed, I shall not take part at all.'

'How unusually democratic of you,' said Natalie, in her deep, hoarse voice.

He ignored her.

'I have listed possible teams,' he continued, 'taking everyone's personal idiosyncrasies into account. Will you hear them?'

They had no objection, though his children were wryly amused to see him setting the course before relinquishing the reins.

Anthony passed a hand over his grey mane, put on his reading glasses, cleared his throat, and read what he had written. 'To keep the balance, there should be one man and three women in each group. Each group should include one of our senior ladies,' bowing to Sybil and Natalie, who were relieved to be separated, 'two members of the Malpas family, and one guest. I suggest Edward as one group leader, with a possible team of Natalie, Blanche and Freddie; while Lydia leads the other group, ably supported by her mother, Katrina and Daniel.'

Thus separating all those who might quarrel.

In quite a jocular tone, he added, 'I have a special word for Freddie. I must apologize for parting you and Lydia, Freddie,' said with a smile, 'but some members of my family do not agree as amicably as you two do, so your companionship is being sacrificed for the sake of peace.'

99

Uncertain laughter from the Malpases. Freddie stood up and bowed in high good humour, and sat again, winking at Lydia.

There was a silence as they all thought through the plan. Then Sybil said, smiling mischievously. 'I think you've been extremely clever, Tony!'

She was congratulating him on his political dexterity, learned through spending years on university committees. Some cheerfully, some grudgingly, the others gave their assent.

'Just a few more moments of your time,' he continued, well pleased. 'There are three ways of playing charades. I think it best to give an outline of the game we play, for those among us who may be unfamiliar with it, namely, Natalie and Daniel. And no doubt,' with a glint of his spectacles, 'Katrina would like her memory refreshed.

'Two teams choose their own subjects. Taking turn by turn, the leader of one team then calls on a member of the opposing team to mime one of the following: a *word*, a *quotation*, a *proverb*, a *popular phrase*, the *name of a person* either living or dead, the title of a well-known *song, television programme, book, film,* or *play.*

'The leader's team has to guess the word correctly, and the length of time they take is noted. All the times are added up in the finish, and the team who made the greatest number of correct guesses in the shortest time are the winners. Any questions?'

'Supposing they can't guess and they give up?' Natalie asked bluntly.

'Then the time they have taken to come to that decision is doubled,' said Anthony crisply. 'Anything else? No? Then, as I have nothing to do, would you like me to be the time-keeper?'

They all agreed. ·

'Good! Now I abdicate. Take over, Edward and Lydia. Yours are the crowns!'

He left his chair and came round to kiss Sybil's hand.

'You see, the old man can change his spots after all!' he murmured to her.

'Don't you believe it,' Natalie said, overhearing him. 'I've studied leopards. The bastards just become more adroit.'

She and Blanche looked at each other simultaneously, and laughed.

'You and I have much in common, Aunt Tasha,' said Blanche.

Natalie covered her pleasure with an abrupt little nod, and turned away.

'Fellow thespians!' Edward cried, savouring his role as leader. 'Pray draw aside and consider your names, quotations, phrases, et cetera! How long shall we give them, Lyd?'

She, too, was elated: speaking more rapidly, laughing more frequently, her voice young and high.

'Oh, half an hour to sort themselves out and rig themselves up. If you want advice you have only to ask for it. As you know, Blanche is in charge of the dressing-up box.'

'My dears, may I interrupt, just for a moment?' Sybil asked, addressing the company. 'Just one little thing! You can borrow any props you need from anywhere in the house – except Tony's study, which is out of bounds. And while you are upstairs, please, *please* be as quiet as you can. We don't want to wake the children.'

Blanche turned to her brother and muttered, 'Oh, doesn't that take you back twenty-five years? And Sybil still sounds as if she and Daddy were running a boarding school!'

But Edward, eyes sparkling, rubbed his hands. 'I've had an amazing idea how to take the old man down a couple of pegs,' he said. 'The hunt's up and I'm going in for the kill.'

'So long', said Blanche, 'as you remain the hunter and don't turn into the fox.'

The adults had become children again. They laid out refreshments: bottles of wine, slices of Christmas cake, German biscuits, Belgian chocolates, marzipan sweets and candied fruits. They hunted up notebooks and biros. They conferred in different parts of the room, heads together, arms round each other's shoulders, whispering intently. They took off their shoes and ran silently up and down the stairs, collecting props. They rummaged in the dressing-up box, asking Blanche's advice about certain costumes, gratefully accepting her ministrations and suggestions.

The tone of the family party was lighter, happier, more ebullient than it had been, and by nine o'clock the charades show was ready to roll.

CHAPTER ELEVEN

Edward and Daniel rigged up two faded green velvet curtains on a rod across the playroom doors, to be looped apart or let fall by means of bell-ropes. Later, these would become actors in their own right, demanding attention and behaving in a temperamental fashion. The two men also shrouded a portion of the playroom with dust-sheets to form a stage and wings; pushed the sitting-room furniture out of the way and set up six kitchen and three dining-room chairs for the audience; and volunteered to be operators and stage-hands until it was their turn to act.

Full of importance, Anthony was making whispered enquiries of the two leaders and receiving final instructions. Then he stood forth, resplendent in his crimson smoking-jacket and braided pill-box cap, and thumped the floor three times with a stout ash walking-stick, as they did in the French theatre, to declare that the play was about to begin. *One, two, three.* Reluctantly, unevenly, the curtains were pulled apart to reveal an empty stage.

'Ladies and gentlemen,' Anthony intoned, 'a coin of the realm has been tossed to determine who shall begin – and Edward has won the toss.'

Edward's eyes were on Katrina. They wavered as she met his gaze steadfastly, and he looked quickly away, rubbing his hands in a parody of good fellowship.

'All right, then, Dan. I choose *you* to begin.'

Daniel's face lit up. He strode forward, held out his arms, and enquired of the audience, 'Now who'll take my place? For I want the curtains closed, so that I can make a proper entrance.'

'Oh, you don't need to bother about the curtains,' said Anthony impatiently. 'You can start now.'

But Daniel lowered his head and repeated obstinately, 'I want to make a proper entrance. And for that the curtains need to be closed.' He elaborated his idea. 'And then I want you, sir, to come forward and thump the floor with your stick, and announce me. And then the curtains open – and there I am!'

His earnestness amused them. He had the fixed demeanour of a man who had been drinking, not heavily but steadily, and was anxious to appear cold sober. As he shook his head from side to side, hands on hips, repeating his request, Anthony frowned and Blanche fumed. But the rest of them began to laugh, and Daniel instinctively threw himself on their mercy.

'I've been hearing what a grand and serious business this charades is, and I'm all for giving you a grand and serious performance. But how can I make a proper entrance without the curtains closed and the thumping on the floor?'

'Oh, for God's sake, somebody, close the curtains, and let him have the thumping on the floor!' Natalie commanded, and raised another laugh.

'Blanche,' Anthony ordered, forgetting yet again that he was no longer master of ceremonies, 'come and help Edward with the curtains!'

'There's a particular way of paying out the rope,' said Daniel, gleaming, coming to Blanche's side, 'that I will show you.'

He put both arms round her waist to assist her, and the laughter redoubled.

She dug a sharp white elbow in his ribs and whispered angrily, 'If you don't stop making a fool of me in front of my family you can damned well go home!'

He whispered back, mischievously, gleefully, 'Ah! You sweet shrew! I can't do that. Your lady mother has invited me to see the New Year in with the family, and I've accepted with what some might call reckless alacrity.'

'Oh, get out of my way,' she muttered, slapping his hands down.

'Yes, take yourself backstage,' said Anthony testily, waving Daniel off as if he were a wasp, 'and then we can get on with the game.'

He bowed low, with a triple flourish of one hand, and obeyed. Blanche, eyes glittering, colour high, gave a curt nod to Edward and they let the curtains shuffle together.

When Daniel came on again he was a different man. He had

103

placed the children's work-table and a chair on the stage, thrown an ancient grey wool shawl of Sybil's across his shoulders, and was holding a spotted bundle.

'This is one word, and with your kind permission I'm doing the first two syllables in one mime,' he announced.

Anthony opened his mouth to object, but Sybil pressed his hand quickly and firmly, and he closed it again.

Daniel wrapped the shawl round him, pulled his hair over his face, became old and bent, turning sideways to the audience, peeping slyly at them. He held up the bundle and shook it, listening to the clinks and rattles with glee. He sat on the chair, tipped out a mixture of real and imitation money, counted it into piles, added them up, and entered the total in a notebook. Finally he rose and bowed to indicate that this part of the performance was over, and held up his hand.

'Third and fourth syllables. And I'm doing them together as well.'

'Oh, look here—' Anthony began, but was again hushed by his wife.

Daniel became a clown. He slipped and slithered on an imaginary banana skin, sat on an invisible pin, set fire to himself with unseen matches, mimed ludicrous joy and absurd terror, fell on his face a fool, got up again a wise man. And bowed.

They laughed and clapped and laughed again, and Natalie cried, '*Encore!*'

Daniel held up a cautionary forefinger, and said engagingly to his admirers, 'I feel it's only fair to say that the fifth syllable represents a letter.'

More laughter.

Anthony was on his feet, despite Sybil's restraining hand, calling them to order. 'One moment, if you please! Everybody – and Daniel in particular – I must point out that charades are meant to be *mimed*.' He made a concession to his errant guest. 'But, of course, we do understand that Daniel – however entertaining – is a novice at charades and therefore unfamiliar with the rules.'

'Oh, stuff the rules!' Natalie said, and Daniel bowed his thanks.

'The lady took the words out of my very mouth,' he said blandly. 'And now, if you'll excuse me a moment, I need a prop – in both senses.'

He returned with a sweeping brush, and announced, 'Fifth syllable.'

His body and the brush formed two sides of a triangle, across the middle of which he stretched one arm. And, lowering one eyelid, invited response.

'A!' his admirers chorused in adoration.

He gave a deep emphatic nod.

Anthony was heard to say to Sybil, 'Oh, this is impossible!' But no one heeded him.

'And the final syllable, gentlemen and ladies,' cried Daniel.

With consummate humility he turned to face Blanche and went down on his knees. Arms outspread, he implored forgiveness. Embarrassed, she stared past him. His arms fell heavily down. He rose, head bent, and walked slowly away.

The applause this time was sympathetic.

Yet he returned, not at all the worse for her treatment of him, and announced, 'Whole word.'

'You're supposed to draw a circle in the air!' Anthony said crossly. 'Not say, *Whole word*!'

'Oh, for Christ's sake shut up, Tony!' Natalie growled.

'I'll thank you not to speak to me like that, and in my house—'

'May I have your attention, please?' Daniel cried loudly, robustly. 'I am about to give you the whole word!'

Again he went down on his knees to Blanche, but this time he had evidently decided that the outcome was satisfactory. He mimed joy and gratitude. He thanked heaven for her forgiveness. He kissed both hands to her, invited the onlookers to share his delight. And walked off a happy, happy man.

The applause was vehement, devoted. Blanche, sensing that her family was on his side and wished him well, let her curtain slump to, and joined the others.

Anthony stood up, watch in hand, and announced, 'Solution, please, Edward's group. I am timing you from . . . now!'

There was a quick whispered conference between Edward, Natalie and Freddie, with Blanche saying self-consciously, 'It's fairly obvious.'

'I guessed the word before I'd worked out the syllables!' Freddie said.

'Are we agreed, then?' Edward asked. And when they nodded he stood up and said, 'Reconciliation. Reckon. Silly. A. Shun.'

'Ah, you're a clever one,' said Daniel admiringly. 'I saw that as soon as I met you.'

'Thirty-two seconds!' Anthony said, disgusted. 'And it was not especially clever of them to guess it so quickly, Daniel. You made the whole thing perfectly obvious. In the art of playing charades there should be more mystery, more skill.'

'He'd have been in line for a jelly-baby!' Edward whispered to Lydia and she giggled.

'I thought it was wonderfully good. Come and sit by me, Daniel,' said Sybil.

'Your choice next, Lydia!' Anthony called.

His younger daughter tapped her lips, saying 'Inky-pinky,' and then, 'You, Fred!'

Freddie pretended to lift up an immense club and bring it down on Lydia's head, but otherwise accepted the choice with her usual good humour.

'Edward and Daniel. Curtains!' Anthony ordered.

'Still organizing the events, despite your supposed abdication?' Edward enquired ironically, as he passed his father.

'I'm only doing my part of the job,' Anthony replied, unruffled.

Fittingly, Freddie had decided to continue the comedy. There was a very long pause, and several whispers of 'Are you ready?' Then from stage left lolloped an incredible animal, composed of a pair of brown trousers and an old brown jersey, and Freddie's woolly-gloved hands holding up a stuffed stag's head that Jack Maddern had once given to the Malpases. This creature, who seemed afflicted with internal amusement, shambled forward, swaying its head from side to side in an engaging fashion, and drew a circle in the air with one paw.

There were one or two laughs. With a saucy flick of the horns, the animal beckoned to Anthony, who came up, smiling a little stiffly. These were not the kind of charades that best pleased him. The head conferred with him, while he put two fingers over his mouth, considering. Finally, he turned to the audience.

'This is an unusual request,' he said, 'but within the rules, I believe. Freddie feels that it is only fair to tell you that the head is not necessarily the animal she is representing.'

A flurry of whispers in Lydia's group.

'I thought the syllable was *dear*. Isn't it?'

'No, it can't be!' Scornfully. 'There isn't a word beginning with dear.'

'*Stag.* It must be *stag* – like stagnation.'

'Quiet, please!' Anthony ordered.

The animal was rousing laughter, cocking its head and wriggling its bottom.

'Give us a song, then!' Daniel cried, in an expansive mood.

'No talking or singing or sounds of any kind are allowed,' said Anthony severely, returning to his seat.

Slowly and clumsily, the creature waltzed round the stage.

The laughter grew. They all clapped. Daniel cried, '*Encore!*' And they echoed him. But, as if realizing that Anthony's patience had been sufficiently tried, the animal stopped obediently, centre-stage, bowed low, and trotted off. There was unanimous applause.

'Well, that was fun!' Sybil said, delighted. 'But what was it supposed to be?'

A zoo of whispered suggestions followed, none of which were likely.

'A performing animal, perhaps? Something to do with a circus?'

The stage had been darkened. The head discarded. But Freddie still wore her brown trousers and singlet, and a scarf tied into a turban. She walked in a crouching, bow-legged style, shielding an imaginary light and peering ahead. On reaching her destination she hammered, lifted and stacked, crawled away dragging something heavy behind her. Finally she sat, unwrapped invisible food, munched it.

Mine or *coal* were the favoured guesses.

'Croust?' Sybil wondered, meaning a Cornish snack.

'There's no word on earth that has *croust* in it!' Anthony said loftily.

'What about *croustacean*?' Daniel suggested mischievously.

There was a longer pause while Freddie changed, for when she returned she was wearing her party clothes.

The third syllable was some kind of competition, because she mimed two different persons laying an imaginary dinner table for an elaborate meal. One of them muddled along hilariously, playing to the gallery without shame, and raising laughs. The other completed the task effortlessly, efficiently, and stood apart, like a magician's assistant, with a smile and a gesture as if to say, 'That's how it should be done!'

Then Freddie stepped forward and drew a circle in front of herself to indicate that she was about to perform the whole word.

In an instant she became a multitude of people. Changing roles in seconds, she stood in front of an imaginary fireplace, and raised unseen coat-tails; lifted an unseen glass in a toast, shook hands graciously, made silent conversation; swept grandly by in a flowing gown, laughed, talked; met invisible guests and introduced them to each other; bustled in from the wings, carrying trays and offering drinks; and finally shook hands with everyone and waved them good night.

Then she turned to face the room, threw out her arms for acclamation like a diva, and bowed very low.

Daniel led the applause, clapping, stamping, crying, 'Bravo! Bravo!' And saying *sotto voce* to Blanche, 'What were you on about, woman? It's as good as a night out in Dublin!'

'That's because you're outsiders, and you aren't doing the real thing,' she answered.

'Wasn't Freddie *clever*?' Sybil was crying. 'Weren't she and Daniel *funny*?'

And again Blanche answered, 'These are Uncle Jack's sort of charades. The Malpases play a darker game altogether.'

'Now, Lydia's group!' Anthony cried. 'Your answer, please! I shall begin timing you in exactly three seconds. One. Two. Three.'

Daniel said immediately, '*Hospitable*?'

'Quite right!' Freddie answered, coming out front.

Anthony said, baulked of a tantalizing wait, 'Two seconds.' And tutted to himself.

The rest began trying it out on their tongues.

'*Hoss*? Oh, yes! Horse! Funny sort of horse! *Spit*? No! No, you're wrong. It's *hoss* and then *pit*. Oh, yes, *pit*. And then *able*. And the word was Freddie being – *hospitable*! Oh, very good.'

'How did you guess, Daniel?' Sybil asked.

'Well, she's a very clever mimic, our Freddie. Did none of you recognize yourselves?' They shook their heads. 'Oh, yes,' he continued, 'we were all there, on our best behaviour. Malpases and guests. She even mimicked herself and Lydia.'

'I didn't know she was imitating *us*!' Anthony said, slightly affronted. He hated not to know.

Daniel remained bland, expansive, and innocent. He turned to Freddie and winked. 'You were taking the mickey out of us all, now weren't you?' he said.

'Of course, she was,' cried Lydia proudly, linking arms with her friend. 'Freddie is the reason we're invited to so many parties.

She can hit any character off. In fact, sometimes she's downright wicked.'

They giggled together, while the others smiled uncomfortably, wondering if they had been insulted. Then curiosity overcame embarrassment. There was a chorus of, 'Oh, do it again. Do the word again!'

But the culprit refused.

Sybil, noting Daniel's beaming countenance and jaunty stance, his close companionship with the whisky bottle, could not forbear from whispering. 'Blanche, do you think Daniel should have black coffee?'

'No,' her daughter replied composedly. 'I think you should see him as he can be, not as you would like him to be. You're inclined to be over-generous in your judgement.'

'Darling!' Sybil said in despair. 'Don't be difficult when we're all enjoying ourselves.'

Anthony had just accepted a glass of Daniel's whisky.

'Is this a new bottle?' he asked suspiciously.

'A new one of mine, sir,' Daniel replied, smiling. 'I took the precaution of laying in a small supply for the holiday.'

'Ah!' Anthony looked at him closely. 'Good idea,' he said amicably. 'Right, who's next? Your turn, Edward. Jump to it, lad.'

Edward's eyes met Katrina's ironic gaze, and exasperation dictated the next choice. 'You, Kat!'

She was looking self-possessed and very chic, Blanche noticed. Formerly her wardrobe had been that of a woman doing her best on a schoolmaster's modest salary. Now she dressed well, but it was the minor details which most clearly displayed her new prosperity: silver-gilt fashion earrings, silk designer scarf, Italian shoes.

'You remember how to begin, I suppose?' Anthony asked.

His tone implied that she did not. He glanced at her over his spectacles as if she were an unsuitable applicant who must nevertheless be interviewed.

'Oh, yes,' she replied coolly, directly. 'How to begin, how to continue, and how to end.' Bowing slightly to the assembled Malpases, she slipped behind the curtains.

'Here we go!' Blanche murmured.

CHAPTER TWELVE

Katrina had learned her first charades lesson well. Remember the rules. Give them no chance to instruct you, criticize you, and gradually whittle away your confidence. Breathe deeply, take your time, be in control of the situation and yourself, and count to ten before you begin. When the curtains jerked back she was waiting for them.

. . . eight, nine, ten.

Katrina threw out her arms, opened her mouth wide and rolled her eyes soulfully at the ceiling.

'Song!' they cried joyfully.

She put up five fingers.

'Five words!'

One finger.

'First word!'

They were enjoying this. And Anthony was heard, quite clearly, to whisper to Sybil, 'Now that's how it *ought* to be done!'

Smiling, Katrina fixed her eyes upon her husband, waved one arm directly at him, retreated step by step into the wings, waving, smiling. And was gone.

A restless, an uneasy silence, followed. But she was with them again almost immediately, holding up two fingers for the second word. She became an automaton, eyes staring ahead, limbs rigid. Stiffly, she stalked the stage. Stopped and faced them again. Changed into a little girl, skipped forward, cradling something precious, holding it up for them to see. Cradled it again. Skipped off.

The other four words were performed just as clearly and economically.

She pointed to herself.

She tousled her hair.

She became a soldier, turned her back on them, heels clicking. They felt, in some way no one could define, that she was turning her back on her husband. She marched off.

She came back for the last time, and pointed to him.

The performance was over.

Freddie, Natalie and Daniel gave one or two perfunctory claps. The Malpases sat as if stunned. Katrina rejoined them, apparently not caring that an immaculate performance was to remain unapplauded. And sat down composedly.

Rousing himself, Anthony said, 'Timing begins now.'

Looking directly at his wife, Edward guessed, '*Goodbye Dolly, I must leave you.*'

'Quite right!' Katrina said, smiling her tight little smile.

'Two seconds,' said Anthony, resigned.

Someone said, 'Oh, well done!' But the effort was half-hearted, and fell flat.

Sybil was clapping her hands again, this time with the commanding plack-plack-plack that Blanche had described as 'running a boarding school'. Her colour was high. 'I think we should take a break before we do a fourth charade. Tony, shall you and I make coffee? No, we don't need any help from anyone, thank you.'

And he, who generally ordered coffee and waited for it to arrive, followed her out obediently.

With Sybil gone the members of the party drifted away from Katrina and formed small groups in different parts of the room, talking in subdued murmurs. Marooned on an island of her making, her expression hardened, but she did not lose an atom of self-assurance.

Edward was sitting by himself, head in hands, elbows on knees, and Blanche went over, mostly to console him but partly to evade Daniel.

Her brother lifted his head and said simply, 'Upstaged and undone. Kat's message could hardly have been clearer.'

'You were hoping for a reconciliation?'

He nodded, and said, 'I thought that was why she came down here. I've been mulling things over, and gearing myself up for another try. For the sake of the kids. But now it looks as though she's leaving for good.'

'Well, she needn't have told you so in public, Teddy. And nobody liked her for it.'

He shrugged, and said, 'She wanted to pay me out. To pay the family out.'

Blanche said passionately, 'I hate charades.'

A large warm hand descended on her shoulder. A persuasive voice spoke in her ear. 'Blanche,' said Daniel, bending over her, 'could I have a word in private?'

She answered without looking at him, though his touch sent messages to her flesh. 'Dan, I've had a long, hard Christmas Day.'

'It's a practical matter entirely.'

Resigned, she said, 'Oh, very well. Excuse us, Teddy.'

Her brother stared up at her absent-mindedly as she rose, and said sadly, 'Be my guest, love. Be my guest.'

'You'll see what I mean when I show you,' said Daniel, lifting the curtain aside and ushering her in.

Blanche stared at the half-lit stage, and was turning to ask him what he was talking about when he put both arms around her, and kissed her long and soundly.

'There,' said Daniel, somewhat breathless, 'that's what I meant.'

Furious, aroused, she pushed him away with such strength that he had to steady himself against the wall. She spoke in a savage whisper lest she be overheard. 'Don't you dare treat me like an easy lay. Now, if you don't behave yourself I shall insist that you leave, and I don't give a shit if you have to *walk* home. Is that understood?'

He looked and felt as savage as she did, but had too much to lose by showing temper. Quietly and with difficulty he said, 'All right then, Blanche. Have it your own way. You tell me how you want me to behave and I'll do it.'

She was slightly breathless herself, but answered with rigid resolution. 'I understand how you feel about Aaron, but you must keep him in one compartment and me in another. I don't intend to jeopardize my freedom by becoming involved with you again, and if I want a lover I can find one – thank you very much.'

He swallowed, and nodded. In the well of the room beyond they heard Sybil say with deliberate cheerfulness, 'Coffee, everybody!' and became aware of social obligations. Blanche whispered, 'Lipstick!' Daniel wiped his mouth with hands that trembled slightly. She, ivory pale, reddened her lips. Assuming smiles, they joined the company.

*

Sybil and Anthony were playing a charade of their own. As she filled the coffee cups her glance reminded him.

'Good Lord,' said Anthony, comparing his fob-watch with the clock on the mantelshelf. 'Look at the time. I had no idea!'

'I really think—' Sybil began.

'Yes, it's too late to go on with the game,' said Edward, pre-empting his father's lines.

'Mummy, let me do that. You must be exhausted,' said Lydia, following his lead.

'And when you're ready I'll run you all round to the pub,' Anthony said. Even his kindness was peremptory.

Edward said reluctantly, 'I can do that.'

'No, no. My turn to play the chauffeur,' Anthony insisted, and glanced at Sybil, who nodded approval.

Daniel thanked him effusively. Natalie raised her eyebrows. Katrina said nothing.

Conversation was stilted, disjointed. The animals had followed the trolley out of the kitchen, and everyone made much of them, using them as cover for their thoughts. They picked up Salome and courted her. She struggled out of their embraces and leaped on Blanche's lap. They tickled Patch in a favourite spot behind his ears. He allowed it. They condoled with Mr Silk, who was yet again in disgrace and grateful for any kind word. Gracie evaded them with dignity, and lay on the floor at her mistress's feet.

Languidly, Sybil sat back and caressed the Labrador's head, mentally removing herself from the company. She was summoning up the last of her energy to round off the day well.

We're all apprehensive, Blanche thought. Kat's set something in motion that we can't stop and we're apprehensive.

'I must look after Aaron,' she informed the room at large, and sat Salome in her place.

Daniel half rose from his chair as she was passing, but Blanche put one hand on his shoulder and checked him. 'Not yet. Give me ten minutes,' she said firmly. 'I'm changing him now, making him comfortable. You can come to say good night to him before you go.'

He nodded, and sank back: just one of many disconcerted people in that room.

The twilight of the bedroom was welcome to her. Her son was heavy, sleepy. She dealt with him automatically, thinking of

Daniel. As she held Aaron to her, alive and warm and smelling of baby powder, she was remembering the warmth and strength of his father, the male scent. So far she had been wholly centred on her baby. Now she needed a lover as well as a child and, even discounting Daniel, foresaw endless complications.

'Oh, to hell with sex!' she whispered into Aaron's neck.

The whisper tickled him and he twitched away from her and flung out one small round arm, which struck her cheek lightly as if in reprimand.

'But without sex – no you!' she said, putting him back in his cot.

Sensing her body alive and responsive after its long celibacy, she felt that long, hard kiss once more, and closed her eyes for a moment, deliciously giddy.

Consequences

CHAPTER THIRTEEN

Boxing Day

'Blanche! Blanche! I've brought you a cup of tea, and the playroom's been turned into a real stage.'

Henrietta was shaking her, and Blanche woke suddenly from a confused dream to a dry mouth and a jumble of thoughts.

'What time is it?' Sitting up. 'Where's Aaron?'

'Everybody's sleeping in this morning. You must have been very late coming to bed. And you needn't worry about Aaron. I got him up all by myself, and changed and dressed him in the bathroom so that you wouldn't be disturbed. Ben helped me to make our breakfasts and we put Aaron in his high chair and he ate a lot. Messy, isn't he? But the fire needs lighting, and the Aga stoking up, and we don't know how, and anyway Gran'ma's got a thing about children and matches. And it's nine o'clock.'

'Nine o'clock? Dear God, I don't know when I last slept as late as that. Henny love, I rather wish you hadn't taken Aaron out of his cot.' And as no small child was crawling or staggering after her, she asked, 'Where is he now?'

'He's practising climbing the stairs by himself,' said Henrietta importantly. 'You haven't got any stairs in your flat, you see, so we thought he ought to learn while he's here. He's doing very well so far. Ben's ready to catch him if he falls. And we wouldn't let him take Ba up with him. So he's quite safe.'

'I am very *angry* with you!' Blanche said abruptly, setting her teacup down with a smack, struggling into her kimono, pushing her hair out of her eyes. 'You had no right to leave him with Ben! He is *not* safe! He could fall. Fracture his skull . . .'

'No, he's quite safe,' the little girl repeated obstinately, though her face was pink from the rebuke, and her mouth quivered. 'He's enjoying himself. He thinks it's a game.'

117

'It is *not* a game, and you're an extremely naughty girl,' Blanche cried, running down the corridor.

Choked with shame, Henrietta followed her out on to the landing, holding the cup of tea carefully so that it did not slop. A furious Blanche was a different and an alarming person.

'Daddy believes in games. He says that learning should be fun. We've been teaching Aaron new words,' she offered, in placation.

Ben, less susceptible to rebuke, hailed his aunt gleefully from the foot of the stairs. 'He's all right, Blanche. Clemmie and me are here, watching him.'

'And Ba's sitting here waiting,' said his sister, near tears, pointing to the knitted lamb which was perched precariously against the newel post, ready to fall on Aaron given the slightest provocation.

'Oh, my God! Aaron! Stay where you are!' Blanche commanded.

Half-way up the staircase, scarlet with effort and excitement, alternately pushing and hauling himself from step to step, the child was tackling a personal Everest. As his mother called to him he came to a halt, stood upright uncertainly, clung to a banister, and pointed an imperious forefinger.

'Go!'

She was about to rush down the stairs and scoop him to safety when Sybil's hand held her back, and Sybil spoke quietly. 'Darling, don't fuss him. He's doing very nicely, and he must learn some time.' Then to her other grandson, in a tone that brooked no argument, 'Ben, leave that hamster in the hall at once, and come up behind Aaron. Just two stairs behind. Don't touch him and don't worry him.'

For the climber was now turning on this new adversary, shouting, 'Go!'

Sybil spoke firmly and calmly. 'Aaron! Don't bother about Ben, darling. He's just there in case you slip. Up you come, my baby!'

Aaron gave her a wet and wavering smile and returned to his task.

'And I'll hold Ba,' said Sybil, catching the toy as it toppled.

Blanche sat down helplessly on the landing and huddled her knees to her chest, saying, 'I'll never trust Henny again.'

'We meant it for a nice surprise.' Henrietta said forlornly. Tears slid down her face and plopped into the teacup.

'You know very well that you shouldn't have taken Aaron without asking his mother's permission,' said Sybil firmly, but put an arm round her grand-daughter. 'Fortunately he's all right.'

'Now what's up?' Lydia asked, joining them, yawning, buttoning her housecoat. Then she laughed, and said over her shoulder to Freddie, 'It's Blanche's little buster, climbing the wooden hill.'

'Attaboy!' Freddie cried robustly.

A sleepy Edward enquired, 'What's all the row about?' And was informed in detail.

Blanche kept her face resolutely away from these spectators who were encouraging her son's progress. To them it was an entertainment. To her it was flesh of her flesh set at risk. Her heart misgave her each time Aaron pressed himself up with one hand and made a hazardous snatch for the next banister with the other.

Three more stairs and he was upon her. Small warm fingers clutched her cold ankles. A triumphant face peered over her knees. All twelve teeth gleamed with achievement.

'Legit!' Aaron said succinctly.

She clasped him to her, laughing and crying. She loved him so much that it hurt.

'Drama over!' Sybil announced, and the family dispersed. She reminded her daughter, 'Poor Henny is watering your tea with tears.'

The adjective *poor* hinted that Blanche had been too harsh. Encircling her son firmly, she held out a shapely hand to her niece. 'Sorry, Hen. You frightened me to death.'

'I'm sorry too. I'll never ever do it again,' said Henrietta penitently, and sat beside her, hiccuping, and drying her eyes.

'What's all the fuss about?' Ben asked, puzzled by these niceties. 'He's learned how to climb the stairs.'

From the master bedroom came the clarion call of, 'Sybil, aren't any of those girls making tea yet?'

'The voice that breathed o'er Eden!' Edward murmured.

'In a minute, darling!' Sybil called. Then, 'Look, Aaron. Here's Ba, saying, "well done!"'

'We'll make the tea,' chorused Lydia and Freddie.

Forgiven, Henrietta asked, 'Blanche, why has the playroom been turned into a stage?'

Stroking Aaron's curls, holding him and his knitted friend, Blanche answered, 'Oh, we were playing charades, and Dan and

Teddy fixed it up temporarily. But the game went on too long and we hadn't the energy to clear up.'

'Oh, don't clear it up, Blanche. It would be such fun. We can all play charades every day, then.'

'I can't think of anything worse,' said Blanche seriously.

But Henrietta had recovered from her disgrace. 'Well, I'm going to ask Gran'ma. I'll bet she lets us.'

'You do that.'

Refreshed after his labours, Aaron scrambled off his mother's lap and pointed to the staircase. 'Down.'

'Oh, not down by yourself, lamb. Let Mama carry you down.'

'No. Down.'

'All right, then. Hold my hand, and I'll hold Ba.'

'He won't learn that way,' said Ben, unmoved by the recent crisis of emotions. 'You should teach him to crawl down backwards.'

'Down. Go.'

Blanche sighed.

'All right then. Turn round and grab the stair with both hands. I'll be right behind you.'

As they made slow, grunting progress, Henrietta said conversationally, skipping down beside them, 'Aaron is very articulate, isn't he? Having older children round him is a good influence.'

That remark comes directly from Sybil, Blanche thought.

'I hope he's not going to be an only child,' Henrietta continued, in her grandmother's vein. 'Will you and Daniel be having another baby?'

'They're not even having sex,' said Ben, before Blanche could answer, 'so how can they have another baby, stupid?'

'Benjamin Malpas,' Henrietta cried in a terrible voice, 'never say things like that in front of a young child. Aaron could be badly shocked.'

'Down.'

'Look, why don't you forget my private life?' Blanche asked, amused and annoyed.

'Oh, all right,' hastily. And then, reiterating her argument, 'But I still think it's a pity for him to be on his own.'

Aaron completed his task, with the remark, 'Legit.'

'Blanche,' said Ben, 'I've taught Aaron how to say Clementine's name. Listen. Aaron, say "Clemmie".'

'No.'

120

'Aaron, who's this? Aaron, look. Who's this watching you?'

Aaron viewed the little brown animal nibbling in her cage, smiled at her, and drew breath to do the word justice.

'K-lemmie.'

'There, Blanche,' said Henrietta, vindicated. 'See how much he's learned, playing with us this morning!'

CHAPTER FOURTEEN

Dilatory though the Malpases had been, their uninvited guests were even more so. Only Daniel showed up at noon, acting as messenger for the others, drawing Sybil aside to confide in her. 'Natalie's staying in bed this morning. I think, between the two of us, that she's not used to young children.'

'Nor to family life,' Sybil added sarcastically, 'but how nice to be able to stay in bed when you feel like it!'

Daniel's answer was automatic, though he gauged the situation shrewdly. 'Ah! There's no fooling you. Anyway, she sends her love and says she'll be here some time after lunch.' He drew closer to her, became more confidential. 'And a word with you about Katrina. She's not too sure of her welcome, but she wants to take the children for a walk by themselves this afternoon. Then she'll bring them back here and would like to talk to Edward privately afterwards. If you don't want her under your roof she says she quite understands, but in that case could the children come to her at the pub about half past two, and will Edward pick them up from there around four o'clock? I offered to deliver your answer.'

Sybil said drily, coldly, 'I find it very strange to have my daughter-in-law making appointments with me through an intermediary.'

'I thought you rated me something more than that,' said Daniel, confronting her.

Their eyes met: his honest and reproachful, hers surprised and suddenly conciliatory. For a moment they connected at a deeper level than the social one.

'So I do,' said Sybil after a pause, 'so I do — but I'm very displeased with *her*. Still, I would rather she discussed family affairs in the privacy of this house. Otherwise the Cornish Arms will be broadcasting the news all over the village. I'll write a note if you will take it.'

'And can I do anything else for you at all?' he asked gently.

She smiled then, for she saw that he was sincere in his wish to be of help.

'I wish you'd drink a little less, my dear,' she answered, just as gently.

He bowed his head, picked up her hand and kissed it.

At ten minutes past four Sybil showed Edward and Katrina into the kitchen, partly because it was the only unoccupied room at that time of the day, but also because she felt that it was a good place for them to be, and would perhaps help them to come to a satisfactory conclusion. She had an affinity with kitchens as a source of nourishment, a recipient of intimate female conversations, and a chronicler of family life from the turmoil of breakfast to the peace of evening hours. And she loved the kitchen at Minions, into which the afternoon sun now shone most promisingly. So she left them in its safe-keeping.

But these two sombre adults drew neither strength nor comfort from the radiant winter light, the white and blue community of china on the oak dresser, the table laid for the children's high tea, the towels drying on the Aga rail. Edward, with automatic courtesy, drew out a kitchen chair for his wife. Katrina said, equally politely, thank you but she would rather stand. This shouldn't take long, she added. And she stood near the dresser, well away from him, which was so discouraging that he also remained standing, and looked anywhere except at her, whistling softly as if he were perfectly at ease.

Edward had never been good at making decisions, and his confidence was not great, so he remained at a disadvantage; whereas Katrina, collected and determined, was well prepared for this final joust. She began by saying sincerely, 'I apologize for last night. It was – unkind – and in poor taste, but there's something about your family that brings out the worst in me.' He made no comment and she added, 'However, I'm not excusing myself. Please will you accept that I'm genuinely sorry?' As he remained silent she continued firmly, 'But I did mean what I said, and I *am* leaving you. For good.'

Her self-assurance angered and frightened him. He began to

grumble. 'It's no more than I expected. You were never satisfied with anything I did. It was always more, more, more. A bigger house, a better district, private schools for the kids. I just hope,' which he did not, 'that this man, whoever he is, can afford to keep you.'

Formerly she would have leaped in at this point with a bitterness that equalled or exceeded his, but now she answered quietly, reasonably, 'His name is Charles Fisher. He owns the company for which I work.'

Defeated, he tried to take his war into her camp. 'I don't give a damn who he is. What we're talking about now is your behaviour. God knows it's been bad enough already, but in the last couple of days you've reached an all-time low. I could have understood your coming here, even without an invitation and without warning, if you were hoping to patch things up. But I shall never understand in a thousand years why you wantonly gatecrashed our Christmas, unsettled Henrietta and Ben, humiliated me, and abused my parents' hospitality.'

Still she did not respond, and now he had to appeal to her. 'For God's sake, woman. What sort of game are you playing?'

'I'm not playing games any longer – apart from last night's charades,' she answered seriously. 'It wasn't my intention to upset everybody, and of course I thought you'd be by yourselves. I didn't reckon on Daniel and Natalie complicating matters. I'd reached an important decision and I wanted to sort things out with you face to face, but sensibly, amicably – not like last night. And I wanted to make my peace with your family, to say I was sorry it had all gone wrong but that needn't mean we were enemies. Oh,' lifting her hands and dropping them, 'I can't explain. I was feeling good, and I wanted everyone to understand. Teddy, our marriage is over, but it deserves a decent death.'

She was so unlike her old fiery self that she unsettled him. He said stiffly, 'What happened to change your mind?'

He avoided looking at her. She consulted the shining toes of her shoes: shoes quite unsuitable for country life, shoes that declared the gulf between them as clearly as she had done the night before.

She said, 'It was the fact that no one else had changed at all. I knew, as soon as I walked in, that I've never mattered to your family as a person, only as your wife. They don't know *me*, and don't *want* to know me, and nor do you. You'd rather muddle on, however wretched we are, and they would prefer us to stay together at any cost. We all know now that you and I should never have married. We were young and unsuited. But there's no point in spending a lifetime making up for a youthful error of judgement. And I've finished paying for that mistake, Teddy. The price is too high.'

Love had long since vanished, but his pride could be wounded afresh and most deeply. He said sourly, 'And you think you've found a better bargain elsewhere?'

Resolutely she replied, 'I came here to ask you for a divorce, because Charles wants to marry me. He's prepared to foot all the legal bills, and you won't be troubled by any demands for alimony.'

Afraid and isolated, he blustered, 'I wouldn't give you alimony anyway, so there's no need to congratulate yourself on being noble!'

She frowned a little, not in annoyance but in perplexity, and tried a different approach. 'Teddy, I know you're hurt and angry, and it's natural that you should be, and I know I've made life difficult for you and the children the last few months, but please let's not have a final slanging match. I had to be sure, before I made a move, that it would be the right one, and now I'm convinced. That's what I wanted to explain to you.' She appealed to him, 'Teddy, you and I were never happy together, except at first. Can't we wish each other well and be happy apart—'

He cut across the rest of her speech, enraged. 'Don't you dare patronize me! And don't try to rationalize your own damned selfishness. You could always prove that what you wanted was best for everyone else, and in one way you're right.' He sought to wound her through her children. 'It may surprise you to know that the three of us don't need you. We've managed very well without you. We have fun together. I'll divorce you with the greatest pleasure, so you needn't have worried, and I shan't grudge you reasonable access to Henny and Ben – provided that you and I don't ever have to meet again.'

'But I love my children, and I want them,' she answered earnestly. 'That was the other reason for my coming down here – to persuade you to do what's best for them. Surely you can't believe that it's good for them to live so scrappily, to depend upon neighbours and domestic help?'

He strode away from her, flinging his arms above his head in disbelief, laughing and shaking his head in fury. 'I can't believe I'm hearing this,' he cried, 'not even from the Queen of Hypocrites.'

Caught up in her plans, she did not heed him, speaking rapidly, freely. 'Children need a stable environment. Charles and I want them to make their home with us. Of course they'll have holidays with you . . .'

Edward stood quite still and listened.

'Charles is a widower in his fifties. He and his wife never had children and he's always wanted them. He isn't just doing this for me. He's very fond of Henny and Ben, and they like him too . . .'

Edward realized that his children had kept this relationship from him, and though they probably did it to save his feelings he felt doubly betrayed.

'. . . a house with a swimming pool and a big garden. We can do so much for them . . .'

She stopped talking, alarmed. He had turned round and was coming towards her, shouting at her, waving his arms. Shouting and waving this monstrous suggestion back into the darkness from which it came.

'You're not stealing my children as well as breaking up our marriage. You're not having *all* your own way. I won't let you. I'll fight you in every court in the country first. But that won't be necessary, because you deserted us. *You* – deserted – *us*. Oh, yes. I shall see my solicitor as soon as I get back. And meanwhile I want you out of here and away from us. You *sicken* me, you materialistic, egotistical bitch. Pack up and get out and fuck some more money out of your rich old man. Get out, I tell you. Get out or I'll throw you out.'

He was beside himself: the veins in neck and head swollen, his face a dull ugly red. Disturbed, she stretched out a tentative hand, spoke to him, tried to appease him; but he pushed her away from him so violently that she fell against the dresser, and in trying to save herself knocked Sybil's soup tureen onto the slate floor where it shattered.

'Oh, look what we've done!' she cried, shocked and sorry.

Her hard, bright carapace had been broken. She tried to shield herself as he came at her again, arms flailing, then scrambled up and fled to the kitchen door, shrieking for him to stop. And still he slapped her face from side to side, and banged her head and shoulders against the door, yelling that she should pack up and get out, get out, get out, while she screamed for help and tried to defend herself.

No one could ignore a crisis that drew the family from every corner of the house, and even brought Anthony stumping downstairs, spectacles pushed high on his forehead in astonishment. Clumsily, he helped Daniel to pinion Edward's arms while Freddie and Lydia lifted Katrina from the floor. Blanche, hampered by Aaron, tried to persuade Henny and Ben back to the playroom, and Sybil caught their hands and attempted to lead them away; but they refused outright, tugging themselves free, and huddling against the wall together, watching their parents with frightened eyes.

Natalie, cigarette in holder, summed up the situation in one word. 'Whisky!' she said to herself, and went to find a bottle.

Edward shook his head as if to clear it, and concentrated on getting his breath back. Gradually his colour subsided, his shoulders relaxed into their scholarly hunch. 'I'm all right,' he mumbled to his captors.

Relieved, embarrassed, they released him.

Sybil helped Katrina to a chair, where she sat motionless, hands clenching and unclenching in her lap, head averted. The others stood round her, not knowing what to do nor where to look. Physical violence was hardly the Malpas style.

'The tot that cheers and hopefully inebriates!' Natalie announced, returning, and poured everyone a drink without asking whether they wanted it or not.

The men downed their whisky quickly, fiercely. Sybil did not touch hers, bent on persuading Katrina to sip and cough and sip again. Katrina at last dropped her head in her hands and began to cry softly. Then Henrietta and Ben sidled forward to the small figure sobbing at the kitchen table, and put their arms round her neck and laid their cheeks against hers.

'Don't lean on her, my loves,' Sybil cautioned them gently, for Katrina trembled and tensed herself as if she were afraid to be touched.

The children moved away, hands locked behind them, looking from their mother to their father, and back. Their eyes condemned him, and still Katrina sobbed.

'We're no use here. Better leave the women to it,' Anthony advised in a low voice.

'Come with us, Ted,' said Daniel, in sorrowful understanding. 'You look as though you need another drink.'

The females gathered round the victim protectively.

The males ushered the wife-beater out as if they too had been found guilty of assault.

CHAPTER FIFTEEN

Sybil, kneeling on the kitchen floor, became aware that a pair of short trim legs, clad in beautifully tailored trousers, had stopped beside her. And looked up.

'Freddie, I really must apologize for that appalling scene.'

'What nonsense!' Freddie said robustly. 'These things will happen, even in the best-regulated families.'

'Which ours', said Blanche, 'is not.'

She was giving Aaron his tea. At the foot of the high chair sat Mr Silk, waiting for crumbs to fall. The two cats were snarling at each other over their respective food dishes. Gracie lay by the Aga, eyes half-closed, meditating.

'This was my mother's tureen,' said Sybil, picking up the shards and regarding them wistfully. 'I remember it from my childhood. So how old must it have been?'

She spoke in the past tense because the pot was past repairing. She did not expect an answer, spoke to herself rather than to her listeners.

'I retired it from daily life several years ago, and brought it down here with some of her other things, to keep it safe. Isn't that ironic? It's not valuable. Not especially fine china, nor made by any grand pottery, but such a graceful shape, such a pretty blue and white pattern. We used this tureen regularly at home, when I was young. My mother used to cook and serve a three-course meal every evening, beginning with soup – and she cooked a midday lunch for we three children as well. How women worked in those days, and with none of our time- and labour-saving equipment. Ah well, times change, and no one eats as much as they used to. Soup is regarded as a meal on its own now. Unless I'm giving a dinner-party, I serve it for a weekday lunch or a Sunday evening supper . . .'

Freddie sat on a corner of the table, swinging one leg. When she thought that Sybil had come to the end of her monologue she began, tactfully, to speak of the present situation. 'Sybil, I came to tell you that things are more or less back to normal. The men have disappeared. Katrina is lying down in our room, and Lydia and the children are with her, and I've been telephoning on her behalf. When she feels up to it we can take her back to the pub and do her packing. She intends to leave tomorrow.'

Sybil sat back on her heels, distressed.

'Is that wise? She's been dreadfully shocked. And imagine spending the night by herself in the Cornish Arms, when everything has gone so badly. Oh, I know that Natalie and Daniel are staying there too, but she needs someone to look after her.'

For Natalie was not by nature a carer, and Daniel, being a man, was out of the question.

'I would keep her here,' Sybil continued, 'but there's no room to spare.'

Freddie thought about this, consulting her swinging foot.

'Is Katrina friendly with Lydia?' she asked. 'Because I'm quite willing to sleep on the playroom sofa, and she can have my bed.'

Sybil pondered this offer, but had been so distracted by breakages of every kind that she looked to Blanche for advice. 'You two girls are quite friendly with her, aren't you?'

Blanche scraped tomato sauce from Aaron's chin with a teaspoon, and posted it into his mouth. Mr Silk pounced on three flattened baked beans and a crust.

'Sybil, don't be ridiculous,' Blanche replied. 'You can't possibly have Kat and Teddy under the same roof.'

'But surely someone should keep an eye on her?'

'She's old enough and independent enough to look after herself. Our main concern is the wife-beater, who must be feeling less than the dust.'

Sybil was disturbed by this reference to her son's behaviour. 'Blanche dear, that isn't funny.' She turned to a more responsive companion. 'A very kind thought, Freddie. But, under the circumstances, perhaps not.'

She switched her attention to the tureen. 'I'm afraid there's nothing to be done with this apart from sweeping it up. Freddie, would you mind fetching that dustpan and brush?'

She moved back to the original problem. 'Tomorrow seems very sudden. Can she cope with a long train journey?'

Freddie answered carefully, testing the delicacy of this ground. 'She asked me to phone her friend Charles Fisher, and he's coming down to fetch her. He lives near York apparently, so it's quite a drive, but he's prepared to start out this evening and stay overnight somewhere along the way. He expects to arrive around lunch-time tomorrow. He asked me if I could book a table for them in a local restaurant.'

Sybil closed her eyes, grimaced, and took a deep breath.

'Oh dear, this is becoming more and more complicated,' she observed. 'There simply isn't anywhere open, and I can hardly ask them to lunch here.' Fragments of her childhood clinked and slithered into the dustpan.

'Of course you can't, and why should you?' Blanche said brusquely. 'This is their problem, not yours. They can have a ploughman's lunch at the Cornish Arms.' Her tone changed to one of pure indulgence, 'Aaron Malpas, you are a grubby, greedy *toad*!'

'Toad! Toad!' Smacking the tray of his chair.

Mr Silk scurried here and there, foraging for flying beans.

'I've seen some messy eaters in my time,' Freddie remarked pleasantly, observing him, 'but I reckon that Aaron takes the prize.'

Blanche laughed. Sybil pondered.

'I think you're right, darling,' she said finally. 'It's dreadful to be inhospitable, but we've had quite enough trouble without inviting more.'

The sound of footsteps in the passage alerted her, and she pulled herself to her feet as the door opened.

Katrina was extremely pale but once more in command of herself. She walked slowly into the kitchen, followed by her two children and an attendant Lydia.

'Sybil, I'm truly sorry about the tureen,' she said at once. 'I know how much you loved it. I'll try to make it up to you in some way.'

'Accidents happen,' Sybil answered stoically. 'Are you feeling a little better?'

'Well enough to be on my way. And I do thank you for your forbearance.'

The children, who had been silent and subdued, clinging to her hands, came to urgent life and begged her not to go. 'You can stay here and sleep with me,' cried Henrietta. She supplicated her aunt. 'Mummy can sleep in our room, can't she, Blanche?'

'I wouldn't dream of it. I've upset too many arrangements already,' said Katrina tightly.

'Oh, please. Oh, please. Oh, Mummy, please. Oh, Blanche, please.'

Katrina's face contracted.

'I'd like you to be here when I wake up tomorrow, Mum,' said Ben humbly.

Henrietta was already in tears, and Katrina seemed about to follow suit.

Wiping her son's hands and face, and those portions of the chair that he was not occupying, Blanche answered as willingly as she could. 'If Freddie would sleep on the sofa I suppose I can move Aaron and myself to Liddy's room – if she's prepared to put up with us.'

Lydia looked as reluctant as her sister felt, but Freddie gave her an encouraging wink.

'I must find clean sheets,' said Sybil mechanically, wondering whether she had enough bedclothes to meet the occasion.

'Don't bother, we can swop our sheets and pillowcases,' said Blanche, reading her.

But Katrina ended this futile discussion. 'Absolutely not, Sybil. I refuse to cause any more trouble.'

The children, who had been ecstatic, were immediately cast down. She hugged them reassuringly and kissed the tops of their heads, then spoke on. 'I shall be quite all right at the pub. And anyhow, Charles . . .' She hesitated how to describe him to her mother-in-law. 'My friend Charles Fisher is meeting me there tomorrow. It would be difficult for everyone if he had to come here.'

Freddie broke in, 'He did ask me to book lunch at a restaurant, but Sybil tells me this is not possible.'

'No, of course it isn't,' said Katrina practically. 'Charles doesn't know what Cornwall is like out of season, bless him. We'll have a bar lunch at the Cornish Arms and set off afterwards. We can take the journey in easy stages, stopping when we feel like it. I expect he'll be tired after that drive, so we can stay overnight somewhere. There's no immediate hurry to get back.'

Her children turned their faces up to hers, wondering if they were included in any way.

Katrina said directly to Sybil, 'I wonder if you would mind speaking to Edward for me? I'd like to say goodbye properly to

Henny and Ben tomorrow. If they came to me about twelve o'clock we could give them lunch in the family room at the pub.'

Henrietta and Ben brightened at the prospect.

Sybil said uncertainly, 'Yes. Yes, of course. I'm sure that will be all right.'

Katrina said, 'Thank you.' Now she bent over the children and spoke to them. 'You two are coming to us for New Year, so it won't be long before we see each other again.'

Sybil did not mean to pry, but was unable to resist the temptation. 'Have you agreed a date for their return? Because Edward didn't seem to have any fixed plans.'

Katrina replied, 'Oh, I made arrangements before I left home, and sorted them out with Henny this afternoon. She knows what to do, don't you, Hen?'

And she, wiping her eyes, repeated parrot fashion, 'Ben and me are to leave on Friday morning to catch the nine forty-seven from Redruth, and Mummy's meeting us in York at five twenty. I've got the tickets in my purse, and the timetable, and the seats are booked.'

'You're travelling all that way by yourselves?' Sybil asked, aghast.

'We're travelling first class,' Ben assured her. 'First class, Gran.' He would have liked her to be as impressed as he was.

Henrietta chimed in, 'And we'll be put in charge of the guard, or some nice lady. We only have to sit there and drink Coke and read our magazines.'

Ben said, 'And Mum's given us ten pounds to buy refreshments. Ten pounds!'

Sybil turned to her daughter-in-law, saying, 'But they're carrying the hamster cage and that wretched stick insect as well as their luggage and presents. Aren't they very young to cope with all that?'

'He's not wretched,' Ben muttered. 'He's a very nice stick insect.'

'Sybil,' Blanche said firmly, 'Katrina has already made the arrangements and Teddy presumably concurs with them or doesn't mind. They know their own business best.' She meant, they are adults, and no longer your responsibility.

Sybil was thinking, but these are my grandchildren and vulnerable, and I mind.

'They'll be perfectly safe, Sybil,' said Katrina, equally firm.

'Edward will see them on to the train and ask someone to keep an eye on them. They've become very independent in the last few months. Very experienced travellers. I live quite a distance from them, you see.'

Horrendous pictures flashed before Sybil's eyes: Katrina delayed by car failure or a car accident; the children waiting in a deserted station at night, not knowing what to do, stalked by night's monsters. Slowly, she swept the remains of the tureen on to a newspaper. Folded it into a parcel. Dropped it in the pedal-bin.

I don't understand this generation, she acknowledged.

She remembered another complication.

'What about the little dog? Mr Silk. Surely, they are not—'

'Charles and I will be taking him back with us, and keeping him for Henny. I didn't expect to leave him with Edward. I have his travelling basket, and food for him.'

Sybil could never fault her daughter-in-law on efficiency. In the past she had been grateful for it, believing that Katrina's capability made up for Edward's insufficiencies. Now she found it chilling.

'Oh, not Mr Silk,' Henrietta cried, beginning another lament. 'I'm his mother. Mummy, *we* can look after him. We can look after Mr Silk, can't we, Ben? Oh, Mummy, please, please let me take him home with me—'

'Henrietta, do be quiet!' said Sybil, in a tone that did not allow of protest or tears. 'There are far more important matters to discuss than Mr Silk. And I should like a word with your mummy by herself, if you please. You'll be seeing her shortly.'

'Bed-time, glutton!' Blanche said to her son.

Ben put one arm round his sister and spoke to her like a kind and sensible adult. 'Come on, old Hen,' he said, and led her out.

Sybil was very much on her dignity.

'Do sit down, Katrina. I don't want to seem inquisitive or unkind, and you must still be feeling shaky, but I need to know what's happening . . .'

Her daughter-in-law inclined her head, and sat and scrutinized her fingernails, which were matchless.

Now how does one begin? Sybil wondered. And tried. 'This – friend of yours – Mr Fisher . . .'

Katrina looked up at her and made a small grimace. 'I wish you'd call him Charles, Sybil. I appreciate your feelings, but Mr Fisher does sound formal.'

I am old-fashioned, Sybil thought. I don't address people by their Christian names unless I know them personally. In my head he will remain Mr Fisher. 'Very well then. When did this relationship with Charles begin?'

Katrina presented her side of the case readily. 'Two years ago. For eighteen months it was an affair. For the past six months we have been living together, to make sure that we wanted a permanent relationship. And I've invited the children to stay with us regularly, to see whether this would work for them as well as ourselves.'

Although Edward was her son and she loved and preferred him, Sybil could not help thinking that he did not know his mind as well as his wife knew hers, and would have been incapable of planning a change of life-style so competently, or so far ahead.

She said, half-humorously, 'You modern women astonish me. How did you find time to run a home, bring up two children, hold down a job, and meet Mr – Charles.'

Katrina almost smiled at her fingernails.

'I've been his personal secretary for the last three years. So we knew each other very well, and could see each other regularly.'

'Was this at the university?'

'Oh, no. I haven't worked at the university for ages. They don't pay well enough. No, Charles is a businessman. He owns this computer company. People think highly of him. He's quite an authority in his field.'

She spoke with admiration, with pride and respect. He came up to her standards, Sybil could see. Whether she loved him was another matter, but admiration, pride and respect might well be equated with love in Katrina's mind.

'Is he – divorced – or . . . ?'

'He's a widower. He was happily married for twenty-five years. His wife died soon after I joined the company five years ago. He has no children, and he's very fond of mine.'

Evidently she felt she had been questioned enough. Her tone became brisk. She drew herself up. 'I came here to ask Edward for an amicable divorce.'

Is there such a thing, Sybil wondered.

Aloud, she said, 'I must say that I don't care for your choice of venue or your sense of occasion. I arranged this Christmas to bring the family together, not to disrupt it further. You would have done better to wait.'

Katrina accepted the rebuke, but said earnestly, 'I didn't come here to ruin your Christmas, Sybil. I came to sort matters out in an atmosphere of seasonal good will. I even hoped that you might see it was for the best, and give me leave to go.'

Sybil said stiffly, 'You were hoping for a great deal too much, in my opinion.'

'Divorce is a much more civilized business these days,' said Katrina, propitiating her. 'We should be able to agree a separation without having to prove adultery or blacken each other's characters.'

'And what is to happen to Henrietta and Ben?'

'Charles and I want them to live with us. That was what the row was about. They can see Edward whenever they like and he can have them for holidays, but I want custody.'

Sybil consulted her hands. Clasped on the table before her, illuminated by a pale shaft of sunlight, they looked old. She folded them in her lap, out of sight.

She said sadly, 'I know Edward's weak points. He underestimates himself and his ability, which means that he doesn't take the initiative in anything, and loses opportunities for advancement.' Her voice strengthened with conviction. 'But although he will never be rich or powerful he has values and qualities that are more important than wealth or power, and his children will benefit from those.'

Katrina dealt with this statement concisely, slightingly. 'Nevertheless, he doesn't look after them properly. And he leans on Henny like he used to lean on me, and that's not fair.'

'Fair?' Sybil cried, with such emphasis that her daughter-in-law jumped slightly. 'What has fairness to do with it? You and Teddy – I make no special case for him – have indulged your likes and dislikes at the expense of your children all along. They are already suffering from divided loyalties because they love you both. And now you are asking them to divide those loyalties yet again, and love *two* fathers. Is *that* fair?'

Katrina did not answer for a moment or two. Then she said, 'We did try to make the marriage work. We've been to Relate and had group therapy and personal counselling. It wasn't wasted as far as I am concerned. I've learned a lot about myself.' She added

135

sourly, 'I wish I could say the same for Edward, but he doesn't like facing home truths.'

'I am not at all sure that this concentration on oneself is entirely wise,' said Sybil drily. 'My generation of women was brought up to think of others.'

'Yes, and that's why my generation of women is now having to fight its way out of a social and emotional straitjacket,' Katrina answered tartly.

Then she made a little movement of the hand as if to apologize, and went on reasonably, peaceably. 'It's not a question of reviving *love*. Edward and I don't even *like* each other any more, and whenever we meet we wage war – as you must have observed. Would you prefer the children to live in that atmosphere?'

'No,' said Sybil, shaking her head vehemently. 'Oh, no. God help them. No, no.'

And they were both silent.

'No, I can see it's gone too far for reconciliation,' said Sybil at last.

And they were silent again.

'There's just one other thing,' said Katrina in an appeasing tone. 'I have a favour to ask of you, for the children's sake. Can you persuade Edward not to fight for custody?' Her voice and eyes implored Sybil to understand, to intervene on her behalf.

'You can hardly blame him if he does,' said Sybil, forthright and unconvinced. 'You were the one who left them.'

'I also left a domestic substitute, so that at least they had a reasonably well-run home,' said her daughter-in-law hardily, 'and I've done what I can from a distance, such as buying their clothes, paying their expenses, and giving them pocket money.'

Sybil could not answer. She was grieving for Henrietta and Ben who deserved so much better than this.

'I love my children,' Katrina said, and the statement was absolute. 'I may not love them in a way you can understand, but I do love them, and I believe I know what's best for them. With Edward they'll simply muddle along, getting nowhere and becoming nobody, and I can't allow that. I intend to have custody, and I shall fight for it, but I don't want to bring the children into court if I can help it.'

Suddenly Sybil saw her daughter-in-law's bruised and resolute face in a new light. 'Are you sure you didn't come down here on purpose to quarrel with Teddy?' she asked sternly.

Katrina shook her head emphatically.

Sybil gestured towards the bruises. 'Has he – done this sort of thing before?'

Katrina shook her head again.

Still, Sybil was thinking, she and this Mr Fisher are worldly people, and they mean to have their own way. That scene and those marks can be used as evidence of physical cruelty, and all of us were witnesses.

'Charles will be a good stepfather,' Katrina assured her, 'and the children like him.'

Sybil's mouth twitched.

'And I shall play fair all the way round. You've been very good to me and the children over the years. We shan't lose touch with you.'

But Edward will meet someone else fairly soon, Sybil thought, because he cannot stand alone. If he hasn't learned from this marriage he'll find another Katrina, because he's the sort of man who needs a strong woman to love and care for him. But if he's lucky he might meet someone who will help him to be his best self. He is only in his thirties. They may start a new family, or she may have children already. And then there will be another branch of Malpases for Henny and Ben to encompass, with all their subsequent ramifications. So many people to satisfy, all living in different places, and some at great distances. Parents, step-parents, step-siblings, grand-parents, step-grandparents.

'Are your mother and father still living in Doncaster?' Sybil asked, remembering them dimly, met at the wedding and never seen since.

'Oh yes, they're still there. We keep in touch.'

'What do they think of your present plans?'

Katrina rose now, politely but decidedly, to indicate that the interview was over. 'They didn't want me to marry Edward in the first place, so they think I'm doing the right thing.'

No more could be said. Sybil straightened up mentally and physically, to end the interview as it had begun, with as much dignity and good will as she could muster.

'Then we must hope', she said, 'that it works out well for you all.'

And discovered that she was exhausted.

CHAPTER SIXTEEN

Wednesday, 27 December

The world opened up again, dispersing the claustrophobia of a family Christmas. Its magical day over, the Christmas tree seemed artificial, superfluous: an illusion, waiting only until Twelfth Night, or the end of this holiday, to be reduced again to a box of ornaments and bonfire wood. Mrs Laity, calling in to offer her services, accepted coffee that she did not need in order to sit a little longer in the kitchen and exchange news and glean information. '. . . and everybody do say how they enjoyed the party.'

Her quick black eyes discovered the space on the dresser. 'Now where be your old tureen, Mrs Malpas?'

'Sadly, broken. An unlucky accident.'

'Too many visitors,' Mrs Laity decided. 'Handsome old thing, he was. And after all the care we took of him. Mary Sampson tell me that Katrina's off today, and her face all bruised, and a gentleman coming from upcountry to fetch her back home.'

Sybil answered automatically, slicing a conglomeration of cold meats, 'I'm afraid so.'

'She and Edward not going to make up again, then?'

'Sadly, not.'

'T-t-t. What I say is, it's the children that suffer.'

'Sadly so.'

'Sad-ly,' Aaron said reflectively, watching and listening from his high chair.

'I seen Blanche and her young man in the shop this morning, and we had a few words. Some 'andsome man. It's to be hoped something'll come of that.'

Evidence was already before her eyes in the form of Aaron, chewing gingerly on a rusk.

'Teething, is he?'

'Go!' Aaron challenged her with the rusk.

'Yes, it's to be hoped something come of it for his sake, poor liddle dear,' Mrs Laity said, hinting at his bastard status. 'Now, Mrs Malpas, what do you want done?'

'If you could hoover and dust the living room and playroom, Mrs Laity, while they're all out, and then clean the bathroom, it would be a help.'

'Sitting room, playroom, bathroom. That sister-in-law of yours,' Mrs Laity said, collecting her basket of cleaning materials, 'would she be a famous lady like your 'usband's a famous gentleman?'

'Famous is too strong a word.' Sybil considered. 'She's well respected in her profession as he is in his, certainly. She's a very fine photographer.'

'We was saying at the party how she do look like him. No mistake.'

'She is his twin. His twin sister.'

'Twins!' Mrs Laity cried triumphantly. 'I never knew you had twins in the family. If Blanche have any more she'll need to watch out!' And she laughed aloud. 'Why, there could have been two of *him*!' indicating Aaron, who had finished his rusk and was in dire need of a face-cloth.

'Two Aarons is quite a thought,' Sybil agreed, preparing to deal with him.

'But we was forgetting that Blanche be adopted,' said Mrs Laity, correcting them both, 'so there won't be no danger o' that.'

Sybil paused, face-cloth in hand. 'Yes, of course. One does forget. With it being so long ago.'

'I remember the first time you brought her here.'

Busy with her grandson, Sybil answered mechanically, 'That would be Easter nineteen fifty-two.'

'Some long time. And yet she do have a family look.'

'That's often the way.' Perfunctorily.

'Like my cousin Betty that couldn't have none of her own and she adopted two – and they warn't related – but the pair of them looked more like my aunt than her rightful grandchildren.' She paused at the door. 'Oh, and one more morsel of news. They do say that Mr Maddern's cousin be in London over Christmas and New Year, and he might be down here before long.'

'Ah!' Sybil said, as if she had been winded.

She stopped cleaning Aaron's face and chair for a moment, then shrugged and sighed and continued to sponge and talk.

'I suppose he'll be taking up residence at Predanick Wartha,' she remarked.

She did not trouble to ask Mrs Laity how she knew. Her sister was the village postmistress.

'I dare say he will. Well, I'll be getting on, Mrs Malpas.'

'Sad-ly,' said Aaron to himself, patting his clean hands on the clean tray, savouring the two new syllables.

'What a lot of new words you've learned!' Sybil said, pleased. 'And it isn't all sad news, is it, my baby? Your daddy loves you and your mummy very much, and we must hope for a happy ending. I wonder', she asked herself, 'whether I should teach him to say Da-da. No,' mentally seeing her daughter's fine black brows drawn together in a fine black temper, 'better not. We don't want to be in trouble, do we, my lambkin?'

And she spread crusts and rinds for the birds on the kitchen window-sill, while Aaron banged the tray, chanting, 'Sad-ly! Sad-ly!'

Mrs Laity was back again, purse-lipped with disapproval.

'Do you want they dusty old curtains taking down from the doors?'

'No, no. It's the children's stage. It keeps them happy. And when they've gone to bed I close the doors and draw the curtains across, to keep out the draughts. They've been acting little plays there.'

She did not say that she had come upon an improvised Nativity play that morning, where Mary divorced Joseph and took custody of Jesus. Mrs Laity would not have approved or understood.

'I don't approve either,' Sybil told Aaron, carrying him to the window to watch the birds pecking up her offerings. 'But I do understand.'

They were the only people there that afternoon. The beach lay pale and cold and gold in the dark embrace of rock, the sea spread out its lace-edged petticoat before them, the sky was a runny water-colour blue with ragged white racing clouds. Sybil, breeze-blown, hands in pockets, walked steadily, with Gracie keeping pace at her side, while the two children ran ahead and called and threw sticks that the old dog ignored. Four sets of footprints formed behind them, oozing slightly since the tide had not long ebbed: a pair of purposeful brogues, four sedate paws, four erratic wellington boots running to and fro, crossing and recrossing, as the children ran their bewilderment out.

'Gran! We should have brought our buckets and spades!' Ben cried, scampering back.

He shouted the news at her, was pretending his excitement. What a marvellous time we're having, he was telling her, and to think that it could have been even better!

'Too cold for that,' she answered, comprehending the depth of his trouble.

He turned his back on her, shouting louder still, 'Henn-y! Race you to the rock!'

But his sister lifted one shoulder, defeated, and trailed back to Sybil, head down, bottom lip thrust out.

'Oh dear me,' said Sybil, teasing her gently. 'Henrietta Malpas has a broken wing and a pout.'

'Well, *why* won't Gracie play with us?'

'She's too old, my love. She just wants a quiet constitutional. Oh, what a cold hand. Let's tuck it in my pocket, shall we?'

They walked along together, less comfortably but more companionably.

'They shouldn't have taken Mr Silk,' said Henrietta, all forlorn. 'The day was bad enough without taking Mr Silk.'

'Did Mrs Sampson give you a good lunch? Don't just nod, Henny. Tell me about it.'

The other shoulder hunched in protest.

'She gave us sausage and chips, and Ben absolutely *poured* Fruity Sauce all over his. I didn't know where to look.'

'I don't expect Mrs Sampson minded. Did you have a pudding?'

'Ice-cream and apple pie. And fresh orange juice to drink.'

'What a pity!' Sybil remarked slyly. 'You won't have an atom of room left, and I brought two Mars bars with me.'

'Mars bars? We've always got room for *them*!' Henrietta cried, making a rapid recovery.

'Then why don't you race Ben to the rock, and we can find a warm place out of the wind and sit and have them?'

She was off in a flash, shouting, 'Ben! Ben!'

Gracie gave a gusty sigh, and plodded on.

*

'I'll bet they've had lots of shipwrecks here,' said Ben, nibbling.

'Oh yes. The cove is cruel as well as beautiful. A ship could break its back on the rocks out there.'

His eyes were too bright and moved too quickly. He nibbled fast, talked fast. 'And when the sailors tried to swim ashore the villagers murdered them. Hit them over the head with axes until the blood ran down, didn't they, and stole all the cargo?'

'That was a long time ago. They don't do that any more. How's the Mars bar?'

'Super-duper-doo.'

But Henrietta laid down her Mars bar and looked at it with distaste. She said, 'Gran'ma, did you know that Mummy's going to divorce Daddy and marry Uncle Charles, and they want Ben and me to go and live with them?'

'Yes, your mummy told me.'

'Uncle Charles has a big house, and a tennis court, and a swimming pool,' Ben cried to the rough wind and the racing sky. 'I'll bet his house is worth half a million pounds.'

'I like going there for the weekend,' Henrietta admitted, and added, 'but I'm not sure I want to live there for ever and ever.'

'I do,' said Ben, nibbling faster and faster, eyes on the rocks. 'I'd like to live there with Dad. They've got a river running past the bottom of the garden. We could go fishing.'

'But that's the whole point, you stupid boy!' his sister cried shrilly. 'You *can't* live there with Daddy. Daddy has to live in our house while Mummy lives with Uncle Charles.'

'Henny, Henny,' said Sybil, putting an arm round her shoulders, 'don't be cross with Ben. Divorce is a very difficult thing to understand and accept.'

'What I'm trying to say is,' in a lower tone, but with a distressed quality of breathing that hinted at tears, 'we can't leave Daddy by himself.'

'I don't see', said Ben stubbornly, 'why we can't all live there together in different rooms. It's big enough. And then Dad could sell our house and make a bomb.' He danced up and down in counterfeit delight, crying, 'A bomb! Get it?' and made bombing noises.

Henrietta screamed, 'It's nothing to do with size. Don't you understand anything?'

His eyes flicked away. He finished his Mars bar, saying, 'Yum,

yum. Are there any more?' He wandered off before anyone could reply, and stood with his back to them, staring out to sea.

Sybil found a paper handkerchief and offered it. 'He knows only too well what's happening, Henny. He's just too upset to face it.'

'But you have to face things,' she sobbed. 'It's no use being an ostrich.'

'What's wrong with your Mars bar?'

'I don't feel like it now, thank you. Please will you keep it for me?'

Sybil slipped it into her pocket, held out her hand and said, 'Then let's walk back to the car. Come along Gracie, old lady. Ben-boy! Time for tea.'

Ben picked up a handful of pebbles and trailed behind them, occasionally stopping to skim one viciously out to sea, while Gracie, finding his pace congenial, walked or sat beside him.

'I've thought and thought about it, ever since yesterday when Mummy told us,' Henrietta continued, 'and there's simply no way round it. I can't go and live with her and Uncle Charles. I shall just have to stay and look after Daddy. He'll never manage by himself.'

Sybil looked down at the thin young face and earnest expression.

'Oh, I wouldn't say that, Hen. He's not very tidy or organized, but I don't think he minds very much. I don't think he notices external things. He's so busy teaching or thinking or reading or listening to music.'

'But he needs someone there to look after him. If he's left to himself he'll just live on take-aways. When we go shopping he doesn't bother about buying healthy food. It's Ben and me who read the list of ingredients, isn't it, Ben?'

The stones had been thrown, the rocks left to their sinister memories, Gracie brought to a reluctant trot to keep up, and he was forgiven.

'We make sure there's no artificial colouring and sweetening,' Ben said, grateful for his reprieve. 'Hen and I are learning to cook. I can cook chocolate blancmange and jelly.'

'He makes good chocolate blancmange and jelly,' Henrietta said judiciously. 'And I can make stew and rice pudding.' Remembering that her grandmother had a thing about children and matches she added, 'Ben's not up to oven cooking, just yet. He does top of the stove cooking. And we're both very careful, and we cook together so's we can take care of each other, and it's an electric stove. So you needn't worry.'

Ben walked by his sister's side, hands thrust in the front pocket of his anorak.

'I won't worry,' Sybil promised fruitlessly, thinking of sharp knives and electric shocks.

Ben said, 'If we live with Mum and Uncle Charles during the week we could live with Daddy at the weekends, and do his cooking and shopping.'

'What? Packing and unpacking, and to and fro on buses or trains every weekend?' his sister asked, but not sarcastically, treating him as an equal. 'It's bad enough twice a month. We'd never manage it once a week. Not with our homework as well. Besides, I don't think they'd let us.'

They were exploring this new terrain, trying out the ground, pondering the maps of old terrains, finding their way; and Sybil walked beside them, privileged to listen but lacerated by the knowledge that they were, as Katrina had said in the narrower sense, experienced travellers.

Ben said dejectedly, 'I liked living with Mum before she left us. We didn't have all this bother about looking after Dad.'

'We had different bother,' Henrietta said, 'being sent out of the room, and sitting on the stairs listening to their rows, or else nobody speaking.'

Gracie pattered mournfully beside them. Sybil did not intrude upon the conversation.

'Except for Dad not being there,' Ben admitted, 'I like staying at Uncle Charles's house. We have fun, and we don't have to bother.'

'It's all right,' his sister said, making the final sacrifice. 'You live with Mummy and Uncle Charles, and I'll stay with Daddy. We'll just have to see each other in the holidays.'

Ben stopped short, and reddened; and Sybil remembered how her father's colour would rush from neck to forehead when he was deeply moved or angered.

'But then *we'd* be divorced as well,' Ben said, visibly distressed.

'No, we wouldn't,' she said in a very small voice. 'We'd be living in different places, but we'd still like each other. That's not being divorced.'

He stood for quite a minute, while Henrietta waited and

shivered patiently, and Gracie sat at his feet and gazed up at him with mournful expectation. He came to a formidable decision.

'No,' he said. 'We'll *both* stay with Dad.'

'I think,' said Sybil, treading delicately, 'that perhaps you shouldn't make up your minds quite so early. The court will decide with whom you live.'

Their faces turned towards her as if they had forgotten her presence.

'But they won't separate us, will they?' Ben asked.

'No,' said Sybil. 'They won't do that.'

'Do we have to go to court?' Henrietta asked, white and sharp and apprehensive.

'Certainly not,' said Sybil. Her own mind made up.

Ben ran forward to escape further discussion, to evade further revelations. Again he half shouted, to prove to them both that he was in full command of himself and life was wonderful.

'Look, Hen, I've found a shell. Hen, let's collect all the shells we can find . . .'

She joined him, high and shrill, dancing and jumping, clapping her hands.

'We can make necklaces and pictures. Come on, Gran'ma, help us to find shells.'

Sybil knocked on the door of Edward's room.

'I don't mean to disturb you, Teddy dear. Just to say that supper will be a little late, and I hope you'll be joining us again now that things are more or less back to normal. We had a very pleasant evening yesterday. Doing our own thing, as Ben says. Freddie played halma with your father, and Blanche was sewing something very beautiful and exotic, and Dan was sketching everyone – so clever – and we watched the television or chatted. And this evening Natalie is bringing over a heap of photographs to show us . . .'

He was very pale and gaunt, hunched over his books, supporting his head with one hand, doodling with the other. Not working, agonizing. He had been a butterfly of a youth: light of heart and head, a creature of the shining moment. Now he seemed wingless, hopeless, spent. Visibly, he roused himself to answer her. 'Yes, I'll be down,' he said with difficulty. 'Did you have a good walk this afternoon?'

'Lovely – except that the children got themselves covered with oil when they were down on the beach collecting shells, and we've had to clean it off with paraffin. Such disgusting stuff. I didn't notice until it was much too late. Hands, boots, coat sleeves, even poor old Gracie's paws. You'd think, wouldn't you, that the authorities would put up a notice, warning people?'

'Indeed they should,' he answered automatically. 'And how are the kids? How are they taking things?'

'Marvellously well,' she cried, carrying a banner for them. 'So grown up in so many ways. And funny, too, Teddy. I've had to smile to myself once or twice.'

He smiled briefly, in sympathy, and then tried to put right a recent wrong. 'I'm sorry about what happened with Kat, Mum. It wasn't – I've never – I don't want you to think – I didn't . . .'

'No, no,' she said quickly. 'She drove you too hard and you overreacted. It can happen to any of us. I didn't condone it, but I did understand.'

'They're such good kids, you see,' he said. 'It hit me badly to think I was going to lose them as well. And I meant what I said. They're worth fighting for.'

Lest she had heard of or observed his limitations as a practical parent he strove to set right that impression also. 'And you needn't worry about them, Mum. I shall do my best for them. We've got ourselves organized now, you know. We've had time to adjust. You must come up and stay with us. You'd be surprised how well we cope. Really you would.' He thought of some other way to reassure her, to prove his stability and worthiness. 'And if you're worried about the kids travelling by train then I'll drive them home on Friday, and deliver them to Kat's door if necessary.'

'No, no,' said Sybil. 'I was overreacting, too. Children grow up quickly these days and Henny and Ben are very self-reliant. Let's not complicate matters by altering their arrangements at this late date.'

She hated saying what must be said, and clutched the door-knob until her knuckles stood out white. 'Teddy – I know how you feel – and you're a loving father – and I'm all for you – but think carefully before you fight Katrina for custody. She means to win at any cost.'

He threw down his pencil, and it spun off an open book and struck the wall. His voice was resonant with misery and anger. 'My dear Mother, a couple of days ago you tore a strip off me because I wasn't facing up to Kat. Now you're asking me to let her have all her own way. Why should she? And why should you assume that if we fought for custody *she* would win? I think I'd stand a good chance. I do my job well. I provide a decent home and income. And the kids love me. Don't forget that Kat walked out on us. The judge will surely wonder what sort of mother does a thing like that? Or are you assuming that mothers are always right, money can buy anything, and there's no justice in the world?'

Sybil stood her ground though his words pelted her like stones. 'I'm thinking of the children, Teddy. Imagine them having to stand up in a court of law and to testify for or against either of you. What would that do to them?'

He said stubbornly, 'That's short-term thinking. Yes, it would be bloody, but the kids are staunch little beggars. Ben's a bit young, but old Hen would speak up for me.'

'Oh, my dear,' Sybil cried, riven for the three of them, 'it would be kinder to let Henny and Ben go rather than crucify them in such a way. And think of the added bitterness between you and Katrina. Afterwards, whichever way the case went, the children would have to cope with two warring parents.'

Tears stood in their eyes but did not fall. Neither of them spoke. Then Sybil went out, closing the door softly behind her, and Edward turned again to stare blankly at his books.

CHAPTER SEVENTEEN

Thursday, 28 December

Blanche and Daniel sat on the floor of her bedroom, which was the only place where they could find privacy, and endeavoured to create a new basis for friendship while looking after Aaron. This was difficult, for the baby wished to be the centre of their world, and insisted upon total participation. Henrietta and Ben had given him a primary-coloured plastic posting box for Christmas, and he had learned how to post different shapes into their matching holes. The toy was, in truth, slightly too young for him. Left to himself he could solve its problems easily, but he had realized that when he made mistakes people paid more attention to him.

On the chest of drawers Blanche's silver mask reclined against the wall, well out of Aaron's range, staring sightlessly ahead, shimmering in the light from the window. Now Daniel got to his feet and motioned Blanche to join him in a child-free space. Smiling, frowning, attracted, uncertain, she rose and stood opposite.

Aaron, watching them both, clapped his hands together and demanded, 'Me! Me! Up!' But his parents were absorbed in each other.

Daniel picked up the mask, held it in front of her face and said, teasing, serious, 'Make believe that you're the Delphic oracle, and tell me what the future holds.'

She made an impatient sound. 'What nonsense! What an infuriating man you are!'

'No! Me! Up!' Aaron clamoured, desiring their company.

Daniel bent down and lifted his son aloft, hushed him gently. 'You can't have your mother all the time, my boy. Let her be, for a few minutes.'

Blanche was about to put the mask briskly back in its place, to show Daniel that she would not be coerced, but hesitated

148

because she did so love it. Her gust of irritation dispersed. Smiling, she disguised her face and cried. 'Bo!' to Aaron. Then turned away and looked at the world from a new perspective.

'I feel wonderfully liberated behind here,' she said, laughing a little, excited, self-conscious, 'as if I had gone abroad or become the Brontë children speaking the truth to their father. I can say what I feel.'

His smile was rueful, tender.

'I thought you always did.'

'I say what I think, that's not quite the same. I don't go down into the depths and speak from there. Goodness! I'd forgotten. Down, down, down, like Alice.'

There was a pause while she contemplated her inner self and they contemplated her. Aaron's expression was anxious, his fingers plucked at the collar of Daniel's blue shirt. He did not know this woman with the silver face and the strange excited voice.

'And what are you seeing at the bottom of the rabbit-hole?' Daniel asked, holding the child comfortably, reassuringly.

She lowered the mask and said abruptly, 'I don't propose to tell you!' And gave another laugh, this time of warning.

He had been careful in his behaviour towards her since the episode of the kiss, and she had relaxed in consequence. So he spoke persuasively, but continued to pursue his original objective. 'I'm prepared to listen to anything, anything at all. I'd like to listen.'

'Why?' Forbiddingly.

He dared say, 'Because I have a notion that I'm down there with you in the depths.'

'You're in my *past* not my *depths*,' said Blanche, marking out his permitted terrain. 'You're someone who once happened to me.'

She could not forget that happening, but did not intend it to happen again.

'That's not true,' said Daniel earnestly, shaking his head. 'We met fathoms down, and I know it. I was there then and I'm there now, and by God—'

He stopped himself, set Aaron on the floor in front of his plastic posting-box, and put a shape into his hand. Then he turned his attention to Blanche.

'We never get a minute together,' Daniel said in desperation,

149

gesturing at the child and the cramped room. 'Could we not go somewhere more private and talk?'

'About what?' Blanche replied, obdurate.

'You could give me a hearing, for God's sake. You could let me explain myself.'

He lifted his hands above his head to show that he carried no weapons.

'In!' Aaron commanded, trying to force a sky-blue diamond into a square hole.

Blanche sat down again on the floor to collect herself. She did not look at Daniel. 'Not that one, chicken. This one,' she counselled the child.

Daniel said to her beseechingly, 'Will you not come for a walk with me? Just for half an hour.'

'Gone!' Aaron cried, and picked up a custard-yellow circle, and jammed it deliberately in the wrong slot and tugged his mother's hand. 'In! In!'

'You were always just,' said Daniel, 'if not always merciful. I'm asking for justice.'

Her black frizzed bush of hair was bent over their son but the thoughts beneath it were of Daniel. She said slowly, 'All right, I'll ask Sybil if she'll have Aaron for a while.'

She swooped on her son and gathered him up. He did not want to be disturbed, and his strength and beauty, as he protested, roused all her love for him. She laughed over his head at Daniel. 'Lord, what a temper! Come along, poppet. Come to Gran'ma.'

'No. There!' Aaron cried passionately, pointing to his patch of floor, the vermilion posting-box, the gaudy wooden shapes.

'He wants to stay where he is,' Blanche translated.

'Then leave him be, and I'll fetch the lady to him.'

He stumbled on Ben outside the door. 'Snooping at keyholes', said Daniel amiably, 'deserves a kick up the backside. And what would Gran'ma say if she heard about it?'

'I wasn't. I wasn't!' Ben defended himself vehemently. 'I was rescuing Clemmie. We were playing in the passage and she got stuck in this corner. Look! There, Clemmie,' freeing her, 'off you go.'

Daniel ruffled Ben's hair, to show there was no ill-feeling; and Clementine's plastic ball whirled past him into Blanche's room with the hamster inside it, furiously pushing her way to nowhere.

Aaron's protests turned to glee. He sat up, rust-red head on one side, a smile on his mouth, watching the transparent sphere bump crazily up against the chest of drawers and wobble over a carpet fringe.

'Blanche,' said Ben, giving Clementine a turn in the right direction, 'my stick insect's dead.'

'I'm sorry to hear that. Accident or natural causes?'

'It just died. Of course. I can't get really upset about a stick insect like I could about an animal, but I'm sorry just the same.'

The hamster roved the room, pedalling ceaselessly, intently; and they watched her until Sybil came in smiling, with Daniel at her side.

'I hear you two are going for a walk,' she said cheerfully. 'Do wrap up well. It's quite cold in the wind. Poor old Hen's off her food and out of sorts but I expect it's a reaction to yesterday's events, including the oil on the beach. I think, as you two will be out of the way, that I'll send her back to bed for a rest. While you and I,' to Aaron, 'will take this beautiful posting-box to the playroom and have lots of fun.'

'Clemmie and me will have fun with you, too,' said Ben, jealous for his lost babyhood.

'That will be lovely, darling.' Absently. To her daughter, 'Freddie and Lydia are driving me into Truro at one thirty this afternoon to do some shopping, so we're having an early lunch and I need you to take over. You and Daniel will have the house more or less to yourselves. Tony will be in his study. Teddy and Ben are going out for a rock scramble. And Natalie won't arrive until the drinks tray appears at six o'clock. We seem,' she added incredulously, 'to be out of the storm for once.'

'Or in the eye of it!' Blanche answered, slightly acerbic.

Sybil motioned them to leave while Aaron's attention was elsewhere, but Daniel, unused to these subterfuges, said, 'Goodbye, my boy!' and rubbed the curly head affectionately.

'No-o-o!' Aaron cried, realizing that his parents were deserting him.

'Take no notice!' Sybil said. 'And close the door behind you!'

Over the child's rising wail of desolation they heard her saying brightly, 'Oh, what a dreadful noise. Now shall we pick up all these pretty shapes and put them in the box?'

'You're supposed to sidle out, unbeknownst,' Blanche told Daniel, as he helped her into her scarlet greatcoat.

She stood back and surveyed him critically. He had abandoned the pin-striped suit since Christmas Day and returned to his usual state of comfortable neglect. This morning he was wearing a pair of shabby green corduroy trousers, a washed-out plaid shirt and a fisherman's jersey. 'You never were a snappy dresser,' said Blanche drily, 'but you seem to have plumbed new depths in the last couple of years. Where do you find these rags, for God's sake? Don't say Oxfam – no charity shop would stock them.'

He pulled on his brown car coat, grinning in his old fashion, and replied, 'I've been out of touch with my *couturière*, and you see the result!'

He held out his hand, but though she smiled she stuck both hers in her pockets. They began to walk briskly towards the village.

'Where are we going?' he asked.

'To a private place where we can talk,' she answered briefly. 'That was what you wanted, wasn't it?'

They left the scatter of cottages with cement-washed roofs, the Methodist chapel, the Cornish Arms, the corner shop and pillar-box, the bus stop and telephone kiosk behind them. The countryside was stark in its winter livery. Occasional farms huddled in their patchwork of stone-hedged land. Fallow green alternated with furrowed brown. Arthritic trees bent the way of the wind. Gulls, driven inland, swooped and cried harshly. In the clean blue bowl of sky a buzzard circled, watching for moving edibles on his table below. The air smelled of damp leaves, of wood-smoke.

'That's Predanick Wartha behind the tall gates,' Blanche said. 'Uncle Jack's house. Lovely house. Lovely man. And there's the barn, on the other side of Mrs Wish's farm. It's a good place to get away from people.'

'Ah, a barn!' Daniel said pleasantly, but his eyes glinted. 'A wonderful place for amorous meetings. Have you ever used it for that purpose?'

She stopped short and faced him. 'Yes, I have. Are you jealous?' she demanded, and her mouth curved in contempt.

'Yes,' said Daniel quietly. 'I'm jealous, God help me. I've sunk that low.'

'Well, haul yourself up again,' Blanche advised. 'What I did, and when, and how often, is none of your damned business.'

'I know that,' he said mock-humorously. 'I have no rights.

This is a woman's world. It's a terrible thing when a man discovers that he's superfluous.'

Mat Kellow passed them on a motor-bike, and Blanche greeted him with a wave, but her smile vanished with him.

'That means the village grapevine will be buzzing in ten minutes,' she remarked, annoyed. 'Anyway, you're wasting your time being jealous. It was years ago. My first love, in fact. No, my first lust. He was one of Uncle Jack's grooms, and I was just eighteen, and we had a brief affair. I know every private place around here for miles. I was potty about him, but it was all over in two months. He was a beautiful black-haired rake of twenty with the body of a god. Now he's middle-aged and grey and growing a beer-belly and he's been soporifically married for years. We hail each other when we meet, but our wild and glorious summer is long since over, and the shiver in the loins is no more.'

It was Daniel's turn to stop and face her. 'You never told me about him before.'

'Why should I? You've never been to Cornwall before. The barn reminds me of my misspent youth, and then I remember him. That's all.'

She stepped over the stile gracefully. Daniel placed one hand on the top, and vaulted. Pleased with his agility, he asked conversationally, 'But why did it only last two months? Why didn't you elope to the Cornish equivalent of Gretna Green and live unhappily ever after? Why didn't you get yourself pregnant?'

'Because I left home in the October and went to a London art school and forgot him. The family must have realized, or were told, what had happened, and asked Uncle Jack to speak to him, because I never saw him when we came down that Christmas, and the following Easter he was engaged. So that was that. Why didn't I get pregnant? Oh, I wasn't his first girl. He took care of that side – a form of contraception that I didn't particularly fancy. When the next man turned up, a few months later, I made sure I was prepared. I went on the pill.'

He glanced at her hopefully, but her face was set against any advance on his part.

The barn was high and wide and old: handsomely built of granite, standing alone at the end of a cart-track. There was no glass in

153

the windows, the dirt floor had been trampled flat by a century of feet, there were pieces of machinery around: to thresh, to grind, to crush. An old unit for a bulk milk tank stood in one corner. Dust prevailed.

'Well, here we are,' said Blanche. 'Do you want to go on chatting about my past, or shall we climb up and make ourselves comfortable?'

He sighed, and mounted the ladder. The hay had a faintly stuffy warm scent, like summer preserved, but their breath steamed on the winter air. Chivalrously, he took off his coat and spread it out.

He began abruptly. 'I've lost my daughter for good and all. Juliet was married in August.'

'Ah!' said Blanche, comprehending a little more. She guessed. 'Did they not send you an invitation?'

He picked up a straw and chewed it, narrowing his eyes at a gap between the roof slates. He attempted a jaunty indifference to cover his outrage and despair.

'Oh yes, I was invited, by Norah and her present husband, to attend *their* daughter's wedding. *Their* daughter! On a great white card embossed with gold, to a great white wedding, and a slap-up feast with waitresses and champagne in a marquee as big as a railway station, and everyone but me dressed up to the nines.'

'Oh dear,' said Blanche, and was sorry but had to hide a smile. 'Well, it was Juliet's day, not yours, and I expect she looked beautiful.'

He nodded, too full to speak.

'Natural prejudices apart, what did you think of the bridegroom?'

Daniel roused himself to answer, gruffly, bleakly. 'She's married a man who will never make the world spin for her, but never harm a hair of her head either. So be thankful for small mercies, I said to myself. But what I'll never know is why I was asked to the wedding. I've never been there before. Was Norah showing me how well they'd done without me? Or did they just do the right thing and hope that I wouldn't come after all?'

Blanche hugged her knees and watched his face. In sadness it showed another side of him: a vulnerability, a depth of feeling, that the joker in him protected.

'Perhaps,' she suggested kindly, 'Juliet *wanted* you to be there.'

He shook his head, not in negation but in puzzlement. 'I'd like to think that but I'll never be sure of it. Still, I took her a noble gift. I chose her the most elegant Royal Doulton tea-service I could find. It was as grand as any of the other presents, I can tell you.'

'Lucky Juliet! You must have been living on bread and scrape ever since,' said Blanche, keeping her tone light. 'She would be thrilled.'

'Oh, she was pleased all right,' said Daniel uncertainly. 'She thanked me nicely – and so did he – and she gave me a hug and a kiss. But she didn't say anything about seeing me again, and I haven't heard from her since.' He added, in a lower voice, 'God, how I hate being patronized. I could have killed the lot of them – except for her.'

She was afraid to show too much sympathy lest he mistake it for reconciliation.

'Did you drown your sorrows in the champagne?' she asked ironically.

He turned his head quickly, angrily, to reprove her, but held his peace. 'I wouldn't have disgraced the girl,' he said.

They sat for a while in silence. He gave her an embarrassed smile. 'But I'll admit that when it was all over I took a bottle of whisky back to the hotel bedroom with me, and I don't remember a thing until I was on the train home. And I stayed drunk for three days after that, because there was no meaning to life at all.'

She made a grimace of understanding. There was another silence.

'I used to take things as they came,' he said, throwing away the straw, 'and call them good luck or bad luck. I never thought they might have happened because of me. But the wedding changed all that, and I started to think.'

Blanche was listening to him with growing concern, for a truly reformed Daniel demanded that she reconsider their situation and she did not want that.

'I loved Norah with a young man's love,' said Daniel earnestly, 'but I wasn't cut out to be a husband and father by nature, and we were no more than twenty when we got married. I crucified that girl by behaving as I did. And it was the same with Juliet. I worshipped the child, I'd have given her anything on earth – except the steady love she needed. You know what I'm like,' appealing to Blanche, 'if it's not new friends and mad parties, and wild goose chases, then it's me shut up for days at a time, working

155

– and biting the head off anyone that interrupts me. So Norah stood it as long as she could, and then she left me for a man who could take care of them both.' A flash of the old Daniel came to his defence. 'Though he's a poor sort of fool that I wouldn't wipe my boots on,' he remarked.

He became serious again. 'You and Norah are as different as two women could be, and the only women I've ever truly cared for – except for my mother. When you and I met I told myself that I'd found the right person at last, as if Norah had been the wrong one. And when we split up I put the blame on you for spoiling a grand relationship by getting pregnant. I'm not saying you're without faults, but I stopped looking at your faults and started to look at mine, and it was a sobering experience, I can tell you. For I'd considered nobody but myself, and though I loved you and was proud of you I'd only hindered you. You said we were hollow, that there was nothing to us, apart from enjoying ourselves. Well, I'd agree to that.'

He looked directly at Blanche, taking a final gamble. 'I was given another chance when I met you, and I made a mess of it again. But there's no sense in life for me if I lose you and the boy. No heart to it, no purpose. Just me working for myself. Blanche, I'm no saint and never will be, but then you were never fond of saints. You can lay down what conditions you like, and I'll do my best for the both of you. And if you catch me playing the fool when I should be serious then give me hell – but let me try again, will you, Blanche?'

She was overwhelmed by an old terror of being trapped in a situation over which she had no control. She attacked him deliberately, coldly, cruelly. 'Like the prodigal son, you return home full of good will only because your luck has run out. Philosophically speaking, I don't doubt that forgiveness is a splendid thing. But to me common sense and experience count for more. I would be a fool to trust myself even to the best of your intentions, and a greater fool to put Aaron at risk as well.'

They were both appalled.

Blanche said rapidly, brusquely, 'I'm sorry, Dan. I don't doubt your sincerity. But it wouldn't work.'

His pallor disturbed her, and she could endure no more.

She burst out, 'Aaron and I were happy by ourselves. For the first time in my life I was content. I was finding myself at last, but you've spoiled all that. I wish that you'd never come here. I wish to God you'd left us both in peace.'

In tears, she scrambled to her feet and began to climb down the ladder. He picked up his old brown coat, and followed her. They stood apart. She dried her eyes and contemplated her handkerchief. He averted his unruly head.

Then he said with quiet dignity, 'You have been less than generous, but I take your point.' He told the dirt floor, 'I'll not be coming back with you for lunch. And I shan't be troubling you further. I'll be off tomorrow.'

Victorious, ashamed, Blanche said, 'But you'll come to supper tonight, won't you? Sybil would be hurt if you just went away without saying anything.'

He scuffed the earth thoughtfully. 'Oh yes, I'll make a good end of it, and behave myself into the bargain.'

Blanche said pacifically, trying to exonerate herself, 'We were beginning to be friends again, Dan. You should have left it at that.'

He shrugged and half smiled. 'Ah, but I could never leave well alone,' he remarked. 'I would always want it to be better.'

And was striding away from her before she could think of anything else to say.

In contrast to the turbulence of Blanche's soul the atmosphere was serene when she plunged into Minions, full of apologies for being late.

'We ate lunch without you,' Sybil said placidly. 'It was only cold meat and salad and there's plenty left. I've just put Aaron down for his nap, and I'm ready for off. Everyone else is either out or gone to ground. Oh, could you pop upstairs with a jugful of lemon barley water for Hen? She won't eat but she's thirsty. I think she may have a feverish cold. Could you take her temperature? I meant to do it but we've been run off our feet.' She meant that *she* had been run off her feet, but was too tactful to say so. Observing her daughter closely, she asked, 'And where's Daniel?'

Blanche kissed her in thanks and apology, and disposed of him as casually as she could. 'Oh, he's coming later on. What can I do for you while you're away? Cook supper?'

'No, thank you, darling. I'll bring something we can heat up,

157

and then we can relax this evening.' She asked of the downcast face, 'Did you have a nice walk?'

'Absolutely lovely!' Blanche lied, and was too wretched to care that she lied and that her mother knew it.

Henrietta, lying in the semi-dark, was grateful for the drink and apologetic about her condition. 'I don't think there's much wrong with me, apart from a cough and a sneeze,' she observed. 'I'll be up and about tomorrow. I expect it's the strain of the last few days.'

Blanche was careful not to smile, though she could hear Sybil in every sentence. 'I expect so,' she said. Then feeling the hot little hands, observing the hectic cheeks and the way the child moved as if her body and limbs were too heavy, was not so sure. 'I think we should take your temperature,' Blanche said.

'Gran'ma meant to do that, but she's been busy with the lunch and Aaron.' Who was fast asleep in his cot, arms outflung, with Ba beside him.

Blanche found the thermometer in the bathroom cabinet, and rinsed it thoroughly because the case was dusty with disuse.

'You needn't worry,' Henrietta assured her, as the mercury rose silently, inexorably, in her armpit. 'Ben and me are not going to leave Daddy by himself.'

'Ben and I,' Blanche corrected her automatically, and then said, 'Sorry, Hen. The Malpases are all pedants. I'm not worried about Teddy, I'm concerned for you two.'

'Oh, *we*'re all right,' said Henny ironically. 'It's the *grown-ups*.' Then she added, 'But I thought you'd like to know, because Daddy's your brother. I would want to know if it was *my* brother that was being left on his own.'

'That was very kind, and I appreciate the thought. Let's peek at the temperature.'

She lifted the corner of one curtain and held the instrument up to the light.

'Is it an *all's well*, or an *oh dear*?' Henrietta asked quaintly.

Another of Sybil's expressions.

'It's an *oh dear*, but not desperate. A hundred. Have you any other symptoms?'

'A headache. And my face seems to have got blotchy since I came to bed. I noticed it in the bathroom mirror when I went for a pee just now, but I expect that's due to the chocolate I pigged over Christmas.'

'Let's have a good look,' said Blanche, drawing both curtains back, peering into the small blotched face. 'Are you blotchy anywhere else?'

Obediently Henrietta hoisted her nightdress, revealing a narrow chest and flat stomach similarly patterned. 'And it feels tender behind my ears,' she volunteered.

Blanche touched the swollen glands. 'I think we must unearth the local doctor,' she said.

Henrietta lay back on her pillows as if she had now done all that was possible. 'So long as it isn't something catching,' she said, and turned her face away, and fell asleep almost immediately.

CHAPTER EIGHTEEN

The doctor left Minions in an uproar. Sybil, returning pink and exhilarated from the freedom of an afternoon out in undemanding company, found Anthony waiting for her in the hall. With typical thoroughness he had read up Henrietta's ailment and possessed himself of the facts. His spectacles mounted his forehead, his stance was truculent, his face suffused with fear and irritation.

'That child has German measles!' he cried accusingly, shaking *The Family Medical Dictionary* at his wife. 'It's highly contagious, and she's been incubating the damned disease for the past two or three weeks. She must have been riddled with it when she arrived, and she's probably infected the entire village as well as this household. I *said* it wasn't a good idea to come down here for Christmas, and I was right. God knows what will happen. We were already overcrowded and now the place will be like a blasted field hospital!' Having flung this last spear he asked pitifully, 'Sybil, have I had German measles?'

'My dear, just give me a minute to think.'

Momentarily at a loss, she wandered through to the living room and sank into the nearest chair, still wearing her coat. Lydia and Freddie carried two large cardboard boxes of food through to the kitchen, and returned to make themselves useful in whatever capacity they could. But Blanche, who had been listening at the top of the stairs, holding Aaron freshly bathed and wrapped in a towel, attacked her father forthwith.

'If that isn't typical!' she called down indignantly. 'I thought you promised to give Sybil a glass of sherry before breaking the news, and instead of that you're blustering at her before she can take off her coat!'

Anthony turned round in the living-room doorway and

shouted, 'If you talk to me like that you can damned well pack your traps and go home for good! For *good*!'

'Good!' Aaron echoed gleefully.

Blanche, ready for a confrontation, cried, 'Why don't you ever think of her first?'

He hovered between hall and living-room, incensed, and put the blame on his wife. 'I told you how it would be if you asked Blanche to come for Christmas!'

'Oh, *please*!' Sybil begged, weary of them both.

The clock struck six. Time for all Malpases to gather together. Outside, Edward backed his Mazda neatly into place behind Freddie's vintage MG, and Ben hurtled into the house as if he had been catapulted, laden with awkward-shaped parcels and already talking.

'Gran'ma. Gran'ma. See what I've bought with my Christmas money!'

'Not just now, Ben dear. Later.'

Edward, following his son, looked round apprehensively and asked, 'Is anything wrong?'

He was answered by his father in forthright fashion. 'Henrietta has German measles. And keep that boy away from me, he's probably riddled with it too!' He glared round, flung his arms up in the air, and paced between hall and living room and back. 'We'll all be penned up here for weeks, like a flock of blasted sheep!' he cried.

Sybil spoke coldly and practically. 'We certainly shall not. We haven't the room to keep open house with a sick child to nurse. Those of us who have had German measles must go.'

Edward stood quite still, plainly shocked and bewildered. From his hands dangled two cheerful carrier bags, bearing seasonal good wishes. 'Is Hen very bad?' he asked.

Sybil said instantly, comforting him, 'No, no. It isn't a serious illness. But she needs rest and care. Don't worry, Teddy. We'll sort something out.'

Before he could respond they were interrupted by Natalie, striding into the hall in her outdated elegance, ready for her evening whisky. 'What a quarrelsome lot you are!' she growled amiably. 'What the hell's wrong now?'

They told her, in different ways, beginning and ending at different times, like an over-zealous orchestra with an arduous piece of music to play.

'Good God!' she said, disturbed. 'Have you and I had German measles, Tony?'

'How the hell do I know?' he answered grumpily. 'But I'm damned if I want to go through it at my age. Is that the disease where your balls swell up?'

'No, that's mumps,' said Edward automatically.

Lydia handed her mother a glass of Tio Pepe, and provoked her father. 'You'll be quite safe with German measles, Daddy, unless you're pregnant.'

'That's not funny!' Anthony said, as they all laughed.

A quick touch on the arm, a quizzical look, distracted him pleasantly.

'Oh, God bless you, Freddie! I have seldom needed a drink more than this!' He swirled the amber liquid round in its glass, appreciatively. 'Good for morale, good for shock, and a natural disinfectant . . .'

Sybil had evidently heard enough. With considerable asperity she remarked, 'Oh, don't be ridiculous, Tony. The child isn't carrying bubonic plague. And as our three children have had every infantile ailment except scarlet fever, and you never caught any of them, we must assume that you are immune – or else,' slightly louder, as he showed signs of protest, 'that you suffered your share of childhood illnesses at the appropriate time. And now I suggest we stop speculating about possible difficulties and deal with the present situation.'

They were all silenced. Blanche sat on the top stair, holding Aaron, and assessed the state of play below.

Sybil sipped her sherry and said gratefully to Lydia, 'Thank you, darling. That's very thoughtful.'

Abashed, Anthony stopped acting out his alarms and wandered over to sit beside her. He said, conciliating her, 'I was only worrying about the extra work for you, after all the trouble you've taken to give us a good Christmas.'

She ignored this dishonesty and answered the real question. 'Our children and their illnesses were never allowed to interfere with your work, and I see no reason why our grandchildren should be an exception.'

She looked at Edward, who was still standing miserably in the middle of the room. Her face and voice softened. She spoke to him as though they were alone. 'You and I can manage this between us, Teddy. I'm perfectly willing to nurse the children here but I shall need you to run errands in your car and help.'

He replied in the same vein, concerned for her. 'Of course I will. But it's too much to ask of you.'

'I shan't mind a bit. It's the most sensible decision, and the most humane one. The alternative is to drive poor little Henrietta back to Yorkshire in her present condition, with Ben probably feeling off-colour as well; and then to organize everything from scratch on the eve of a Bank Holiday, and nurse the pair of them. That *would* be too much.'

He stood forlornly, holding his jovial carrier bags, thinking. He managed a smile. 'I take your point. Thanks a lot. I'll help in any way I can.'

She nodded, satisfied that the first problem had been solved.

Anthony cleared his throat, not peremptorily, almost apologetically, but she answered his next question without listening to it and without looking at him.

'It really would be best for you to go back to Clifton early, Tony, because we obviously can't celebrate the New Year as we planned. Mrs Lees will be coming in to look after the house and your laundry. I'll telephone tonight, to make sure you have the essentials. You have only to take care of yourself. I'm sure lots of friends will invite you over for meals, and otherwise you can eat out or buy ready-prepared food and heat it in the micro-wave.'

His comforts had never been disposed of in this way.

He attempted to justify himself. 'I find it difficult to work down here, Syb. So many people. And the study isn't sound-proof.'

Sybil's reply was cool and deliberate, and she would not return his gaze, which was by now beseeching. She reproved him with courtesy. 'My dear, as I have said, there is no need to interrupt your work, and to be quite truthful I no longer have the energy to look after you and nurse sick children as well. Those days are over.' She gave a brief sigh, as if acknowledging the heroic endeavours of her youth. 'So you are free to return to Clifton whenever you please. Tomorrow, if you like. You can leave Gracie with me, and then you are not encumbered. Let me know what you decide.'

To Lydia's considerate enquiry, she replied, 'Yes, I will have another sherry, thank you, darling. I'll take it with me, while I feed the animals.' She rose to her feet and departed for the kitchen, followed by the dog and both cats, and leaving a glacial gap behind her.

Anthony accepted a second whisky and brooded over it.

Freddie raised her eyebrows to Lydia, who whispered, 'We'd better do drinks all round.'

They called upstairs, 'Gin and tonic, Blanche?'

'Yes, please,' replied a distant voice, 'if someone will bring it up.'

'I'll take it up,' said Edward, setting down his carrier bags. He addressed Anthony apologetically, 'We've bought a thank-you present for Mama. Do you mind if we hide it behind the Christmas tree?' Anthony grunted. 'Thanks. We'll give it to her later.' And as the drinks tray was being prepared he said to himself, 'Poor little Hen. She must have been feeling rotten, and she never said a word.'

Ben had kept a judicious silence while the adults stated their claims and drew up their battle-lines. Now he gave voice to his personal preoccupations. 'Daddy! Do hamsters catch German measles?'

'No. They have their own diseases.'

'Daddy! Can I come up with you to see Hen?'

'Yes, why not, old son? You've probably got it anyway.'

Anthony moved restlessly and muttered something about too many people.

Freddie and Lydia came and sat on the sofa, one either side of him. They exchanged perceptive glances. 'Lydia and I have had a chin-wag,' Freddie began. 'And our conclusion is the same as yours, Tony. The best thing we can do for Sybil is to clear the decks and leave her to it.'

'Ah!' Anthony said, grateful to have his wife's decision accepted as his own. 'Yes. Well, it does seem the most sensible solution.'

'As you so wisely remarked,' Freddie continued, 'there are too many people here.'

'Quite so,' said Anthony, brightening up as his face was saved.

'So we think we should clear off after supper, and leave our room vacant for Blanche and her little buster.'

'Ah . . . not sure what Sybil will think about that, but I see your point. Yes.'

'Glad we agree,' said Freddie, smiling. 'We'll just pop along to the kitchen to tell Sybil, and help with the supper.'

'What are we eating tonight?' Anthony asked, anxious for his stomach.

'Chinese. Lots of miscellaneous dishes.'

'Ah!' Anthony said. 'Good!' he added, disappointed.

Lydia bent and kissed his cheek. He returned the kiss absent-mindedly, and spoke directly to her friend. 'Sybil and I have been genuinely delighted to meet you, Freddie,' he announced, 'and we hope that this is only the first of many visits. As soon as Sybil is home again we'll give you a ring, and you must come for a long weekend at our Clifton home. Oh, and,' as he remembered, 'bring Lydia with you, of course.'

His younger daughter's mouth dropped open. Behind his back she made a clown's face of disbelief and mimed 'Who's Lydia?' Freddie hurried her away before they both erupted into laughter.

'Well now,' said Natalie affably, sitting in the chair Sybil had vacated, 'how's my favourite brother?'

She leaned forward and patted his knee affectionately. He murmured something sorrowful and indistinct.

'I'll tell you how you are,' she said, 'you're fed up with bloody domesticity. Why don't you drive us both off to my bolt-hole in London for a spot of fun and culture?'

He shook his grey mane from side to side: a loyal, husbandly lion, woefully tempted.

'What difference will it make to Sybil?' Natalie asked. 'She's not going back to Clifton. From the sound of it, you'll be by yourself for at least two weeks.'

Mournfully, he muttered that he had to look after the house.

'What a load of pee,' said Natalie forcibly. 'I heard Sybil say that your Mrs Whatsit took care of the house. And besides, there are those two married students I spoke to, living in your basement. They sounded house-trained and Sybil-brainwashed to me.'

'Pressure of work,' he said, and sighed.

'Another load of pee,' said Natalie. 'You're retiring next summer. You can't be doing anything but winding down and handing over.'

'Must get on with my book.'

'You've got the rest of your life to finish that.'

'Sybil might be upset.'

'On what grounds? She's doing her own thing. Why can't you do yours?'

He shrugged, and glanced sideways, smiled unwillingly.

'Don't be so damned selfish. Think of me for a change,' said Natalie, grinning, rallying him. 'You know I'm not welcome here, and I certainly shan't stay when you've gone. We can fly further afield than London, if you like. Take one of those winter bargain breaks. Venice will be too wet underfoot at this time of year, but we could have a week in St Petersburg and wallow in the Hermitage. Find the sun and fly to it. Stay in Paris at a small hotel and live it up generally. You name it, we'll do it.'

Blanche had come downstairs and was standing beside them, waiting for an opportunity to speak, holding an irascible Aaron, who plunged and writhed in his restricting blanket.

'Sorry to interrupt,' she said, and her expression was unfathomable, 'but it's a matter of some urgency, because I want to put this horror to bed.'

'Yes, yes, yes, of course,' Anthony replied with laboured cordiality, assuming a new role as indulgent parent and grandparent.

To Natalie, he said, as of an unimportant matter that concerned her rather than himself, 'I must give your idea some thought before I can make a definite decision.'

And to Blanche, 'Yes, my dear. How can I be of assistance?'

Her eyes were fiery and contemptuous, belying the smooth beguiling tongue.

'Sorry to butt in. Hen needs a room to herself and Aaron shouldn't be exposed to infection. Could he and I sleep in your study? If we move your bookcase and desk on to the landing, we could get his cot and my bed into the room.'

Although Anthony's eyes met hers in black understanding, his reply was just as honeyed and politic. 'I have no objection, but it may not be necessary. I believe that Freddie and Lydia are leaving tonight in order to let you have their room. They're in the kitchen, helping your mother. Why not ask?'

'Oh, that would be wonderful. Thank you.' Charmingly.

'No!' Aaron said, honestly.

Natalie laughed. 'I'm no sentimentalist about children,' she said, as Blanche walked away, 'but I rather like that one. He has character. What do you feel about him?'

'I? I hadn't thought about him, one way or the other,' he said abruptly, and rose and stalked the room again, chin at an angle, restored to his old self.

'And Blanche? Haven't you thought about her either?' Natalie asked, not at all discomposed by his attitude or response.

'Blanche?' he growled. 'I can hardly help thinking about her, now can I? She's inclined to force herself upon my attention.'

'You're a damned peculiar father to her,' said Natalie frankly.

He tossed his mane, deliberating. He was impatient. 'She's always been a difficult child.'

'But you're not a great success with Edward either, and I find him quite charming.'

'Oh – he's – he's – he's got no ...' Anthony gestured to heaven, as if appealing for divine suggestion, and then found his word '. . . backbone.'

'And your attitude to Lydia I would describe as being one of easy indifference.'

He considered this. His laugh tried to be light, but was not amused. 'Yes. I suppose that sums it up.'

'In fact,' said Natalie conversationally, 'you're a total failure as a parent, which bears out an old belief of mine – if you don't want 'em don't have 'em.'

He answered in a leisurely, malicious fashion, 'What a comfort it must have been to you to know that you abided by your beliefs, my dear, while your brother was trapped into betraying his.'

She watched him, hawk-like, half smiling. 'Anyway,' she said, 'they're all grown up now, for better or worse, and the trap is open. In fact, it's been open for several years, so why didn't you walk out?'

Blanche paused in the doorway, taking a fresh grip on Aaron, waiting to speak. Anthony raised a beleaguered head. 'Yes, Blanche?'

'Sybil has persuaded Lydia and Freddie to stay tonight. She wants us to have an official farewell evening.'

'Oh, Christ!'

'My feelings exactly,' Blanche replied. 'Anyway, as they're not leaving until tomorrow they'll be using their bedroom. So, for the second time of asking, please may we sleep in your study?'

'Yes, God damn it! Yes.'

'Thank you so much.' She departed with dignity, untamed head erect, the child balanced on her hip.

Anthony strode the room restlessly, muttered indistinctly.

'As I was saying,' Natalie continued blandly, 'why didn't you opt out? And please skip the usual excuses. You could work anywhere, sell up and split up, leaving Sybil enough to live on, and be true to the black-hearted, unprincipled old bastard that I always loved. Why not, Tony? Why not?'

She had pushed him too far. He said coldly, formally, 'I find this conversation both pointless and disagreeable. If you'll excuse me, I must go upstairs and make sure that Blanche isn't deliberately wrecking my study.'

His footsteps retreated, heavy, deliberate. From the kitchen came the sound of laughter. The laughter grew louder as the door opened, softened again as it closed. More footsteps: light-hearted, brisk. Sybil came smiling down the hall and popped her head round the doorway. Restored, she had thought to see her husband, to smooth over their recent difference of opinion. The smile was immobilized as she saw Natalie sitting there alone, selecting a cigarette from her silver case, tapping it.

'Oh,' Sybil said. 'I thought Tony was here.'

Natalie inserted the cigarette in her holder, lit it, and inhaled, before she replied.

'He's upstairs, probably having another row with Blanche. I must say, Sybil, I'm astonished that a peace-at-all-costs person like yourself should produce such an aggressive family. How *do* you do it?'

They had doffed their social tone and were speaking as they felt, with deep dislike.

Sybil said coolly, 'In this case all the trouble has been occasioned by outside influences.'

'You'd managed to keep everything under wraps until we arrived?' Natalie asked genially. 'Well, this particular outside influence will be departing some time tomorrow, as soon as she's collected her ancient bones and her few traps together.'

Sybil said, making no attempt to pretend regret, 'I think that would be best. And now, if you'll excuse me, I must see what's happening upstairs.'

Sounds of voices arguing, of furniture being moved, could be heard from above.

Sybil mounted the stairs resolutely, wearily, to sort out the mêlée.

'At the last count,' Natalie called after her, 'there were three children, three adults, two opposing camps and a furniture removal going on up there. I think you may find it rather congested.'

Then she refilled her glass, sat and sipped, smoked and coughed, and laughed.

CHAPTER NINETEEN

Daniel arrived at seven, spruced up for this final occasion in his pin-striped suit, pale and troubled. He exchanged a polite 'Good evening!' with Blanche, who was laying the dining-room table, and approached the living room as though it were a den of lions.

Sitting at the bottom of the stairs in the hall, counting his pocket-money, Ben said conspiratorially, 'Grandpa gave me fifty p to stop asking him questions, and Aunt Tasha gave me fifty to stop hovering about. And Dad gave me fifty p to go away.'

'Well, don't try anything on me,' Daniel replied automatically, though there was no zest in his voice, 'because you're more likely to get a sock in the jaw!'

Ben sniggered, and departed to his bedroom, whistling.

Downstairs, the atmosphere of the living room was that of a public library. In one corner Anthony read a geographical magazine. In another Natalie pored short-sightedly over a photograph album. Both of them wore horn-rimmed glasses and looked incredibly alike. They glanced up at Daniel, nodded, and returned to their books. But from the playroom Edward called to him in friendly tones. 'Ah, there you are, Dan! Just the man I need! The lady of the house has given orders to take down the velvet curtains and declare the theatre closed.'

Daniel came forward, rubbing his hands and smiling in imitation of his usual self.

'How about a drink first?' Edward said, sensing that he was wretched and ill at ease. 'Allow me to regale you with whisky, and impart news of the latest Malpas crisis.'

Upstairs, Aaron took possession of his grandfather's study, commenting on this new change of environment in monosyllabic words, unaware that he had shattered a long tradition; Freddie and Lydia packed all but their toilet bags; and Sybil made

Henrietta comfortable for the evening. Everyone felt bruised, and yet a certain measure of peace was stealing over the family because its members would soon be parting.

Sybil had found *Lolita* lurking, unloved and unread if she did but know it, beneath her granddaughter's pillow, and confiscated the paperback without fuss or reproach.

'I should wait until you're a little older,' she had explained, 'and as you're feeling if-ish would you like me to read to you like I used to? Let's find an old favourite.'

Really, the holiday hasn't been so bad after all, Sybil thought, as she opened *The Lion, the Witch and the Wardrobe*.

Henrietta had not expostulated. Indeed, she was glad to be rid of *Lolita*. So she lay back, eyes closed, and drifted into the childhood that Sybil evoked and reclaimed for her.

Family tales could follow, Henrietta thought, if she played her cards right, and if her grandmother were not too preoccupied with supper preparations: tales of Blanche and Edward and Lydia at Minions; of Sybil and her brothers further back in history; of Grandma Outram, who was born before Queen Victoria died; and of *her* father who became a master letterpress printer; and of *his* mother who taught herself and him to read and write; and of *her* parents who were cotton-workers, with nothing to sustain them but Christian faith. Brass-nailed clogs, grey shawls, wet cobbles and dark satanic mills dominated her dreams after these stories, but the good always triumphed, the humble were exalted, and all the endings were happy ones.

'Gran'ma, excuse me interrupting you,' she said fervently, 'but if Ben catches German measles can he please be ill in another room? I don't mean to be unkind, but I couldn't cope with him and Clemmie in my present state of health.'

'Oh, I should think so. We shall have the house to ourselves. We can do what's most convenient for us,' Sybil answered. And smiled to herself, partly because her granddaughter was comic in her earnestness, and mostly because she saw the time ahead as a wide, unruffled pond of domestic peace.

In the pleasant room overlooking the paddock and back garden, another crisis was in progress. Freddie sat on the edge of her bed, hands clasped between her knees, and watched Lydia stuffing underwear and woollies haphazardly into a suitcase.

'Would you like me to do that?' Freddie asked, for she had packed her own clothes neatly and efficiently. 'They'll be all wrinkles when you take them out again.'

Lydia shook her head and wiped her eyes. She had lost her pretty air of inconsequence. Her mouth was set in suffering. Her carefully careless hair was just plain tousled.

Freddie drew a quick breath through her nostrils, and kept her patience. She said, 'I respected your wishes as far as this visit was concerned because you said we shouldn't be asked again. But Sybil and Tony have welcomed me into the family circle and now they want to know me better. I can't hide behind a front of ordinary friendship. I must be truthful with them.'

'But to be truthful about yourself you have to be truthful about us,' Lydia said, and her bottom lip quivered, 'and how they'll take *that* little piece of news I daren't think.'

Freddie said hardily, 'How they take it is another matter, but at least we shall have behaved honourably.'

'Well, you might feel honourable but I certainly shan't,' said Lydia in desperation. 'I've never been a success, and they didn't approve of the men I knew or the way I lived, but at least they were natural relationships. I'm sure they'd think this was a hanging offence.'

Freddie looked bleak. She had never got used to being branded abnormal.

'They simply wouldn't understand!' Lydia cried. In a different tone, at once of wonder and exasperation, she said, 'I don't know that *I* understand it.'

She struggled with herself, not wanting to hurt Freddie, but needing to explain. She said diffidently, 'I don't want them staring at me as if I was peculiar.'

Anguished, she folded the Bruce Oldfield creation in three and pressed it down on the muddle. Freddie rose, patience exhausted, and came to the rescue. 'No,' she said firmly. 'The dress deserves better treatment than this – and so do I.'

Lydia's eyes were full of tears. 'Oh, don't be cross with me. Listen to me,' she pleaded, clutching Freddie's arm. 'We've been so happy together, and if you tell them about us it will all change. Why can't we just go on as we are? Why do you have to spoil everything?'

Freddie disengaged her arm gently, emptied the suitcase on to the bed and began to repack it.

Lydia drifted over to the window, to look out on the paddock of her childhood. In pain and perplexity, she communed with herself aloud. 'I've always been the odd one out in our family. I'm not brilliant like Daddy, or talented like Blanche, or wise like Mummy – and though Teddy and I have always stuck together he's much cleverer than me. And everyone treats me as if I'm a fool, or not there – like Daddy this evening saying, "Oh, and bring Lydia, of course." I made a joke of that but you get very tired of making jokes at your own expense . . .'

Freddie folded the gown with care, interleaving it with sheets of tissue paper, closed the lid and locked the case, listening to Lydia's monologue.

'. . . but you've always treated me as if I was special, and made me feel I was somebody. And offered me real work. I really appreciated that, because it wasn't the sort of job my friends usually give me – meaning something brainless where I have to look decorative and be nice to people. You assumed I would want to learn about the trade, and I *am* learning, Freddie, all the time – and I love it. It's a new world for me. And you said I was good with the customers, and you were pleased with me about that ormolu clock . . .'

Freddie came over to the window and put one arm affectionately round Lydia's shoulders. Her eyes were loving, but she remained objective. 'You're not brainless, Lyddie, you're just plain lazy! And you've been Sybil's little girl for too long. She's a wonderful person but she's never pushed you out of the nest. No, don't cry,' as Lydia's tears welled up again, 'I'm not trying to hurt you. I'm trying to explain you to yourself.'

Lydia swallowed a sob, and nodded. Freddie patted her shoulder and moved away, hands in pockets.

'Our partnership is important to me,' she continued. 'I'm prepared to acknowledge it freely to anyone and to defend us if necessary. But how do *you* feel about it? Am I important to you or am I a temporary convenience?' And as Lydia gave her a tearful, imploring look, Freddie said seriously, 'I need an honest answer. Here, use this!'

Lydia dried her eyes with the proffered handkerchief. 'Are you going to sack me and throw me out on the street if I deny you thrice?' she asked, trying to laugh.

'You should know me better than that,' said Freddie. 'You can keep the job as long as you take an interest in it, and live in the rooms over the shop, rent free. But we shan't live together any more or see each other except on business matters.'

Lydia reproached the crumpled handkerchief, 'I never thought you could be cruel.'

Freddie replied factually, 'You can't run away from trouble all your life. Just for once you must make a stand.' She would have liked to stroke Lydia's hair and comfort her, but did not.

'I'm off downstairs now, to see how I can help Sybil,' she announced. 'When you come down we'll talk to your parents. Either we tell them we're splitting up, and blame me – if that makes you feel better. Or we face it out together. It's up to you.'

Lydia said desolately, head bent, 'It's exactly like coming home from school with a bad report, and being frightened of upsetting Mummy and getting Daddy in a wax.'

Freddie said impatiently, 'But that's precisely the point I am trying to make. You're acting like a child, instead of an adult who is responsible for her own actions.'

'You don't care,' Lydia cried, seizing on an excuse. 'You simply don't care.'

Freddie stood up, clenching her hands in her trouser pockets, and looked at the tousled head with love and sorrow. 'Oh, I do care,' she said finally. 'I care too much to pretend we are less than we are.'

Edward determined to conduct the telephone conversation with Katrina factually and unemotionally. He had hesitated for more than an hour before ringing her, fearing that Charles would answer the telephone, and wondering how they could deal with each other. But Charles was civil and matter of fact, received the news with the correct amount of sympathy and regret, explained the circumstances to Katrina in a few concise sentences, and handed him over to her.

Edward said to Katrina, abruptly, awkwardly, 'Before I say anything else, I want you to know that I'm sorry for what happened.'

After a moment she answered, 'I accept your apology.'

He said curtly, 'But I shall contest you for custody of the children.' And heard her quick, sharp intake of breath.

She gave an enraged little laugh, and answered, 'Do you really think that's wise, considering that you assaulted me, and I've got bruises and witnesses to prove it?'

Charles's voice in the background apparently checked her. She continued in a more pacific tone. 'I'm sure you don't want to wash all our dirty linen in public, any more than I do. I promise that you'll have plenty of access, provided they can live here with us.'

'And I promise you exactly the same thing,' he replied inexorably.

'Then you're asking for trouble!'

Charles advised her again, and she spoke more quietly. 'Oh, well, this is the wrong time to talk about it. We're both still upset at the moment.'

She fell into their old routine of using the children as a means of communication. 'Charles tells me that the children won't be with us for New Year because Henny has German measles. How is she?'

Feeling he had gained a point, Edward answered in a lighter tone. 'Not too bad, actually. Looking at her rash and crying woe unto her.'

'Poor old Hen! And how did Ben take the news?'

'His reaction was to talk so much that three of us, unknowingly, bribed him to shut up.'

Katrina laughed: a lovely sound which ran up four notes. Furious with himself, sorry for himself, he missed her sharply. She relayed the information to Charles before picking up the conversation. 'Ben's bound to catch it,' she said, 'so they'll be down with Sybil for a couple of weeks at least. It's very good of her. I'll send her some flowers. Oh, and I'll post a surprise parcel to the children next week. They'd like that, wouldn't they? And I'll have them here to convalesce.'

The quiet background rumble of Charles's voice modified this remark.

'That is, if you want us to help you out. Convalescent children are fairly demanding, you know, and you'll be back at school by then – but it's entirely up to you.'

Edward said cautiously, 'That might be a good thought. Shall we talk about it later, when they're ready to travel?'

Katrina was running on, as she did when seized by an idea. 'You can bring them straight here, if you want to, and have a meal with us. Or we'll drive over and collect them. Whatever you want to do.' She heeded her adviser yet again. 'Charles would like us all to be on friendly terms . . . and so should I, Teddy.'

A long pause.

'I'll keep in touch,' said Edward. 'Thanks, anyway.'

'Oh, and tell Henny that we're house-training Mr Silk and he's having a wonderful time here. It's an enormous garden and he loves exploring it—' This time she stopped herself. 'Just tell her he's absolutely fine, and longing to see her again. And, Teddy, may I ring tomorrow evening to ask how she is? And will you give her and Ben our love? And do thank Sybil for being so kind.'

He put down the receiver with some triumph and some regret. He had done better, far far better, than he expected. Katrina was vulnerable after all, and Charles had a restraining influence upon her and was evidently not raring for a fight. Mourning for the lost marriage would take its toll of Edward before he could be truly comforted; but something had been salvaged, something achieved, however hard and grievously.

He took the stairs two at a time, almost cheerfully, to tell his daughter that Mr Silk was running free in a splendid garden and panting for her return.

Daniel was aware of a green scent, a glittering jacket, a charismatic presence, a shy touch and an apologetic murmur. It was Blanche, in her brocade coat and gold lamé trousers.

'Could I have a word with you in the kitchen, Dan?'

He followed her, bemused: afraid to hope for better things, fearing worse to come.

'I'm sorry you weren't here in time to say good night to Aaron,' she began diffidently. 'He missed you. He asked for you.'

The news was sweet to him, and sharp too. He blurted out the truth, 'I'm not brave enough to say goodbye to him as well as yourself.'

'Oh, Dan,' said Blanche, penitent.

She could not find the words she wanted, and he had no more to say. She put her hand on his sleeve. He looked at it and then at her, uncertainly.

'Dan, I didn't mean to cut you off from Aaron. I only meant . . .'

She was not sure what she *had* meant, and began again.

'You're as important to him as he is to you. Of course you must see each other, and know each other. I would never prevent that. It would be wrong. And I'm sorry I was unkind – no, let me be honest and say "brutal" – this afternoon.'

He was full of joy, and fearful of that joy.

'I'll not be a trouble to you,' he promised her, and patted the hand tentatively.

Blanche bit her lip and wondered how to put this trickier proposition. 'I did say,' she ventured, 'that we were becoming good friends again . . .'

He would have helped her if he could, but was himself tongue-tied. He squeezed the hand optimistically.

'I'd like us to be friends,' said Blanche.

He lifted the hand and put it to his lips. Then relinquished it, stood back and gave a little bow, to show her that he knew how far to go, and when to stop.

Blanche said again, 'Oh, Dan!' Rueful over him and herself.

The kitchen door swung open and Sybil hurried in crying, 'I'd forgotten about the custards!' She snatched an oven cloth from the rail. 'Oh, pray not!' she cried to the contents of the simmering oven. And then, 'Oh, thank heavens. They're just right!'

Her presence relieved them. They both laughed.

'What's this about custards? I thought you weren't going to cook this evening,' her daughter remarked.

'It's really for Henny,' Sybil replied defensively. 'Children are picky when they're ill. A personal baked custard is so tempting. And if she has one, then Ben must.'

'Served with a spoonful of raspberry jelly in a small blue bowl,' Blanche remembered, and stood dreaming, hand on hip.

'What a grand pair of women you are!' Dan said, smiling on them. 'I'd love to take you both to County Meath and introduce you to the family.'

'Oh, that *would* be delightful,' Sybil cried. 'Wouldn't it, Blanche?'

'I'm not being involved with any more families,' her daughter said, determined. 'One is enough.'

But Sybil glided over this reply, and asked Daniel about his mother, and elicited a description of a large and sprawling household ruled by a food-conscious matriarch, which, Sybil said, reminded her of her Cheshire home. So they wandered for a while

177

in green hills, soft rain and family recipes, while Blanche put a pile of dinner plates into the simmering oven to warm and Daniel opened the evening wine.

Now Anthony wandered into the kitchen, under pretext of offering his assistance, actually to find out when supper would be served. He stared at Blanche and Daniel with mild displeasure and, seeing that he wanted to speak to Sybil alone, they moved towards the door in unison. As they closed it behind them they heard the opening speeches.

'Tasha says she's going tomorrow,' Anthony announced belligerently.

'Very sensible.' Briskly.

His tone changed, became injured. 'I can't think why she came in the first place. *I* didn't ask her.'

'I didn't suppose you had,' Sybil replied caustically. 'Even *you* have limits.'

'That's a damned disagreeable sort of remark to make . . .'

'The Malpases rage on!' Blanche said, and sighed. 'I shall be glad to go home and leave them to it. I'll be leaving fairly soon, I should think. If Aaron's caught the plague I'd be better off nursing him at home, and if he hasn't then I'd best get him out of the way.'

'Would you mind if I stayed until you left?' Daniel asked cautiously.

'No, of course not. I was rather hoping you would.' She thought for a moment or two and then said, 'I can give you a lift home in the car, if you like.'

Their conversation was interrupted by Freddie and Lydia, walking one behind the other, heads down, unusually subdued.

'Is Mummy in the kitchen?' Lydia asked warily.

'Yes, and Tony's with her, and they're fulminating.'

Lydia said, with sorry vivacity, 'They'll be fulminating even more when they hear what we have to say. We'll probably be thrown out. I wonder if they'll let us take our Chinese take-aways with us?'

'We'd like a private word with them,' Freddie explained, keeping an even tone.

'Anything wrong?' Blanche asked.

Freddie put one hand on Lydia's arm, as if to reassure and protect her, and replied for them both, 'Something that needs clearing up. That's all.'

'It isn't all, at all,' Lydia remarked. 'It's like the party that Mac and the boys gave Doc at Cannery Row, when someone lit the string of giant fire-crackers!'

'Oh, good!' Natalie cried, relieved, as Blanche and Daniel entered the living room. 'I've been parked here like an unwanted ornament for ages. No one's spoken to me, apart from Ben, and I paid him to go away and shut up. I'm leaving tomorrow.'

'So we heard in passing. Sorry about all this,' Blanche answered, amused, and sat by her aunt on the sofa. 'I expect you're faintly shell-shocked. You have just experienced one of the Malpas's more chaotic Christmases, and even the ordinary sort can be quite chilling. Something always does happen, but not usually all at once and to everyone, with German measles thrown in for good luck.'

'I like you,' said Natalie sincerely. 'You take life on the chin instead of taking it to heart or in the stomach. I like him, too,' she added, nodding at Daniel. 'He's all right.'

'Another whisky, ma'am?' he asked courteously, reviving.

'God, I've drunk enough to float the Queen Mary already. Yes, why not? Sybil never liked me and now Tony's keeping away from me. Thank you, Dan. Here's a happy New Year to you both and to your little battler upstairs, and sod the rest of them!'

Lydia hung back, but Freddie was a lone and doughty warrior, well schooled in the art of confrontation. Legs slightly apart, hands clasped behind her back, she faced an astounded Sybil and Anthony, and delivered her message succinctly.

'I want you to know,' said Freddie, 'how very much I appreciate your asking me into your home at Christmas time, and making me so welcome.'

Sybil was painfully aware that Malpas Christmases tended to be lacking in good will and merriment. 'My dear,' she said truthfully, 'we should have been lost without you.'

'I'll tell you something, Freddie,' said Anthony confidentially. 'You're the first friend of Lydia's who has come up to scratch, and Sybil and I think you're a damned good influence on her, and we hope to see you both again often.'

'That's rather the point,' said Freddie bravely. 'I can't sail under false colours, and I regret that I shall have to be blunt with you. I'm one of the Sapphic tribe, you see – to give it a nice name. Or, not to mince words, a lesbian.'

Sybil and Anthony stood like Greek statues, still bearing the stamp of former beauty, holding up a temple which time was fast eroding, receiving yet another unwanted tribute from a passing sea-bird.

As Lydia did not speak or come forward, Freddie shouldered the responsibility. 'I don't want you to blame Lydia,' she said quickly. 'It's not her fault. She needed a good friend, but now our friendship is at a crossroads because I love her. It's up to her to decide whether she wants it to continue or not. If she does, then I can't accept your hospitality unless you know the score, and I apologize for misleading you.'

'My dear Freddie,' said Sybil helplessly. And to her daughter, 'My dear child.'

Anthony cleared his throat, rocked back on his heels, and pronounced judgement. 'We're all adults here, I hope,' he said. 'No apologies necessary.'

Lydia left the safe haven of the kitchen door, and dropped her usual mask. She looked all of her thirty years, and hers was a sad face: one that had been slapped many times, literally and meta-phorically, to be prettied up again with fresh paint and a little-girl smile, and used to catch another man. Now she stood by the side of her friend and faced her parents with some dignity. She said, 'Freddie's covering up for me. I went into this relationship with my eyes open. The idea of – love – is new, but we've been – lovers – for a while now.'

The effort was very great, but the thought of loss still greater. She drove herself on. 'I've never been as happy with anyone as I am with Freddie,' she said, appealing to them for understanding and clemency. 'I'm learning about the antique business, and I mean to make a go of it. And I feel safe, as I did when I was a child. I'm safe – and happy.'

Another truth was being demanded of her, not for her parents nor for herself nor for Freddie, but for the partnership that was to be. 'I don't think I am a lesbian by nature,' she said honestly, 'but I've never been much of a heterosexual either. Sex was something I did because men wanted it, and I can't say they lit any lamps for me. But it seems right with Freddie.'

Their silence compelled her to add a rider. 'I should be very sorry to think that you didn't want to see me again, but Freddie is right. We mustn't pretend. And it was my fault that we did. Freddie is a very honest person. She only kept quiet because of me. I love and thank her for that, as for everything else, and I ask her to forgive me.' She held out her hand, and burst into tears, and Freddie clasped it and looked round as if ready to wield a thousand swords in her defence.

Sybil was the first to speak. 'There was no need,' she said, though stunned by their frankness, and indeed she would rather they had said nothing and let her deduce the situation gradually, 'no need to distress yourselves so. Tony and I . . .' She looked to him to finish her sentence.

'Yes, of course,' he said, equally stunned. 'Realized the state of affairs all along. Adults. Modern age. Say no more. Invitation still stands.'

'Thank you,' said Freddie gravely, gratefully. 'Thank you both very much.'

A brief embarrassed silence followed. It was Sybil who brought them all back to a matter of immediate importance. 'And now it really is getting late and everyone will be hungry, so I feel that supper shouldn't be delayed a minute longer. If you could ask Blanche . . .' She remembered who had helped her all along, and she smiled upon them. 'Why on earth do I need Blanche when I have you two to buttle for me?' she asked engagingly.

Relieved, reprieved, accepted, Lydia and Freddie began to carry plates and dishes into the dining room.

CHAPTER TWENTY

Thursday evening

The photographs she spread over the floor of the living room were the best of Natalie's working life and represented nearly forty years of wandering. The company had pushed back their chairs to view them clearly. Anthony and Sybil stood some way apart, he with his hands in his pockets, she with hers clasped as if in prayer, and they gave praise because praise was deserved: on his part with enthusiasm, on hers with reservation. Blanche walked round the pictures slowly, hands on hips, exclaiming over those which caught her imagination, examining others carefully to learn more about her aunt. Freddie and Lydia made admiring little comments. Edward picked out those he liked, and paid charming compliments. But Daniel, as an illustrator, showed the closest professional appreciation, and he and Natalie became a group of two who understood each other.

'What a terrible desire you have to seek out the truth,' he said sombrely. 'You present your subjects stark naked. I clothe mine in fantasy. If I have to present the truth I'll see that it's dressed for the occasion!'

'If you're talking about these,' she answered, indicating a series of refugee photographs, 'they're political news, therefore instant and sold as such. I have lighter subjects for other markets, as you can see.'

'But you're serious with all of them. Ah! I feel like throwing my work on a bonfire and learning to see again – not even to draw, just to see.'

'I'm afraid I don't know your work,' Natalie replied in her abrupt fashion.

'I'd send you one of my books,' he said sincerely, 'if I had the courage.'

Touched, Natalie said, 'But I should like that.'

'Tony and I are very interested too, Daniel,' Sybil interposed, for he was her guest, and in a way her son-in-law, and she did not see why she should be left out. 'We know nothing of your work, only of yourself...'

'My work *is* myself,' said Daniel, absorbed, 'which gives me pause to think.'

'In which case, we should like to know more about both.'

He roused himself then, and said cheerfully, 'Then I must send a selection to you.'

'We'd love some too!' Freddie and Lydia cried, almost simultaneously.

Not knowing what he asked, Edward held up a hand, saying, 'Blanche tells me you write and illustrate wonderful children's books too, so don't forget Henny and Ben.'

They all gave him their names and addresses, which Daniel wrote down earnestly.

Sybil said to Blanche in an undertone, 'But, my dear, we should buy them. He can't afford the trouble and expense to send to so many people.'

'I shouldn't worry about that,' her daughter replied, smiling. 'His intentions are excellent, but he's unlikely to carry them out. Except for...'

Except for Aunt Tasha, she thought, but did not finish her sentence.

'Oh, I see,' said Sybil, perplexed. 'Then, perhaps he'd be kind enough to give me the titles and I'll order them from our local bookshop.'

Natalie, now overshadowed by the promise of Daniel's publications, was collecting her photographs together. Sybil, obedient to her principles of making a guest feel appreciated, even though she were disliked and unwanted, said, 'These are really wonderful, Tasha. I know you haven't brought your camera with you but Tony would lend you his — it's quite a good one — and perhaps tomorrow you could take a group photograph of us all, as a memento of the occasion?'

Natalie paused for a moment, head bent, thinking. Her answer was unexpected, almost pitiless in its candour. 'That's not possible. I have cataracts in both eyes. They're at the early stage, so I have to wait some time before they can be removed. Meanwhile my vision isn't good enough. That's why I didn't bring my camera with me.' Her tone was factual. 'The specialist tells me I shan't die of it, and there are all sorts of aids like contact lenses and special glasses. They can sometimes implant an artificial lens, but not always.'

To Daniel she said, 'But when your work is you, what's left when it's taken away?'

He had no answer.

She said to her sister-in-law, 'So I'm afraid someone else will have to wield the camera, Sybil.'

And told herself, holding the photographs, 'Somehow I have a feeling that these are the last of me.'

Her tone did not ask for sympathy, in fact it indicated that sympathy would be most unwelcome. All but Anthony were stricken to silence, and his reaction was equally pitiless and unexpected. He reddened and roared as if Natalie had attacked him personally. 'What the hell do you mean by coming out with it like this, Tash? Why the devil didn't you tell me about it before? Why didn't you come to *me* first?'

Natalie ignored him, speaking drily to the company at large. 'I may not like the bastard but I still love him. It's one of the things about being a twin.'

Anthony strode out of the room, slamming the door behind him. Natalie jumped up, letting the photographs fall where they could, and followed him. Sybil sat down very slowly, knotted her hands in her lap and gazed fixedly at the carpet. The others looked to Blanche for orders.

'Tea?' she suggested, motioning them out to the kitchen and out of the way.

Then she sat by Sybil and put one warm hand on her two cold ones.

Without looking at her, Sybil said in low, emphatic tones, 'I will do whatever is humanly possible to help her from a distance, but however much he pleads I *will not* take her into my home. I will not have her in our life at all, and I said so from the beginning. She is possessive and destructive. And if he insists then he will lose me. I shall leave him.'

Blanche, aware that this decision came out of a past she knew nothing about, warmed Sybil's hands in hers and did not comment.

'I would walk out this minute,' Sybil was saying, trembling, speaking to herself rather than to her daughter. 'I would go to Mrs Laity's cottage and ask if I could stay with her tonight, in spite of all the gossip it would entail, but I can't leave Henrietta and Ben and worry poor Edward. It's always the same. One is tied by one's responsibilities, and no amount of fine talk about self-belief and self-fulfilment and sexual equality can alter that.'

Blanche said gently, 'You can sleep in my bed, in the study with Aaron, while I sleep on the playroom sofa. I'll deal with Daddy and Aunt Tasha too, if you want that.'

'I *must* be by myself,' said Sybil, distractedly, not heeding her. 'I can't pretend that nothing has happened, and make small talk and pour tea.'

'Come and lie down on my bed. No one will disturb you there.'

Sybil looked up and focused on her daughter's concerned face. 'But I don't know where Tony and Natalie are, and I can't bear to see them.'

'Then I'll find out where they are, and make sure you *don't* see them. Wait here, while I explain to the others.'

The four of them were warming themselves over the Aga, speaking in subdued voices.

'They're walking up and down the paddock, talking,' Edward told Blanche. 'Dad came in here for the torch, and went out with Aunt Tasha. He said that they weren't to be disturbed, and we knew Sybil didn't want us in the living room. So we stayed put.' With restrained humour, he added, 'And a happy New Year to all Malpases!'

Lydia, standing close to Freddie for comfort, said forlornly, 'I don't know why our family meetings always end like this.'

'Not quite like this,' Blanche answered cryptically. 'This is a new one on me.'

'Wouldn't it be easier for everyone if Lydia and I cleared off?' Freddie said. 'I don't mind driving at night and the roads will be empty.'

Blanche said, 'Actually, Freddie, that would solve a practical problem. We're short of space.' She turned to Daniel, and her voice softened. 'Dan, I know my family even if I don't know what all this is about. I'm afraid we're in for a force ten gale and I must stay here until it blows out. But if I were you I should go home tomorrow. I'll ring you when we get back.'

Daniel made his declaration lovingly, firmly. 'I'll not interfere, but I want to stand by you and the boy. Your family is part of you, and so it's part of me. We'll see this through together.'

'Good on you, Dan,' said Edward, comforted by the prospect of masculine support.

Now Lydia spoke up, nervously but with conviction. 'I think we should stay too, Freddie, I mean,' being honest, 'I'd much rather go home because this sort of thing frightens me to death, but Mummy's upset and I feel I should look after her.'

'That's all right by me,' said Freddie.

'And while we're together,' said Lydia, gaining strength and confidence, 'I think we should tell them, Freddie, about us.'

Blanche said, amused and touched, 'There's nothing to tell, love.'

'Nothing at all,' said Edward. 'You daffy old duck!'

They laughed at her and hugged her, and smiled at Freddie.

'This girl is a nut-case,' said Blanche, 'but an endearing nut-case — I'll say that.'

'You go home, Lyd,' Edward advised. 'We'll take care of Mama, and there won't be so many bodies to litter the stage in the last act.'

'Anyway, we need your room,' said Blanche, teasing, forthright. 'So let's make you a flask of hot coffee and cut a few sandwiches for the journey.'

Daniel asked, 'Now what can I do for anyone? Should I sit with Sybil?'

'No, thank you,' Blanche answered him kindly. 'I'll take care of her. But I expect these two ladies could use a porter to carry their luggage downstairs.'

Sybil was still sitting in the same position as Blanche had left her, bruised and passive, a delicate plant beaten down by wind and rain, and Blanche hesitated to disturb her. Still, it must be done.

'Freddie and Lydia have decided to leave, after all. So I'll make up a bed for you in their room with clean sheets and pillow-cases. They'll be off in a few minutes. I thought you would want to say good-bye to them.'

Sybil, drawing on depleted energies, replied, 'Yes, of course,' and was standing up, pale and smiling, when they appeared.

Lydia said, embracing her, 'Darling Mummy, you've been so wonderful and we've tired you out!'

186

Freddie shook hands, saying, 'The invitation works in reverse, don't forget. Any time you want a holiday, Sybil, come and stay with us. We'll make you very welcome.'

'We have a lovely flat,' said Lydia, 'and I can show you the antique shop.'

All Sybil could manage, despite her steadfast stance and smile, was, 'Thank you, Freddie. Bless you, Lydia. Goodbye, and a happy New Year to you both. Blanche will see you off, if you'll excuse me.'

At the front door Lydia turned to her sister and said, 'Let me know what it was all about, will you, Blanche? Here,' rummaging in her handbag and producing two cards, 'this is our home address, and this', rather proudly, 'is my place of business.'

'Our invitation extends to you and the little buster – and Dan, of course,' Freddie continued. 'Any time. Just give us a ring beforehand, so we can lay in a supply of gin, rusks and baked beans.'

Blanche said, 'Thanks, Freddie. When summer comes we may well wend our way across London, or meet somewhere for a picnic.'

Daniel and Edward now appeared to make their farewells.

'Best of luck, Teddy!' Lydia said, hugging him tightly, kissing him on both cheeks. 'Say goodbye to your darling Henny and Ben for us, and if ever you're in London . . .'

'. . . and if ever you're in Yorkshire . . .'

Christmas had brought them all closer and their invitations were sincere. But they would probably not see each other again until Sybil took the initiative and provided the venue.

'Goodbye! God bless!' Daniel cried. 'This may be the first time we've met but it surely won't be the last.' He followed the flight of his fancy. 'I'll tell you what, why don't we all go over to Ireland to see my mother? She'd love that.'

They kissed and embraced, laughing a little at the expansiveness, the sincerity, the impracticality of this suggestion.

'Do you need me?' Edward asked Blanche privately. And, as she shook her head, added, 'Then I'll go upstairs and make sure that the kids are all right. Children are sensitive to bad vibes, and they've had more than their share already.'

Her nod of understanding gave him full permission and he left her to deal with their parents. But Daniel linked her arm and came out into the driveway to wave Freddie and Lydia off.

As the tail-lights disappeared, Blanche sighed. 'I shall miss Freddie. She's been a tower of strength. And Lydia was sweet, wasn't she? Trying to tell us what we all knew! Standing her ground like a valiant mouse!'

The night was cold and clear and windless, studded with stars. The silence was underlined rather than broken by the occasional bark of a dog. The peace was deceptive, screening a multitude of conflicts.

'And now all you're left with is me,' said Daniel humbly. 'It's Hobson's choice, I know that, but I'll do my best.'

'I would rate you a good deal higher than Hobson,' she replied soberly, touched by his dedication. 'And I'm glad you're staying with Aaron and me.'

She leaned against him then, because she was weary and the evening stretched before her demanding heaven knew what, and because she trusted him.

He kissed her gently at first and then long and deeply. This time she put her head on his shoulder and stayed there, and he spoke softly into her frizzed black bush of hair, stroking the back of her neck, holding her close. 'We never quarrelled in the real sense of the word, now did we? Never tore lumps out of each other like those sad people in there. Oh, we've had a fight now and again, but both of us enjoy a good clean fight, now don't we? And we've missed each other, haven't we?'

Mesmerized, she listened to him. Her breathing softened. She could have stayed there for ever in the warmth of him, listening to his body telling her body the story it wanted to hear. But they must look after Sybil, so after a while she kissed him to remind him, and they joined hands, wordless, and went inside.

While they were heating milk on the Aga in quiet contentment, the kitchen door opened and Anthony and Natalie came in.

Immediately, Blanche was on guard. She kept her tone neutral, spoke over her shoulder, gave her message casually, briefly. 'Freddie and Lydia have left, after all. They asked me to say goodbye and thank you very much and they'll be seeing us again. Sybil's gone to bed. She's very tired, and she'll be sleeping in their room tonight. I'm making milk and honey for her.'

Anthony raised his arms heavily and let them fall. He looked old and drained and gaunt. A small pageant of expressions crossed Natalie's face: contempt, despair, stoicism, sadness.

'Now can we do anything for you, sir?' Daniel enquired, gravely polite.

Anthony roused himself to answer just as courteously, 'I don't think so, thank you. Natalie and I will drink a nightcap in the living room – by ourselves, if you'll excuse us – and then I'll take her back to the pub. It's been a long evening and it's very late. Will you be up when I get back? Because I'd like to go straight to bed.'

'Oh yes. Dan and I will be talking for quite a while yet,' Blanche said, 'so I'll look after Gracie and lock up, if you like.'

She kept her face averted from her father, and he avoided looking at her. They were being careful with each other. There had been trouble enough for one night.

'I would appreciate that,' said Anthony. 'I'm extremely tired. Thank you.'

Natalie said to her niece's back, 'I'll be off tomorrow, Blanche, and I haven't seen as much of you as I should like. Could we have a walk together before I go?'

Daniel consulted Blanche's face, which was struggling to reconcile her liking for Natalie with her loyalty to Sybil.

'That's a cry from the heart,' he said to her, very low, 'and she's got no one but herself. Don't turn her down. I can look after the boy and keep an eye on Sybil.'

She swallowed, nodded to him, turned to Natalie, swallowed again. 'Yes. By all means.'

'Good,' Natalie said. 'I shan't come back here so perhaps you'd meet me at the Cornish Arms? My train leaves from Redruth about three o'clock – no thanks, Tony,' as he began to protest. 'I'll order a taxi. It will save a lot of difficulty.' And to Blanche, 'Why don't you meet me at eleven o'clock and then we'll have lunch at the pub afterwards? Mrs Sampson makes a substantial sandwich.'

'It would be easier for everyone,' Blanche said quickly, 'if I came back here for lunch and dealt with Aaron. We should still have plenty of time together.'

For she needed to limit this meeting which made demands on her affection and divided her loyalties.

'As you please,' Natalie answered, discouraged.

They were all at a loss how to end the conversation.

Then Natalie held out her hand to Daniel, and said with forced good humour, 'Best of luck, Dan. May your whisky bottle never be empty!'

He put both arms round her and gave her a bear hug and kissed her cheeks, and answered seriously, 'Goodbye, and God bless you until we meet again.'

A wounded bird of prey, nevertheless she continued to pounce. 'I have no God, and I doubt that we shall meet again – but I've been glad to know you.'

They had sat together by the Aga until Anthony put his head round the door to say good night.

Then Daniel asked, 'Where can we go?' Looking hopefully round the kitchen as if it might turn into a four-poster bed and draw the curtains on them.

Blanche answered firmly, 'Nowhere in this house.'

His fingers slid caressingly down her arm, leaving a trail of goose-bumps behind. He said, 'And I doubt I could smuggle you into my room at the Cornish Arms, even by the backstairs.'

'We could try the barn again, but we'll have to climb over a gate and approach it from the far side, otherwise we'll rouse the farm dogs. Are you game?'

'I'm game', said Daniel, 'for anything!'

They had the world to themselves out there. The moon shone over a sleeping village. They walked quietly, spoke softly, flitted across a field, keeping close to the hedge, and mounted to their eyrie.

Blanche said, 'I wasn't expecting you, so unless you've come prepared, we're taking a risk.'

He said, 'I'm sorry you don't fancy the method, but I had hopes, so I *am* prepared.'

She leaned forward and kissed him full on the lips. 'Damn the method. I fancy *you*,' she said, 'very much indeed.'

They stayed mouth to mouth and closed their eyes, hearing and feeling the twin race of heartbeats, prolonging the delight of waiting.

'And you were ready to take a risk?' he whispered at length. 'Why was that?'

'I'm a great risk-taker,' she answered airily, though her breath came more quickly. 'Did you never find that out?'

They made a nest for themselves under the window at the back of the loft and spread their coats under them.

'Don't take off more than necessary. It's too damned cold and the straws stab you,' said Blanche breathlessly. 'And you can forget the preliminaries. This is neither the time nor the place, and I don't need arousing.'

'Ah, there's no beating an honest fuck,' said Daniel, 'and abstinence is a fine sauce.'

She opened her legs to receive him and cried out with joy.

Later, relaxed and leisurely, they made love again and more slowly, savouring their reunion, recalling other liaisons. A double bed in Paris. A blue pool in North Wales. A Spanish beach at night.

'We've made the sun run in many a grand place,' said Daniel reflectively, 'and there's never been a woman to match you.'

She smiled then, turning her face to his, splendidly complete. 'And have you been faithful to me – after your fashion?'

'I've been entirely faithful,' he swore, hand on heart, but could not resist mocking her. 'I can't remember the name nor the face of any woman I've had since we parted.'

She regarded him placidly, lazily. She spoke with loving sarcasm. 'That's what I call true fidelity. But I must confess that though I have been chaste in the flesh, since we parted, I have been totally unfaithful to you in spirit. Aaron and Aaron's welfare came first, and the responsibility made me choosy. I've had real battles with myself, trying not to sleep with unsuitable men whom I desired greatly. And won every one of them.'

'You didn't desire them,' said Daniel, bending over her. 'You were only driven by appetite. You were anhungered, my darling, as I was. But when you saw me again you desired me. Oh, yes, you did. And I desired you, and do desire you,' preparing to mount her again, 'greatly . . .'

191

The Party's Over

CHAPTER TWENTY-ONE

Friday, 29 December

They left Blanche's car parked on the cliff top and made their way down to the beach. They did not speak, as they negotiated the precipitous path, until the descent was behind them and the long wet stretch of sand before them. They strode together rhythmically, easily, on a cold grey day where sky merged imperceptibly into sea, and the wind tugged their head-scarves. Lumps of glistening brown seaweed, left stranded by the retreating tide, smelled as rich as Christmas pudding.

In the distance, behind them, a solitary man walked a dog, which barked and scampered and wagged his tail, dashing in and out of the waves that rushed towards him as rough and playful as himself.

Natalie opened the conversation. 'How's Sybil today?'

Blanche gave an answer that was no more than sufficient. 'She says she slept quite well, and she's certainly looking brighter.'

'Are she and Tony on speaking terms?' Natalie asked directly.

'Not yet,' said Blanche, 'but that's usual after a bust-up.'

Natalie laughed hoarsely. 'I'm not a hypocrite, so I won't pretend to be sorry about anything that happened,' she said contemptuously, 'particularly as I'm getting the rough end of the pineapple, as usual, but I need to regain your good opinion of me before I go.'

As Blanche continued to walk on, mouth set in a tight line, not answering, Natalie said passionately, whole-heartedly, 'I believed us to be friends.'

'It's difficult', said Blanche, tight-lipped, 'to be friendly with someone who causes my mother such intense pain, and brings out the worst side of my father.'

With a flash of temper, Natalie cried, 'Of course, if you've made up your mind that Tony's a blackguard and she's a saint I'm wasting my bloody time!'

Blanche stopped, so that Natalie had to stop too, and looked point-blank at her aunt. 'I don't know what's happened between the three of you, but I don't like the tensions you bring with you, and I doubt if any explanation could change my feelings about my parents or their marriage. My father takes up more time than any child ever could – one woman's lifetime, in fact. Sybil could have been a person in her own right if she hadn't met him. She had great potential. She went to university as a highly promising English scholar. She was – is – beautiful, intelligent, diplomatic, capable. She could have used her talents in a dozen ways, to delight and fulfil herself and numberless others. Instead they were dedicated to my father and, in my opinion, cruelly squandered.'

Her voice had become more reasonant as she voiced an old wrong that she was still righting in herself.

Natalie's smile was a grimace. 'You don't resemble her,' she said. 'Sybil would have found a tactful way to say that, if indeed she had said it at all. But I don't pull punches either, so I'll be as forthright as you. I agree about Anthony. I love my brother as I love myself, but I know he's a selfish bastard. And any woman who became seriously involved with him would be crossing out a life of her own from the start. I also would agree that Sybil had the potential, *and* the opportunity – that you didn't mention, and the two do not always go together – for making her mark in the world. What she lacked was the guts to do it.'

Blanche's colour rose, her eyes glittered. 'She fell in love,' she cried. 'Uncle Jack was unofficially engaged to her, and he was the man she should have married, but my father broke that up.'

Natalie was amused by her vehemence, dismissive of Jack Maddern. 'Any fool who can't keep a girl deserves to lose her. Yes, I suppose that Sybil should have been allowed to sink back into a lifetime of rural comfort and obscurity, but Tony wanted a woman who would adore him and further his career, and Sybil was an ideal choice. Oh, I'm sure he was fond of her in his way, but he would never have allowed love to overcome ambition, whereas she . . . excuse me, a moment. I need a mild fix.' She stopped to light a cigarette, shielding the little flame in the bowl of her hands, screwing up her eyes over the smoke, inhaling deeply.

Behind them, the man grew larger, the dog nearer, the barking louder.

Looking sideways sharply at Blanche, Natalie said, 'A woman must be particularly canny about falling in love – as you know. Otherwise you wouldn't be in two minds about that engaging Irishman. I understand your problem. You're weighing the cost of keeping Dan against the cost of losing him, but Sybil isn't like you and she wasn't entirely innocent of that broken engagement. She fell in love with Tony and then let him take her over. So don't blame him entirely.'

Blanche strode on, staring ahead of her, eyes brilliant with anger at the double thrust.

'I admit that Sybil has great qualities,' said Natalie, coming as near to a pacific tone as Blanche had heard, 'though they may not be the sort that I admire. Feminine women bore me, you see. So let's look at it from a different angle. You and I have a strong masculine streak. I don't mean we've gone over to the other side, like Freddie, but we've got a lot of man in our make-up. Wouldn't you agree?'

'I'm the only member of the family who can stand up to my father, if that's a lot of man,' said Blanche grimly.

'That's part of what I mean, but only a part. You and I like men, we get on well with men, we prefer their conversation to female chitchat, and most importantly we can look after ourselves. Apart from the tenacious Daniel, I would guess that you chose men who could be manipulated. If you couldn't manipulate them you discarded them, or they had the balls to leave you. Am I right?'

Blanche was silent, walking along the desolate shore, thinking of the men who had come into her life and either departed of their own accord or been summarily despatched. She answered reluctantly, 'I suppose so. But I dislike the idea of manipulating anyone, and I don't agree that I do. I make sure my partners know the rules, so to speak, but if we differ in principle then it's better to split up.'

'That's a nicer way of putting it,' said Natalie bluntly, caring very little for niceties, 'but I call a spade a bloody shovel, and I say *manipulation*. It may not be pretty, but it happens. Look at Sybil and Tony, twisting each other to their own ends—'

'Which are always *his* ends!' Blanche cried furiously, stopping again in her tracks and forcing Natalie to stop also.

'*Their* ends,' said Natalie imperturbably, face to face and eye to eye. 'That's what I'm trying to tell you. Yes, he needs her to bolster him up, but by God she needs him to need *her* and to acknowledge her supreme importance to him. She's prepared to pay a price that neither you nor I would contemplate, because she doesn't want to go out there herself and make it on her own. Shit, Blanche! She's made a *career* out of looking after him!'

'And you think *nothing* of that achievement?' Blanche cried, enraged. 'Well, how could you? My God, you're his sister through and through. You've looked after number one and let everyone else go hang. But now the party's nearly over you find you need other people besides yourself. So you turn for home, and invite yourself to a Christmas that Sybil has created – and I mean *created* – with love and care and skill and imagination and dedication. Like an artist. Just as she's created their marriage and his image. And I wish you could appreciate the immensity of that achievement. But you're like *him*. You think it happens by itself. You set her down as a Martha, and think yourself a superior Mary. Well, I'll tell you what I think about Martha and Mary – *and* Jesus Christ, patronizing the poor wight when he had eaten her supper! – I think your *attitude* is shit! And I said as much to the Sunday School teacher when she told me that story, and she sent me home with a warning note. And after three warning notes I was expelled.'

She was close to tears.

'Don't you dare belittle my mother to me!' she cried. 'Ever!'

Natalie waited the requisite seconds before aiming her reply to the heart. 'But she's not your mother, remember?' Natalie said evenly. 'You were adopted.'

The tears came, hovered, slithered softly down. Blanche wiped them furiously away with the back of her woollen glove, swallowed, controlled herself. 'Do you know,' she said, when she could speak, 'after all this time – and despite the ongoing family battles – I'm so much a Malpas that I tend to forget I was adopted?'

She could face Natalie again, and deliver the next two shots in her usual trenchant fashion. 'But when I *do* remember, I take great comfort from two things. Your brother is not my real father, and I thank God for that. And although Sybil didn't give birth to me I am her daughter by choice, and the product of her upbringing, and I have a greater right to call her my mother than any natural child, because she *chose* me.'

The man had caught up and they exchanged a brief, banal comment about the weather. The dog ran past them, barking joyfully, skittering to a halt by the water's edge.

Natalie's expression was unreadable. An ageing eagle, gaze failing, wings less powerful, she waited until the walker was out of earshot, hooded her eyes, and said, 'Shall we go on?'

In the ensuing silence Blanche realized a truth that had eluded her.

Sybil is one reason why I had Aaron, she thought. I was a damaged child who held a grudge against life from the beginning, and she suffered me while I expiated my parents' sins. In Aaron I could repeat the mothering, and make sure there was no father to spoil things. Oh, I wanted him for his sake and mine, but I also wanted to show Sybil that good works bore good fruit, that loving-kindness was not wasted.

The day was obdurate, the air moist and chill and salty, but Blanche lifted her face to receive it. She trod the wet dark sand exultantly, and revelled in the feeling of completion that yesterday's lovemaking had bestowed on her; from which thought she came naturally to Daniel in the role of lover and father, and from there to the relationship between her own father and herself. The palimpsest of Daniel with Aaron was gradually imposing itelf upon that of Anthony with Blanche. She was resolving something. The father image could be good.

Natalie's harsh deep voice fetched her back to the walk, the talk, the winter morning. 'So you cast Sybil as the angel of the house and Tony as the heartless villain?'

'Neither heartless nor villain,' Blanche said impatiently, resentfully, 'but demanding and destructive, yes, and emotionally immature.'

She improved on this. 'Children need approval and encouragement, need to shine in their parents' eyes. Sybil made us feel we were important, but he set standards too high for us to achieve, and then showed his disappointment when we failed. He could devastate us.'

'And he is the reason why Teddy lacks confidence in himself, why Lydia stopped trying altogether, why I thought, "Sod you! I'm going to be a success, doing things you couldn't possibly approve of – because I want to make you bleed."'

Natalie's voice interrupted again. 'And yet you want to shine in his eyes?'

'That's not true,' Blanche answered peremptorily.

Then realized that it was. She experienced again the deep slow glow of delight when she saw that her father thought Aaron a fine boy, and herself beautiful, and was glad to see her again. He had received her Christmas gift gracefully, worn it with pleasure, allowed her to adjust the smoking cap.

'So you think me a Victorian patriarch?' he had said, appreciating the sly joke at his expense.

And yes, even her gift, meant to be an acerbic comment, was in truth hopeful, affectionate, conciliatory.

Blanche swerved away from this revelation. Her pace quickened. 'Anyway, he can't harm me now because I know myself,' she announced, as if that were the end to any argument.

'Do you indeed?' Natalie drawled, relishing the words as she spoke them. 'What a wise young woman you must be. Who are you?'

The words *I am Blanche Malpas* died unformed on her lips, but anyhow Natalie did not wait for them.

She said, 'Have you no curiosity about your real parents? Surely you must have wondered? The world is littered with adopted adults, searching for a lost childhood.'

A sense of deep unease had been growing in Blanche throughout their conversation. Now her pulse hammered the same question, rapidly, urgently. Who are *you*? *Who* are *you*? *Who are* you?

She answered firmly, trying to talk herself back to normal. 'Naturally, I was curious, and as soon as I was old enough to understand what it meant Sybil told me I was adopted. Later, when I asked further questions, she told me that I was the result of a love affair between two university students. That was as much as she knew. The adoption people apparently match the child as best they can with the adopted parents, but they don't disclose names or identities.'

'You were quite old, when they adopted you.'

'A few months older than Aaron is now,' said Blanche, tight-lipped, dry-mouthed.

'Too young to remember anything about it?'

Again Blanche swerved away, in life as in mind, and stumbled on a piece of driftwood as hard as fossil, that had been tossed up by the sea.

'Steady!' Natalie cautioned, taking her arm.

'Fucking flotsam!' Blanche said, and kicked it aside, and released herself rather forcibly from Natalie's support, and strode on, faster. 'I do remember one thing,' she cried, over her shoulder. 'Sybil saved my life.'

Natalie dropped her cigarette end and ground it into the sand with the heel of her boot. Then, panting slightly from cigarette smoke and exertion, she caught up Blanche, coughing and laughing, but as if the laughter hurt her.

'Saved your life?' she managed to say at last. 'Isn't that rather melodramatic? I understood that you were living with a reputable foster mother.'

The breath was suddenly knocked out of Blanche and she began to wheeze as if she had been running away from a memory that now held her at bay.

She heard a voice that hurt her, hit her, with words that were blows. She felt uncaring hands lift her up, set her down, dispose of her as they would. She smelt the damp cold air of the room to which she was confined. And the time of day was always dusk. As if light would never penetrate.

The memory enfolded her, making respiration difficult, and she remembered something else: the attacks of childhood asthma through which Sybil nursed her until she was ten years old. Against the screaming struggles for air that only calmness and common sense could prevail.

'Sybil saved my life,' Blanche repeated with difficulty, suffocating afresh.

Now as far ahead as they had been far behind, the solitary man walked on and his dog ran to and fro, challenging the sea.

Blanche drew a lungful of merciful air, and turned on Natalie, crying, 'This is a subject that I will not discuss.'

CHAPTER TWENTY-TWO

November 1951

The terraced houses of South London had been built on a grid pattern at the turn of the century for white-collar workers. Streets intersected streets in miles upon miles of sturdy replicas, each containing three or four bedrooms, a parlour with a bay-window, a front-door with a stained-glass pane and a brass knocker, a strip of sour soil at the front and a longer strip at the back. Here pretensions to gentility waged a daily struggle against poverty, and conventions were rigidly observed. In the early nineteen-fifties, respectability reigned.

The tall fair young woman who stood on the whitened doorstep, impeccably dressed and gravely pretty, was hampered by a large paper parcel and a half-grown golden Labrador. One gloved hand hauled on the puppy's lead, the other lifted the glistening knocker and rapped twice, not too loudly, just firmly enough to state *I am here*. Then she drew a deep breath to steady herself, and straightened up to give the impression of maturity and authority.

The woman who opened the door had no such need to compose herself. Her steps were brisk, her sensible shoes brightly polished, her face shining with soap and water, her hands hard-worked. Durability was woven into the hand-knitted pink jersey and home-sewn brown skirt. Her blue overall creaked with starch. Her hair was confined in tight grey waves. An honest clean industrious person, one thought at first glance. But Sybil, looking into North Sea eyes, suffered misgivings and ruined her introduction in consequence. Besides, the puppy was young and still frisky, despite Tony's training.

'I've come to see – it's about – that is, my name is – down, Flora, down!'

Mrs Newton set her right on all points, drily and directly.

'You're Mrs Malpas, aren't you? Come to see the little girl. I'm afraid you'll have to leave the dog outside. I don't allow animals in the house.'

'Oh. Yes. Of course. What shall I do with Flora?'

'I should fasten the lead to the porch, if I was you.'

'Oh, but she's very young and strong and not used to being left by herself. I'm afraid she might pull free and run out into the traffic.'

Mrs Newton sighed and said, 'Then you can bring it through and tie it up in the backyard.'

'I do hope I'm not inconveniencing you,' said Sybil, slightly breathless with the puppy, 'I know I'm a few minutes early.'

She had been nearly an hour early: sitting in the municipal park on a chill bench under the winter trees; thinking over the reasons for her decision and the scene between herself and Anthony that had preceded them; waiting out her time before daring to cross the road.

'You can't inconvenience me,' said Mrs Newton, pleased to advertise her efficiency. 'I'm always ready. That's what I tell people. Anybody can come whenever they like. They may find me working, but they'll never find me wanting. Would you like to step inside?'

The hall of the house was bleak and brown and cold.

'You'll excuse me if I show you into the kitchen,' said Mrs Newton, 'but it's the cosiest room downstairs. I don't light a fire in the parlour until four o'clock. Mr Newton comes home at six, you see, and we sit there of an evening when the children are in bed.'

The kitchen managed to have all the ingredients of cosiness without achieving either its feeling or effect. Looking round, Sybil felt that the room had been cleaned and tidied into total submission, and wondered whether Mr Newton was in the same condition.

'Is this one of your foster children?' Sybil asked politely, of the small boy standing by the french window, forehead pressed glumly to the glass.

'Yes, this is Arthur. Where's your manners, Arthur? Say how-do-you-do to Mrs Malpas.'

He repeated the question dully, and Sybil acknowledged it gracefully.

'And let the young lady through while she ties her dog up.

203

Think, Arthur! Think of others! Now, Mrs Malpas, tie it up to that hook by the coal-bin.'

Sybil did as she was told and returned with dirty gloves. Behind her the puppy leaped and yelped inconsolably.

'Arthur's been sent home from school. Stomach pains again,' said Mrs Newton with obscure satisfaction. 'But it isn't pains, it's shamming, isn't it, Arthur? You and I know better than Miss Jenkins, don't we? We've been to the doctor and he says it's all in the mind.'

The boy hunched his shoulders, and stared apathetically out on to the concrete backyard.

'I hope he'll be better soon,' said Sybil, disquieted. 'Are you looking after many children now?'

'Just four of them. There's a brother and sister at school. They come of a problem family. They'll be in at four o'clock. And then Arthur and Blanch.'

She pronounced the name as if it were akin to *blench*, and so lost all its grace.

'I see. Where is Blanche? Is she having a nap?' Sybil asked.

'She's in the back bedroom, in disgrace,' said Mrs Newton, very bright and self-righteous. 'I may be old-fashioned, but I believe in punishing children when they do wrong. That's the way they learn to do right. Arthur was a wrong-doer. You were a wrong-doer, weren't you, Arthur?'

The boy breathed on the glass and rubbed it clear with his cuff. He said, 'Yes,' indifferently, to the grey concrete bunker, the high black fence, the whimpering puppy.

Mrs Newton drew herself up. Her voice was strident, her stance formidable. 'Arthur! Turn round and answer like a gentle-man when I'm speaking to you. And kindly remember my name, if you please.'

Obediently, sullenly, he presented an unsmiling face, resentful eyes. 'Yes, Mrs Newton. I was a wrong-doer, and I'm sorry for it.'

'Tell the young lady how naughty you used to be.'

'Oh, there's no need,' said Sybil quickly. She smiled at him, to show that she was friendly, but he would not respond. He knew better than to trust an adult, though that adult was young and lovely and her goodwill shone in the dark kitchen.

'There's no need,' Sybil repeated. 'I had two older brothers.

204

Both, tragically, killed in the war. And I remember them as very *mischievous*.'

She stressed the word gently, and smiled upon Mrs Newton to show that, though no reproach was intended, one should not transform a minor peccadillo into a major transgression. Her eyes were frank and untroubled, her cheeks still faintly rounded, her mouth full-lipped and generous. She had chosen to wear her best suit, hoping to look older than her twenty-four years. The slender waist cinched in by a narrow corset, the long full skirt swirling above slim ankles, the pretty blouse and stiletto heels betrayed instead a youthful love of dress and a pleasing vanity. She was everything that Mrs Newton was not, and had never been.

'Boys *are* mischievous,' Sybil insisted.

'This was more than mischief,' said Mrs Newton, refusing to be robbed of her prey, determined not to have his sins diminished. 'Wasn't it, Arthur?'

She folded her hands over the stomach of her blue overall and stared him down. He hung his head.

'Well, whatever it was,' said Sybil, determined not to be used as a whip, 'I'm sure he won't do it again.'

Mrs Newton considered her ironically. 'You've never had much to do with children, I dare say.'

'I taught children in my father's Sunday School, and I teach schoolchildren now.'

'Ah, but you only have them part-time. When you've got them full-time they need discipline. I never lay a finger on them, mind!' Drawing herself up, as if in outrage that anyone should imagine she did. 'I don't have to,' she added grimly. 'I keep them properly fed and washed and clothed, and nobody could say I didn't.' These facts settled, she confided her invincible remedy. 'I control by will-power. Sheer will-power.'

You break their hearts and spirits, Sybil thought. She said firmly, 'If you don't mind,' inventing an excuse, 'I have another appointment to keep, so please may I see the little girl?'

Cheated of her effect, Mrs Newton replied sarcastically, 'Oh, you can see her all right. No trouble about that. But she's a right little vixen, I'm telling you. I'd be less than honest if I said she wasn't. You won't take to her – nor her to you, if I know anything. She's not your sort. I won't give a bad child a good character for the sake of getting her adopted. I'm not one of them that sheds their burdens easy. I was always a one for telling the truth.'

'Nevertheless, I should like to see her, if you please.'

'This way then,' said Mrs Newton, in a voice that despaired of those who would not be advised for their own good.

The house, with its downtrodden carpets, its hushed net curtains and uncertain wallpapers, had a dejected atmosphere, and this spiritual misery was enhanced by its state of cleanliness. The worn linoleum shone, the drab furniture covers were brushed threadbare, an odour of carbolic soap and bleach predominated. November seeped through the walls and numbed the air.

From the landing window a thin cat could be seen rummaging in the backyard dustbin.

Mrs Newton rapped on the windowpane. 'Dirty habits,' she explained, 'I will not tolerate.'

The cat slunk away.

The back room was no more than a box, frigid, murky and desolate, and had probably been chosen for just these reasons. The cheerless rayon curtains were closed, but did not quite meet across the window, so disclosing a timorous splinter of light. The walls had been distempered during the war when materials were short and choice limited. The result, an uneven cream colour hand-blocked with a sponge dipped in green paint, resembled parsley sauce. A stolid brown cot stood in the middle, battered by years of imprisoned occupants, its side pulled up and firmly locked. There were no pictures on the parsley sauce walls, no carpet on the scrubbed wooden floor, no shade on the dim electric light bulb in the ceiling, no other furniture, no sign of a toy or cuddly animal. There was nothing for any scapegoat to do here except to contemplate its solitary wretchedness.

Driven back upon her resources, the child had shown her rage and frustration by the only means left open to her. She had managed to tumble her pillow and eiderdown over the side of the cot, to tug off her shoes and socks and throw them out too; and then, these tasks accomplished, had cried herself out and fallen asleep.

'Temper, temper!' Mrs Newton whispered to herself, picking up the fallen objects, savouring the evidence of natural viciousness. 'Now do you see what I mean?'

But Sybil stepped softly forward, almost holding her breath so

206

as not to disturb the child, and looked down on this rejected fruit of a casual union.

Arms outflung, she sprawled like an abandoned rag doll. A black fuzz of hair, an ivory skin, a small pink mouth pursed up with suffering, cheeks streaked with grief.

'She's defiant,' said Mrs Newton, 'that's what she is. Defiant. But give me time,' she promised herself.

Probing Sybil's silence, she added, 'Dark, isn't she? I did wonder whether she hadn't a touch of the tar-brush. I'll not go so far as to say Negro, but it might be Pakistani.'

'A touch of the Mediterranean, perhaps,' Sybil corrected her crisply. 'Spanish or Italian babies are very dark.'

Mrs Newton sucked her lips together. 'The mother was ladylike,' she conceded, 'but you never can tell these days. Some white women like to go with black men, you know.' And she screwed up her eyes. 'Perversion, I call it. And the bloods don't mix.' She surveyed the present culprit. 'It would explain a lot,' said Mrs Newton, standing in judgement on a case not proven.

She bent over and shook the child awake before Sybil could cry, 'No, please don't disturb her!'

For the sleep was sound and deep and sorely needed.

'Get up, Blanch,' Mrs Newton urged. 'There's someone to see you.'

The child came to consciousness with a sob, saw her jailer, and began to pull herself up by the bars of the cot, crying, 'No! No! No!'

'What did I tell you?' Mrs Newton demanded, hands outspread, vindicated.

Now the child turned its head to see the stranger, and Sybil found herself staring into a pair of shining dark eyes. Shock on one side, curiosity on the other held woman and child silent and motionless for several seconds.

Then Sybil said, 'Hello, Blanche?' And looked to Mrs Newton for permission. 'I've brought her – could I give her . . . ?'

'So long as it isn't sweets,' said that lady, who could take control of any other gift when the visitor had gone.

For once they were in agreement.

'Oh, not sweets,' Sybil protested. 'So bad for their teeth and appetites. A soft toy.'

The child was standing up, holding the cot-rail, observing them closely.

'She's got plenty of toys,' Mrs Newton added, 'and clothes. The mother sends them. None of them suitable. She's got no idea. Expensive, too. They're all in the cupboard. You can see them. I say to everyone, you can search the house, I've got nothing to hide.'

'I've brought a teddy bear.'

The first friend of childhood.

'She's got one already,' Mrs Newton said triumphantly. 'Haven't you, Blanch? Tell the lady you've got a teddy.'

The child's face became the face it should have been, open and joyful. 'Tedd-y! Tedd-y! Tedd-y!' she cried, and beat the rail with one small soft fist.

Under guise of instructing the child, Mrs Newton gave Sybil the benefit of her long experience with malefactors. Her tone became silky, insinuating, faintly obscene in its malice. 'Teddy's been shut in the cupboard because you've been a naughty girl, hasn't he? When you're naughty we punish poor Teddy too, don't we? Oh, dear me, poor Teddy. Locked away in the cold and the dark.'

The child's mouth opened and shut silently over words whose meaning was known, even if their pronunciation was uncertain. Cupboard. Naughty. Punished. Locked away.

'Poor Teddy!' Mrs Newton crooned. 'Is Teddy crying, do you think? Have you made poor Teddy cry, Blanch?'

The child sat down suddenly and began to wail. Tears slithered down her face: abundant, transparent, twin-tracked. Her mouth squared with grief.

'Yes, you're sorry now, aren't you?' Mrs Newton said, relishing the spectacle she had provoked. 'Sorry you were a naughty girl. Tell me you're sorry, Blanch. Say *sorry*!'

Sybil could bear the inquisition no longer. She bent forward and picked up the sobbing child, laid a warm cheek against the wet cheek, cradled the racked body. Young and inexperienced as she was, she knew that adoption would not simply be a question of asking and receiving, but a long, slow, official process. Until the child became theirs Mrs Newton was in charge of her, and Sybil guessed how much power the woman could wield, how many difficulties she could cause, how many torments she could inflict.

So she thought, as she continued to hush and soothe Blanche, that she must placate the monster for the child's sake.

'How long have you been a foster-mother, Mrs Newton?'

'Over twenty years,' was the answer, delivered curtly.

'And how many children have you had in that time?'

'I've stopped counting.' Curtly again. Then, curious, incredulous, 'Are you sure she's prepared to sign? The mother, I mean.'

Sybil could not bear to look at her, and spoke into the black fuzz of hair.

'Oh, yes. She is a relative. As you probably realize. From the name. The name being unusual.'

'I see,' said Mrs Newton, and evidently saw a great deal more than she said. 'You've been long enough making up your minds, then?'

'I'm afraid I don't quite understand you.'

'If you knew about Blanch why didn't you adopt her when she was born? That's what I mean.'

Sybil hesitated, and then admitted, 'I – we, that is – didn't hear about Blanche until recently.'

'Ah!' Mrs Newton said, satisfied. 'Then I'll give you some good advice. Number one: from what I know of the mother, she could change her mind right up to the last minute. Number two: if she doesn't, then make sure she keeps her disance, because she's one of them dog-in-the-manger types. Don't want the child herself and won't let nobody else have her.'

Sybil said diplomatically, not committing herself, 'We shall do our best for Blanche, in whatever way is necessary.'

'Yes,' mused Mrs Newton. 'I dare say.' She picked up the pillow and eiderdown and smoothed the wrinkled undersheet. She retrieved the shoes and socks from where they had fallen.

Blanche had quietened and was lying on the shoulder of this sympathetic stranger, giving an occasional hiccup or snort of grief, sucking two fingers noisily.

'Aren't you going to give her your lovely new teddy bear, then?' Mrs Newton asked slyly.

'No, I don't think so. She wants her own bear.'

Mrs Newton permitted herself a small tight smile. 'It's just as well. She'd only have thrown it down,' she admitted. 'She's chock-full of defiance and bad temper, you see.'

'I would call it intelligence,' said Sybil, 'and loyalty.'

She tried out her own authority. 'Blanche is quiet, now. And I think she's been punished enough, and learned her lesson, don't you? So could she have her own teddy bear back?'

Something about Sybil must have impressed Mrs Newton because the woman opened a cupboard in the wall, and held out the missing companion. He was almost as large as the child: silky-furred, suede-pawed, beautifully stitched, with a neat black nose, quizzical boot-button eyes and a wide confident smile.

'*She* sent it,' said Mrs Newton. 'The mother. Blanch thinks the world of it. What she won't do for me she'll do for Teddy. Funny, isn't it? How their minds work.'

The mother had spent a great deal of money on this toy, an aristocrat among bears. Sybil could imagine her walking into a shop and saying imperiously, 'I want a teddy bear. The best you've got.'

He made nonsense of the humble, sunny creature that Sybil had chosen, and for which she had paid thirty shillings: one half her week's housekeeping money. She resolved to donate the inferior bear to the Christmas raffle at her father's church.

'There,' said Sybil, giving the beloved one into Blanche's arms, trying to set them both down in the cot. 'There he is. Safe and sound.'

But the child held fast to both Sybil and the bear, and would not let go.

Natalie said, seemingly at random, 'Have you still got the teddy bear I gave you for your first birthday?'

It was shocking to have her thoughts invaded in such a way, and Blanche stammered, 'The bear? The bear?'

'I expect he's showing the length of his days, by now,' said Natalie conversationally.

Blanche replied with difficulty, 'Still lovingly preserved.'

'They told me he was your favourite toy.'

More than that, much more, Blanche wanted to say, but could not. They had walked almost to the end of the beach, and she began to perceive.

'Let's sit down for a minute,' said Natalie, indicating a granite boulder. 'I have something I must tell you.'

'I can stand,' said Blanche loudly, moving away, clenching her hands in her pockets.

She managed to keep her voice under control. Her scarlet

greatcoat blazed against the grey seascape. She said, through stiff lips, 'I can guess what you are going to tell me.'

Natalie also stood. They had both lost their colour, were the same shade of old ivory, against which the lipstick flared gallantly. Blanche's black unruly hair had youth and life, but was still akin to Natalie's wild white mop. They were both tall and fierce, and they faced each other as adversaries rather than mother and daughter.

Blanche said bitterly, 'But after all this time, to what purpose?'

The question covered past, present and future.

CHAPTER TWENTY-THREE

'It's all gone wrong,' said Natalie, with savage regret.

She would have liked to hold her daughter's arm or stroke the untamed head, and dared not, knowing that intimacy was forbidden, that she had barred herself from it.

'I've angered you, talking about Sybil, instead of setting myself right with you,' she cried. 'I never meant the conversation to go as far as this, I wasn't going to tell you. I just wanted us to be friends.'

Blanche made a gesture that repudiated the excuse.

Natalie said, 'Well if you won't sit down, I must.' And lowered herself stiffly on to the boulder. She watched Blanche humbly, fearfully.

'You must have the impression that I came down here to make trouble,' she began, 'but I didn't. The party, as you so aptly put it, is nearly over for me. I was facing a solitary Christmas and an eye operation that will at best leave me partly blind. But don't mistake me. I never intended to mention that either. I didn't come begging for pity or charity. I just felt that it was time to reconcile myself to Tony and Sybil, to see you and the boy, to draw a little comfort and goodwill from the family circle, and to go away again without upsetting anybody or asking for anything. And instead of that I've stirred up a lot of old trouble, alienated you, and betrayed myself.'

Blanche said drily, not looking at her, 'Perhaps you are not entirely to blame. There's something about the Malpases at Christmas that brings out the worst in everyone. Katrina wanted to make her peace and incited war.'

Natalie said to herself, 'In one way or another, the three of us came here to be reconciled.' She shrugged, sadly, philosophically, rummaged in capacious pockets for her silver cigarette case.

'It wasn't what I expected, anyhow,' she said. 'Remembering Christmas Past, wondering about Christmas Future, having Christmas Present rammed down my throat.'

She fitted the cigarette into its holder, sat smoking and thinking.

'Everything had changed,' she said to the glowing tip. 'Tony used to be a man of power. Electric. He could have lit up New York. Ruled the world. I used to wonder how Sybil would manage to contain him. She didn't, of course. She was too clever to try. She let him out on a long lead, and made herself a cosy little nest and lined it with children, and eventually drew him back. She's done that for forty years, gradually making herself indispensable to him, shortening the lead, fetching him home. And now, by Christ, when she's about to have him chained up for good, she's not so sure she wants him!'

She gave a loud harsh laugh, then coughed and coughed. She gasped for air, apologized. Tears glittered in her eyes.

'I'm all right!' she cried fiercely, as Blanche made a half-hearted move towards her. 'The smoke went down the wrong way.'

She coughed again, smothered the cough, brooded, inhaled less deeply.

'That's why I'm against marriage,' she said. 'It's all about conformity, whittling people down to fit some mediocre image, rather than expanding to contain them both. Tony didn't need a wife. He should have had a faithful housekeeper and a string of fascinating mistresses. You didn't know him when he was young. He was brilliant, handsome, charming – a bastard, as I've said, but an outstanding man. Sybil's turned him into a crusty old curmudgeon who can't manage without her for a couple of weeks.'

She looked up at her daughter, and grimaced a smile. 'That's the other side of the picture,' she said. 'No doubt you will disagree.'

Blanche said critically, 'I heard you persuading him to go on holiday with you.'

'Yes. Why not? I was his favourite companion once. But I'm old now, and he's older still. I can't prise his carpet slippers off the hearth.'

'It sounded', said Blanche, 'as though you'd done this often.'

'Quite right. We had.'

'And yet family legend has it that you, personally, disappeared into the wild blue yonder in your youth, never to be seen again until this Christmas Eve.'

'Family legend was meant to do just that. In fact, Tony and I kept in touch for years. His work sometimes took him abroad, and I was freelance, so I could join him for a couple of days or for a holiday. Later I was able to afford a modest *pied-à-terre* in London, and we met there. We'd been very close, you see, until his marriage. Occasionally he told Sybil he'd seen me. Most of the time he didn't.'

'Was all this secrecy necessary?'

Natalie took a last deep puff, dropped her cigarette butt, and ground it out on the pebbles with the heel of her boot.

'Well, yes it was, rather,' she drawled, 'because Sybil was very possessive and Tony was afraid of upsetting her. So I went along with that. For his sake, of course, not for hers. And all that about her choosing you was sweet Fanny Adams. The choice wasn't hers. It was mine. I chose to give you away.'

Blanche took a few steps nearer, guarded but curious. 'But if you dislike her so much then why did you allow her to adopt me?'

Natalie shrugged, and said roughly, 'It was Tony's idea. Tony thought it the best solution. He was my confidant, you see. In those days it was social death to produce an illegitimate baby. Nowadays, as you know, you're accepted as a single parent – and probably you can get a grant for doing it!' She laughed and coughed. 'Anyway, your worries and Sybil's more or less coincided. Sybil miscarried their first child and had some kind of breakdown, and you were giving a lot of trouble to the foster-mother – Mrs Whoever-she-was – and I was broke and living abroad, which meant that Tony was responsible for everybody. He had his work to do, and this wasn't his scene anyway. He couldn't cope. So bringing you and Sybil together solved our problems. And, as I've said, I acknowledge her qualities. I knew she'd make a good traditional mother. Besides, the other choices would have been fairly dreary for you – staying in care and belonging to no one, or being adopted by strangers. At least you were in my brother's family.'

Blanche thought of the child whose interests had never come first, whom these adults had ignored or used, and said sorely, 'I never knew that.'

'There's a lot you don't know,' said Natalie forcefully, 'and I've told you more than I intended to, anyway, so let's leave it at that.'

She saw Blanche's face set against the world and turned away from her, saying, 'It's done me no good, as usual. If I were inclined to be paranoic I would judge that life put me up in order to knock me down. And now I think we should go back.'

She got to her feet with some difficulty, brusquely refusing Blanche's reluctant hand, and dusted the back of her cloak.

'Growing old is a bugger,' she said stoically. 'You get stiffer and tire more quickly, you need your comforts, you can't hold your drink like you used to, and you can't pick up men unless you pay them. I've never had to do that, and I'm not starting now, but it was damned good while it lasted.'

Her enemy now, Blanche said coldly, dangerously, 'Was *I* the consequence of picking up a man?'

Natalie's face was colourless. 'Good God, no. He was the love of my life. A brief but beautiful affair,' she said wryly, beginning to walk away. 'The best things never last, but crap sticks to you for a lifetime.'

Slightly mollified, Blanche asked cautiously, walking by her side, watching her old, cold face, 'Who is or was he?'

Natalie answered more gently, 'That – if you'll forgive me – I can't tell you.'

'Why not?'

'Because it would invade his privacy.'

Blanche said angrily, 'I have a right to know about him, just as he has a right to know about me. He and I have rights that are nothing to do with *you* . . .'

And stopped, thinking of Daniel and Aaron.

'Your father knew that you existed and where you were,' Natalie said abruptly. 'He could have introduced himself if he wanted. It was his decision not to do that. Sorry! I didn't mean to hurt you again. I should have stayed away and kept my mouth shut.'

Raw at heart, white-faced, Blanche strode on.

'I'm as selfish as Tony,' said Natalie, making a dreary joke of a sad truth. 'I go my way and damn the consequences, and then the consequences catch up with me. It seems ironic that the best thing I ever did for you was to hand you over to Sybil.'

Again she would have liked to touch her daughter's hand, to

dissolve the distance between them, to be friends again; but did not know how to and so reverted to herself. 'No, let's face it, I wasn't cut out to be a mother. I'm one of life's wanderers.'

She laughed then, matching Blanche stride for stride, boasting to keep up her spirits. 'God, what a life I've led. Staying up all night and working the next day. Travelling to assignments, or wherever my fancy led me. Making friends and acquaintances all over the world. I can set foot in most countries and know someone who'll offer me a bed for the night. How many people can say that?' She paused. 'And I'm glad I didn't stay in England,' she said defiantly. 'Too insular for me. Too claustrophobic. It was more difficult to track you down to Cornwall than it would be to hop off to Istanbul.'

The man and his dog had left the beach and were half-way up the cliff path. They could hear the dog barking faintly. The light was poor, the shore uninhabited, the sea comfortless, the coast line forbidding. Natalie absorbed the scene for a few moments: old and wild and desolate. 'I expect they tart this place up for the holiday season,' she observed contemptuously, 'but I'd rather see it at this time of year, particularly as I shall never see it again. I prefer beauty to be stripped and stark.' She stopped to face her silent daughter. 'We've said the important things, and you're sufficiently like me to despise small talk. Just drive me back and let me go. No insincere farewells.'

At half past noon the telephone rang at Minions.

'Sybil?' High and strained. 'It's Blanche. I'm phoning you from the village kiosk. Look, I shan't be in for lunch. No, don't save any. I don't want it. Can you manage without me for a couple of hours or so?' With grudging good manners, 'Thanks. That's much appreciated.' High again, 'What's happened? Natalie's spilled the beans about my adoption and I'm too sick to face the family right now.' Adamant, 'No, you can't do anything for me, apart from looking after Aaron. I need time to myself.' With angry impatience, 'Of course, I'm upset. I'm so bloody upset I can't think straight. Sybil, I can't talk any more. Good-bye for now. See you later.'

*

At two o'clock the mouse-coloured felt hat, coral scarf, bottle-green coat and a whiff of patchouli, announced that Mrs Laity had arrived to give and to glean.

'Mrs Laity!' Sybil cried, her trance broken. 'I didn't expect to see you! Do come in.'

'I come as soon as I could,' said Mrs Laity, unwinding her coral scarf. 'Mary Sampson tell me that your 'usband's sister is off upcountry today, and the doctor called here yesterday, and the little girl got the German measles. Is that right?'

'I'm afraid so,' Sybil replied automatically. Her thoughts were sombre, and with Blanche. Yet in spite of her trouble the speed of the village grapevine entertained her.

'Shouldn't be surprised if Ben don't catch it, too,' said Mrs Laity cheerfully. 'Ye-es. You looking after her here, are you? I thought so. I tell Mary, "Mrs Malpas won't let Edward go home with one sick child and another sickening. She'll stay on and look after them here." So I come to see what I could do for you, and I called in at the post office to see my sister Chrystal, and she say you don't have to bother none about shopping. You just phone your order through and Josiah'll bring it over.'

'How very good of her. Oh, you are kind, Mrs Laity!' Sybil cried, and despite the impending crisis with Blanche she felt relieved and grateful, because help was forthcoming when most necessary.

'Well, we known each other some years now, Mrs Malpas,' hanging her hat on a hook behind the kitchen door, 'and it aren't the first time we've been through this!' Significantly.

'I'd forgotten,' said Sybil, helping her off with her coat. 'Blanche and Edward!'

'The master was in America, and you was on your own down here, expecting Lydia.'

'Easter, nineteen fifty-nine.'

'And then there was that New Year when they went down with the chicken-pox.'

'And Tony had to go back to Bristol for the beginning of the spring term.'

Seasoned warriors, the two women had taken up arms in many a domestic battle.

'He'll be returning to Bristol tomorrow,' Sybil said, putting the kettle on the boiling plate. 'Blanche moved Aaron's cot and

217

her bed into his study last night, you see, and put his bookcase and desk on the landing.'

They exchanged a look of complicity. Mrs Laity tittered. 'Well, men aren't no use at times like this. Best get them out o' the way. No, no, don't you bother with no tea for me. I had a cup just now with my daughter Phyllis, and told her the news. Her girls sent some comics for 'Enrietta.' She produced them from her patchwork holdall, and received thanks graciously. 'Now, where do you want me to start?'

'Could you strip the bed nearest the window in Lydia's room and make it up afresh? I'm going to put Henny in there, and then if Blanche decides to stay on for a few days she can have her room back. There should be enough sheets and pillowcases for that, but I'm on the last of everything now. and I haven't a clean towel in the place. I wasn't expecting to need so much extra linen. I wondered if the launderette was open in Helston, or if the laundry van would call—'

But Mrs Laity waved these ideas away.

'Oh, don't you bother about tha-at. Mat Kellow's mother'll do your washing. She don't do no bed and breakfasts this time of year, and she's got that big machine of hers. She won't charge as much as the laundry, and they'll be done, dried and ironed, and back for New Year's Eve. If you bag everything up I'll tell Mat to call round and collect it tonight.'

That problem solved, she donned a floral overall, picked up the vacuum-cleaner, and departed to make order out of chaos.

'All right then, 'Enrietta?' Sybil heard her call cheerfully, as she reached the top of the stairs. 'And how are you today? Feeling better, are 'ee? I brought you some comics from our Susan and Angela.'

'Oh, how *sweet* of them, Mrs Laity! I haven't seen Susan and Angela for *ages* . . .'

Sybil closed the door on the rest of their conversation, and the smile that Henrietta always brought to her lips gradually faded. Then she sat at the kitchen table, hands clasped in front of her, and waited for Natalie's daughter to come back.

At three o'clock Blanche walked in, white-lipped and unforgiving: the injured child who had been rescued more than thirty years ago. And it was to the child that Sybil spoke, standing up to face her, using an old phrase from their past.

'Is it to be *my* fault?' she asked gently.

In Blanche's expression hostility strove with remembrance. Assailed, she cried, 'It was wrong to hide the truth. You should have told me.'

'*When* should I have told you?' Sybil asked composedly. And as Blanche sought for an answer, she said, 'As a child? You were too insecure to have your identity threatened. As an adolescent? You might have nourished some romantic notion about Natalie that would have been – I can assure you – most cruelly dispelled.'

Still Blanche clung to her rage as to a spar. 'You could have told me when I was an adult, at any rate. Why not?'

Sybil echoed Blanche's question to Natalie. 'After all that time? To what purpose?'

The silence between them was a wrestle of wills.

Then Sybil said, 'I don't claim to be a perfect mother and Tony was not the best of fathers. But parents are not gods – only human beings who can make mistakes. You know that, being a parent yourself. So tell me what really troubles you. Oh, my dear, don't look like that!'

She held out her arms, and Natalie's daughter came into them like a child, and cried out her accusation. 'You didn't choose me, like you said. No one chose me. My mother didn't want me. My father wouldn't acknowledge me. Daddy – Tony – thought of me as a problem to be solved. And you accepted a second-hand child because you had lost your own. I wasn't special, as you always told me. I was nobody. And nobody wanted me. And though it's ridiculous, and I've been telling myself for three hours that it's ridiculous, I mind. I bloody well mind.'

'*I* wanted you,' said Sybil, 'and *I* chose to adopt you. And though one should never have favourites, you are sometimes closer to me than my natural children.'

Blanche sobbed as she had once sobbed for the loss of her bear. 'But I feel adrift, lost, as if I don't belong to anyone. I'm remembering what it used to be like. The nightmares, the asthma, the terror of being locked away and forgotten, of being lost. I thought I'd been cured of that. I love my son and I love my work – I even love that daft Irishman. Why am I not cured?'

'I don't think we are ever cured of childhood traumas. We

learn how to cope with them, even to put them to good use, but they're always there.'

'Like the teeth planted in the earth that grew up overnight as an army of soldiers. I loathed that story. I used to dream about it.' She sobbed again. 'And I feel exactly like I used to: unlovable and unwelcome. It makes a devil of me! No wonder Daddy – Tony – and I fought. He didn't want me, and I didn't want him, and we were stuck with each other.'

Sybil's embrace was warm and soft and resolute. She smelled faintly, deliciously, of the lemon verbena sachets she hung in wardrobes and tucked at the bottom of drawers. 'That's not so,' she answered, keeping her tone sensible, neutral. 'You're the child of his twin sister. His niece. A blood tie. You and he fought because you were too much alike. And he *is* proud of you, and he *does* love you – and I believe that he loves Aaron too, though he wouldn't admit that, even to himself.'

She rested her chin on Blanche's wild head and held her more closely. She patted her back softly, rhythmically, soothing her. The closed door and the distant noise of the vacuum-cleaner gave them a measure of privacy, preventing Blanche's deep, torn sobs from being overheard.

CHAPTER TWENTY-FOUR

October 1951

The letter from Natalie, bearing an Austrian postmark, arrived on a Saturday morning in the second month of Sybil's retreat from life, and Anthony read it over his solitary breakfast, frowning. His sister wrote as she lived: largely, expressively, directly, with force and passion. Her writing drove across the pages.

Angie's place

Dearest Tony,
I'm screaming for help! Mrs Thing – I never can
remember her name, but you know it anyway, and
have her address – has written another stinking letter. She
says Blanche is destructive and aggressive, and Mrs
Thing's nerves won't stand for it. She says she'll have to
charge an extra five pounds a month if she's to go on
fostering her, and I owe three months' keep anyway, and
if I don't do something about it she'll be forced to
reconsider the present arrangements. Etc. That kind of
crap! Actually, I don't think she'd refuse to keep Blanche,
she seemed a penny-pinching conscientious sort who
would put up with anything if she were paid enough.
Which brings me to the other point. I'm broke, Tony
love. Not my fault, either. I've been camping here on
charity, bread and scrape for weeks, waiting for my
Russian visa to come through. The moment it arrives I'm
off on an assignment, so I can't deal with Mrs Thing and
Blanche. Will you cope? I know you will! A thousand
thanks and may God bless – even if I don't believe in
him. I'll send you a postcard from Leningrad. My love,
always, Tasha

For several minutes Anthony brooded on the unexpected and unwanted turns of fortune, and how trouble begat trouble, and why a desired child should die and an unwanted child persist in surviving. 'As if I hadn't enough problems!' he remarked bitterly. 'Just when I need to concentrate on this new project. And there's the blasted shopping to be done this morning, and yet another hour of tedium at the launderette!'

An intellectual Gulliver, tormented by Lilliputian domestic worries, he raged outwardly and inwardly. During the last six weeks, since Sybil miscarried their first baby, he had become aware of the numberless demands made upon a woman's time. True, the district nurse called in regularly, and a temporary help cleaned their flat once a week, but for the most part he was forced to look after himself and Sybil, and the pettiness of a housewife's world astounded him. He was aghast at the hours consumed in mundane tasks and the mindless slog of doing them repeatedly. He was further infuriated by the lack of female family help, to which a man was surely entitled in times of crisis.

There was Sybil lying upstairs since the first week in September, no use to herself or him. It had been a bad miscarriage, and the doctor advised them to wait a year or two before trying again, but she was physically recovered, thank God. Yet instead of coming to terms with the loss and the deferred hope, she stayed in bed in a silent stupor, or cried at nothing at all. She should have been on her feet a month since. Still, that was that, and when the wife didn't come up to scratch a man should be able to turn to his mother or mother-in-law, but where were they, damn it?

Mrs Outram was busy nursing Sybil's father, who had suffered a mild stroke, and Mrs Malpas was no damned good as a mother and never had been. A remarkable woman, mind you. Handsome, high-handed, quick-witted, a first-class brain, but useless with children. He and Natalie had stumbled up, rather than been brought up, with a succession of amateur nursemaids who seemed interested only in alcohol or men. He could not have been more than six years old when he heard one neighbour say to another, 'That Mrs Malpas is no better mother than a cat!' He had observed cats closely after that remark, seeking the truth of the statement, but as all of them appeared to be devoted to their offspring he failed to understand the analogy. Now, for a few moments, he pondered the saying afresh, wondering why this animal should be so slighted, and actually looked up 'cat' in *Brewer's Dictionary of Phrase and Fable.* Failing to find the appropriate phrase, he returned to his present tribulations.

The financial situation was a thorny one. Tasha was no good at managing money. Never had been. He'd helped her out and more than helped her out, several times before, as well as giving her all his savings when the child was born. And now he had to cough up three months' keep and renegotiate the terms. How did Tasha suppose he would do that on an assistant lecturer's salary of four hundred and fifty a year, with Sybil no longer working as a teacher? The truth of the matter was that Tasha did not think at all. What a lot of problems it would have solved if she had miscarried and Sybil's baby had been born.

He indulged himself for a while, musing on this happier prospect, before connecting one with the other. He sat for a long time while the temperature of his coffee dropped from lukewarm to cold. Then he drew a deep breath, smoothed the mane of black hair with both hands, adjusted his tie in the mirror, and walked slowly and thoughtfully upstairs.

The bursar's secretary, acknowledged as an expert in such matters, had described him as the handsomest man on the staff. Sybil, turning wearily, hopelessly, towards him, thought him the handsomest man in the world. The first sight of that lordly head and imperious black eyes, that air of total self-possession, the hawk-like features, his stature and bearing had changed the course of her life. Inwardly, she knelt before him.

The Labrador puppy for which she had longed, which had indeed been bestowed on her as a consolation for losing the baby, was lying on the bed beside her, equally dejected. It opened its eyes as Anthony dominated the little bedroom, and then closed them again, renouncing hopes of a walk. The atmosphere became tense, and Sybil, watching her husband stride up and down, was reminded of a lion stalking its cage.

He paused before her breakfast tray and assessed her appetite. 'You haven't eaten anything!' he said accusingly.

Two thick unevenly sliced rounds of blackened toast dotted with unsoftened butter, and a dollop of jam on a saucer, lay untouched. A cup half full of chestnut brown tea also bore witness against her.

'I didn't . . . feel like it,' said Sybil diplomatically, and could not have been blamed, but was.

'You *must* make an effort, Syb,' he said reproachfully.

Her eyes filled with tears that she tried to hide. He sat beside her and lifted one limp hand to his lips, then fondled it. He hesitated. He plunged.

'Syb, I've had an idea that you may or may not like, but whatever decision you take – and the decision is entirely yours – this must always remain a secret between us. In fact, but for the special circumstances in which we now find ourselves, I should never have mentioned it even to you.'

She pushed herself up on one elbow. He had intrigued her.

Considerate now, and charming, Anthony said, 'Before I begin, let me fluff up the pillows and make you comfortable. Then you can sit up while I tell you a strange tale.'

Sybil was crying again, yet in a way that gave him hope, for these were not the weak despondent trickles of loss but tears of rage and compassion. Now she accepted his handkerchief, blew her nose vigorously, wiped her eyes decisively, and attacked him.

'As you know, Natalie and I do not get on. I *did* try, though I didn't like her, but *she* wouldn't try at all. She's always treated me as a fool, and I think she's a hard case. In that, at least, I am right. I find it impossible to understand any woman who would abandon her baby. And then to lean on *you*, to make *you* responsible for her inadequacies. Why weren't your parents told? Why didn't you trust *me*? Why did you keep it secret from everyone who could have helped?'

Such were the signs of recovery, perhaps of acceptance.

He produced his defence. He prepared to be censured. 'My dear Syb, you know as well as I do that a cat would make a better mother than mine, so it was of no use telling her. She would only have advised what Natalie did, which was to have the child fostered or adopted. As for my father, no one ever tells him anything and he doesn't want to be involved anyway. Besides, you know as well as I do what it would have cost Natalie to acknowledge the child in the first place, and in the second to keep it – even if she were capable of such devotion, which I admit she is not! And, though you don't like each other, and I accept that,

224

she is not only my sister but my twin – a stronger bond than the ordinary one. She turned to me as the one person most likely to help her, and so far as I was able, I did – and shall continue to do so.'

Sybil's expression conveyed love, understanding, admiration and puzzlement. One hand began to stroke the puppy's head, languidly at first and then more firmly.

'But why should the father get off scot-free? He should be the one to help her. Why won't he marry her?'

Anthony said brusquely, 'There was never any question of that. Tasha doesn't like the idea of marriage.'

Sybil's voice shook with anger as she said, 'No, I suppose not. She wants love without responsibility. But who is he? Is he married already? Is it Brian Dilling?'

He was restive, discomfited. 'Natalie won't say,' evasively. Then abruptly, 'And there's no point in guessing.'

Watching him closely, she did hazard a guess. 'Is she not sure who the father is?'

He shrugged.

'Women like Natalie should never have children!' Sybil cried vehemently.

Anthony's feelings for his sister and his wife were at war with one another. He remained silent.

'And you say the child's name is Blanche? Did Natalie name her?'

'I expect so. It's a name we both liked in the past.' He lifted his face a little, musing. 'The first wife of John of Gaunt was called Blanche, and she had silver hair.'

He felt more comfortable, connecting the name with a historical fact rather than discussing the child herself.

Sybil brought him back to the point somewhat impatiently. 'It's a pretty name,' she agreed. 'And is the child fair?'

'I've never seen her. I don't know. I never thought to ask.' And as Sybil was plainly shocked by these omissions, he added quickly, 'Natalie had the baby in some special hostel for unmarried mothers. I didn't know when it happened. She rang up a few days later and told me Blanche had been born and she'd arranged for a foster-mother to take care of her. A Mrs Newton. I have the address, but I don't deal with the woman directly. I write or telephone when necessary – as now.'

Sybil was almost herself again, exercising qualities of shrewd-ness and perception. 'I wonder why she chose a half-way house? Why fostering? Why not have the child properly adopted? Does Natalie intend to have her back at some stage?'

Anthony spread his hands, expressing bewilderment. 'I can't imagine that. She's never seen her since. But I do know that she wouldn't let go completely. She couldn't bear to lose the child altogether, if you understand me.'

Sybil sat thinking, hands clasped round her knees, and nodded. 'Yes, knowing her, I can see that. She's possessive, if not respon-sible.' She turned to him, saying, 'And what makes you think that she would let *us* have her?'

He replied honestly, 'I can't say whether she would or would not. I'm simply proposing what might be the best solution for everyone.' He felt obliged to add, 'But you may not like the child. Apparently she's difficult to handle, very aggressive.'

'Is she indeed?' Sybil said tartly, massaging the puppy's neck. 'One can hardly blame her. Swept off to a foster-home as soon as she was born, and kept there by an uncle who has never seen her at all.'

He bent his handsome head again, submitting to her rebukes, and she softened. 'Well, well, recriminations are useless. You did your best.' A little smile flickered across her mouth. 'Actually, you've done very well, Tony, because this sort of thing is not your province.'

He looked up then, heartened by the lilt and life in her tone. He said spontaneously, 'I'm sorry about the baby, Syb.'

A spasm of grief crossed her face, and was suppressed. She spoke matter-of-factly. 'Tony, would you be kind enough to make me a pot of Earl Grey tea? Earl Grey. It's in the white caddy decorated with primroses. I can't drink tea as strong as you like it.'

'Certainly,' he said, jumping to his feet. 'How many spoons?'

'Just one level caddy spoonful, in the small china teapot. And the pot should be heated before you put in the leaves. And I think I'd like some fresh toast. Lightly browned, this time. In fact,' throwing the bedclothes aside, 'I'm getting up.'

The puppy woke immediately, and ran to and fro, yapping dementedly. She would be a large dog. Her paws were too big for her body.

'There, my darling. There, Flora!' Sybil said soothingly, kneeling down and embracing the animal.

Astounded, delighted, relieved, Anthony cried, 'But, my dear love, are you sure you feel well enough?'

Her eyes were the vivid blue he remembered. He had given her hope and a fresh purpose in life. 'Oh, yes,' she said decisively. And then, 'Tony, I'm prepared to think seriously about this adoption, but of course I must see Blanche first. And if I do make up my mind to take her it will be on one condition. Natalie must renounce all rights in the child. I couldn't have her influencing Blanche or interfering with her upbringing in any way – and I'm sure she would try. So, in the event of adoption, I shall not see your sister again. Indeed, to be truthful, I should prefer not to see her anyway!'

She had astonished him once more, and he was silent.

'I know how close you are to Natalie,' Sybil continued, tender towards his feelings but determined to stand her ground, 'and I understand that you will want to keep in touch with her. That's only natural. But you must meet elsewhere.'

He said helplessly, 'I don't know how Tasha will feel about that. She isn't without fondness for the child. She gives her presents.'

Sybil's eyes blazed. Her grip tightened round the puppy's neck and it whimpered, afraid. 'Instead of love and care?' she cried scornfully. 'You say she hasn't even seen her since she was born.'

He was nonplussed. 'Well, it's difficult, you see, with Tasha travelling about . . .' He thought of a more acceptable explanation. 'And perhaps she thinks it would unsettle the child. Yes, I expect she thinks it wiser to stay away.'

Sybil said coldly, 'On that point I agree with her entirely. So there should be no problem in the future.'

She soothed the puppy and it licked her hand. There was another silence, during which Anthony was completely at a loss how to deal with the situation. Discerning this she took pity on him again. 'If Natalie wants to be a distant philanthropic aunt, and send Blanche presents, then that's fair enough. And of course you will want to send photographs and news of the child to Natalie. That would be fine by me, because I don't intend to correspond with her.'

She appealed to him out of the knowledge they shared. 'Tony,

227

devoted though you are to your sister, you must admit that she is both wilful and unpredictable. This child is obviously disturbed and needs a secure background. I couldn't risk Natalie coming to see her on a whim, and playing whatever role appealed to her at the time. That would be disastrous for Blanche and utterly unfair to me.'

As he continued to look undecided, she said immovably, 'If I do take responsibility for Blanche then she will become our daughter and Natalie's niece. I accept her wholly or not at all. And that is my final word.'

Then Anthony bowed his head, and promised, 'It shall be as you say.'

And it was.

CHAPTER TWENTY-FIVE

Friday, 29 December

The sun straggled through the clouds that afternoon, as if to show that light and warmth still existed even when they were in abeyance.

Upstairs, Henrietta bathed and changed and was transferred to Lydia's room, overlooking the paddock. Sybil made fresh orange juice for her, collected all the Narnia books together, and lined them up on the window-sill with the pot-plant that Mrs Laity had given her for Christmas. Salome, padding in from the garden, leaped up on the chest of drawers to act as supervisor; and Patch jumped on to the invalid's bed and kneaded the coverlet with predatory claws.

'Goodness,' said Henrietta, restored in spirit if not in health, 'it's a treat being ill at Minions, isn't it?'

Downstairs, Aaron was put in his playpen, while a mute Blanche helped Sybil to sort out the laundry, dealt with the daily washing, checked the contents of cupboard, refrigerator and larder, and wrote out two shopping lists, one for the village and one for Helston. By half past four she had achieved a measure of tranquillity, and felt able to take Aaron on her knee and join the others at the kitchen table, as they prepared to drink tea and trawl the teeming seas of village gossip.

'You're looking whisht, Blanche,' said Mrs Laity, observing her fixed smile and drained demeanour. 'Not sickening for nothing, are you?'

'Only a quiet life,' she answered wryly.

Mrs Laity dismissed this notion with contempt. 'Won't none of us get that until we'm underground!'

And turned to more interesting topics.

Blanche was thinking that Natalie's train would be crossing the Tamar about this time, leaving Cornwall behind her for ever.

In a sense, all Natalie's journeys would be final ones from now on: last looks at this place and that. Blanche could imagine her making her arrogant way to the buffet bar for an early evening whisky: the fur-lined cape displacing small objects on passing tables, the leather boots treading down or kicking aside anything in her path, frizzy white hair escaping the confines of her Russian fur hat, head held high.

Mrs Laity was saying, '. . . but it depend on the amount of death duties whether that new heir,' she pronounced the h as if Jack Maddern's nephew were possessed of a good head of the same, 'sell the home farm or not. And then he might not want to live over here in that great house. Might sell up altogether, they say – and then where shall us be? Hard times, Mrs Malpas. Hard times. And Mr Jack warn't old. Not what you call old. Not for down here. Live for ever down here, we do.'

Sybil sighed, and traced an invisible pattern on the scrubbed table. 'I cannot believe he would leave so much to chance,' she said. 'Surely . . .'

Outside, the light was failing now, as it failed in Natalie's personal world. When she reached London it would be dark. Between train and taxi cab Blanche trod every uncertain, haughty step with her. Would she have a meal out or go straight to her bed-sitting room and make a hot snack? No, Blanche could imagine her being impatient with cooking. Too much trouble. She would eat out somewhere, nothing elaborate, nowhere grand. And then what? A long silence in a solitary room.

'Well, you cain't tell. Even the best of folk say more than they mean. And Mr Jack cain't have known, when he left here, that he would be took sudden. Food poisoning, was it?'

'A clot in the lungs,' said Sybil, knowing the truth.

'Well, that's what we been told, but you do never know with foreign food, and some say he was poisoned.'

Preferring drama, and a proverbial warning never to leave Cornwall.

Blanche decided that when Dan came in she would tell him about Natalie. The thought of sharing her trouble lifted her spirits. The dread of losing independence cast them down again. She loved him but feared to entrust herself. And yet, what else was there? The boy on her lap growing up and growing away. Solitude. Darkness. The everlasting dark.

'Natalie should have gone by the morning train,' Blanche said, breaking into the others' conversation. 'She would have reached London while it was still light.'

Sybil replied coolly, 'She was always a law unto herself, and she knows that we must abide by the laws we make. She'll survive.'

'Any old how,' said Mrs Laity, 'they saw the lady off in style. Some lovely car!'

Blanche, seeing Sybil bite on the question she wished to ask but would not, asked it for her. '*Who* saw her off in style?'

'Why, the master and your young man, and Edward and Ben, come round in Edward's new car. I was sitting in the kitchen at the Cornish Arms with Mary Sampson, and Jack come in and tell us.'

'Amazing', said Sybil to herself, 'that someone is always on the spot at the right time.'

'You didn't know that?' Mrs Laity enquired of them, incredulous.

Blanche answered for them both. 'Natalie told us last night that she was going by taxi. They probably dropped in to say goodbye and decided to take her to the station instead.'

'Well, that's what happened,' said Mrs Laity, amazed at their lack of information. 'We didn't see them, mind, only heard from Jack when he come into the kitchen. "They come round for Miss Malpas in Edward's new car," he said, "and the lady went off in style!"'

Mrs Laity re-enacted the scene first from the landlord's side and then from the viewpoint of herself and Mary Sampson, to clarify the situation, ending with '. . . and now I must be going, Mrs Malpas. Friday night is pasty night, and if my 'usband don't have his pasty there'll be hard words before bedtime. You want me to clean downstairs tomorrow, do you?'

Sybil was again in command of herself. She had had so much practice. 'Only if you are *sure* you have the time, Mrs Laity. Don't forget that it's the last shopping day before New Year.'

'Get my shopping done in the morning and be here by two o'clock.'

'Then I look forward to seeing you. And thank you again.'

While they were bathing Aaron, Sybil said, 'That must have been Tony's idea. He organized the drive on the pretext that it would

231

give me a clear afternoon. I don't in the least mind his taking her to the station, in fact I think he should have done. But I mind his deceit very much. Very much indeed.'

'Yes,' Blanche said thoughtfully, 'there's been too much deceit. All the way round.'

When Anthony walked in at half past six he was smiling affably, too affably, as if he guessed that the news had preceded him.

'Here we are, Sybil, all safe and sound!' he cried, and kissed her averted cheek. 'And I've brought you some flowers. First of the season.' Producing a bouquet of daffodils from behind his back.

'Thank you,' Sybil said, unmelted.

'Oh, by the way,' he continued, as Daniel helped him off with his coat, 'we called in at the Cornish Arms to say goodbye to Tasha. She said she was ordering a taxi, but I couldn't have that. So we drove her to Redruth and gave her a decent send-off.'

'Gran'ma,' said Ben, claiming her attention, 'we had to wait twenty minutes before the train came in. So Grandpa bought me an orange juice and a chocolate wafer from the refreshment room, and Aunt Tasha bought me a *Dandy* so's I wouldn't be bored.'

'How very kind of them,' said Sybil coolly. 'And what did you all do for the rest of the afternoon?'

Daniel, appointing himself as chief mediator, said, 'Ah, we had a great time. We went on to Truro to look round the shops, and ate a grand cream tea.'

'Oh, you've had a cream tea as well? What a lot of treats!' said Sybil, arms folded. 'Where did you go for that?'

'A jolly little tea-shop up a side-street,' said Anthony heartily, 'called Tea-cakes or something like that.'

'Muffins,' Ben corrected him. 'And Grandpa bought us presents, Gran'ma. More presents!' Brandishing a box-shaped parcel.

Anthony patted Ben's head, to please Sybil.

'Yes, we've had rather an extravagant Grandpa in charge of us this afternoon,' Edward added gallantly.

Clearly, they were defending him.

'I'm so glad,' Sybil said.

'They've started the New Year sales already, Gran'ma,' Ben

clamoured, unwrapping his loot. 'Guess how much this Lego cost. Just guess. You'll never guess in a million years.'

He tugged at her sleeve, and Sybil put one arm round him and smiled into his clear grey eyes and kissed his freckled forehead. 'Ben,' she said, 'don't think so much about money. The price isn't important.'

'It is to me,' he mumbled, slightly crushed.

'He's just excited, aren't you, old chap?' Edward said. 'He didn't expect Christmas to happen all over again.'

'We chose a jersey, if that's what you call them these days, for Henrietta,' Anthony said, pulling it from a large carrier bag. 'I'm not too sure about it myself, but Ben told us it was all the rage.' He looked doubtfully at his wife. 'Bit on the gaudy side, eh?' Displaying a garment that would have shamed Joseph's coat.

'A little too bright for our taste, perhaps. But probably not for hers.'

'It's fab!' Ben assured them. 'Absolutely fab!'

Anthony turned to his silent daughter. 'What does our fashion expert say?'

Blanche roused herself. 'Oh, it's the in-thing among the young. Hen will love it.'

'Told you,' Ben muttered.

Anthony held the garment at length and surveyed it critically. 'It doesn't seem to have a coherent pattern either,' he said. 'Just blobs of colour.' He rolled up the sweater and stuffed it back into its glistening carrier bag. 'I wonder why anyone would want to wear that?' he asked himself.

He turned to his daughter again, as if magnetized by her silence 'We've bought a wooden train for Aaron. He can push it around and crawl after it.'

Daniel removed the train from its long box and displayed its talents on the kitchen floor. 'What do you think about that, now?'

'Wonderful!' Blanche said, summoning enthusiasm with difficulty. 'Aaron will love it.'

Daniel's face shone with pleasure. He slipped one arm round Blanche's waist, trying to engage her full consideration. She accepted his hug and kiss and tried to match his mood. 'What a marvellous expedition you've all had,' she cried.

'And so unexpected,' Sybil remarked, slicing daffodil stems with a small sharp knife.

Anthony glanced at her apprehensively.

'When you told me you were going for a drive,' she added, over her shoulder, 'I'd imagined a nice long run round the coast, with perhaps a short walk between.'

The mellifluous voice of Daniel came to Anthony's rescue. 'We played it by ear,' he said joyfully, 'didn't we, sir? Followed the mood of the moment, and nobody more surprised than ourselves at the result.'

Sybil put the daffodils in a blue pottery vase, stood it on the dresser, and rewrapped Henrietta's present. She did not answer.

Blanche stared at her hands, found a speck of something on one nail and rubbed it off.

Anthony said, 'Good heavens! Nearly seven o'clock. Time for a noggin. Blanche, would you like to buttle for me?'

Obediently, she took a tray of ice cubes from the freezer compartment and followed him into the living room.

He said uneasily, confidentially, 'I know I'm in the dog-house about taking Natalie to Redruth, but I couldn't let her go off by herself, now could I?'

Blanche's tone was cool but not unfriendly. 'You did the right thing, but in the wrong way. You should have told Sybil.'

Twisting the cap of a new bottle of gin, Anthony admitted, 'I didn't want to risk another explosion.'

Blanche shrugged, and said, 'You pays your money and you takes your choice. Do you have the row before or after? That's what I ask myself in the same predicament.'

He said drily, 'You don't know the degree of row we're talking about.'

With her new-found wisdom Blanche answered, 'No, I don't suppose I do, but you should have remembered that the village grapevine never sleeps. Mrs Laity sprang the news on us and made us look a pair of fools.'

Anthony said sincerely, 'God damn Mrs Laity!'

Blanche's smile was wan. He glanced at her, uneasy, apologetic. He poured her drink first. 'Here you are. You look as if you need it.'

She nodded, swallowed, and closed her eyes momentarily as the alcohol began to smooth out an exceedingly rough day.

He followed her example. They contemplated each other steadily: he with sympathy, she amazed at his perception.

'I gather there were major revelations from Natalie,' he said.

She nodded again. He made a sound of exasperation. 'It's all been handled very badly,' he said. 'You should have been told years ago, but your mother – Sybil, that is – won't give an inch to Natalie. I've had to lead a double life to keep in touch with my own sister. Ridiculous!'

He was striving to make a dangerous situation commonplace, to disguise wounds as scratches.

'Anyway, Tasha feels the same way about Syb,' he said, 'and I could never influence either of them.' With rare honesty he added, 'I may have a good brain but I'm a fool at dealing with women.'

He poured out two generous whiskies and a schooner of Tio Pepe.

'Shall we take those in?' Blanche asked.

'Not yet. Let's have another first.'

This time she smiled spontaneously, and he smiled back at her.

'The presents for the children', he explained, 'aren't bribes. They're apologies. I'm inclined to be impatient with Ben – which is understandable! – but I was harsh about poor Henrietta, which is not. Unfair to blame her for catching German measles. My only excuse is that there were far too many people here, and all of them with problems.' He shrugged in resignation. 'With rare exceptions, I find most people a waste of time, and I detest organized family gatherings. I expect that's where charades came in originally – something to do that involved thought and effort instead of this endless chit-chat and breast-beating. Still, Sybil loves it all. So . . .'

From behind the sofa he brought out a small package, gift-wrapped. 'I wanted to offer you an apology, too. Something small and witty and apt – like a miniature version of Dan's silver mask. Couldn't find a damned thing. So – this is a sort of joke. Remember?'

January 1952

Mrs Newton delivered her monologue in one long moan.

'She's been pestering me to put on her new hat and coat since breakfast, so in the end I dressed her up. The mother sent the clothes for her to go home in. Foreign-looking, they are, and fancy. And Blanch won't eat nothing and I can't make no sense

235

of her.' Uncertain whether to accuse or regret. 'So don't blame me if she looks like something out of a circus and says she's hungry.'

'She's excited,' said Sybil. 'And so am I.'

'Is Mr Malpas not coming in?'

'No, he'll stay in the car with the puppy.'

'Oh, yes, that dog of yours,' said Mrs Newton, preceding Sybil down the bleak brown hall. 'I was expecting your husband to carry the luggage. There's a box, as well as that suitcase you brought last time. I suppose I'll have to help you.' Aggrieved. 'And I've got a bad back. I shouldn't be lifting things.'

She opened the kitchen door, crying, 'Here's your new mother come to fetch you, Blanch.'

The child sat on a kitchen chair, legs dangling, clutching the teddy bear. She was wearing a burnt orange double-breasted coat adorned with brass buttons, and a dashing orange beret. Her brilliant black gaze was fixed on the door.

'She's been sitting there like that since eight o'clock,' said Mrs Newton. 'Waiting.'

The child dropped her fur friend to the floor, scrambled down after him, picked him up by the ear with one hand and ran unsteadily towards Sybil.

'Oh, what a welcome! Give me a gorgeous hug and kiss!' Sybil cried, smiling into those frighteningly familiar eyes.

She lifted the child up, saying, 'I've brought your new daddy with me today, and Flora the dog – who wants to be friends with you – and we're all going to drive home together to Oxfordshire. Home, Blanche.'

The child said nothing, but clung round Sybil's neck with all her might and would not unclasp her hands.

Sybil said with difficulty, over the stranglehold, 'You needn't trouble yourself about the box and the suitcase, Mrs Newton. As soon as I'm in the car I can look after Blanche and the dog while my husband fetches them.'

Deprived of one grievance, the woman looked for another.

'Aren't you going to walk like a big girl, Blanch?' she demanded.

A muffled but emphatic, 'No!'

'That's all right, Mrs Newton,' said Sybil peaceably. 'I'll carry her.'

'Oh, yes, you'll carry her all right,' Mrs Newton prophesied.

'I've thought from the first that you didn't know what you was taking on. You've picked up a burden that won't be put down, I'm telling you.'

And unfortunately she was quite correct.

From the beginning, Blanche divided her new parents, demanding an inordinate amount of attention from both of them, which Anthony at least was not prepared to give. In fact, once the child was adopted he showed no further interest in her, and resented the way she monopolized his wife; and Sybil took exception to his behaviour on both counts. By the time Edward was born, two years later, their marriage had almost foundered beneath the load of Natalie's daughter. Sheer necessity brought Anthony and Blanche unwillingly together.

Again it was a Saturday, he was at home and unable to concentrate on his work, and Sybil was lying upstairs in bed with her new son. But no situation repeats itself exactly. This time he was enduring the assistance of his mother-in-law as well as a visiting midwife and a home help; and he had company in the shape of an exhausting four-year-old, even more devastated by Sybil's situation than he was, and both articulate and vociferous in her objections.

'Tony dear,' said his mother-in-law, who had too much to do, 'would you like to take Blanche out for the afternoon?'

He considered the proposal with some distaste, saying, 'What should I do with her?'

Mrs Outram, like Mrs Laity, thought men were a domestic hindrance and best out of the way. She answered with patience, but with firmness too. 'You could take her for a walk in the park and give her tea in a nice tea-shop.' Adding, with as much conviction as she could muster, 'You'll both enjoy that.'

After the obligatory scene with Blanche, who, like himself, was unconvinced and unwilling, they set forth together. It was their first open encounter. Sybil had shielded them from each other.

Standing on the pavement outside the house, Anthony said, annoyed and helpless, 'What park is she talking about? I've never been there.'

'Yes, you have,' said Blanche, important with knowledge. 'You go with my mummy and me sometimes on Sundays.'

'I don't remember it. Anyway, I don't know where it is.'

'I do,' said Blanche. She assessed him shrewdly. 'You don't know how to get there, do you?' she said. His ignorance aroused her interest. 'I'll show you. Do you know your road drill?' And as he continued to be perplexed, she said, 'I do!' She clasped his hand in hers, saying, 'Hold on tight and look both ways. Now we can cross safely.'

For the next hour she took charge of Anthony and forgot the loss of Sybil. She showed him the ducks, and deplored the lack of bread with which to feed them. 'Mummy should have given us a bagful!' She led him to the playground and instructed him in the art of pushing her on a swing, and watching over her as she negotiated the slide. She did not allow his attention to wander, and expected considered replies to her questions. He took her out to tea to shut her up.

They passed the toy-shop on the way home and by this time she had schooled him sufficiently well to cater to her needs. Anthony waited with commendable patience, hands in the pockets of his duffel coat, as she pressed her nose to the glass and told him what she would like for Christmas. He was reflecting that the afternoon had not been entirely wasted. Minus the frown and the tantrums, she was a vivid and unusually attractive little girl. He was surprised and delighted by her intelligence, the length of her memory, the extent of her vocabulary, her capacity for self-expression. Plans for her future education formed and re-formed in his mind. Sybil was teaching her the basics, arithmetic, reading and writing, but already he looked further ahead. They must find a good school for her. He could coach her, keep an eye on her progress. Sybil had done a decent job so far, but he, Anthony, would do better.

Mentally, he was giving and receiving praise at Blanche's graduation ceremony when an imperious childish voice startled him by saying, 'What's that stripy thing with a little tiny window in it?'

And tumbled him down to the present moment and her immediate needs and desires. So he clasped her hand and answered, 'Come into the shop and find out.'

More than thirty years later, Blanche accepted her second kaleido-scope with the same sensation of astonished rapture. Imitating the child she had been she held it up to one eye and discovered a brilliant mandala. Shook it gently and found another. And another.

Then she lowered the toy, smiled at him widely, radiantly, as she had done in the toy shop, and said again emphatically, 'I *like* it!'

Still she feared that this rare feeling of affinity might go the way of all others, turning into gruffness on his part and asperity on hers.

But Anthony asked frankly, 'Where did you and I go wrong?'

Blanche answered gently, 'It must have been further back than I can remember, and for reasons I don't know. Sybil says that you and I fought because we were alike, and I can see that. I recognize much of myself in Natalie, and she's very like you – but far more vulnerable.'

His arrogant head was humbly bent. He made a gesture of the hand, but whether in agreement or repudiation she could not tell. Blanche endeavoured to cement this new understanding. 'Sybil said you had made yourself responsible for me more or less from birth, because Natalie ...' she found a bearable reason '... because her work kept her away. Sybil said that you paid the bills and acted as go-between and suggested the adoption.'

She felt the old fingers of suffocation seeking for a grip on her throat, and forced them off with words. 'I don't remember my foster-home but I know it was a bad inheritance because I've suffered from it and Sybil took the brunt of it. But you must have suffered too. Children aren't exactly your scene and you gave me a home. So I thank you for that.'

This time his gesture brusquely disclaimed her thanks.

Blanche paused for a few seconds, thought, swallowed, and then said, 'They must be dying of thirst in there. I'd better take their drinks.'

As she reached the doorway, he said, 'Blanche!' Peremptorily.

She stopped and turned. His tone belied what he wanted to say. He was struggling to express his inmost feelings and finding this extraordinarily difficult.

Finally, he said, as if he were accusing her, 'You stayed away too long. I missed you.'

Gently, she answered, 'I missed you, too.'

Then he made a declaration from the centre of himself. 'We must never let this happen again.'

'We won't,' she assured him.

239

She would have liked to set the tray down and go over to him and put her arms round his neck and lay her cheek against his, but she saw that he could not deal with more emotion at the present. So she smiled at him, and went out.

Consolation Prizes

CHAPTER TWENTY-SIX

Friday evening

The house party was gradually winding down. The children ate their supper in Henrietta's bedroom, so the adults' evening meal was a subdued though civil affair. At eight o'clock Katrina rang to enquire about the invalid, and Ben thundered downstairs in his pyjamas to speak to her at length, recounting the treats of the day and their prices.

On her way to the kitchen to make coffee, Sybil was relieved to hear how breezy he sounded: an impression that she amended on the way back.

Ben was saying pensively, '. . . and I'm keeping my fingers crossed that I don't catch it, because we'll be home sooner then, and we can come and stay with you, Mummy. Oh, well, I suppose I'd better be going. Yes, I'll tell her. Night night. Sleep tight.'

Hearing his grandmother approach, he became brisk and facetious. 'And make sure the bed bugs don't bite! 'Bye, Mum!'

Swaggering upstairs, a devil of a fellow, he called to Sybil off-handedly, light-heartedly, 'Oh, Mum says to thank you for looking after us so well. G'night, Gran!'

She knew he was distressed, otherwise he would have hovered round her, asking questions and bringing forth excuse after excuse to stay down a little longer, and she resolved to pay special attention to him when they were by themselves. But her mood was mellow as she presided over the coffee pot in the living room, and she surveyed her family with an affection that was all the deeper for knowing they would soon be gone.

'Tomorrow is Departure Day,' she announced brightly, 'and I need to make various arrangements. So what time are you travellers leaving?'

Daniel looked at Blanche, who looked uncertain. Events had followed, one upon the other's heels, all week, and today had been the most fateful occasion. She lacked the energy to make yet another decision, and her instinct was to stay on at Minions and sort herself out under Sybil's wing. 'We haven't actually discussed dates and times,' said Blanche defensively.

'But you were concerned yesterday, about Aaron catching German measles.'

'Yes, but I haven't thought about it since.'

'I should, my dear, because if you don't go tomorrow there's no point in leaving before next Tuesday at least.' Displeased. 'What about you, Tony?'

Anthony, stirring the rough, sweet fragments of sugar into his coffee, said incisively, 'I've decided to stay here and see you through this, Syb. And then, when it's all over, I can help you to pack up and we'll drive home together.'

His eyes sought approval from her.

Sybil said automatically, 'That's a very kind thought, Tony . . .' then added truthfully, 'but I don't think it would be such a good idea put into practice.'

He addressed her as if there were no one else in the room. 'You'll have our car at your disposal, and I can take you shopping while Edward keeps an eye on the children.' He threw in a final inducement, in which there was a shadow of reproach. 'I'm not asking for special treatment. If I'm going to pig it in Clifton, with fry-ups and take-aways and such, I can pig it just as well here.' Pacifically, he added, 'And I shall have your company.'

Plainly she was not enraptured by this change of heart and mind, but nothing could be done about it – short of an argument – and there had been too many arguments already.

'Well, stay and see the New Year in,' said Sybil, making the best of the situation. 'And afterwards, if you find it too much . . .'

Anthony said, 'I think that Blanche and Daniel and Aaron should stay on, too, and see the New Year in with us.'

They were all astonished.

'But if Ben falls ill he'll need Blanche's room . . .' Sybil began, visibly put out.

He had thought of this and answered calmly but authoritatively. 'Then Blanche and Aaron can join Daniel down at the Cornish Arms as my guests. Most probably it would suit them better than being separated, as they are at present.'

'But I must have a room to myself,' Sybil insisted, 'so that I shan't disturb you if the children need me during the night.'

He was leaning slightly forward, regarding her earnestly. 'That is a specious argument, and you know it, Syb. You never have disturbed me. I sleep like the proverbial log.' He added in a lower voice, 'And I want you back in our room, not punishing me by sleeping apart.'

She flushed up angrily, crying, 'I have to be with Henrietta during the night, in case she wants anything.'

And sat, head bent, sipping her coffee for comfort.

'The child is not as ill as all that,' Anthony remarked, and turned to his daughter, speaking persuasively, 'I realize that you and Daniel have work to do and homes to go to, and that you're concerned for Aaron, but I should like you to stay here for New Year if you feel you could.'

They exchanged looks. They nodded. She answered for them both. 'We'd love to, but only,' with a doubtful glance at Sybil, 'if you are *both* quite happy about that.' Careful not to accuse, she appealed to him, 'You know what we can be like as a family. I don't want to supply further ammunition.'

Sybil set down her coffee cup on its saucer with a little smack. Very pale, very rigid, she turned her head to address her daughter directly. 'I am always happy to have *you*, and you know that. You help and sustain me. My problem lies elsewhere,' indicating Anthony, 'and has no bearing on whether you go or stay.' Now she looked directly at him and spoke to him as if they were alone. 'You know perfectly well how I feel and what the trouble is about. Promises have been broken, rules transgressed, half-truths have disguised downright lies, and wickedness has been paraded as fond attachment. But if you think to evade central issues by pleasing me with a false show of family affection you are very much mistaken.'

She had pierced him to the core and he blazed up, shouting, 'My affection is not a show, and it is not false!'

He had silenced her for the moment. He drew breath in a deliberate effort to collect himself. He spoke to them all, then, in a quieter tone. 'I have no gift for easy family relationships. I lack Sybil's patience and perception. But my affection is not false.'

Blanche, Daniel and Edward sat in appalled silence. Sybil recollected herself. 'I'm sorry to bring up such personal issues in

245

public, but matters have gone too far for once and we must talk them out.'

Edward said under his breath, 'Why, *for once?*' But only his companions heard him.

Anthony turned towards them, speaking courteously but firmly. 'Blanche, my dear, Sybil and I need to talk things over. I'd be very much obliged if you could take these two cavaliers down the pub for the rest of the evening. And, if you still want to see the New Year in with us, you may as well book your room there as from tomorrow night. Tell Mary Sampson to send the bill to me.'

Again Blanche and Daniel communed, and again Blanche spoke for them both. 'We'd love to stay, provided the Cornish Arms can put us up.' She added, 'But I can pay for Aaron and myself.' Then, afraid to disturb their present harmony by so much as a breath of disagreement. 'Truly, I'd like to!'

He answered her kindly. 'I dare say you would, but this is my suggestion and I should prefer it to be my treat.'

She bowed her head in acknowledgement, and thanked him. Inside her, an imp mocked and capered at this unusual display of daughterly behaviour, but the moment was too precious to allow it freedom. And so far had she moved back into the past that, in giving Sybil instructions, she addressed her in past style. 'Mummy, if Aaron wakes he'll need changing – you'll find a packet of disposables on the window-ledge.'

Sybil inclined her head.

'And speaking of treats,' Anthony added, taking out his wallet, 'I should like you all to have the first round on me.'

He handed a five-pound note to Edward, who received it in amazement and stammered his thanks. Then the three of them, slightly distrait with the speed and course of events, put on their outdoor clothes and disappeared into the night.

11 o'clock

As soon as Anthony answered the front door, Blanche and Edward knew that the quarrel was over. Gracie padded out into the hall to greet them, and Salome leaped onto Blanche's shoulder. An air of tranquillity prevailed. Their father's expression was absent-minded, amiable, carpet slippers on his feet, spectacles thrust up on his forehead, grey mane slightly tousled. Immediately he asked

246

the question of them that they would have liked to ask of him. 'Everything all right?'

'Absolutely fine,' Blanche answered. 'And Mary Sampson is giving us the family room, which comes complete with cot. Oh, and Dan says thank you very much indeed.'

Nervously, for he had always been afraid of his father, Edward made light and humorous conversation as Anthony took Blanche's coat. 'I thought that Mrs Sampson might find Blanche's request somewhat unconventional, but she took it without a lift of the eyebrow or a nudge of the elbow. Do I gather that the Cornish have cottoned on to the idea of single parents and unmarried couples?'

'Oh, I expect so,' Anthony replied, not caring one way or the other. 'If it doesn't happen to them they see it on the television and probably think it should. And judging from the current displays of sexual activity on the screen, nothing should surprise them. In my youth you had to visit Soho for that sort of thing.'

'Everything all right here?' Blanche asked, and added quickly, lest he think she was prying, 'All the children asleep?'

'All quiet on this western front,' he answered easily. 'Sybil's rather tired after the efforts of Christmas week, so I persuaded her to go to bed.'

'Quite right,' Edward said, placating him. 'We must all look after Mama.'

Anthony preceded them into the living room, saying over his shoulder, 'You'll find it a lot warmer in here. Would you like a final nightcap with me, or have you had enough to drink?'

No, no, they said. They had drunk very little. Talked mostly. A nightcap would be welcome. They followed him, patting Gracie, stroking Salome: glad of a lull in the warfare.

'With regard to tomorrow, Sybil was thinking,' Anthony continued, measuring modest tots into tumblers, 'that Edward and Daniel could perhaps shunt the bedroom furniture back into place while I take her shopping. Then we'll all have an early lunch and clear out of the way, to allow Sybil and Mrs Laity to set the house in order. We can do something together or separately, as you wish. Is that all right by you?'

Indeed, they said bemused, it was. An excellent idea.

Anthony sat back in his chair and propped up his feet on the brass fender. He did not look at them as he said, 'Sybil and I have been talking of many things . . .'

Edward glanced at Blanche and mouthed, 'Of shoes and ships and sealing wax!'

She mouthed back, 'Of cabbages and kings!' With the glimmer of a smile.

'. . . but mostly about Minions. I don't know if you are aware,' said Anthony, clearing his throat, speaking to the fire-irons, 'that she and I have been under some considerable strain for the past two months, wondering what to do about this place.'

They had thought perhaps that was the case, they murmured.

'It means a dickens of a lot to Sybil,' said Anthony gloomily, 'and she's not leaving without a fight. At the moment she can't find anyone else to tackle so she's fighting me. I've had the lot thrown at me tonight – including Ben's mythical twenty-five thousand pound profit!'

Blanche and Edward sat in fascinated silence. This was the first time that he had ever confided in them. His opinions were usually made known in public as orders, complaints or denials.

'To put it concisely, she wants me to sell the Clifton house and buy Minions. With this twenty-five thousand pounds profit, and my savings and pension, we can live like lords. I shall write my book in the perfect environment, and I can travel to and from Minions, whenever and wherever I want to, to keep in touch with colleagues and events. Meanwhile, she says, she will be able to lead a quiet life and have time for all the things she wants to do.' His tone was affectionate, ironic. 'Fair enough. She's worked damned hard for forty years – and so have I. She's entitled to retire – as she says – *properly*.'

He turned towards them now, and spread out his hands in entreaty. 'Believe me, both of you, if I thought that I could write my book in peace down here, and make occasional forays to the outside world, I would consider it seriously. But Sybil's notion of a quiet life is not mine. I know damned well that if we *did* make a good profit on the sale she would spend it on Minions. She'd be turning those outhouses into extra rooms, so that she could invite everybody we've ever known to come here for a restful weekend or a recuperative holiday. The place would be a madhouse full of lame dogs, screaming kids, and people with personal problems.'

Blanche laughed aloud. She could not help it.

'What's so damned funny?' Anthony asked testily.

'It's funny because it's true,' she said.

He addressed himself to them earnestly. 'Sybil loves domestic life, you see. But I love the life of the mind. I need either to be completely alone, or to be somewhere where things are happening or I can make them happen. I like to keep my finger on the pulse. That's why I must stay in Clifton. Besides, there'd be nothing here for me. It's all very well for Sybil to say that I'm an important man and people will always want to meet me, but I can't see ardent admirers trekking down to this neck of the woods when I've retired. And although Jack was good company, within limits, he's gone now.'

'You've never shared our feeling for Cornwall, have you?' Edward asked cautiously.

Anthony considered this question, mouth pursed, nostrils flaring, but answered urbanely. 'I do enjoy it. In small doses. Preferably alleviated by the company of lively minds. But I couldn't live here permanently. Could you?'

'Oh, yes,' said Edward, and his tone was heartfelt. 'Very easily, and with great relief and pleasure after present day city life. In fact, now that Katrina and I are finally splitting up, I'm thinking seriously of applying for a teaching post in this part of Cornwall. If I win custody it would be a good place for Henny and Ben to live, and if Katrina wins custody then at least the kids will have Cornish holidays. In fact, I've been discussing the pros and cons with Blanche and Dan this evening.'

'Good God!' Anthony said. He surveyed his son with renewed wonder. 'Would you really do that?' And then again, 'Good . . . God!'

A brief pause. It was evident that the two men would never have anything in common.

Anthony asked bluntly, 'What about you, Blanche?'

She stirred restlessly. 'I'm ambivalent. Like you, I need the passing show, and I can't live here anyway because my work is in London. But losing Minions would be like losing a piece of myself. My childhood roots and centre are here, with Sybil.'

'Bless my soul!' Anthony murmured, and was lost in thought for a minute or two.

He asked, 'How important is Minions to Lydia?'

Blanche said affectionately, dismissively, 'She's a creature of the moment, and she revolves round people rather than places. Right now life is all Freddie. So she would be sorry but not devastated.'

Again they were silent while Anthony mused over his tot of

whisky. Then he roused himself once more. 'Anyway, you'll be relieved to hear that eventually your mother and I came to a compromise – I find that marriage is largely a matter of compromise! – and we've decided to sell the house and buy a flat in Clifton. I don't really believe in Ben's twenty-five thousand as devoutly as Sybil does, but we should do pretty well on the sale, so we are going to ask Jack's nephew if we can rent this place at a price reasonable for both parties, and pay for it out of our profit. My pension will cover our living expenses quite comfortably, and Sybil has a little money of her own, left by her mother.'

He was looking to them for approval, and saw by their expressions that he had done the right thing. Gratified, he continued, 'We don't know much about this nephew, except that he lives on the other side of the world – Australia or New Zealand or somewhere – and what Sybil has found out recently comes from Mrs Laity through Jack's housekeeper, so take it with a hefty pinch of salt. Apparently the nephew's mother, Jack's sister, was a rum customer. Some colonial made her pregnant and she ran away with him.'

He mused for a while, swirling the golden drops round and round in the heavy glass.

'The fellow left her in the lurch, I believe. Old Jack stepped in and did what he could, but he never talked about it. She wouldn't come back home. Didn't want to face the music, I expect. She's been dead for a few years now. The nephew manages a sheep farm. Still, Jack paid for his education at a good school over there, so he's probably quite decent.'

Blanche and Edward exchanged winks.

'Jack acted as a sort of father at second hand to the boy. Visited him from time to time. Kept in touch with him. What the fellow will make of life as a member of the Cornish gentry I don't know – or what they'll make of him, for that matter. Anyhow . . .' A longer pause.

Then he went off at a tangent. 'Sybil kept coming back to the fact – or the fancy – that Jack intended her to have Minions. But, as I said to her, this is a legal business. If he wrote nothing down then nothing is what she will get, whatever he meant to do. Still, I don't mean the nephew to snap up the house as easily as that. Sybil has put a lifetime's work into this place, and a lot of our money, and I feel that her part in the restoration should be acknowledged. It was a mud hut when we first arrived.'

'Oh, Daddy!' Blanche demurred. 'Minions was never a mud hut.'

He shrugged off this mild criticism.

'Anyway, he must be made to understand that he's better off with established tenants who are prepared to pay a decent rent. I believe he's coming down here for New Year, so I shall be able to interview him myself.'

He paused again, finished off his whisky with a little toss of the head.

'Sybil was pretty well done up when we'd finished talking, but I thought you'd want to know what we'd decided, so I stayed up to tell you. And now I shall follow her to bed.'

He pushed himself to his feet saying, 'Edward!' in his abrupt manner.

His son jumped up, glass in hand: a puppet yanked by the paternal string.

'Perhaps you'd be kind enough to lock the place up and so on?' Anthony asked.

'Yes. Yes, of course, Dad.'

Anthony turned to Blanche, and his face and tone softened. 'Good night, Blanche!'

His lips touched her cheek uncertainly, but she put both arms round his neck and kissed him whole-heartedly. She said, 'We're delighted about the room. It will make such a difference to us.'

He was pleased and moved, saying, 'Good, good.'

Wanting to express affection for his son, he managed an awkward, 'Good night . . . my boy.'

As he made his way to the door, shuffling slightly in his aged carpet slippers, he said mildly, 'I'm glad you're both here with us, to see in the nineties.' And remembering a decade of family disasters, added drily, 'The eighties have been a bit of a bugger.'

Shoes in hand, so that she would not disturb anyone, Blanche waited until Edward's bedroom door closed softly behind him. She listened at the door of Lydia's room, then noiselessly turned the knob and peered into the half-light. Henrietta was fast asleep, but the bed that Sybil had occupied as night nurse was empty.

Anthony had not only mollified his lady, he had also persuaded her to return to the matrimonial couch.

CHAPTER TWENTY-SEVEN

Saturday, 30 December

The weather was mild for the time of year, the afternoon sunny and breezy, the song-birds hopeful and enquiring. Upstairs, Henrietta dozed over *The Horse and His Boy*, and Patch slept at the bottom of her bed. Downstairs, Sybil sat in a kitchen full of winter sunshine, tasks completed, hands folded, eyes closed, a smile touching her mouth, listening to Minions. Thoughtful creaks and cracks came from beams and slates as they adjusted to the change in temperature. Sifting and trickling and crumbling suggested mice or decay. Occasional moans and sighs betokened wind around the eaves. Woman and house were at one.

August 1949

'I'm afraid it's in a fairly primitive condition,' Jack said, taking her elbow, guiding her over the threshold. 'My father had tenant farmers here for donkey's years, and though they looked after the land and their immediate comforts they didn't do anything for the house. But I thought, before I let it again, that it might be worth doing up for you – and – and Tony, of course. See what you think.'

Sybil, back from her honeymoon and doubly beautiful, inspected the flagged hallway and dim, neglected rooms, the single water tap in the kitchen, the long tin bath hung on the lime-washed wall of the outhouse, and the chemical closet next door to the coal-shed.

They wandered out into the paddock.

'I've been thinking ahead, you see, Belle,' said Jack, taking her arm again on a pretext that the ground was uneven, 'and I believe

I can prophesy a couple of things quite accurately. Tony is going to make his mark in the world.'

She turned her radiant new face to him, saying, 'Oh, he is. Yes, he is.'

'In that case,' said Jack, suffering from love of her, and from her lack of love for him, 'he will need to take every opportunity that comes his way – and make a few if necessary.'

'Oh, of course. And I mean to encourage and help him as much as I can.'

'Which means,' Jack said, 'that Tony's career must come first with you both. That he'll have trips abroad, and not be able to take you with him. That he'll be working at home as well as at college, and you won't see much of each other. And that you'll move from place to place as he gets bigger and better appointments.'

Though she held her belief in Anthony aloft like a banner, Sybil was losing some of her glow and Jack hurried to restore it. 'I'm only stating obvious facts,' he said. 'I'm not talking about your love and happiness and the success of the marriage – all that goes without saying. But I do have a concern for *you* in this.'

His hand moved from her elbow to clasp her fingers.

'With everything concentrated on Tony's career, who will take care of *you*?'

She moved away from him, dimmed again.

He added hastily, 'I mean, when Tony isn't there.'

Her face cleared a little, and he ventured closer. 'May I tell you my plan? I thought that if there was a second home to which you could come for holidays and short breaks . . . and somebody around on whom you could rely . . . if you see what I mean. But, of course,' kicking a tussock, 'it will take a lot of time and hard work on both our parts to bring this place up to scratch, and you may not want to bother.'

Sybil did not reply directly, exclaiming instead at the beauty of the Virginia creeper, whose autumn flames were licking across the granite walls. She was seeing the house not as it was but as it could be, opening it up in her mind, making the rooms light and warm, furnishing them. She pictured children, running out into the summer air, followed by the family dog, watched by the family cat. As an afterthought she put a pony in the paddock and rows of vegetables in the kitchen garden.

Jack was saying, '. . . and though one doesn't care to discuss money – so vulgar, as my father used to remark! – there is the consideration that Tony will be years and years before he earns a decent salary. A permanent holiday home would be a great advantage, and I'm not thinking of making a profit from it. If you'll pay for the electricity you use . . .'

To Sybil it was already her first home. For she could hardly call two furnished rooms, with kitchenette and use of bathroom, a home. 'Nonsense! You must let it to us, Jack. Tony would insist upon that,' said Sybil staunchly. 'He's so proud and independent, you see. Otherwise, he might think it was charity.'

'Then I'll charge him a peppercorn rent to keep him happy,' said Jack easily. 'This is a two-way bargain, remember. I shall provide the essentials, but you will be doing the planning and beautification.'

Mindful again of her new husband's pride and independence, Sybil said, 'Naturally, I shall have to discuss this with Tony before we agree to anything.'

'Yes, of course, I understand that.'

But she was speaking on behalf of a man who expected the best of everything and always found other people to supply his wants, so the outcome could be foretold. It was her decision that counted and Sybil and Jack knew it, yet must play a little social game to satisfy the proprieties. This done, he would assume an important role in her life: the husband Anthony would never be.

But she cast the game to the winds, crying, 'It's a wonderful idea, Jack! How good you are to me – to us! I should so love this house. Oh, how soon can we begin?'

Now she said aloud, 'Ah, my dear Jack!' Full of remorse.

For her power over him had been great, and he had shaped Minions according to her wishes and in her image. And Minions had provided the stability and sense of continuity that would otherwise have been lacking. For Jack's surmise was correct in every detail. Once the honeymoon was over, Anthony pursued his career with relentless ardour. Looking back, she saw even that happy first year in furnished rooms as flawed, already presaging troubles to come. He had been impatient to return to work, reluctant to take holidays; and, though she had not known it at

254

the time, the secret responsibility of his sister's child was taking its toll of them both.

In the second year she had miscarried a baby Anthony did not want, but had allowed her because she pleaded for it. In the third year Blanche was admitted into their marriage at a terrible cost. This had not been eased by the unplanned advent of Edward; nor alleviated by the birth of Lydia, their reconciliation baby; because Anthony regarded his children as rivals for Sybil's affection. As well as these stresses, and the thrust of his ambition, they moved from one form of temporary accommodation to another.

'It's like being married to a member of the forces,' Sybil said, packing yet again.

Over the years they improved their residences and inherited parental furniture. But Blanche had left home, Edward was at college, and Lydia engaged, before he accepted his final appointment and bought a house at last.

So Cornwall had been a haven for Sybil and her children.

'Minions will always be yours,' Jack said once. 'I shall make sure of that.'

But people in love make promises they may not be able to keep, and though Jack was the most generous of men he lacked patience with detail. He would mean to do something, but postpone the doing. Also, death had surprised him.

And may well surprise me too, Sybil thought. So who am I to complain? I have benefited from this home and Jack's love for forty years. Many people have no home at all, few have such good friends. I am a fortunate woman.

Then she ended the conversation in her head, seeing that it was time for her granddaughter's afternoon tea and for the washing to be brought in.

CHAPTER TWENTY-EIGHT

March 1953

Jack Maddern's housekeeper would have known that Sybil Malpas was at Minions, even if her arrival by taxi, the previous evening, had not been noted; even if a sealed letter, addressed in her handwriting, had not been delivered by young Mat Kellow soon after breakfast, for his air of suppressed excitement, his preoccupation, and the absent manner in which he ate his midday meal, betrayed him.

Miss George was an elderly woman who had come to the big house as a scullery maid, long before he was born, and she took a personal interest in his welfare. She thought it a pity, though she was careful not to gossip outside, that he should be enamoured of a married woman; firstly because it might lead to scandal, and secondly because nothing could come of it, and he should be thinking of settling down and getting himself a son or two for Predanick Wartha.

Sybil's letter had been with him since it arrived. Miss George had caught him reading it between courses. Now he consulted the sheet of paper openly, took out his father's gold fob-watch and compared its time-keeping with the dining-room clock; preparing – she would bet a pound to a penny – to tell her that he was going out and would not be home for tea.

'Was everything all right, sir?' she asked, hands folded in front of her, for he had eaten very little.

'Splendid. Splendid. By the way, Mrs Malpas has arrived unexpectedly with her little girl, and I need to see Will Kellow about those shelves you mentioned, so I shall be dropping in at Minions. Don't expect me home for tea, Miss George.'

'No, sir.'

256

So little said, so much known, and even more pondered and considered.

The afternoon was breezy, spring-like, bracing, and Jack decided to walk to his assignation. On the outskirts of the village, fields of daffodils danced a minuet with the wind. In the village itself he kept his patience, while making a leisurely affable progress towards Minions: stopping and being stopped, answering questions, acknowledging complaints and requests, exchanging good wishes. Like his father before him, he performed the double duty of magistrate and landlord, and owned most of the local property, so the demands made upon him were many and the responsibilities widely spread. Indeed, he often wondered who owned whom, for he served harder as a master than any of his servants. But at last, his business done, he was able to think of pleasure, and turned down the side lane to the house and knocked on the back door. Familiar as he had become, he did not wait for a response but lifted the latch and walked into the kitchen.

Sybil was standing at the stone sink, washing small garments and crying over them. The child, Blanche, was nowhere to be seen, hopefully taking an afternoon nap. Grateful to have Sybil to himself, sorry to find her in this state, he knew better than to ask what was wrong. Only Anthony could make her cry like this.

So he said amiably, 'I should have thought there was enough water about, Belle!' And made her dry her hands, and brought her to the warmth of the fire, and stood beside her, one arm about her shoulders, while she sobbed herself out.

A coal tumbled from the grate on to the rag rug, and as he stooped to lift it back with the tongs he went into a Minions reverie, though always mindful of Sybil's grief. He really must, he reminded himself, do something about the kitchen this year. The place wasn't fit for more than picnicking. Not that Sybil allowed its deficiencies to make any difference. She produced appetizing meals and clean clothes as if she had the finest equipment in the world, but he hated her to drudge. She had to boil every drop of hot water, the floor was damp and uneven, and the Cornish range too small and antiquated. One of the museums might like it, or some little restaurant looking for a quirky symbol, and then he could put a four-oven Aga in its place.

That damned fellow Malpas did not seem to mind at all, if indeed he noticed. He was away most of the time. They had come down for a month's holiday last summer with Blanche, who was wearing Sybil out. Anthony had stayed for a week and then driven off with a wave of the hand, leaving her, as it happened, short of money as well as without transport. Of course, he must have known that Jack would ferry her and Blanche to and fro, and look after them, but didn't that make matters worse? And then there was the child herself: a responsibility that Sybil should never have accepted. She had confided in him, of course, and he had thought it a great mistake from the beginning. Adoption was a risky business at the best of times, but to take on the by-blow of a promiscuous woman like Natalie Malpas and some unknown blackguard was bound to lead to disaster.

'Is everything all right between you?' Jack had asked Sybil.

But she replied, as always, 'Oh, yes. Tony is just very busy at the moment.'

Loyal to him. And he did not deserve her loyalty.

Then the fellow had driven them all down for Christmas and gone back before the New Year. And yesterday she had arrived here without him, quite unexpectedly; travelling half-way across the country, encumbered with the child and their luggage, because Anthony had gone abroad for three months. Not good enough by half.

As if she had divined his thought, Sybil dried her eyes and said simply, 'I think I'm at the end of my rope, Jack.'

Usually he could tease her out of this mood by minimizing Anthony's defects and calling up her virtues, but this time good humour and common sense failed to work.

Sybil said, looking away from him into the fire, 'Tony's gone too far this time.'

She stood twisting the little handkerchief in her fingers, while he wished it were Tony's neck, and then she burst out, 'I haven't positive proof and he swears that there is no one else, but something has been going on in a clandestine fashion for a long time.'

Ah! Probably a secretary or one of the students. Jack had heard rumours about Anthony's conquests when they were all at university together, but Sybil would not have given them credence even if he dared tell her. Part of the man's attraction was his ability to make a girl feel unique, and as long as any girl thought she was *the* one she didn't mind if there had been others. And then, he was an arrogant devil. Like that sister of his. Two handsome, arrogant, mesmerizing black devils who could have anyone they fancied, or almost anyone. The pair of them should have been strangled at birth.

'I shall never forgive him,' Sybil was saying. 'I told him I should leave him.'

'Well, you can, you know,' said Jack promptly. 'You can move down here permanently whenever you like and let him go hang. I'll look after you. If you divorce him I'll marry you.'

She turned to him then as if he had been a priest offering sanctuary. 'But what about Blanche? Because I'm all she has.'

Personally he thought that the child was a bigger problem than Anthony, but knowing Sybil's feelings on the matter he could not say so. 'Blanche, too,' he said, steadfast in his love, and crossed his fingers surreptitiously.

She said he was so good, so very good, and then began to cry again. 'I've told him that our marriage is in name only, from now on.'

Yes, it would be like Sybil to say that: putting the matter delicately even *in extremis*.

'What did he say?' Jack asked.

'He said . . . he said . . .' swallowing a sob '. . . that we'd discuss things when he came home, but he had to catch his flight.'

'Bastard!' Jack muttered.

'But I shan't discuss it,' Sybil said more firmly, and wiped her eyes. 'As far as I am concerned we have separated. And to make sure that I don't go back on my word—'

She broke down again, and he put both arms round her. 'What dreadful deed have you done, Belle?' he asked her tenderly.

She answered with a laugh and a sob that threatened to strangle her, 'I've given the landlady a month's notice. We haven't a home anymore. There's no turning back.'

Jack stared at her top-knot of fair hair, shocked, incredulous, delighted.

'You mean you *have* come down here for good?'

She nodded, and then shook her head. 'Not exactly. I shall divide my time between Cornwall and Cheshire while I work out what to do. I can help my mother to look after Daddy. He's been almost an invalid since the stroke, and she and I have always got on well together. She'd be glad of the company. But this all happened in such a rush that I knew I had to think about it carefully before I said anything to her. So I came here first to mull things over. I don't want to worry her.'

He could understand the hesitation. Blanche was not an easy house-guest. Still, Sybil was here, and dependent on him, and that damned fellow was abroad for three months.

'I knew something was wrong,' he said with satisfaction, and embraced her more warmly, and closed his eyes, and wished.

It was one of those cold, bright, Cornish days when the promise of spring is not yet made manifest. The wind was up and the house responded to it with a long and passionate conversation, conducted in the rafters and down the chimneys and through the cracks in the window-frames and beneath the doors.

Sybil was quiet now, and they stayed together in a trance: he yearning, she resting against him. A sudden vicious puff of smoke from the range made them both cough, lift their heads and look at each other, and laugh ruefully.

'That's better!' Jack said, glad to see her smile again. 'I really must—'

He was about to say 'pull out that range and buy you an Aga,' but the sight of her face just below his, still bearing a trace of tears, and yet so tranquil, so Sybil, made him forget that intention and fulfil another. He kissed her in tribute to her beauty and his love. And when she did not protest or move away he kissed her again, in hope; and again in an exploratory fashion, to discover when she would move away. Her skin was as cool and smooth as cream. Her lips did not so much respond as allow him to partake of them. She smelled faintly, deliciously, of lemon verbena. Her body was young and warm and yielding.

In truth, she was so grateful for Jack's loving kindness and so bruised by Anthony's lack of it, that she permitted him to cross the line between friend and lover almost without thought, as if he deserved to be so rewarded.

He whispered urgently, as they reached a point of no return, 'Where's Blanche?'

'Sleeping,' Sybil whispered back languidly, and granted him ultimate access while the wind roamed round the house.

Afterwards, they were both a little shaken and incredulous: he at his good fortune, she at her transgression. And both were ravenously hungry, for he had eaten little since her note arrived, she had eaten nothing all day, and it was almost six o'clock.

So while he telephoned Miss George to say he would not be

back for dinner, Sybil cooked copiously and imaginatively for the three of them: a quick meal of catholic tastes, incorporating the child's whims and fancies and their favourite dishes, so that all three could dip and taste and try as they pleased. And they made much of Blanche, who had wakened at last, flushed with sleep and wailing over past sorrows and present surroundings, and sat her between them at the kitchen table so she could share the feast. And Sybil made up a story about the wind, and pretended to answer the questions it asked of the house. It was one of the happiest evenings in all their three lives.

Anthony did not discover for some weeks that his wife had left him, because he was extremely busy and a perfunctory letter-writer. Her lack of communication penetrated his consciousness slowly, bringing with it a whiff of foreboding and then, as her silence continued, reducing him to a state of panic. Finally he made an international telephone call and discovered that he no longer had a home as such. She could not have vanished with a three-year-old child, and she had no money of her own, so he deduced that she was either with her parents or at Minions. When at last he returned to England, and tracked her down in person, he was almost abject: not quite so abject as to overlook the involuntary light in her eyes when he appeared. Otherwise, all was changed.

Jack had made more improvements to Minions in those three months than in the past three years. His plans for its future were ambitious, and already being considered by Kerrier District Council. And Sybil was looking wonderful. She had put on a little weight, and it suited her. She moved more slowly, smiled serenely and often, no longer accorded Anthony her instant attention when he spoke. And the child, Blanche, was quieter, too. She and Jack had come to some sort of understanding. She liked him, climbed on his lap, made the small demands upon him that a loving and beloved daughter will make of her father. He, Anthony, had been cut out.

But all was not lost. Sybil was bound by her initial love of him and the sacrament of marriage, and Jack was too decent to rob him of the opportunity to make amends. Anthony took full advantage of them both. So it came about, as the Cornish summer moved to its zenith, that Sybil and Jack met one more time. And she gave herself to him — it was an expression that Jack had not fully understood until now — with such generosity that he thought the scales were dipping in his favour. But it was only her way of thanking him, and making reparation.

As they lay together in a cove, far away from his villagers' prying eyes and whispering tongues, staring up into the blue Cornish heaven, feeling the warm damp mattress of sand beneath their backs, interlacing their fingers, she delivered the *coup de grâce* as kindly as she could.

She said, 'You've made me very happy, Jack, and you know that I love you in the finest sense of the word, but Tony is truly sorry, and Blanche is sleeping right through the night, and life will be easier at home now.'

Jack gave up hope then, and though remaining constant in his friendship and devotion to Sybil, and his role as the perfect uncle to her children, his romantic regard for women changed and he took no more emotional risks. Certainly he did not remain celibate, but he made sure that the question of marriage never entered into any future liaison.

And Sybil exacted the last ounce of retribution from Anthony before mending their quarrel. She insisted on the provision of a rented house that they could begin to furnish themselves. She exacted a full confession of his past sexual misdemeanours, so that in sentencing him she might take other offences into account. And finally she announced, without preliminary discussion or even an apology, that she was expecting the baby he had hoped to postpone indefinitely.

Edward was born the following April, a little early according to Sybil's reckoning. It seemed in retrospect quite out of character, for in life he was always a little late.

CHAPTER TWENTY-NINE

When Ralph Maddern arrived that Saturday afternoon Sybil was in the paddock, unpegging a line full of small garments. She had not heard the front-door bell, and though Henrietta was kneeling up in bed, hammering on the window to attract her attention, her thoughts were far away. So he walked round to the back of the house to announce himself.

She was exactly as he had expected her to be, with her unselfconscious beauty and humility. His uncle had once described her as 'A goddess burdened with unconsidered trifles!' But goddesses did not age and Sybil had done, which was something of a shock, for Jack always spoke of her as if she were perennially young. Yet beautiful still, and – observing the pegs and the mound of damp clothes in the wicker basket – still burdened with unconsidered trifles.

'Mrs Sybil Malpas? I hope I haven't come at an inconvenient time. My name is Ralph Maddern.'

'Oh, Lord!' Sybil cried, dropping Ben's pyjama jacket.

A long, lean, sunburned man in his early forties, with light-brown hair and light grey eyes was leaning on her garden gate. He had a definite look of Jack-when-younger about him, and otherwise was dressed as perhaps he thought he should be, in a tweed jacket, cavalry twill trousers, a polo-necked sweater and brown leather brogues, all looking new and carefully chosen. Sybil was at once delightfully surprised and deeply ashamed of herself. For what had she expected of this nephew from the other side of the world? A stage colonial, brash of speech and manner, beer can in hand, corks bobbing round his hat? Indeed, she admitted, she had not thought at all, only nourished her prejudices because Jack was dead and Minions lost. So her conscience pierced her.

She picked up the jacket, saying distractedly, 'Mr Maddern. Of course. How good of you to call. No, not in the least inconvenient. Please excuse the domestic details,' indicating the wash-basket and her apron.

Behind her a bedroom window was being pushed up, and she turned, crying, 'Henrietta Malpas, close that window at once. You'll catch cold!'

The window went down with a disconsolate thump, but Henny remained with her face pressed to one pane, contemplating the visitor.

'I'm afraid my granddaughter', glaring at her, 'has German measles. But, as you can see, she is feeling brighter.'

Ralph Maddern gave Henrietta an amicable wave, which she returned vivaciously.

'Bed!' Sybil commanded. The face disappeared from the window. She continued, 'So far it has missed my grandson Benjamin, who is out at the moment with the rest of the family, and I have been catching up with the chores – it being New Year's Eve tomorrow – and was not expecting – not that you aren't very welcome, of course . . .'

Sybil paused to draw breath, put one hand to her lips to still her nervous volubility, and became herself again.

'You've come at exactly the right time,' she said, smiling. 'I was about to make tea.'

He was amused, relieved, delighted. If he had worn a hat he would have lifted it in tribute. Instead, he strode forward to pick up her wash-basket and follow her into the kitchen.

But how strange, Sybil thought, feeling him walking behind her, that he should come here now, looking so like Jack, after I've been thinking of Jack all afternoon.

Her shoulders felt cold. The nape of her neck prickled. Imagine, she thought in wonderment, that the flesh remembers after so long a time.

And then chided herself for being an old fool.

Anthony and Blanche and Daniel and Edward and Ben, back from an afternoon messing about in rock pools, found Ralph Maddern and Sybil in the living room, talking like old friends, while Henrietta sat tucked up on the sofa, feeding a buttered scone to Gracie.

'Tony, you must meet Jack's nephew!' Sybil cried, jumping up, shining with pleasure. 'Ralph, this is my husband Tony . . .'

Reserved dignity on Anthony's side. Wary politeness on Ralph's part.

'My daughter Blanche and her – Daniel – and their son, Aaron.'

Blanche came forward to greet him, because Aaron was sitting on Daniel's shoulders, covering his father's eyes with the knitted arms of Ba.

'My son Edward . . .'

They shook hands: two long, thin, quiet men with fine brown hair that inclined to fall over their foreheads.

'. . . and my grandson Ben.' Smiling at him meaningfully.

Ben shook hands like a gentleman, but burst forth into speech immediately afterwards.

'Why is she downstairs?' pointing to his sister. 'She's supposed to be ill. And she shouldn't feed Gracie between meals.' Then, overlooking these iniquities, 'Look, Hen,' thrusting a slopping red plastic sand-bucket under her nose, 'I'll bet you'll never guess what I fished up—'

'Not now, Ben,' said his father, putting one hand on the crown of his head and turning him towards the door. 'Take that bucket into the kitchen and stand it in the sink, and wash your hands before you come back.'

'And then shut up,' Henrietta added, 'because the grown-ups want to talk.'

'I can see you're feeling better, Spotty Face,' said Edward, and put up his fists and threw a punch or two in her direction, saying over his shoulder, 'I hope you'll excuse my obnoxious kids, Ralph. They have no manners.'

'Ralph has children of his own,' said Sybil, radiant with inner knowledge, 'and understands the occasional lapse.'

'Occasional?' Henrietta cried pertly. 'Ben's mannerless all the time.'

'That's enough, Hen,' said her father good-naturedly.

'Ralph only arrived here last night, and came over as soon as he could,' said Sybil, 'with the most wonderful news. Blanche, I've left a trolley laid in the kitchen. If you'll bring it in, with the electric kettle, Ralph will tell us everything while I make fresh tea.'

Aaron ceased tormenting his father and shouted, 'Tea! Tea! Tea!'

'Tea for me, too,' Ben cried, charging back. 'Gran, are those cream splits on the trolley for us? Salome was licking one of them, but I smacked her and she ran off.'

Sybil was saying, 'No, Ralph, I insist that you sit down. Visitors are not allowed to help.'

Anthony's ironic black glance met that of his daughter. She winked at him and shrugged. He smiled.

Blanche said, 'In the interests of peace and propriety, Sybil, I think I should feed Aaron in the kitchen. You can tell me the news afterwards, although I'm panting to hear it . . .'

But Sybil would have none of it. They must all be there. So Daniel carried in the high chair, and Blanche spread newspapers underneath it, and Edward wheeled in the trolley.

Ralph sat forward, hands clasped on his knees, smiling round on them all. He was moved and astounded by the fact of being in Cornwall and meeting the Malpases at last. They had been part of Jack Maddern, with Predanick Wartha, Minions, and the village; and though he knew that he was his uncle's heir he had never expected to realize all this and them so soon. In fact, he had listened to Jack rather as one listens to a story-teller: living the tale but not expecting to take part in it. Besides, there was only twenty years' difference in age between uncle and nephew. Ralph should, by rights, have been a far older man before he came into his inheritance.

Sybil sat opposite him with a little sigh of triumph, and her radiance returned. Gracie sank down at her feet. Patch jumped on to her lap. Salome leaped effortlessly to the top shelf of the bookcase and sulked. Ben sat on the sofa by his sister's feet. The others brought chairs into a wide circle round the fire.

'What a pity that Lydia isn't here with us,' Sybil observed. 'Ah, well, it can't be helped. Now, Ralph, would you like to begin?'

His voice was warm and slow, the colonial accent giving it a slightly laconic tone. He looked round on them all and smiled. 'It seems that I know all you far better than you know me. But, then, my mother kind of upset the family apple cart, so I expect he kept pretty quiet about the pair of us. But he often spoke to me of Sybil, and it was clear to me that he intended her to have this house for life. We talked this over, as I remember, the last time that we met — about eighteen months ago. I thought he would have written a codicil to that effect, but I reckon that he didn't expect to die so soon.'

He veered away for a while, to give them an insight into his own affairs. 'The news took us by surprise, I can tell you. Lu and I have a lot of thinking to do before we pull up roots. We were both born in New Zealand, and that's our country. So I may put a tenant in here for a few years while the kids grow up, and then retire early. I'm playing it by ear right now.'

He returned to them. 'So I've come over to sort everything out, and I got here as soon as I could. I'm the manager of a sheep farm in New Zealand, you see, and you can't drop that kind of job in five minutes. I had to make arrangements.'

The silence was intense. He smiled round on them all, and Sybil was reminded of the way Jack would stretch out the news of a forthcoming treat.

Ralph Maddern said succinctly, 'The tenancy of Minions is to remain with Sybil, rent free, during her lifetime.'

No one spoke for several seconds. Then Sybil said, 'And after my death, Ralph. Tell them what happens after my death.'

There was a concerted wail from the sofa. In the delight of Minions' reprieve, Sybil had forgotten her grandchildren, who were now confronted by the prospect of a further emotional upheaval. 'Oh, nonsense!' Sybil chided them briskly. 'I shan't die for twenty years yet! I come of a long-lived family.' For the deaths of her brothers had been untimely, and her mother would have lived longer had she not mourned the premature death of Sybil's father. So she offered them a fable to reassure them. And they were heartened, because twenty years were beyond their comprehension and they would be old by then. But their father knew that with Sybil's death would come the end of his extended childhood, and he must begin to prepare for that.

Ralph said to him, 'Well, if you and I are still tottering around then, Ted, I'm sure we can come to some arrangement about the tenancy.'

'There!' Sybil said, as if a prophecy had been fulfilled. 'What do you think of that news, as a beginning to the new decade?'

There was a confused babble of amazement and delight, over which Anthony's voice rose as official representative for the occasion. 'Ralph, this is an extraordinarily generous offer. We all love Minions and should have been sorry to lose it,' grandly, 'but

I know I speak for the family when I say that we are grateful to you for Sybil's sake . . .'

Henrietta and Ben cheered.

'. . . and I find it particularly edifying,' Anthony continued, frowning them to silence, 'in such a materialistic age, to honour a wish that was not legally binding . . .'

This time he was interrupted by the recipient of his thanks. 'Of course it was binding,' said Ralph tersely. 'I gave him my word. I believe you call it a gentlemen's agreement over here.'

Ben said under his breath, 'Pow!'

Blanche and Sybil cried in unison, 'Tea, everybody?'

Her house repossessed, as it were, Sybil was now free to worry about other members of the family. Sitting on a cork-topped stool, with Gracie beside her, she posted Aaron's limbs into his sleeping suit while Blanche let out the bath water.

'It's all very well for Tony to send you off to the Cornish Arms,' she said, 'but it won't be easy for you to cope with Aaron while you're living in one place and sleeping in another.'

'It's only for three nights, and we have cots in both places, so I shall put him to bed here first,' said Blanche reasonably, 'and then we'll take him across with us when we leave you at eleven.' As Sybil opened her mouth to protest she added firmly, 'Many years ago, as I remember, the three of us were packed into the back of whatever ancient car Daddy was running at the time, dressed in our pyjamas and dressing gowns, and driven two or three hundred miles overnight down to Cornwall, were we not?'

'Well, yes,' Sybil conceded, holding Aaron up. 'I was just thinking about his routine, and where you would keep his clothes . . . but, yes.'

'So things are not so very different, after all,' Blanche remarked, receiving her son.

Aaron opened one fist and dropped a damp chewed rusk on the bathroom floor in front of the Labrador, who stared at it disdainfully and then looked away.

'Don't you want to eat that nice biscuit, Gracie?' Blanche asked ironically.

'No. She's too old. She can't be bothered,' Sybil replied absently, hanging the damp bath towel on a rail, picking up the rusk and putting it on the window-sill outside.

'For the birds,' she explained, and took a plastic bottle of bath-cleaner from the shelf and said, 'Darling, have you thought any more about your future – with Daniel, I mean?'

'Who speaks my name?' a caressing voice asked from the doorway.

'Da. Da. Da,' Aaron replied, twisting round to see his father, looking at him, laughing.

Blanche turned her head, her smile inviting him to come to her, lifting her face for his kiss. Then spoke to Sybil teasingly, naughtily, knowing her news would displease. 'We've made temporary plans,' she answered. 'We're trying out a new method of partnership and parenthood. Each of us lives in our own flat, and we look after Aaron between us, and stay with each other when we feel like it. So, as you see, hopping between the Cornish Arms and Minions will be good practice.'

Sybil dropped the plastic bottle in the bath and retrieved it with a vexed pounce, suffering the exasperation of one who does not understand the present generation. She straightened up to face her daughter. 'How do you mean look after him between you?' she asked sharply. 'The child is already ferried between you and Mrs Patel, and now you offer him a third home. He won't know where he belongs.'

Gracie pricked her ears, got slowly to her feet and padded out of the bathroom.

'Of course, he will,' said Blanche easily but firmly. 'He belongs with us, wherever we are. Now, sir, shall we brush our teeth?'

But Daniel took pity on Sybil and came to soothe her. 'Now you're not to trouble yourself,' he said earnestly, taking her free hand between both of his, where it lay like a dried white leaf. 'You've only seen my social side, so far, but there's a lot more to me than that. I mean to be a good family man. I work at home most of the time and I can fit my schedule around Aaron, just as Blanche does . . .'

Sybil was remembering his foray into their society on Christmas Eve, and all that had ensued in the six days since then. Her hand trembled. He squeezed reassurance into it.

'Up and down, Sunny Jim!' Blanche was saying, wielding the toothbrush.

'Up. Down. Zhim,' Aaron sputtered indistinctly.

Daniel was saying, 'I'll be there to fill the gap when Blanche works late or she's too tired, or whenever they both need me. I can baby-sit for her if she has to go out in the evening, and the three of us will spend our weekends together at her place or mine.'

'Mostly at mine,' said Blanche, brisk and unrepentant, 'unless your housekeeping has improved considerably.'

Sybil liked Daniel very much, but he did not inspire her with the same confidence as a professional child-minder. She addressed her daughter. 'What about Mrs Patel? Surely you won't get rid of her?'

Blanche said determinedly, 'Mummy, we're at the experimental stage. I'm not getting rid of anyone. I couldn't manage without her. Dan isn't taking Mrs Patel's place. He's adding another dimension to Aaron's life and mine.'

'And the boy will see more of me than most sons see of their fathers,' Daniel added.

'Oh, that's true. That is indeed true,' Sybil said, turning away from him, wringing her hands without realizing it. For Anthony had never been there with his children while they were growing up, except during enforced holidays and grudging weekends. It was Jack who taught Blanche how to ride and bought her a pony; Jack who taught Edward how to play cricket; Jack who taught Lydia how to swim, when no one else could coax her into the water; Jack who drove them all out for picnics and days on the beach, took them to fairs and shows; Jack who was the true father of their childhood.

'And when Aaron's with me I shan't be ignoring him or sitting him in front of the television,' Daniel pursued. 'I'll be encouraging him to draw and paint and make a mess, which children like to do. And I can cook for the pair of us. I'm a good plain cook. Blanche will tell you.'

Anything that can be fried, Sybil thought. The child being fed straight cholesterol.

'And he'll get me out of the flat, because he needs fresh air, and off we'll go together.'

'Where to?' demanded Sybil, thinking of Chicago in the nineteen twenties, hooch drunk out of teacups, and hoodlums with names like Two-fingered Jed Pastrami.

'Oh, all sorts of places. Parks.' The child lost. 'Rivers.' The child drowned. 'Cafés.' The child's teeth ruined by shop cakes.

'Children,' said Sybil, entreating them, 'need stability. They should be reared by two parents in the family home.'

'Oh, my very dear Mama,' said Blanche, amused and sorry,

taking compassion on her. 'We were reared in a lion's den while the lion roamed elsewhere. I can't believe you don't know that — even if you won't admit it.'

'What nonsense!' Sybil cried, knowing she had lost the argument. 'How you dramatize things!' She pulled on a pair of rubber gloves with great emphasis and wielded the bath cleaner with tremendous spirit. 'Isn't it time that child was in bed?' she asked.

Behind her back, Blanche and Daniel winked ruefully at each other.

Grandmother and grandson kept each other silent company: he fast asleep, arms outflung; she sitting by his cot, hands clasped in her lap, meditating on past and present.

The door was pushed quietly open, and Blanche peered round it. 'We wondered where you were,' she whispered. 'Is anything wrong?'

Sybil shook her head. 'I just needed to be by myself for a while, and ponder.'

Blanche crept in and sat beside her penitently, and held her hand. 'I know I can be a bitch, but you mustn't fret about me,' she said.

'No, no. I wasn't worrying about you. I was thinking of poor Jack. Poor Jack.'

She was silent for some moments, and then gave soft tongue to the thoughts that had occupied her. 'It was Jack and I who restored Minions and brought up you three children. Tony didn't lift a hand unless he felt like it. He didn't have to. He could always find someone else to labour for him.'

Blanche squeezed her fingers.

'I actually left him once, you know. I almost divorced him and married Jack.'

Blanche put one arm round Sybil's shoulders and kissed her cheek.

'I left Tony again and again, in my mind, and in many ways — like the other night. I've been trying to understand why I always came back. I suppose, despite the terrors and frustrations of marriage and its periods of boredom — as well as the good things — it becomes a habit. Not in the sense of taking each other for granted so much as becoming part of each other, however different you may be. Sharing a life that only the two of you can

271

make between you. And the web grows wider and larger and more closely woven the longer you are together. Until, in the end, to destroy it would be to destroy yourselves or to leave you mortally wounded.'

Aaron stirred in his sleep, smacked his lips, curled his fingers. She lowered her voice still further. 'My parents were enlightened people, who believed that daughters should be given the same educational advantages as sons, and that girls should be able to earn their own living. They used to say that if you educate a woman you educate a family. But they also expected I should marry and that marriage would then be my prime responsibility. I accepted that without question. And in those days the roles of husband and wife were quite distinct. The woman created the home and family. The man provided for them all.'

They were silent again, sitting head to head, hands entwined.

'But marriage did not mean that we sank into mental slothfulness,' said Sybil. 'An intelligent woman went on learning. I taught full-time when we were first married, and then part-time when you children were at school, until Tony was well paid. I kept up my interests and read widely, and when you no longer needed me I was able to do much more.'

'Like learning German, and reading Goethe in the original language,' Blanche said.

Sybil's smile was vivid. 'Yes. Yes. Like that.' Gradually the smile faded away. 'Of course, there were exceptions in my day,' she admitted. 'Women who didn't marry or were childless, a few highly talented women who put their careers before their families. But for the majority of my generation, the family was our reason for being. It is my reason for being.'

Blanche said gently, 'But I have my own reason for being, and Daniel and Aaron are additions to it.'

Sybil paused for thought, then said to herself, 'No, neither you nor Lydia would be capable of that dedication, but I feel that Henrietta might be.' Her smile was amused as she contemplated the years ahead. 'Yes, she has all the makings of a grand matriarch.'

Still gently, Blanche said, 'This is a changed and changing world, Sybil, and the idea of the family must change with it.'

They sat together in the room, feeling the chill on their limbs and the warmth where their bodies touched; listening to the sound of Aaron's breathing. The night-light fluttered on its saucer of water in a sudden draught. Ghostly scents of baby powder and Samsara haunted the air. Peace, lulling all the senses, pervaded them.

Sybil began again. 'Oh, I know that mine is an unfashionable idea, and women now expect to pursue a career as well as bringing up a family. But women are not immortal and invincible.' Her voice strengthened with her convictions. 'They have only twenty-four hours in the day and one pair of hands, after all. Something must go. And that something is time for themselves. This sort of time.' Her free hand indicated the half-lit room, the sleeping child, the chair in which she sat. 'Time should be like a good apple harvest,' Sybil said. 'Enough to eat, enough to give away, and enough to lie on the ground.'

Blanche had no answer to this, and Sybil did not ask for one. She released herself from her daughter's embrace and stood up a little stiffly.

'Human beings take many years to mature, and they need help, encouragement and support all the way. There are no short cuts and no royal roads.'

She removed Ba to the end of Aaron's cot and tucked him in more firmly.

'Or else, my dear,' she said, looking straight at Blanche, 'children must tumble up by themselves, and homes become lodging-houses.'

CHAPTER THIRTY

New Year's Day 1990

The telephone rang at five minutes after midnight, and Blanche elected to answer it, champagne glass in hand. Behind her, a shaft of roseate light from the open door of the living room cut across the hall floor. Strains of a Scottish television broadcast mingled with the Malpas's final rendering of Auld Lang Syne. A delicious odour of roast pheasant still clung to the air. Ralph Maddern had spent a carefree evening with them, and the family had been at its finest.

In the dim semi-privacy of the hall Blanche cried, 'Happy New Year, whoever you are!'

The familiar hoarse deep voice wiped out her smile and filled her with anger, pain and compassion.

'I was hoping it might be you,' said Natalie gratefully, then added with her usual arrogance, 'but I would have asked to speak to you anyhow!' She softened again, spoke slowly, choosing her words carefully. 'Look, I know you can't forget what happened. Only a fool would expect that. But – can you think of it as if it were a tale you had been told?' Blanche said nothing. 'I don't feel like a mother anyway. Try to think of me as you used to – the legendary absent aunt.' She beseeched Blanche. 'Do you think you could do that?' She ventured a mild joke to release the tension between them. 'And then all need not be lost, as they say in Victorian melodramas.'

Blanche roused herself. 'Yes. Yes, I expect I can. I'll try anyway,' she answered, her voice and intentions far ahead of her feelings.

'Because we did like each other at first sight, didn't we?' Natalie continued. 'We were friends, weren't we?'

This time Blanche found it easier to say, 'Yes, we were indeed.' She was reluctant to commit herself, yet unable to ignore the plea, and continued, 'I have been thinking about you. Wondering how you were. The eye operation and so on.'

'Sod the operation!'

Blanche laughed a little, and asked, 'When is it likely to be?'

'No idea. I'm seeing the specialist again early in February. Forget about it. And when it happens don't send me one of those bloody get-well cards.'

'I won't,' Blanche answered, smiling, 'but I'll wish you well, just the same.'

'I thank you for that.'

They had said everything they could for the moment, and after a pause Natalie asked, 'Have things calmed down over there?'

'Yes, quite considerably. We're all on our best behaviour. Would you like to speak to Tony?'

A pause.

'Better not,' said Natalie, 'it will only cause trouble. Just say "Happy New Year!" to him from me – and to anyone else who might be interested. And love to you and Dan and the boy. Take care of yourselves and each other.'

Anthony was refilling their glasses when the next call came, and Edward answered it, speaking politely, remotely, as if his former wife were a former acquaintance.

'Oh, hello, Kat! And a happy New Year to you, too. Yes, we're all here, and having a high old time – apart from the kids, who are in bed.'

'Charles and I just wanted to wish you all the best for nineteen ninety, and we look forward to entertaining you here with Henny and Ben some time.'

'We'll see how things turn out,' he said stiffly.

As both of them wondered what to say next they were saved by a voice from the head of the stairs calling softly, seductively, 'Dad, is that Mum? Hen and me aren't asleep. We're here on the landing.'

Edward's smile of relief was evident in his voice. 'Hang on a minute. It seems that the kids aren't in bed, after all. Come on down, you rascals, and speak to your mother!' More easily. 'Here they are! They must have been waiting up! Goodbye, then. Yes, all the best.'

From the living room Sybil called, 'Are they wearing their dressing gowns and carpet slippers?'

And from Anthony, 'Do those children never sleep?'

Edward came in smiling shyly, and Henrietta darted after him, saying over her shoulder, 'You can talk to Mummy first, Ben! And keep your voice down!'

To their new friend, 'Happy New Year, Uncle Ralph!'

To Sybil reassuringly, 'Yes, Gran'ma, we're all warm and wrapped up.'

To Anthony reproachfully, 'Grandpa, we've been asleep for hours and hours, but Ben had to go to the bathroom and then he came to see me and woke me up.'

To them all, 'Oops! Ben's calling me. Back in a minute.'

They heard her say, 'Hello, Mummy! Yes, it's me, Hen! How is my darling Mr Silk? Well, put him up to the phone and let him hear me speak. Hello, Mr Silk. Oh, Mummy, he knows me. He's barking to say hello!' Squeals of delight. 'Bye-bye, Mr Silk. Oh, yes, feeling much better and being spoiled rotten. Yes. Yes, I will. Lovely to hear from you. Lots of love and a happy New Year to you ...' in a husky tactful whisper, '... and Charles!' Then commandingly, 'Benjamin Malpas stay there and don't you move until I tell you!'

She bounced back, aglow with impending news, holding an invisible trumpet to her lips. 'Tah-rah! Happy New Year, everybody! As I was saying, Ben had to go to the bathroom and then he woke me up because he needed my expert advice.'

Anthony gave a snort. Sybil hid a smile. Blanche laughed aloud.

Henrietta surveyed the circle of adults much as her grandmother would survey a circle of children. And in Sybil's manner, she asked, 'Have you all had a nice party?'

They assured her that they had.

'Then that's the good news,' said Henrietta briskly. 'Now for the bad news.' She called, 'Ben! You can come in!'

Out of the dim hall into the brightly lit living room crept a figure all forlorn and uncertain of its reception.

'Look!' Henrietta cried, exhibiting her brother with all the pride of a circus owner showing a peculiarly repulsive freak. 'Lift up your face so they can all see you, Ben. Roll up your sleeves. Undo your pyjama jacket. Show them!'

He tried to adopt a swaggering air, but his underlip quivered.

'No, no,' said Sybil, smiling, drawing him to her. 'There's no need, my love. It looks like a first-class case of German measles to me.'

Ben wound his arms round her waist and hid his head in her midriff.

'He woke up feeling sick about half an hour ago,' his sister informed them, 'and he did his best to get to the bathroom, but he wasn't quite quick enough. Some of it's on the floor. But we waited until after midnight so's we wouldn't disturb you.'

'I'm sorry, Gran,' said a muffled Ben. 'I couldn't help it.'

'I'll sort the floor out, Sybil,' Blanche said, and went to find a mop-bucket.

'Why is he upset?' Henrietta asked, eyes fixed on her brother's heaving shoulders.

'He's been very brave,' Sybil said, stroking his head, shielding him, knowing that he did not want anyone to see him cry, 'and he's tired and he's not feeling at all well. So he and I are going upstairs to make him comfortable. Please excuse us, everyone.'

'G'night!' Ben said gruffly, keeping one arm over his eyes.

Henrietta followed them, chattering up the stairs and along the landing. 'I expect he's upset thinking about being all alone, but he needn't be, because I've got two beds in my room and I've had the German measles already, so I can't catch it any more, and he can have the other bed, and then I can keep an eye on him. I don't even mind if he brings Clemmie in with us! Poor old Ben, don't you worry, Hen will look after you. And when he's feeling better in a day or two we can push the beds together and play some of those old-fashioned board games that you've got here. What about Monopoly? We've never played that. I know where you keep it. On the top shelf in Lydia's room. I stood on a chair and just peeped inside the lid, and it's all full of paper money, and Ben's interested in money. Gran'ma! Gran'ma? Are you listening to me . . . ?'

Downstairs, Blanche stood in the doorway, bucket in hand, and raised her mop in salute. 'Tiny Tim wishes all Malpases a happy New Year!' she cried, grinning, 'and says God help us — every one!'

CHAPTER THIRTY-ONE

February 1990

'Damn you, whoever you are!' Blanche cried, as the doorbell sounded for the second time. 'All right! All right! I'm coming!' Impatient of interruptions.

Anthony stood on the doorstep, carrier bag in hand, travel bag by his side, clearing his throat, lifting his chin, looking splendid, giving a tremendous performance of a man who was in full command of himself and the situation. So she guessed he was uneasy.

'Tried to ring you from Paddington,' he explained, 'but your telephone is out of order.'

'No, it's off the hook,' she answered briefly, 'but do come in.'

'Ah! Yes. Thank you. Your mother – Sybil – said you were always in on a Tuesday.'

'So I am. And what brings you here? Let me have your coat.'

'Ah! Thank you. Sybil sent a country bundle for you,' holding out the carrier bag, 'primroses from the garden, and home-made jam and things, and there's a letter.'

The primroses, held to her nose, gave forth an earthy scent and a promise of spring, and Blanche smiled into them.

'Just dropped in for a moment,' Anthony explained.

'How very nice,' she said, bemused. 'Come through and thaw yourself out. Have you had lunch?'

'Sybil made sandwiches for me, and I bought a plastic cup of hot brown water in the refreshment car. Don't know what the hell it was.'

'Would you like some decent coffee?'

'If it's not too much trouble,' he replied gratefully, on his nicest behaviour.

He rubbed his hands, warming them over the Scandinavian wood stove, looking round the large light room with its bright

278

creative clutter. From her winter perch at the end of the mantel-shelf, Salome turned satanic eyes upon him, the blue infernally lit with crimson.

'This is a very pleasant place,' he said, smiling at Blanche. 'I don't think I've been here before, have I?'

'I shouldn't think so,' she replied, wryly amused. 'You've never visited me before.'

'No, so I haven't.'

He wandered over to the shelves of books and squinted at their titles, pulled one out and returned to sink into an armchair, took out his reading glasses, put them on, opened the book. When she came back he was totally absorbed.

'I didn't realize you still had *Tales of Greece and Rome*!' he remarked.

'You used to read them to me when I was a child.'

He glanced at her over his spectacles, murmuring. 'Yes. So I did. You had an excellent memory, and used to correct me if I missed anything out. (Two spoons of sugar, please. Can't abide this dietary nonsense!) I remember your stopping me once about the Sphinx when I read, ". . . and she licked her lips".'

They chorused, 'and she licked her *cru-el* lips!' and laughed.

He read on, sipping his coffee occasionally.

Blanche sauntered the length of the room, arms folded, turned round and came back to him, puzzled, intrigued.

'What brings you to London?' she asked. 'Business or pleasure?'

He shut the book, as if he had been waiting for her question and could now answer it. 'Neither. I'm flying to Munich to look up an old colleague, and Natalie sees her specialist in Bern on Friday so I'll cross the border and stay with her for a week, hold her hand, cheer her on, and find out what she needs. Probably short of money.'

'Have you told Sybil the whole story?' Blanche asked ironically. 'Or are you slipping in this act of charity unbeknownst, as Dan would say?'

'No, no. Sybil and I discussed the matter at length,' Anthony replied, relaxed and easy now. 'We both agreed that Natalie could not be abandoned, as it were, though Sybil is not prepared to deal with her personally. So I'm doing what I must, and Sybil,' he paused, searching for a suitable expression, and finally choosing one of Ben's phrases, 'is doing her own thing. She's going down to Minions today, as you might imagine. She says the daffodils will be up in the garden. Do read your letter, by the way. She was up until well past midnight writing it. I'm quite happy sitting here . . .'

Dearest Blanche,
Communications since New Year have been so scrappy,
and you and I so occupied with our many concerns, that I
am sending the latest news and a bagful of jollies via
Tony. He really has been extraordinarily understanding,
because I spent most of January at Minions, looking after
the children and then helping Ralph with his affairs,
while he fended for himself here in Clifton.
    The German measles — so glad Aaron escaped! — was
a wonderful opportunity for Edward and me to make
friends with Ralph and introduce him to the way of life
here. The two men get on so well together, and as the
children were in quarantine rather than being truly ill,
and the weather was mild, we enjoyed lots of trips. I was
able to do more for Ralph when we were on our own,
and to impress upon him the value of the roots of his
inheritance, and the importance of his young son and
daughter spending their childhood here, rather than
thinking of Predanick Wartha as a place for occasional
holidays and eventual retirement. It is a momentous
decision to make, but I think I made my point, and he
promised to discuss it seriously with Lucy — his wife.

Blanche said, reading this passage aloud in horrified admiration, 'Sybil is *ruthless!*'

'Oh, unquestionably,' Anthony replied. 'And that fellow's hooked. Still, it depends how his wife feels. If she's as tough as Sybil, and against the idea, then I wouldn't like to be in his shoes!'

He helped himself to more coffee while Blanche read silently on.

    Edward and I had a long telephone conversation last
night. He intends to work and live in Cornwall, and he
has made up his mind that it will be less traumatic for the
children to be based with Katrina in Yorkshire while he
has them for Cornish holidays. I do thank God for that

*decision, and feel it is right, though of course she doesn't
deserve custody – but I have noticed that go-getters
always seem to get!*

*I rang Lydia to exchange news, when I had spoken to
Edward, and she sounds very happy and busy. She and
Freddie are coming for the weekend as soon as Tony and
I get back, so we are looking forward to that.*

*I had a thank-you letter from Ralph yesterday –
though no thanks were needed! – and he is giving me the
little runabout which Jack let me use when we were on
holiday. Do you remember Jack teaching me to drive?
You and Teddy thought it was much funnier than I did!
So instead of being dependent on Tony I shall have my
own car, and can go where and when I please. The sense
of freedom is enormous. I am slightly apprehensive about
tackling the two hundred miles or so back to Clifton,
because I've never driven further than Truro, but it will
be an adventure and I can take the journey in stages.*

*My heart is light to think that this afternoon I shall be
sitting in the kitchen at Minions. The house will be full of
the spirits of you children at all ages. I could wish that
Henny and Ben were here in the flesh, but before too long
I'm hoping that Aaron will be old enough to stay with me
by himself. You and Dan could bring him, and then have a
little holiday somewhere else by yourselves. Think it over.*

My love to the three of you, as always, and God bless,

Blanche folded the letter and smiled. The king was dead, long
live the king. The queen still reigned.

'What time is your flight?' she asked Anthony amiably.

'Oh, early this evening.' He laid aside the book. 'Thought I'd
give myself plenty of time. When does Aaron come home?'

'I collect him from Mrs Patel at six o'clock. And Dan's coming
to supper tonight. Until then I'm by myself,' said Blanche lightly.
And though she was glad to see him she could not help giving a
wistful glance at the silk shirt on the work-table, which she had
been cutting out.

He caught the glance and looked at her, very bright and quick
and understanding. 'I appreciate that I'm robbing you of precious
work time, Blanche, but I need to tell you something of importance. In fact, I planned my flight round the opportunity of having

you to myself.' He added hastily, 'This won't take more than half an hour or so, and then if you like I'll be on my way. I can always find something to do or see in London.'

A slight chill crept into the warmth generated by Sybil's letter.

'Ah!' Blanche said, more to herself than to him. Lest he think he was unwelcome she smiled again, and added, 'You couldn't have come at a better time. I've been slaving all morning, and was about to take a break.'

And she drew the ottoman nearer the wood-stove, and hugged her knees, prepared to listen.

He began, 'Do you remember my parents – your grandparents?'

'Vaguely. I remember that she always wore a hat indoors, and the house was rather grand and gloomy, with books piled on tables and lining the walls. Rather disorganized, too, and the food wasn't great. We three children didn't like visiting them, and they weren't very thrilled to see us either.'

'No. They wouldn't be. They had no time for Tasha and me as children, only as adults. They were both intellectuals, and quite frankly we bored them. I can understand that,' he said honestly. 'Children bore *me* unless I can teach them.'

He went off at a tangent. 'I expect that's why I never came close to Edward and Lydia. He was frightened of me and she was a lazy little beggar!'

He continued, 'I don't doubt that my parents loved us, and I remember loving my mother from a distance, but there were no shows of fondness, only of pride in our achievements. Failure, of course, was treated with contempt.

'Nor were we fortunate in our nursemaids. So Natalie and I became dependent upon one another for spontaneous affection. We brought each other up. At university we were nicknamed the Inseparables. Oh, I don't mean that we made a company of two and excluded the world. Tasha and I are far too fond of holding court for that!'

And he smiled grimly to himself, as he acknowledged this vanity.

October 1946

'Ah! Here come the Inseparables,' Jack Maddern said sarcastically. 'Holding court, as usual.'

He had no patience with those people he designated as 'arty types', being at heart and by upbringing a country gentleman. But Sybil's imagination was stirred. Watching the pair of them pause in the doorway of the tea-shop and present themselves, as it were, to an audience, before bringing their train of followers chattering and laughing behind them, she was reminded of a travelling theatre company at the turn of the century.

'Who are they?' she asked. For she was in her first term at college, away from home for the first time, revelling in a freedom that had never before been hers, and life was a jewel chest that she constantly plundered for more brilliant and costlier gems.

Jack answered reluctantly, because the couple were an anathema to him. 'Anthony and Natalie Malpas. Tony and Tasha, as they are known to their friends. Both very bright. He's in his final year, and they reckon he'll get a first. She should have done the same, but they caught her climbing into her bedroom window at three in the morning, so she was sent down. But,' anticipating Sybil's next question, 'she came back the following term to study photography at the polytechnic, and they share a flat, so her peccadillo hasn't made a ha'porth of difference, though,' with gloomy relish, 'she's bound to come a real cropper someday.'

The Malpas party, numbering eleven, was taking over the tea-shop, distributing itself among the customers, to the accompaniment of high young voices and much laughter. Their presence was devastating. Two people moved elsewhere, to allow them to sit together. A waitress found more chairs. Finally they settled down; five at one table, six at another, and discussed the menu in voices they did not trouble to lower.

Brother and sister had a lively dress sense. In those first drab years just after the war they stood out like peacocks against so many homely hens. Both had evidently been patronizing wardrobe dealers, for their clothes were eccentric in the extreme. Anthony was a dandified, immaculate Victorian, and wore a stock and cravat that Sybil thought very dashing. Natalie was dramatically robed in damson silk fringed with jet, her handsome, reckless face framed by a wonderful black crushed velvet hat, whose brim was pinned back by a huge brooch shaped like the sun.

Jack, who dressed according to type in slightly shabby, well-cut, expensive tweeds, whispered, 'Oh, God, aren't they awful?'

Sybil, shyly observing Anthony, parried this remark by saying, 'Don't they look amazingly alike?'

283

'Yes. And they are both beyond the pale. He's ambitious and takes care not to be caught but she sticks her neck out for the hell of it. You're not eating, Sybil. Would you like a cake?'

She shook her head.

Fragments of conversation from the Malpases' tables drifted across.

'What an extremely pretty girl!'

'Look at the squire chatting away regardless.'

'She's wearing a college scarf – must be a fresher.'

'D'you think he'll get lucky?'

Then the deep hoarse tones of Natalie, rousing a wave of laughter. 'Never in God's name. She's probably his vicar's daughter.'

Sybil and Jack looked at each other, feeling the same suspicion.

'For two pins I'd go over there and speak to them,' said Jack, 'but . . .'

'Oh no,' said Sybil hurriedly. 'We may be mistaken. And they could deny it anyway. And in either case they would laugh at us.'

Annoyed, helpless, he said, 'If you've finished, we might as well leave.'

Keeping as much distance as possible between themselves and the Malpas tables, they made their way to the door. But Anthony was there before them. They were afraid that he intended some public mockery, and Jack clenched his fists, aching for the opportunity to knock him down, but he proved them wrong.

Bowing low, one palm upon his breast, Anthony took Sybil's hand in his and kissed it reverently. She blushed and smiled, embarrassed, exhilarated. Over the thick black mane of his hair she saw the imperious face of his sister set implacably against her; but the touch of his lips on her hand, of his fingers on her fingers, kept her in thrall. He straightened up. She gazed fascinated into a pair of bright black eyes. He clicked his heels, opened the tea-shop door with a flourish, and bowed her out.

'Ass!' Jack muttered, as soon as they were on the grey autumnal streets.

But Sybil did not reply. The even tenor of her ways had changed for ever.

Anthony said to Blanche, 'I knew I had met my future wife, and it wasn't just her beauty that decided me – though I could never have married a plain woman – it was what she promised to be. I had an exciting future ahead of me and I needed to take risks and play it for all I was worth, but I needed anchorage, and the home I sensed she would provide – a home I had never had. Also she was naturally good and I never was. Goodness in a beautiful girl is an enormous attraction for your average male sinner.'

'Well, well, well,' Blanche said, and laughed a little, beguiled by the tale and his honesty. 'Poor Uncle Jack!'

Anthony shrugged, and repeated his sister's words. 'If he hadn't the guts to keep her he deserved to lose her. Anyway, she never felt as much for him as she did for me. He was primarily a good catch, to put it crudely, and her parents were pleased about it. And Sybil was very fond of him, no mistake about that. So she was floating along with them. Until I arrived on the scene.'

He grinned in reminiscence. 'There was hell to pay all the way round. Jack. The Outrams. My parents. Tasha. God help me, we stood against the lot of them. We wanted to marry the following summer, when I graduated. I was given an assistant lectureship while I wrote my thesis, and we could have scraped by on it. Sybil was willing but she was only nineteen and they wouldn't give her permission. So we had to wait until she graduated. None of my family was very nice to her. Tasha was openly disagreeable, and my parents – though polite – would have preferred an older woman, an established academic, for instance, who could have pulled strings for me. None of them gave a damn for Sybil's qualities. They saw that she wasn't one of them and dismissed her as a nobody.'

Blanche remembered Katrina's bitter denunciation on Christmas Day, 'As soon as Sybil and Tony realized I wasn't one of them they had no more time for me!'

But she said nothing, and listened.

'Anyway, I intended to marry her, and if the others didn't like it they could lump it.'

Blanche remembered walking along the windy beach with Natalie, hearing her version of the tale.

'Sybil and Jack weren't in our set, but when Tony brought her into the picture we were forced to adopt her, and Jack hung round us to be near Sybil. It ruined everything. Tony and I had been so close. We understood each other, shared all we had, gave each other complete freedom. Marriage is a non-starter compared to a relationship like that.'

Anthony had been sitting back, reviving the memory of his courtship with the pleasure of a story-teller who knows that his story can only delight his listener, but his face was now sombre. He no longer looked at Blanche, but sat forward, head bent, hands knotted between his knees.

'Our engagement was a damnably difficult, long drawn-out struggle. At the end of the first year I graduated, and our personal group broke up. In the second year, Natalie and I quarrelled over Sybil, and she moved out of the flat she shared with me and began an affair with a lecturer at the university, Brian Dilling, a married man with four young children. He wasn't in Tasha's class. She swept him off his feet. And as everyone liked his family she was highly unpopular. Most people cut her dead. And she and I had stopped meeting and speaking. Then late one evening in the spring of nineteen forty-nine, she turned up out of the blue.'

He digressed for a moment. 'Sybil was on the eve of her finals, swotting in her room at the hostel. Poor Syb. She never stood a chance of proving what she could do. There had been too many emotional demands made upon her.'

In her defence, he added a rider. 'I know that the same pressures hadn't prevented me from achieving my goals, but Sybil was too feminine to fight for herself. She had put me first, and so came second. It was a tremendous pity. She should have done so well.'

He thought about this, but evidently came to the same conclusion now that he had done then. 'I was sorry about it – but there was nothing I could do, because I had to get on.'

He drew a deep breath, gave a quiet sigh, shook his head, knotted his hands afresh. 'Anyway, I was alone in the flat when Tasha turned up.'

CHAPTER THIRTY-TWO

May 1949

Natalie was in a scintillating mood, composed of pride, fury and recklessness. She was cloaked and hatted like a highwayman, in deepest black, and beneath the cloak wore one of her wardrobe bargains: a Fortuny-style tunic and gown. Indeed, it may have been a genuine Fortuny. The violet silk gauze showed signs of frailty, some glass beads on the trimming were missing, but the tunic fell beautifully from the shoulders and the gown followed and enhanced her every movement. Silvery metal bracelets ringed one bare arm half-way to the elbow. A rope of imitation amethysts swung from neck to waist.

In her hoarse deep voice, she challenged him, 'How are you, you old devil? I've brought a bottle of bubbly with me.'

For a moment Anthony was silenced by the suddenness of her appearance, and the emotion it aroused in him. It was as if a missing part of himself had been restored.

He slipped again into the old smooth shell. Smiling, courteous, amused, he said, 'I'm well. Busy, of course. Allow me to take your cloak, Tasha. And how are you?'

'I've been jilted!' she cried forcefully. 'That little swine has gone back to his wife.'

She swept across the room, dropped into Anthony's one easy chair, and lay back: beads tinkling, bracelets jingling.

'Ah!' Anthony said, finding two glasses. 'So Brian finally returned to his senses?'

'What senses?' she demanded bitterly. 'Creeping off to a woman who hasn't the guts to kick him out again? Making up to the forsaken brats? Probably producing a fifth brat to celebrate the reunion? What sense is there in that?'

Anthony said firmly, 'Brian Dilling wasn't your type, Tasha, and you know it.' Removing the foil from the bottle, easing the cork skilfully. 'It's only your pride that's hurt.'

'Only?' she cried. 'Only? My pride *is* me! How dare he! How bloody dare he!'

She brooded, picked at the glass beads on her tunic.

He poured, without losing a drop.

She said aggressively, 'And I don't like my champagne opened as if it were plonk. I like a celebratory bang and a whoosh!'

Anthony smiled at her. Offered her an immaculate, delectably sparkling glass.

She laughed, and returned to the subject of her ex-lover. 'Yes, you're right,' she said. 'He was beginning to bore me. But I wish I'd chucked him instead of the other way round.'

'You might have found yourself lynched, if you had. Your latest escapade hasn't been the most popular one.'

'Well, I'm going to clear out, anyway. Then they'll never know which one of us chucked the other. I've had enough of the groves of academe and all that crap. This is a small-minded parochial place with morals to match. Come on, drink up! The night's young and the bottle's two-thirds full.'

'So where are you going?' Anthony asked, recharging their glasses.

She flung up her arms as if to say, 'Who knows?' And the material rose and fell in shimmering violet folds, emanating a subtle scent.

'What's that perfume you're wearing?' he asked idly.

'L'Heure Bleue,' she replied indifferently.

He smiled to himself, because he knew she had chosen it as carefully as her costume. Her mood was exhilarating, frightening, like an electric storm. Her presence at once magnetized and repelled. He found himself thinking, 'Splendid as an army with banners.'

'You and I were given a good grounding in Greek and Latin,' she said reflectively, 'and I can speak French, German and Italian fluently. So I should get by – even pick up a few more languages on the way . . . and a few decent men, for a change!' The old swagger was evident here.

Anthony sat in the less comfortable chair and crossed his legs. 'I've missed you,' he said simply, 'and I'm going to miss you.'

She turned on him angrily, crying, 'It's your fault that we have to live apart, you idiot!' And plunged straight into controversy. 'Are you really going to marry her, and turn into a domestic jackass like Brian?'

His colour rose but he kept his temper.

He said, 'I shan't discuss Sybil. Let's finish the champagne and talk about you.'

Natalie brooded again. Then her face cleared. She smiled, held up one ringed hand, looking even more like a hierophant, and said, 'Pax!'

The evening grew late. At her request Anthony opened a bottle of wine, and they drank that and opened another. They relaxed into their old way of being, a unique experience in which they picked up and explored each other's thoughts, inhabited a realm of two people who had shared the same womb and travelled through the same childhood. And over this personal kingdom Natalie glittered like a dark star.

They were both slightly drunk, totally at home with each other, admiring their mirror images. So they had often sat, discussing sexual conquests, projecting themselves into mythical futures over which they ruled like little demi-gods. Anthony rode the waves of conversation in an exalted mood, but the current of Natalie's wrath and humiliation was running deeply, dangerously beneath. She no longer came first with either her lover, despised though he might be, or her brother, whom she adored. Worse still, two women she held in contempt had triumphed over her.

Her eyes glinted. She stood up and began to dance round the room, slowly, provocatively, taunting Anthony, flaunting the beauty that Brian Dilling had rejected. 'No, but do confess. People have been telling me hilarious stories about you. Is it true that she won't sleep with you until the ring's on her finger?'

Irrationally, he was as furious with Sybil then as with Natalie. His fingers twitched with temper. She twirled round and laughed at him.

He said deliberately, 'No one has told you anything, Tasha. You're a social pariah. You must have made that up.'

Eyes of jet impaled him. Predatory white teeth jeered at him. 'I can't believe it!' she cried to the universe, hysterically diverted. 'Tony Malpas conquered by a virgin. Tony Malpas celibate! Unless, of course,' pointing at him, arm extended, 'unless you have a girl or two on the side. Have you? Do tell. You know you can tell me anything.'

The swirling violet silk gauze, the evocative scent, tormented him.

'It's none of your damned business!' he shouted.

His anger delighted her. She stopped in front of him, grinning, goading. 'You haven't, have you?' she persisted. 'You're keeping yourself pure – well, as pure as you can be, knowing your proclivities! – for the great day and the great night.'

Her merriment was helpless, noisy, maddening. The sound, the scent, the silk, the motions of her body, brought him to such a pitch of rage that he could have killed her.

'Oh, Christ!' Natalie cried, almost sobbing with laughter. 'Three years of sexual frustration for a helping of English milk pudding!'

He jumped up and slapped her cheek so hard that she staggered.

'Bastard!' she gasped, recovering her balance with difficulty, and slapped him back.

They were beyond and beside themselves: hitting, scratching, tearing, raging, then forgetting, clinging, urging, gloriously riding, and finally being swept from the sublime sea on to a dark reef.

They moved away from each other, silent and appalled.

For many months there was no communication between them. Anthony had no knowledge of Natalie's whereabouts, and no desire to find her. She had vanished as if she had never been.

Sybil graduated without honours and they married in the July, but did not move into his flat as they had planned originally. He had left it two months earlier and was living in lodgings. As an excuse he said it would have been too small for them, but Sybil never understood this reasoning, because they moved into two furnished rooms with kitchen and use of bathroom that were smaller still.

Early the following year he received a personal call on the departmental telephone, and a familiar hoarse voice said, 'Tony. It's Tasha. Don't hang up.'

His heart seemed to beat in his throat. 'I won't,' he said. 'How are you, Tash?'

'I'm in a bit of a jam,' she said. 'I've managed by myself so far, and I wouldn't bother you, but there's nobody else. I need help, and money if you have it. I'm in London. Can you meet me somewhere there, as soon as possible?'

He lied to Sybil and took the day off: a fact that would later come to light and be misinterpreted by his wife.

He met Natalie in the prosaic surroundings of the British Museum tea-room, and amid the commonplace clink of tea-cups, discovered the depth and extent of their trespass. The disgrace of his sister producing an illegitimate child was great, but deeper, greater and more horrifying was the thought of that child's parentage, and he sought to place the onus on her previous lover. But she would not reassure him.

Natalie said with emphasis, 'I have always taken precautions with Brian. I took none when visiting you. Why should I? Even I', she added solemnly, 'would not have contemplated a sin of that magnitude.'

So he attempted to make amends as best he could.

Anthony said, 'You are *our* daughter, Blanche.'

Blanche drew a deep breath and could not answer. For a time neither of them spoke. The winter sunlight revealed the kinship between them, even to their attitudes of contemplation. Inside the wood-stove a log fell softly into its own ash. The cat yawned wide and pink and insolent, on her perch.

Anthony spoke again. 'I hid the truth from everyone for reasons which will be obvious to you. But when Natalie gate-crashed at Christmas she opened up a Pandora's box of old wrongs, and I began to think again.'

Blanche sat in a silence that pressed upon her, thickly, softly, suffocatingly, like the beginning of an asthma attack. Her sight dimmed. Her heart beat faster, more insistently. Afraid of losing control, she tried to draw long, slow breaths while her father's voice penetrated the fog around her.

Incest, she thought. I am the product of incest. I am niece and daughter to them both. What does the Bible say? And the sins of the fathers shall be visited upon the children, even unto the third and fourth generation. Upon the children.

He watched her humbly, lovingly, and did not spare himself or her.

'I never intended to tell you. But there is a practical reason for speaking out, and an explanation to make. Your former way of life, though it angered me in one way, relieved me in another. Like Natalie, you preferred a single, untrammelled existence, and as you grew older and remained childless my concern lessened. Then, just as I thought all would be well, you decided to become pregnant . . .'

Slowly and with infinite grace, Salome stood up, arching her back, stretching her legs.

'. . . and I was terrified – afraid of what you might produce. A middle-aged mother, carrying a double burden of family weaknesses and defects. I had been lucky with you, but the next generation might show up something that was best hidden.'

The beast, Blanche thought, slouching to Bethlehem to be born.

'I panicked,' said Anthony simply. 'I refused to have anything to do with you or the child.'

He lifted his hands in a gesture of regret, and let them fall again lightly upon his knees.

'But gradually Sybil brought us together again, and when you turned up with Aaron at Christmas I saw that I'd been lucky a second time. Of course,' he added, with a hint of his old pride and vanity, 'both Natalie and I are strong and healthy. I've never had anything worse than a bout of flu, and until this business with her eyes I don't think she's had a day's serious illness – and you can set the cataracts down to *anno domini*. But no sooner had I breathed a sigh of relief than you showed signs of settling down with Daniel.'

He shrugged away the doubts and terrors that had besieged him since. He looked at her humbly, beseechingly. 'Sybil says you sound very happy together – and I'm glad of that. I like Daniel. He's his own man. But one of the hopes she's nourishing has driven me into the open . . .'

And yet he could not say it. Numbly, Blanche said it for him.

'No more children.'

He nodded.

The cat leaped noiselessly down and sat in front of them, cleaning its paws.

Blanche's pulse was slowing to normal, her eyes clearing, her breath under control, but now the need for tears asserted itself, and she fought this also.

He looked at her steadily, though she could not return his gaze.

'Are you all right?' he asked her gently.

She nodded, and swallowed. He paused for a moment to reassure himself that this was true, and then went on. 'I have another and equally important reason for burdening you with this confession. Natalie's revelation helped you and me to come to a new understanding.' He hesitated. 'I felt that this was partly because you thought you owed me something. That I had taken responsibility for you when I need not have done.' His hands moved softly, nervously together. 'But, of course, the responsibility was mine in the first place. You owed me nothing. And I owed you more than could ever be repaid.'

Blanche picked up Salome and held her close.

'I believe that secrets fester. Certainly, this one has done. It pervaded my marriage and my family relationships, made a liar out of me. Your presence was a constant reminder of my guilt. The damage done to you was partly my fault. Nor did Natalie and I ever face more than the superficial facts. Once the initial shock was over, we talked about you as if you were a shared niece instead of our child. And when you grew up, wild and headstrong like the pair of us, I censured you far too harshly, because — though I couldn't admit it — you were too like us. Blanche, you have paid our debts over and over again, and I regret that bitterly. Bitterly.'

She made a little movement of the hand that encouraged him to continue, and drew a breath that sounded like a sob.

'But once Natalie had told you her part of the truth, I think that you and I both realized how much we cared about each other.'

She nodded and sobbed outright this time, cradling the cat in her arms.

'I thought long and deeply about this, too, ' said Anthony, 'and I came to the conclusion that a half-truthful relationship was another quicksand into which we could sink at any time, and then I should lose you for good.'

He paused, but she could not speak.

'I might have lost you anyway,' he said, 'but I believe that you should know what I am, rather than revere me for what I am not.'

He made a final visible effort. 'And if you reject me in disgust I shall understand that, too.'

Blanche wiped her eyes and gave a long low sigh. She set

Salome down and looked at him gravely. She felt the weight of her father's guilt then, as he had felt it for nearly forty years.

She asked, 'Does Sybil know?'

He roused himself to answer, though this was not a question he had expected. 'No. I'm sure not. She arrived at the truth at one point, but glided off at a tangent. She actually left me once, because she suspected that you were not Natalie's child but mine. Nothing hides the truth so well as a near miss. But I never told her. Good God!' Anthony cried, horrified by the thought. 'Can you imagine her reaction if I had?'

Blanche gave a tremulous laugh, and he glanced at her doubtfully. 'Best let sleeping dogs lie, eh?' he asked.

'And dogs of that breed, most certainly,' Blanche answered.

She was jaded with emotion, unsteady in mind and body, and this was reflected in her voice and movements. Later, she would relive this scene many times, and agonize over its disclosures, but for now she had suffered all she could bear. She rose and stretched, folded her arms, walked the room, head bent, setting her thoughts free.

'Isn't it odd,' she mused softly, wearily, 'that for years and years I used to wonder who my father was, and imagine him to be as different from you as possible? And yet I know now that it *is* you, and could have been no one else.'

Anthony had risen from the chair, as a prisoner rises in the dock, and was looking directly at her, ready to receive the verdict.

'I can't describe how I feel,' said Blanche honestly, turning towards him. 'Shocked. Empty. Battered. Stupefied. Any adjective that covers those emotions.'

He bowed his splendid head and awaited his sentence.

'It will be – hellish – for me to adjust to this,' Blanche said, and her voice shook. 'I shall need time. A lot of time.'

She said sadly, quietly to herself, 'I have found life hard to live.'

There seemed to be no more to say. Anthony nodded, indicated that he would go, was afraid even to touch her hand, and so made a gesture of farewell at once clumsy and moving.

Then she turned, crying, and held out her hands to him.

'But I shall not reject you,' said Blanche.